The Race for Autumn's Glory

Crossway books by Doris Elaine Fell

Seasons of Intrigue Series

Always in September
Before Winter Comes
April Is Forever
The Twelfth Rose of Spring
To Catch the Summer Wind
The Race for Autumn's Glory

SEASONS OF INTRIGUE

BOOK SIX

The Race for Autumn's Glory

Doris Elaine Fell

CROSSWAY BOOKS • WHEATON, ILLINOIS

A DIVISION OF GOOD NEWS PUBLISHERS

The Race for Autumn's Glory

Copyright © 1997 by Doris Elaine Fell

Published by Crossway Books
          a division of Good News Publishers
          1300 Crescent Street
          Wheaton, Illinois 60187

Cover illustration: Chuck Gillies

Cover design: Dennis Hill

First printing 1997

Printed in the United States of America

Library of Congress Cataloging-in-Publication Data
Fell, Doris Elaine.
   The race for autumn's glory / Doris Elaine Fell.
      p.   cm.—(Seasons of intrigue: bk. 6)
   ISBN 0-89107-926-2
   I. Title.   II. Series: Fell, Doris Elaine. Seasons of intrigue ;
bk. 6.
   PS3556.E4716R33 1997
   813'.54—dc21   96-53869

05	04	03	02	01	00	99	98	97
15	14	13	12	11	10	9	8	7	6	5	4	3	2	1

Let us run with perseverance
the race marked out for us.

—Hebrews 12:1c (NIV)

To Bob Jugan
who introduced me to the Tour de France
for his contagious enthusiasm
• • • •
To Greg LeMond
the American winner of three Tours
for his memorable triumphs
• • • •
And in memory of Fabio Casartelli
Motorola Team, Tour de France, 1995
for his unforgettable smile

Prologue:
The Greek Islands

Salvador Contoni stood at the helm of his vessel and shoved his blue-and-white skipper's cap back from his forehead. Monique Dupree, a Renetti yacht, and the lure of the Greek Islands—what more could he ask for? The woman and the ship— both of them sleek and elegant like royalty, eye-catching and glamorous. He owned neither one, possessed neither of these two beauties that touched him most. He glanced down at Monique. She stood out on the deck, her narrow waist pressed against the rail, her shiny black hair blown back from her face by the gentle sea breeze. She turned, and those enormous brown eyes looked up at him. She was beautiful, even more lovely as she smiled.

"Sal, why are we going to the island of Corfu?" she asked.

"I have an appointment with a rich Athenian in the privacy of his villa. I'm counting on him chartering this yacht."

"A friend of yours?"

"I've never met him. His oldest son made all the contacts."

"Why such a clandestine meeting?"

"So no one will recognize him."

A dark shadow blocked Monique's smile, twisting her lovely features into a frown. "You should have stayed in your father's vineyards. You risk your safety in international waters."

"The man will pay me well."

"A few thousand lire? You take too many risks, Sal."

"But all of them for you."

The yacht and Monique—both of them *grandi Italiane*—except, of course, Monique was French-born. Her coral midriff and gleaming white leggings made her look trim and tidy, swank like a ship being launched on its maiden voyage and sailing gracefully through the turquoise waters. Odd—odd that he always saw his yacht as a beautiful woman and this beautiful woman as a magnificent, luxurious vessel.

"You take too many chances, Sal," she told him again.

The stakes are always high, my love, he thought. *But if I get involved in another arms deal, I will surely lose you.* His body quailed against the alternative—the rest of his life hiding out in his father's vineyards, harvesting grapes, being the heir to his father's winery. Yet Sal would consider returning to the vineyards just to spend his life with Monique, but not before he tracked down Drew Gregory—the American CIA officer who had struck him such a bitter blow. The whole mercenary camp in the Pyrenees had been shut down because of Gregory, and Sal's luxurious lifestyle had been snatched from him. And now the Athenian in Corfu had promised him vengeance against Gregory.

When he saw the worry in Monique's eyes, he thumbed the chain around his neck and pulled it away from his chest. "I wear my madre's St. Christopher's medal. Nothing can happen to me."

She blew him a kiss, stirring an overpowering longing inside him. He wanted to anchor the ship and let it bob in these cool, clear waters so he could run down to the deck and take Monique in his arms. He had always boasted that he took what he wanted, but he must not take this woman against her will. She must long for him as he did for her—must love him as he loved her.

"What are you thinking, Sal?"

"About you. About us," he said huskily.

"Don't. Please don't."

"Why not? My parents like you," Salvador called down to her.

"They barely know me."

"They want to know you better."

Her laugh was curious, accusing. "Did you tell them that I'm five years older than you?"

"It wouldn't matter to them. They say I've changed since you came into my life."

"I'm only here on holiday," she reminded him.

"Stay. Marry me, Monique. I'm almost thirty-four. It's time for me to settle down."

"Really? Did you tell your parents about my boys?"

"Madre saw their picture on the dresser when she put the fresh flowers in our room." He grinned. "She says, 'When your Monique sleeps, she looks like an angel.'"

"Do your parents know that I'm a widow?"

A rich widow, he thought. *A spectacular asset for my dwindling account.* "My madre asked when she saw your diamonds."

Sal's grin widened. "She said, 'Marry her, Salvador. Monique will take good care of you. You will never have to work outside your padre's vineyards again.'"

"Working? Is that what she called skippering my husband's yacht—taking him on rendezvous so he could sell arms to foreign countries and man a mercenary camp?"

"My mother doesn't know about those things, Monique. But I had to skipper the yacht for your husband. Harland made a poor sailor—always seasick himself."

Again her face clouded. "Harland never really trusted you."

"Not where you were concerned." *Harland Smith, the American millionaire arms dealer.* "He gave you everything, even the city of Paris."

"Almost," she agreed. "It was part of his promise when he rescued me from the hills of Normandy."

An innocent beauty thrilled with the promises of Paris. Why else would she have married a man twice her age? "Did you know he sold arms to foreign countries when you married him?" he asked.

"I knew little about him—but my husband adored me."

"Then why do you go by your maiden name, Monique?"

"For the boys," she admitted. "I do it for the boys."

Sal's palms felt sweaty on the wheel. Anzel was going on fourteen and ashamed of his father's past; Giles was still five and a mama's boy. Good-looking boys—more French than American. "My mother would like grandchildren," Sal said. "The boys can live with my parents in the villa. Madre would like that."

"And your padre?"

Sal's muscular shoulders tensed. "My father wants me to work with him in the family business."

"In the vineyards—away from the sea?"

"The Contonis sell the best vintage," he assured her.

She shook her head. "No," she said softly, "you are too restless for the vineyards, Salvador. Restless like Harland."

Sal resented the comparison, but a man could be softened in Monique's presence. Enticed. Trapped. Lured. Salvador understood this. Even now he'd willingly give up the old ways just to win her hand. Why then was he sailing steadily toward Corfu, risking her safety as well as his own to meet with a wealthy stranger?

"Sal, turn the yacht around. Let's go back to Athens."

"We've come too far, Monique." *I can't turn back.*

They had sailed leisurely up the western coast of Greece, and now as the bow of the ship sliced the turquoise waters, Corfu loomed ahead. Sal licked the salty taste from his lips. He was to travel to Corfu alone. *But why Corfu?* he wondered.

"Why Corfu?" she asked, startling him. "Why not meet the man in Athens where he makes his home?"

Vasille Golemis belonged to the New Democratic Party; he was an outspoken advocate for NATO and the European Union. "He's a well-known politician, Monique, an honored member of Parliament."

"All the more reason to meet him in public. Or is that a threat to the new government?"

Sal smiled at that. Papandreou had fallen from power early in 1996. Or was it longer? Time ran a fast race in the political world. The fact that Vasille Golemis had survived the takeover of the new leadership was a vote in his favor. Or maybe he was holding on to his spot in Parliament by a hair. Golemis had opposed the election of Costas Simitis as prime minister. As far as Sal understood, it was Golemis's personal aggravation that he had not fallen heir to the promotion himself. Still the prime minister had definite plans to lead Greece into a starring role in the European Union. Golemis readily backed Simitis in this, but Monique was right. Why would a deputy in the Greek Parliament plan a secret rendezvous with Sal in Corfu?

"I'll stay alert," he promised her. "No amount of money or threats from the Athenian will keep me on Corfu against my will."

She shook her head. "Of course not. Salvador Contoni does

only what pleases him. Takes only what he desires. Risks only those assignments that leave him with a pocket full of lire."

You know me so well, he thought. "We'll be safe," he said. "But I'd turn around right now if you promised to marry me."

"Sal, I won't take my boys away from France, not until this mess about Harland's estate is settled, and the bank accounts and the houses in Spain and Switzerland and Paris are legally mine."

"What about the castle in the Pyrenees?"

"I never want to see that again."

She didn't want the castle where he and others had trained mercenary soldiers. But she wanted everything else, including that fabulous luxury vessel anchored in the Monaco harbor.

"Will you ever get the yacht back?" he asked.

He saw a flicker in her eyes and knew that it was already free. But forget the houses and yacht. "I love *you,*" he said.

"Oh, Sal, I don't think you know what love is all about. No, you love the sea. You would never be happy far from it."

The sea was his life, his escape, his past, and his future. He had felt this magnetic enchantment since boyhood. From that first day, when his father took him from the city of Milan 140 kilometers to the Ligurian Sea, the power of the crystal waters had captivated him. His family wealth and the guaranteed opportunities in his father's vineyards were nothing once Sal felt the power of a yacht bobbing beneath him.

He saw the yacht and Monique as one. He had met her in Monaco, standing in a receiving line beside her husband. With Harland glaring at them, Sal had danced with Monique in the crowded ballroom on board the yacht. As he swung her around, he had blotted out every face from his mind but hers, but when the waltz was over, she went back to stand with her husband.

No other woman stirred such longings in Sal. Life without her was like being constantly seasick. The seasick feeling rose in him again now. He sought safer ground. "Sell the *Monique II* to me," he begged. "I can run charters here in the Greek Islands."

"It's not for sale. The boys want it when they grow up."

"We can buy them another one then."

If he had been standing closer, he was certain he would see tears in her eyes. "Sal," she said, "the yacht is one of those good things their father left behind. I want them to have it."

Elegant and royal like Monique.

"Then I'll come to Monaco and do charters for you there."

"You can't. Interpol is looking for you. And Spain."

"Not very aggressively," he said. "I've been quite visible. I was openly with my family in Milan."

She was silent for an instant, and then raising her voice above the sound of the sea, she asked, "Sal, what is that hollow log beside your navigation charts?"

"The one in the cabin?"

"Yes, by that mysterious black box."

"That's nothing for you to worry about, Monique."

She tilted her head back and laughed softly, her long, slender neck gleaming white in the sun. "I'm not worried—just curious."

"It's the famous Contoni interceptor," he boasted. "A bit more work on that, and I will be able to interrupt anyone's transmission and substitute my own."

Her arms went tightly against her chest. "Why would you want to do that?"

"It's my ticket to success, Monique. It will be useful at sea—listening to the frequencies, blocking them if I have to. Someone will pay me well for my system. The Athenian perhaps."

"Is it like a surgical bypass so you can escape detection?"

Sal saw her shiver. He wanted to be down there with her, holding her, hugging away her fears. "Why not?" he asked airily. "Salvador Contoni was meant to live free."

She turned away and let the open sea spray her face. "We seem to be taking forever to reach Corfu."

"I thought we had forever. But we'll be there soon."

"I think I'll fly home from Corfu. This is the longest I've ever been away from my sons." The sea breeze snatched at her words. "I need to be there to protect them from the endless taunts against Harland. They never give up—"

"They?"

"The Americans. The French. Interpol. There are those who want to silence you, too, Sal."

The Greek politician? he wondered. Vasille Golemis favored American bases in Greece and cooperation with other countries. Had Gregory or Interpol set Sal up for this rendezvous in Corfu?

He set his yacht on automatic pilot and leaned forward, listening to her as she said, "Harland never trusted you, but you have always in your rough way been a gentleman to me—ever since we met in Monaco." Was there a catch in her voice? Surprise? Caring? "And you've been so kind to my sons."

Is that all I matter to her—someone who has been kind to her children? Not someone who has fallen in love with her.

"Sal, you can't risk going back to Monaco. I won't let you. You mean more to me than that."

"But not enough."

"Not enough," she whispered.

"Then why did you come to Milan to see me?" he asked.

Her thickly lashed eyes misted. "You asked me to come."

"I asked you several times, and you refused."

"And then your madre invited me. Did she mind my sailing to the Greek Islands with you?"

"Would it matter?"

"Yes, I liked her. I want her to like me."

"She does."

"She won't. Not when she learns why I came here." A humorless ripple stuck in her throat. "Salvador, what would you say if I told you the American CIA sent me?"

"I wouldn't believe you. You hate them as much as I do."

"But my sons are quite fond of Drew Gregory."

Drew Gregory. The taste of gall filled his mouth. "Monique, why would you help Gregory?"

"To guarantee the safety of my children."

"Is that what Gregory promised you if you betrayed me?"

"You put it so coldly. But, yes, Gregory was certain you'd go back to Paris with me."

And then they'd arrest me. Her betrayal tore at his gut.

"You're not working for him?" He sensed a fresh hardness that would turn his eyes a steely gray. "Tell me it's not true."

"No, I'm not working for Mr. Gregory. I could never do that. But the CIA promised me a quick release of all of Harland's property if I helped them—if I persuaded you to go back to France with me."

"Did they pay you well?" he asked harshly.

"I didn't take their money. I just wanted to put the past to rest so I could live out my life on my parents' farm with my sons."

She struggled with her windblown hair. "The boys still talk about you, Sal."

"Do they?"

"Mostly about yachting and skiing with you."

"But the high speeds on the mountain slope frightened Anzel. That's why I bought him a soccer ball."

"I know. You were sweet to do that."

She retreated from him, backing away, wrapping her arms across her chest again. "I don't want you to risk going to Monaco or France. Ever. Promise me you won't go—please."

"Why?"

"I don't want the American to find you, Sal."

"If it meant being with you, I'd take the risk."

"And I don't want you to get involved with this Athenian. If you need money—let me bring the *Monique II* to you. You could do charters for me here in the Greek Islands where you'd be safe. Would you like that?"

"Not without a permanent arrangement with you."

Her liquid eyes swam as they met his. "Just the yacht, Sal." More gently, she warned, "Don't anchor in Corfu. You may be walking into danger."

"What does it matter? If I'm losing you, Monique, I have nothing else to lose."

Chapter 1

In silence they approached Corfu from the sea. The sun-drenched island was verdant with cypress trees and gnarled olive groves that rose from the rippling bay to the emerald hills above them. Fleecy clouds and chicory-blue waters added to the quiet enchantment as they drifted along a stretch of sandy beach toward the harbor where lesser yachts than Sal's lay anchored.

As he maneuvered their vessel into the harbor, Monique could not take her eyes off Salvador. She liked watching him. A thin fuzz of blond hair covered the back of his broad hands as he held steady to the wheel and eased the yacht between a multicolored ferry and a bobbing fishing vessel. She wanted to remember him like this at the helm of a ship, standing tall and good-looking with a white polo shirt stretched across his broad chest. The Mediterranean sun had creased his face, leaving it bronzed and weather-ridged around his eyes and mouth.

Once they docked, Sal strolled across the shiny deck to stand beside her. He was a strapping, well-muscled sailor, a rugged man who was both tender and brash, cruel and unforgiving. Long strands of sun-bleached hair brushed his forehead. Unruly like his personality; wild and windblown like his spirit. He leaned against the railing, his hands clasped, his elbow touching hers. Cool gray eyes—with no blueness to them—sought hers.

"Monique, I loved you," he said.

"Past tense?"

"I'm not sure." The old hardness marbled his profile. "I'll ask you once more. If I turned around right now, Monique, would you go back to Milan with me?"

Her pulse quickened. "I can't go back there."

"But you liked my family."

"Very much," she whispered.

The kinder his family had been to her, the more disloyal she felt. Whatever their son had become, the Contonis loved him. They had welcomed Monique into their home as Sal's potential bride. She could still hear Mrs. Contoni's words as they said good-bye. "If you love my son, Monique, don't ever betray him."

But she intended to leave him in Corfu and fly back to France. *Be truthful with yourself,* she scolded. *You wanted to be with him, to sense his need of you, to feel alive and protected with a man at your side. And now you're running away from him.*

"We were happy at dawn this morning," he said.

"I know."

That's when they had left the port of Piraeus and turned away from the roar of the Aegean waves to cruise through the Corinth Canal. Once Sal negotiated the canal, they had sailed along the western coast of Greece, north to this enchanting island.

Now as she finger-combed the hair that ran the length of his muscled arm, her skin prickled at the thought of never seeing him again. "I'll miss you," she admitted.

"Then don't go away."

"I must. It's best for both of us."

In the stillness that followed, they searched the faces on the dock—tourists and islanders in short pants and white shirts, giggling girls in sun hats, boys on bicycles, lovers arm in arm, families with small children in tow. Only one Corfiot gave them so much as a glance. He was overly dressed for the weather—a summer business suit, a starched dress shirt, a white handkerchief in his pocket, a flat briefcase in his hand.

"That must be my contact, Monique. Vasille Golemis's son."

"Is he to come on board?"

"No."

"Then what are we waiting for, Salvador?"

"For you to make a move? Isn't this where the CIA told you to bring me? 'Lure Salvador Contoni to Corfu, Madame Dupree,'" he mocked, "'and we'll have someone waiting to pick him off.'"

"I never saw that man before."

"Really? Weren't you given the same description? A handsome Greek in his mid-thirties, dressed in a business suit, and carrying an attaché case—with a multi-caliber Astra A-100 inside."

"Don't even think that, Sal. The CIA didn't know I was coming to Corfu. I didn't even know the place existed."

"You disappoint me, Monique. This is paradise to the international jet set. Surely Harland brought you here many times."

"Harland dreaded crowds."

"Or dreaded exposing you to younger men?"

"Both. But even if Corfu had been in my plans, I begged you to turn back to Athens an hour ago." *Because I knew then that I could not betray you. No matter what I promised Gregory,* she thought, *I want to protect you.* "Please believe me, Sal. I want to keep you out of the hands of the French and Americans."

"I want to believe you. But I wanted to marry you, too."

"I won't marry anyone, not until my sons are grown."

"As young as Giles is, that could be another twenty years."

"And with the risks you take, you won't be here then." Surely Salvador's flaunting the law would cut him down before his time, before he could even peak forty. "Go keep your appointment, Sal. I can catch a taxi to the airport from here," she told him.

He turned and faced her. Dark weather lines formed half-moons beneath his wistful eyes. "You really are leaving me."

"I just came for a week, Sal."

"I wanted it to be longer."

He cupped her chin and ran his thumb over her lips. She knew if he took her in his arms and kissed her—as he had been doing all week—this time he would know that she cared as much for him as he did for her. She had not fought his signs of affection; she had invited them, needed them. He made her feel alive again, fulfilled. Her husband's death had left her empty; but Salvador had brought her back from the abyss, back from the shame of Harland's dying, back from the terrible loneliness.

For a whole week she had responded to him, but it hadn't just been for herself or for Sal. She really was here on Drew Gregory's marching orders. "Beguile Salvador Contoni," Gregory had said. "But get him back to Paris so we can arrest him."

"Why would I do that, Mr. Gregory?" she had protested.

"It's the only way my Agency can help you, Mrs. Dupree."
Gregory had helped her from the chair. "Do what we ask," he said.
"Interpol has already released your yacht. It's yours. But it will be
best if you anchor it somewhere other than in Monaco."

"And my Swiss chalet? And the house in Seville?"

"I have a man working on the house in Seville."

That would be Colin Burdock, she thought. The American
Intelligence officer who had known Harland—and hated him.
Burdock was younger and better-looking than Gregory, and yet at
this moment Gregory seemed fixed in her mind's eye. She had
looked up into Gregory's stoic face, different somehow these
days. His voice kinder. His gaze softer. "Some religious experience," Burdock had told her apologetically. "The old boy went
religious on us up on the mountain at Sulzbach."

In Austria? But not on the assignment in which Harland had
been killed. Back then, Gregory had seemed totally committed to
the CIA, but if Burdock was right, the Agency was vying with God
now for Drew Gregory. And winning? She could not be certain.

As he stood to leave that day, she had asked, "What about my
condo in Paris—is it still under surveillance? And the bank
accounts—still frozen?"

"Give us Sal Contoni, Madame Dupree, and within six months,
we guarantee that everything will be cleared. The estate closed.
Otherwise," he had warned, "this can drag on in the French
courts for years."

"You would like that, wouldn't you, Mr. Gregory?"

"It would be out of my hands. Everything in six months—
except the castle in the Pyrenees. That's up to Spain."

"I don't want the castle."

"Not even for your boys?" he asked.

"There are some parts of Harland's life that I want to wipe out
of their minds forever. The castle—that miserable mercenary
camp—is one of them."

She had not even seen Gregory to the door, but had listened to
it close quietly behind him. From the farm window in Isigny, she
had watched him strike out over the front lawn to his car. He had
stopped abruptly as her sons ran toward him. Even Anzel's face
had brightened as Gregory opened his arms to them.

As she remembered the scene, a sudden chill ripped through

Monique's body; the sea breeze at Corfu felt like ice chips against her bare midriff. She didn't dare risk the possibility of Gregory stealing her sons' affection away from her. The CIA was using her. They would use her again, finding a new excuse the next time or possibly even allowing harm to come to her sons.

Gregory, she thought bitterly, *you are no better than Harland. And now I must outsmart all of you—tell lies about seeing Sal again. Keep my possessions if you must, but I will not betray Salvador Contoni. And I will not lose my sons to your Agency, no matter how many promises you make to me.*

She could taste the urgency of fleeing Corfu—of leaving Sal while he still had his freedom. For Sal's sake and for her sons, she must make Corfu the place for their final good-bye.

"Sal," she whispered, "I'll be gone when you get back from your meeting with the man from Athens."

"No, Monique. You will have to go with me. You are my safeguard out of Corfu."

"Don't use me, Sal," she begged.

"How touching coming from you." Wearily he said, "Let me check the cabin, and then we'll go."

"And if I run away while you're gone?"

"I'll find you."

When he came back on deck, she could see the gun holster outlined beneath his jacket. "Why, Sal?" she asked as he slipped a lacy cape over her shoulders.

"It's my insurance policy. I intend to leave Corfu safely." He caressed her hand. "The meeting won't last long. After that, if you still want to leave me, I'll take you to the airport."

Would he? As he helped her step from the yacht, young Golemis walked away. "Sal, he's not even waiting for us."

"Then we'll follow him."

Sal tucked her arm in his and guided her along the winding cobblestone alleyways of the Old Town, stepping to the blaring Greek music. The smells changed with each unfamiliar block—from the tempting sweet fragrance of bread baking in an outdoor oven to the stench of the fish market and from the tantalizing scent of lemon oil and garlic coming from the Venetian tenements to the foul odor of a poor drainage system. As they crossed onto the broader avenues of New Town, the man ahead stopped to haggle with a fishmonger over the price of octopus per kilo. Moments later, he disappeared through the mosaic doors of the Greek Orthodox church, the smelly sack in his hands.

They followed him inside and found him talking to a priest with a long beard as dark as his black cassock. As they stepped toward the pair, the cathedral door opened behind them. Sal went for his revolver and aimed it at the priest.

Unruffled, the priest extended his hand. "Your gun, Mr. Contoni. It is safer to travel on the island without a weapon."

As Sal waved the pistol, Monique cried, "Sal, give it to him. You can't shoot a priest. You'll have us both in trouble."

"A wise suggestion," the priest said, his kind expression magnetic. "Mr. Contoni, Thymous tells me you have an appointment with his family. The Golemis villa is always heavily guarded to ward off vandalism. They want their guests to come unarmed."

Sal backed away, half turning, his gaze fixed on the church gardener and the priest's assistant who blocked his exit.

"Just a precaution, Mr. Contoni. I am a man of peace, but you have quite a reputation." He gripped Sal's arm with surprising strength, wrestled the gun free, emptied the chamber, and slid the gun up the sleeve of his robe. As calmly, the priest said, "You are safe with Thymous."

Thymous's dark eyes mirrored deep pain. "Father Papanikos will return your weapon on your way out of Corfu."

"Without questions?" Sal asked, tight-lipped.

"Without questions. But, Mr. Contoni, you were to come to Corfu alone. Your wife's presence will displease my father."

"I'm Monique Dupree, not Mrs. Contoni!"

"Right now," Sal snapped, "there is no Mrs. Contoni."

Thymous seemed pleased. "Shall we go? My father doesn't like to be kept waiting."

"Your father could have saved time by meeting me in Athens."

"But the problem lies on this island, Mr. Contoni. Besides, we come here to oversee the family olive orchards." He led them toward the back of the church and out a narrow exit to the compact Fiat parked in the rear. "Allow me," he said, offering Monique his hand as she slipped into the backseat.

As Thymous took the coastal curves at full speed, Monique was certain they would crash into the medieval sea wall and spin off into the emerald sea. Twenty minutes outside of town, he snaked his way up the mountain road and passed through the gates of the Golemis Olive Orchard.

The isolation of the spacious whitewashed villa was guaranteed by the cypress trees that surrounded it. One armed guard stood near a fenced cemetery with a single grave, a lonely shrine in the middle of all this wealth. Catching her eye in the rearview mirror, Thymous said, "Alekos is buried there."

Alekos. Monique shuddered. *The problem lies on this island.* Monique stretched her neck for another glimpse of the grave site, hidden now by the winding tree-lined road. Who was Alekos, and how was Salvador tied in with the person lying there?

Thymous parked between two Mercedes Benzes and then led them through the house past a dining table spread with lamb and seafood, eggplant, and zucchini. Sal plucked a slice of goat's cheese and an olive from the salad and popped them into his mouth as they entered the well-lit sitting room.

Thymous's father sat behind a marble-top desk, the solemn face of the cyclist in the portrait on the wall behind him as mute as his own. Vasille Golemis was stocky, his face ashen, his hair and mustache a silvery gray. He made no effort to stand as he asked, "What kept you, Thymous?"

"Your guests were late in arriving."

Sal stepped forward. "My apologies, Mr. Golemis, but I took the liberty of bringing my friend Monique Dupree with me. We can speak freely in front of her."

"And this," Golemis said, pointing to the heavyset woman beside him, "is my wife, Olympia."

As Monique took Olympia's chubby hand in her own, she saw the resemblance between Mrs. Golemis and the portrait of the young man on a bicycle with his back to the sea. His thickly pursed lips and the shape of his nose were like his mother's, his drooping eyelids like the father's, his Grecian coloring and his hooded, well-set dark eyes exactly like his brother's. She knew with a mother's intuition that it was his grave they had just passed.

"That's our son Alekos," Vasille said. "He's dead." He turned to Salvador. "Mr. Contoni, I want my son's death avenged."

Sal's eyes narrowed. "That was not the agreement—"

Vasille waved his hand for silence. "Hear me out." He spread several pictures on the desk and thumped each one. "My son was to have ridden in the Tour de France this year, but he was killed in the Austrian mountains a few months ago."

"Alekos's death was an accident," Thymous said.

Golemis ignored him. "This is my son's cycling team. I want you to recognize each one of Alekos's teammates, Mr. Contoni, *especially Ian Kendall.*"

Sal sauntered over to the desk, Monique behind him. "What's so important about Ian Kendall?" Sal asked.

"If it were not for Kendall, my son would be alive." He poked the air toward Thymous. "Thymous wants no part of avenging his brother's death. That's why I need your help, Mr. Contoni."

Thymous's answer was tempered with sadness. "Kendall was Alekos's friend, Papa," he protested.

"What kind of a friend would take my son to that mountain to die? Alekos could have won the Tour de France this year."

Thymous's lips drew together, deepening the cleft in his chin. Monique imagined him weeping at his brother's death, crying even more at being displaced from his father's favor, his importance as the firstborn son fading. What good would the profitable olive orchards do this young man if he felt rejected—the son who had stood by the family business, by his father's side?

"Death is cruel," she said to Thymous's father. "But is it right to seek vengeance and put your family honor on the line?"

"What would you know about death and vengeance?" he asked.

She thought of the grief that Harland's life and death had brought to her and to her sons. "I'm a widow," she said.

She pitied him as he turned back to Sal. "Stop Kendall from winning. He has no right to take my son's place in that race."

"Papa, Alekos had no chance to beat Kendall's splendid riding record. Alekos always rode support for Ian."

Vasille pointed angrily at Thymous again. "Our family always stood by each other—" He groped for words to describe Thymous's betrayal. "And now it's as though both of my sons are dead."

Thymous stood motionless by the verandah door, looking like one of the marble statues that decorated the room. Monique saw the pain in those rich dark eyes, yet his features seemed cut from stone—the strong unbroken lines of his nose, the firm cheekbones, and the square well-chiseled jaw. It was as though his heritage went back in time beyond the Golemis bloodline to the mythical origin of Apollo and Zeus. *And what of Salvador?* she wondered, stealing a glance at him. Both of these men had been born into rich families—both primed to take over the family business. But Salvador was like Poseidon, the god of the sea. She was confident that if Salvador could sail all of the waters of the world, he would consider it nothing less than his right.

Salvador tossed the pictures back on the desk. "This was not our agreement, Mr. Golemis." His thumb pointed back to Thymous. "Ask him. Thymous promised me vengeance in another way—not against some young cyclist I've never heard about."

"I followed my father's instructions."

"Then you carry them out, Thymous, but count me out. I have no intention of killing this Ian Kendall for you."

"Sit down, Mr. Contoni," Vasille demanded. "I don't want Kendall to die. I want him to lose the race."

"Be reasonable, Golemis. If Kendall wins, then claim it as a victory for your son. If he loses—and that's a possibility—then you have accomplished what you want without breaking the law."

Vasille's mouth twitched. "I can't count on him losing." He gripped Sal's wrist and slammed it against the desk. Sal jerked free as Golemis roared, "Do you know who I am, Contoni?"

Sal nursed his wrist. "A member of the Greek Parliament, so why risk yourself politically or ruin your family business?"

"That's why I'm hiring you, Mr. Contoni." He reached into his desk drawer and passed an envelope to Salvador. "We agreed upon $250,000 to a Swiss account." He tapped the envelope. "A deposit receipt for half that amount is in here. The other half will be deposited when the job is finished."

"The terms have changed. Half a million. Everything up front— if I agree to do it." Salvador flicked the deposit receipt in Golemis's face. "The rest in cash now."

"Don't, Sal," Monique begged. "Let's leave."

"He can't, Madame Dupree. I know Mr. Contoni is wanted by Interpol . . . by the French." He snapped his fingers. "One word from me, and he will not leave Corfu except in custody. Only my money and political power can protect him right now."

As he reached for the phone, a dark-haired beauty came into the room carrying more food to the well-laden table. "I'm Zoe," she said as she stepped behind her father and rested her hands on his shoulders. "Let's eat, Papa. I'm sure our guests are hungry."

"Starving," Salvador agreed.

"We'll settle this matter first, Mr. Contoni. I can offer you $350,000. No more."

Golemis unfolded a well-worn cable, his large hands caressing it gently as he passed it to Salvador. "But perhaps this will convince you to help me."

Salvador's brows arched. "A sympathy cable from Drew Gregory. Did Gregory know your son?"

"It seems this Gregory was a tourist in Sulzbach at the time, but why would a tourist trouble himself about my son's death unless he was involved?"

"You tell me," Salvador said.

"According to my lawyers, Mr. Gregory has lived abroad for a number of years—American Intelligence, I suspect."

Monique felt the color drain from her cheeks. "Don't get involved, Sal. Let Mr. Golemis's lawyers handle it."

"Madame Dupree, we did file a wrongful death suit, but my son died in Austria. Since his death, Austria has become a member of the European Union, but now I cannot wait. Kendall rode well in the Italian race—came in second. He has every chance of winning in France when the Tour begins in three or four days."

"In six days, Papa," Zoe corrected. "My father's lawyers are trying to freeze the Kendall assets in England, but Papa will not wait for the wheels of justice to turn. That's why Papa insists that you help us, Mr. Contoni."

Monique felt numb. This whole family was diabolical in its thinking. She put her hand on Sal's arm, but he pulled away and held his hand out to Vasille. "I'll take my money now, Golemis."

Vasille snapped his fingers. "Open the safe, Thymous."

Monique cringed as Thymous swung back his brother's portrait and opened the vault. *You are fools,* she thought. *Salvador will come back someday and rob you.*

Thymous slapped the packet of bills into Sal's hand. "So my father's money has persuaded you to help the Golemis family?"

Sal caressed the money. "Why not?"

No, Monique thought. *I know you too well, Sal. This is not for the Golemis family. You see this as a chance to get even with Drew Gregory. I saw it in your face when you read Gregory's cable. Yes, you will take Golemis's money, but you may not carry out his wishes. You don't care who wins that race. All you want to do is destroy Gregory. Why do you hate him so?*

Sal didn't count it. His eyes remained fixed on Zoe as he took the deposit receipt and shoved it into his money belt along with the cash. He patted the bulge. "For you then, Miss Golemis, I will try to stop this Kendall before he gets to the race."

"No. Papa wants you to wait until Ian wears the yellow jersey. And he will wear it at some stage in the race."

"My daughter is right, Mr. Contoni," Golemis roared. "I want Kendall to taste victory. I want him to suffer. And when he's wearing that jersey—when he thinks he is winning—when he's ready to cross the finish line with arms outstretched, stop him."

"The winner's jersey? Then Ian Kendall is a good rider?"

Zoe masked her pain. "One of the best, Mr. Contoni."

۞۞۞

As they stood to leave the villa, Vasille looked up and smiled. "*Buona notte. Buona fortuna,*" he said. "Take the Fiat. My son will pick it up at the dock later."

"You trust me, Mr. Golemis?" Salvador asked.

"I have friends all over the island."

As they passed the table, Salvador grabbed a plate and stacked it with eggplant and spinach and a heaping portion of Greek salad with its chunks of goat's cheese and tomatoes glistening in olive oil.

"You can't take that china with you," Monique warned.

"Why not? We can leave the dirty dishes in the Fiat."

He forked more lamb and pork for them both and threw a broiled fillet of fish on top. Grinning, he grabbed a carafe of white wine and followed her outside. As they came down the steps, Zoe called, "Mr. Contoni, I must speak with you."

Salvador turned with his mouth full. He liked beautiful women, and Zoe Golemis was exquisite in her tight knee-length dress. Her wide, dark eyes were thick-lashed and enormous like Monique's, her even teeth gleaming like the villa walls.

She glanced at Monique as she reached them. "I must speak to you alone, Mr. Contoni. I only have a few minutes before my father misses me."

Sal kissed Monique's cheek. "Wait for me in the garden."

As Monique turned the corner, Zoe said, "Salvador, I beg you, please don't harm young Kendall."

"Has your father changed his mind?"

The same brilliant sun that put sweat beads on Sal's forehead had put a sheen to the flecks of auburn in Zoe's long dark hair. Strands of cultured pearls lay against her graceful neck, an emerald in the middle. "Please, Mr. Contoni, you must promise me that you won't hurt—that you won't kill Ian."

"Your father wants vengeance."

"For an accident? Ian Kendall was my brother's friend. They rode for the same team. Believed in the same goals."

"It didn't sound that way inside."

"My papa is sick with grieving. But if any real harm comes to Ian, it will only double my father's grief."

Sal patted his money belt. "I promised your father."

"Do you always keep your word, Mr. Contoni?"

Seldom, he thought. "I'm committed to finding him. Your father said Kendall just came off the Giro d'Italia; he gave me several addresses." He crammed his mouth full of fish, the boneless piece that he had intended to give to Monique. "Zoe, I'll try and warn Kendall off first. Scare him enough, and he will cancel out of the race."

"Ian won't quit. He likes to win." Sadly, she added, "My brother rode well, but not as well as Ian—and still they were good friends. What my father wants you to do is destroy another young man. What good would that do?"

For one, Sal thought, *it would pain Drew Gregory.* Sal popped another piece of lamb into his mouth and licked his fingers.

"I don't understand your indifference, Mr. Contoni. Why are you willing to destroy my brother's friend?"

It is not Kendall I want to destroy, he wanted to tell her. *It is Drew Gregory. With Gregory gone, I would have a chance with Monique.*

Aloud he said, "If Alekos and Kendall were such good friends, why hasn't Kendall been in touch with your family?"

Her face turned crimson. "He came here to Corfu for Alekos's funeral, but my father ordered him off the property. Thymous and I were so ashamed—but what could we do?"

"Did Kendall really cause your brother's death?"

She looked surprised. "He wasn't anywhere around when Alekos fell off the cliff. Please, if it's more money you want, my brother and I will pay you not to harm Ian."

So she really thinks it was an accident! Sal mused. "And what happens when your father finds out you offered me money?"

"By the time the race is over, maybe some of his pain will be gone. . . . I promised Alekos that I would attend the Tour." She handed Sal a name and address. "This is a hotel near one of the mountain stages in the race. I have a reservation there."

"Does your father know?"

"It would break his heart if he thought I were going, but I often visit friends in France. Maybe I will see Ian there."

"And warn him about me?"

"Unless you agree to my terms."

Sal's charm went into a smile as he tucked the address in his pocket. "I never turn down a pretty lady. Why don't I meet you at that hotel, Zoe, and we can discuss your plans again?"

As she waited for Salvador, Monique wandered along the flowered trails in the villa gardens where the air was scented with almond and nutmeg, lemon and sweet alyssum. Crocus and delicate violets peeked out from the rockery. Off the path a gardener dug in the soil, his side glance taking in Monique's move toward the tulip beds that formed part of his landscape.

She glanced back after passing him in time to see him lift the trowel and talk to it. A senile gardener? Or was he sending a message to the villa that there was a stranger in the gardens? She increased her pace and climbed the hill through the latticed arbor alive with fragrant wisteria and rambler roses, a glorious red in color. From the comfort of the marbled love seat she took in the stark white villas that lay scattered over the emerald hills and the tranquil sea rippling beyond the sun-baked cliffs.

She stirred as someone crunched over the gravel and came around the marbled bench to face her. "Oh, Thymous, I thought it was the gardener coming to spy on me."

"Andreas is harmless." Thymous's eyes were sad as he took her hand and kissed it. "I thought I would never see you again, but Andreas told me you were up here—alone."

He sat down beside her and stretched his lanky legs. "You don't approve of my father's plans, do you, Madame Dupree? Please forgive him. Everything ended for him when my brother died."

"He has the rest of you."

"We're not enough. You must understand, Monique, Alekos was my father's joy."

"His favorite son? But what about you, Thymous?"

"He has no reason to grieve over me. I have always done what he asked. Always."

"But to plan this revenge. Hasn't the Tour had its share of tragic deaths—including that British rider on Mount Ventoux?" She sighed. "Poor Kendall. Does he have a wife and children?"

"Zoe says there's an American girlfriend. My sister keeps up on things like that ever since Alekos introduced her to Ian."

"They were friends?"

"Good friends once."

"Then your father's plans will crush Zoe."

Thymous sat taller. "I won't let that happen."

"You can't stop Salvador. I know him. For money, he'll carry out your father's wishes—even if it means taking Ian's life."

"Contoni is just afraid of my father's threats."

"Salvador is afraid of no one. There's another problem—"

"I know. I saw Contoni's face fill with hatred when he read Drew Gregory's cable. Papa must have known that Salvador would do anything to get even with Mr. Gregory. . . . What are you doing with a man like that, Madame Dupree?"

"I've always made poor choices," she said softly. *Harland. Salvador. Listening to Gregory. Coming here.*

"Do you love Contoni?" he asked.

She smothered her embarrassment. "I told you. I often make poor choices."

"Madame Dupree, no matter what Salvador Contoni means to you, I won't let him hurt Kendall—or my sister."

"Will you go against your father's wishes?"

"I have to. My father's devotion to a dead son will kill him."

"It will destroy all of you. What can you possibly do?"

His gaze strayed toward the olive orchards. "Nothing will ever bring Alekos back, but I intend to uphold the Golemis name—until my father can remember what we have always stood for."

He broke off a rambler rose from the trellis and handed it to her. "Monique, may I see you again?"

For a second she buried her face in its sweet fragrance. "That's impossible, Thymous. I'm flying back to Paris today."

"With Salvador?"

"No. He's only taking me to the airport."

He leaned closer. "Let me take you. Tomorrow. The next day."

She smelled the rose again. "No, Salvador is a jealous man."

"Then give me your address in Paris."

"I have nothing to write it on."

"I have an excellent memory." At the sound of Zoe's footsteps tapping along the path, he said, "Quick, Monique. Tell me. The others are coming."

"After Paris, I'm going back to my parents' farm in Isigny. The Dupree farm. My sons are waiting for me there."

He showed no surprise. "Will I like them?"

"I don't know," she said, flustered.

Again he lifted her hand to his lips. "We'll be in touch. Soon."

"You can't—"

"I must. Zoe and I will be in France anyway."

Chapter 2

An hour after a light breakfast, Ian Kendall and Basil Millard rode out of Carpentras and the herb-scented hills of southeast France, leaving the rest of the cycling team on the sun-golden beaches of Provence. Ian set the pace. It was in him to ride hard as they left the lush vineyards in the valley and sped toward the peak of the glaring white granite hills.

As they neared the windswept summit of Mount Ventoux, Ian glanced back. Basil struggled behind him, his bicycle wobbling erratically, his face the twisted mask of an exhausted rider. "Just a few more kilometers," Ian called.

He noted Millard's jaw sagging as he gulped for oxygen in the mountain-thin air, his miniature Minolta bobbing against his breastbone. One false move on the hairpin curves, and either of them could plunge over the cliff into the deep gorge. Millard pedaled doggedly, as if they were actually in a race and he still had the chance to come in second. They rode alone with no cheering fans lining the road to deaden the pain of the climb.

In spite of the leg spasms, Ian forced himself to keep on pedaling. A kilometer from the crest he braked and lowered his bike to the ground. The scorching sun burned his bare arms as he walked to the marbled memorial with the silhouette of Tom Simpson engraved on the granite. Thirty years before Britain's cycling hero had struggled for a place in Tour history. Ian envisioned Simpson with his features contorted, his heart hammering, his jersey soaked with sweat. Fans had pushed his bike, trying to help him. Twice he fell. "Put me back on my bike," Simpson had begged. Moments later, a mere kilometer from the finish line, he collapsed and died.

Ian wiped his brow. It was hot—95 degrees—but not as hot as that day when Simpson rode this mountain in 110-degree heat. Ever since, the wind had roared around the granite slab; even now the dry winds chafed Ian's cheeks. Out of respect, he removed his helmet and pulled some wilted flowers from his jersey and laid them on the rock.

"You had to be crazy, Ian, wanting to come up here to this barren ash heap," Millard said. "Ventoux isn't even on the schedule for this year's Tour. Why did you come?"

Ian turned. He wanted to tell Millard about the threat taped inside his helmet—wanted to admit that a note delivered to his hotel room in Carpentras had lured him up the mountain. *Simpson never made it to the summit. Neither will you.*

He wet his lips. "I came here for Alekos, but you didn't have to come with me, Basil."

Millard sat on his saddle, one foot braced on the white gravel, his chest heaving. He was a solidly built young man from Birmingham, England—fair-skinned and blue-eyed behind those dark glasses. A sweaty mustache coated his upper lip. "You heard Coach Skobla this morning. No one was to go off on his own."

"Alekos and I came here together once. He told me that he hoped they'd put up a memorial like this for him one day."

"He always had weird ideas about missing the summit."

"Like Tom Simpson. It gets to me that Simpson didn't make it to the top."

"Ian, I think you respected him more than I did. And you aren't even British."

"Part of me is," Ian defended. "England is my grandfather's country. My dad was born there, too—in the Cotswolds." He gave a wry grin. "I think Simpson was one of the cycling greats."

Basil considered. "He would have been if he had lived longer."

"That's what I thought about Alekos."

"Thinking about them won't help you win the Tour, Ian."

"I'll shake it before the race begins. We've got five days."

"Good." Millard lifted his camera to his eyes and squinted. "Strike a pose at the rock, Ian. I'll catch this for posterity."

"Make it quick. We've got company."

Ian nodded toward a dark blue van disgorging its twelve passengers into the blistering sun. As the tourists ambled over to the monument, Ian stepped back to give them room. One man circled around the memorial. He was fortyish, as snow-blond as Millard, an acrid expression on his face as he glanced their way.

Ian picked up his bike. "We'd better go. Coach Skobla is catching a domestic flight out of Avignon in the morning. I can't miss that. I'm hooking a ride to London with him."

"When you call Chase Evans," said Millard, "tell her my wife will make room for her in the hotels along the Tour route."

"I will—if those bomb threats haven't scared her off."

Even behind the dark glasses, Ian saw surprise in Millard's eyes. "Don't take those seriously, Ian," he said. "Threats of sabotage are part of our history. Why, the first time I rode in the Tour, Basque terrorists threatened to bomb the mountain stages in the Pyrenees. The gendarmerie stopped that one."

Ian squeezed his arm. "If we ever need a new team leader, you're my choice. You've never ridden to your full potential."

"You know I'm a sprinter, Ian. I fade out in the mountains."

"You hung in there this morning."

"Better than I expected. Maybe something will inspire me, and I'll be King of the Mountains someday. My wife thinks I'd look good in the polka dot jersey." He shrugged. "But it doesn't work that way. You're the team leader. We ride *domestique* for you."

As the tour van rumbled up the road toward the summit, Ian walked his bike around the memorial, Millard close behind him. A chalk message had been scrawled on the back of the granite slab: *You will never make it to the summit, Kendall.*

Ian's flesh prickled. He grabbed for the handlebars and turned the wheel sharply as Basil stammered, "What the—? Who?"

"Maybe one of your Basque terrorists," Ian said, his tongue thick in his mouth. His gaze strayed toward the blue van already at the summit and turning around. The sweat on his neck turned cold. He sprang on his bike. "Let's make skid marks, Basil."

They descended the mountain, Ian never braking as they sped toward the safety of Carpentras. Behind them, he heard the grinding engine of the van closing the distance between them, and he pedaled faster.

🥠🥠🥠

By the time Ian reached the lush English countryside two days later, the expectation of seeing Chase Evans neutralized the fears that had stirred at Mount Ventoux. As he turned off the motorway and bumped over the rocky, winding road toward the Eagle's Nest, he felt rhapsodic, merry as a cricket. He started whistling one of his grandmother's old favorites, "Got a Date with an Angel."

That's you, Chase Evans, he thought.

The Eagle's Nest lay upcountry, nestled in a sleepy valley north of Oxford, surrounded by shade trees and bushes of flaming bougainvillea that climbed the south wall. Ian broke the tranquillity as he roared into the parking lot in his grandfather's Rolls Royce. The powerful wheels spun against the gravel as he squealed to a stop beside Chase's rented Renault. He hit the ground running, burst through the lobby door, and struck palms with the old man with red-rimmed eyelids. "Give me five, Frank," he said.

For a second the trembling fingers locked with Ian's. Then Ian was off again. Ignoring the Quiet Please sign, he sprinted by a couple of wheelchairs and rounded the corridor on the double, slowing to a subdued walk in front of the nurse's station. "I'm here to see Beatrice Thorpe," he announced.

"You're back again! How nice, but Mrs. Thorpe has company— that young woman from America."

Thanks, nurse. That's what I wanted to hear, he thought.

He had spent the morning tracking Chase down and, dismayed, had even called her home in Long Island, New York. He counted on the maid answering the line, but it had been Chase's mother.

"Nola Evans," she had said sleepily, a middle of the night worry in her voice.

He had forgotten the time change between countries and considered hanging up, but then mumbled, "I'm looking for Chase."

"So are we," she laughed. "We're looking for her to come home soon."

"She doesn't plan that until late August."

"If you knew that, young man, why did you call Long Island?"

"I just thought you'd know where she is now. You see, I'm only in London a few hours, and then I'm flying back to France."

"Oh. Perhaps if you stayed in one place, she'd find you."

"Chase doesn't know I'm looking for her." He tried to picture the mother that Chase had described, a soft-spoken woman with a happy smile, someone with boundless energy bouncing between golfing with the girls and gardening for pleasure. He had a feeling that those blue-gray eyes could see him over the phone wire. "My name's Ian Kendall, ma'am. Maybe Chase mentioned me."

Her pause was significant enough to put sweat in his palms before she admitted, "I recognize the name." The midnight worry had crept back into her voice. "You must be the cyclist?"

It had sounded like an accusation. *I don't measure up,* he thought. "Sorry to have bothered you, Mrs. Evans."

"If you get in touch with Chase, tell her to call collect."

"I'll do that."

"And, Ian, Chase stays with the Nigel Hamptons in Oxford."

"She wasn't there."

"Well, she has a friend at the Eagle's Nest. Try there."

He had smiled into the phone. *Beatrice Thorpe.* Why hadn't he thought of that himself? "I'll try there next."

"I wouldn't suggest waking anyone up," she warned.

Right now, as he slid to a stop in front of Beatrice's room, he couldn't remember if he had even thanked Nola Evans, so anxious was he to borrow his grandfather's car and drive to the Eagle's Nest. He pocketed his Gainsborough cycling cap and popped in a breath mint before doing a quick self-inspection. He rubbed his freshly shaved chin. Finger-combed his thick hair. Straightened the collar of his polo shirt. Did a spit polish to the toes of his shoes. "Good luck, old boy," he said to himself.

He pushed the door open. Bea and Chase sat facing the window, Bea's cane and knitting needles on the table beside them. He stole across the room. "Guess who?" he said, covering Chase's eyes.

Her laugh came quick and breezy. "My cyclist in shining armor. I saw your reflection in the windowpane."

He pulled her to her feet, spun her around, and drew her into his arms. He kissed her soundly, his mouth lingering on her yielding lips. As he released her, he said, "I've missed you. I called your folks at two in the morning trying to find you."

Her wide brown eyes danced. "You didn't. If you rallied my dad from his sleep, he'll never forgive you."

"Your mom answered. You're to call her collect." He touched her cheek where the soft skin had turned a copper tan from the sun. "Have you told your parents about us yet?"

Dark lashes flickered. "I rarely write letters."

"Ian, is that you?" a gravelly voice demanded.

In the excitement, he had forgotten Beatrice. He kissed the top of her silvery hair and then knelt beside her. She was wearing her favorite royal-blue blouse and long beige skirt, her laced shoes poking out beneath the lap robe. He tilted her sagging chin toward him until he was level with those marvelous innocent blue eyes. "Where's the hat, sweetheart?"

She pointed to the derby monstrosity on the table.

"Were you out for tea?" he asked.

"We've been in the gardens looking for you."

"I've been with the cycling team. Hooked a ride to London with the coach. But I fly back to France tonight."

"So soon?" *Was that disappointment in Chase's voice?*

She had captured his heart, this attractive five-foot-five beauty, long-legged and well-figured. He outplayed her in tennis, but he found himself tongue-tied when he considered the degrees behind her name. Ian had never cared about a girl before, not like this one who seemed so intelligent and sure of herself. She was out of his league politically, too, but the whole time he raced the Giro d'Italia in the Italian Alps—and the whole preparation period for the French Tour—he couldn't get Chase out of his thoughts. "Chase," he said, "I had to see you. You didn't answer my letters."

"You didn't give me a permanent address."

She tucked a strand of hair behind her ear, hair the color of chestnuts. Unexpectedly he remembered his grandmother's last Christmas and her humming the song about chestnuts on an open fire. Huskily, he said, "Well, Chase, answer my letter now."

"About the weather?" she asked coyly.

"No."

"Oh—my research project is coming along just fine."

He checked his aggravation. "I don't remember asking you about your studies."

"Really?"

"Don't tease, Chase. I asked you to marry me."

"Oh, that."

"Well, what did you decide?"

"Ian, I can't marry you. I barely know you."

"It doesn't take all that much time to decide you love some-one." He wanted to remind her that she had researched the Kendall history so thoroughly for her Ph.D. that she knew all of the family secrets. "The Kendalls aren't a bad lot," he said.

She blushed on that one. "But I need more time to know you."

"Why? You've met my blue-blooded grandfather Uriah. And you know enough about my grandmother to know that I look like her. That's my background." With a grin, he flexed his muscles. "You've seen me riding my cycle. That's my career."

"But I don't know you, Ian."

"What do you want to know?"

"Everything."

He rattled off his birth date, driver's license number, and his addresses in Belgium and Maryland. He threw in his physical statistics. "I'm five-foot-eleven, give or take a fraction, and 155 pounds, give or take an ounce. And I love skiing, tennis, and cycling—the Tours and world championships mostly."

"Don't forget gardening," Beatrice said. "You planted the bougainvillea here at the Eagle's Nest."

His grin turned crooked. "My grandmother taught me about lilacs and roses when I was a kid. Guess I never outgrew them. Sounds out of character, doesn't it?"

"No," Chase whispered. "It—it sounds nice."

They were both embarrassed. He'd be stuck with the yard work if they married. "I asked you something else."

"I told you. I'm going back to New York at the end of August."

"That leaves July. Come to the Tour with me. I need you."

"Ian, you wouldn't even see me in the crowd. I'd be a blur as you sped by. And I won't go alone."

"Some of the wives and girlfriends are going."

"I thought Gainsborough forbids distractions at the race."

"Jon sponsors the team—pays our salaries, but he doesn't own our personal lives." *Not yet.* "Basil Millard's wife and daughter will be there. And Robbie's wife."

"Standing in the crowd in the sweltering heat?"

"Or the rain. They've made reservations in some of the hotels along the way." He was hit with uncertainty as he thought of Marcus Nash, one of the last-minute replacements on the team. A dark choice. "Marcus Nash's fiancée will be there, too."

"You don't sound pleased."

"He replaced my friend Alekos. Nash is not a team player. But I'm sure the ladies will make room for you."

"I like traveling first class, Ian, with a bed to myself."

"Come down to where the rest of us live, Chase. I've holed up in some of the worst hotels in the world on the Tours. You sacrifice when you have to and you survive."

"Anything for the glory of a race?"

"It's my job."

"Researching is mine. My father would have my neck, to say nothing about wanting his credit cards back if I took off for a three-week marathon."

"Take me," Beatrice said. "I don't mind third-rate hotels."

He swooped her out of her wheelchair. "That's my girl, Bea, but the mountain air in the Alps would snatch your breath away."

And you're fighting for every breath now. He cradled her against his chest and carried her to the bed. "Nap time, Bea."

"I'd like to go in Olivia's place," Bea said wistfully. "She promised you she'd be there."

Yes. He remembered sitting across from his grandmother at the Fox Hunt Restaurant in London. "Ian, win the Tour de France for me someday," she had told him.

"Grams, will you be there?" he had asked.

"Just try and stop me." Death had stopped her.

Bea's eyes glazed with longing. "Someone has to be there to protect you. I know about the bomb threats against the race."

"I'll be all right," he said gently. He sent Chase a warning scowl. "Have you been worrying Bea about those rumors?"

The beginnings of a frown formed on Chase's brow. "Bea brought them up. How serious are they, Ian?"

He shrugged. "Every race has its crackpots."

But this was the first race where he had been personally threatened. He carried the Mt. Ventoux chalked message in his mind and another written warning in his pocket. *Kendall, if you compete in the Tour de France, you risk your own safety.*

He had hitched a ride home from Avignon with Coach Skobla, determined to discuss these threats with Drew Gregory or Dudley Perkins at MI5; in the safety of his grandfather's cottage in the Cotswolds, he had changed his mind. Why risk being pulled out of the race when he was prepared to give winning his best shot?

Her frown deepened. "Why don't you pull out of the race?"

"We'll be safe. The Tour has its own police force."

"So does New York City," she said.

"The worst that can happen to me is a flat tire or oxygen deficit."

"What about broken bones if you crash in the mountains?"

Had he mentioned his dreams in his letters? The pileup on the mountain curve and his grandmother in white waving to him? No, he was certain that he hadn't bothered Chase with that ridiculous dream—that recurrent nightmare.

"Ian, you lost a rider a couple of years ago, didn't you?"

She said it so casually, but she was talking about a man he had ridden with. He couldn't even choke out the name Fabio, so he said, "We've lost more than one man over the years."

"You knew him," she guessed. "Oh, Ian, I'm sorry."

He licked his upper lip. "Fabio was a friend. I speak enough Italian so we got on well." Once started, Ian was able to say, "He was an Olympic road race champion."

"A gold medalist, the papers said."

"Yes. I met him at the Tour of Switzerland. He was a good rider. Came in second." His voice caught. "Fabio had everything to live for—a wife and baby, a good career ahead—"

Softly Chase asked, "Then why did he come speeding down a mountainside without a helmet?"

"They aren't mandatory in European races. No one dwells on crashing. It's one of the risks we take when we ride in the mountains. Fabio knew it. I know it—"

Bea fidgeted with the button on her sleeve as she stared up at Chase. "Olivia was going to be at the race for Ian. Won't you go in her place?"

"Ian, is that why you asked me to go—in your grandmother's place?"

"I asked you because I want you there." He brushed the thin strands of hair back from Bea's wrinkled face and pulled up the side rail. The image of his grandmother dressed in white and waving at him came back forcibly. "Chase, I'd like to tell the team that my girl is there, cheering me from the sidelines."

"I'm not your girl," she reminded him.

"Then I'll tell them you're my friend."

"That's all we can be—just friends. Nothing more." Without thinking she said, "And I won't be your live-in girlfriend."

He shrugged. "All right. We'll save all that for marriage."

⚭⚭⚭

A hot flush turned Chase's cheeks scarlet. She picked up a ball of yarn and tossed it. As Ian ducked, it fell to the floor and unraveled beneath the bed.

Bea rattled her side rails. "Now you pick that up. That was the beginnings of my next lap robe."

They both crouched down, and as Chase lunged for the yarn, Ian's hand came down on hers. "Chase, it won't be easy for me, but I'm willing to wait for you until marriage."

Another hot flush warmed her face as his sea-blue eyes watched her. "Is that what you tell all your girls?" she asked.

"There was never a girl like you before."

"And you're not like the boys back on Long Island," she admitted. Ian would never court her just to be a weekend guest on her father's yacht or a dinner guest at the family mansion.

Ian's hand tightened possessively. "Apparently not. Or you wouldn't leave them behind and travel to Europe so frequently."

Thanks to my grandmother's generosity and my father's credit cards, she thought. What would Ian say if she told him she was part of the New York Bartholomew-Evans clan, her family as well off as the Kennedys of Massachusetts? In her cramped position on the floor, she was convinced that she had put permanent dents in her kneecaps. "Ian, I have plans, and marriage isn't one of them."

"What are you going to do twenty years from now? Sit alone by the fireside with a row of framed sheepskins on the wall?"

"At least I won't be like Mom. Dad gives her the dregs of his time—a minute here, a minute there. That's all the time he can spare."

"Does he love her?"

Their eyes held. "That's why Mother puts up with his hours."

As the side rails rattled above them, Ian released her hand and scooped up the yarn. They stood again on opposite sides of the bed as Bea's gnarled fingers wrapped around the ball of yarn.

"I have to go, Bea," he said. "I have a dinner date in London before I fly out of Heathrow. Stay well, sweetheart."

He glanced across the bed at Chase, and with a shrug of his shoulders and a carefree wink, he said, "See you."

"Be careful. Stay safe, Ian."

The catch in her voice startled her. She imagined that her father had been much like Ian in his youth. Charming and cocky, stubborn and defiant. Her father had gone off to Vietnam in the early years of that conflict, a brash marine convinced that if every other man in the unit died, he wouldn't. That was like Ian—if every man on the team crashed on the riding circuit, he wouldn't. She asked lightly, "By any chance, Ian, are you having dinner at the Fox Hunt with Miriam and Drew Gregory?"

"How did you guess?"

"Miriam called this morning and insisted that I join them."

"Tonight—you're driving into London?"

"As soon as you leave the parking lot."

"Drive down with me."

She started to say no, and then told him, "I'd have to change first."

"Go on then. Pretty yourself up for the drive."

As she slipped into a dinner dress and heels, she knew that the part of Ian that she wanted to know was locked inside him in secret compartments. Come this far, no further. Ian would not admit to his fears, would never admit to defeat. An enigma. Like her father, Ian was a self-made man who faced life on his own terms. He had tossed aside the cushioned life that was his and had made his own way into the professional world of cycling. Ian seldom mentioned his father, rarely acknowledged his brother Grover, but he spoke highly of his grandparents and of his teammates who rode support for him.

But would she ever understand his need for winning?

Moments later as they drove away from the Eagle's Nest, Ian's eyes searched hers. His boy-next-door quality blurred as she pictured his pensive face grease-streaked as he repaired his cycle. And then she imagined Ian's sweaty face as he broke away from the rest of the riders to descend a mountain curve without braking—risking his safety and life. Tears stung the back of her eyes as she tried to visualize him crossing the finish line in Paris with his arms held high and the fans screaming. Ian's world was full, centered as it was on international cycling, reporters, and fans. Would there ever be room in that world of his for her?

❦❦❦

Long Island, New York. After the phone call from Ian Kendall in London, Nola Evans turned to her husband. "That was Chase's young man in England. He's trying to locate her."

Seymour poked his king-sized pillow and glared at the alarm clock in the darkness. "At 2 A.M. in the morning?"

"I don't think Mr. Kendall considered the time change when he dialed us. But he sounded nice, Seymour."

"Nothing sounds nice at this hour."

"You're just an old grump, dear." She cradled the handset. "I'm going to have some hot milk. Care to join me?"

"Come to bed, Nola. We'll talk about Kendall's phone call in the morning."

"I'm thinking about it now. You did things like that when you were dating me."

"I don't remember."

"Dear, you don't remember anything but business statistics and how to land the best contracts in Washington. But I do. I think about the old days a lot lately." She slipped into her satin robe and tightened the sash. "You called me from Honolulu on your way home from Vietnam. At three in the morning."

"Did I? Really? I must have been crazy."

"No, you were in love with me then and not with your job. You asked me to marry you as soon as you reached San Francisco."

"Then why didn't you?"

She sat beside him. "My parents tore up my plane ticket."

"That was a long time ago, Nola."

"Thirty years—but it seems like yesterday."

"It would be nice to start over again with you, Nola."

In three hours he would be the meticulous businessman again, driven by work and power, this moment of vulnerability gone.

She liked him best now with his silver-fox hair uncombed, his dark brown eyes watching her, his attention all hers.

"Let's go away together this weekend," he suggested.

"I'd like that." But she knew it would never happen. The job would demand his time. She offered him the chance to retrieve his offer. "Seymour, maybe we should stay home in case Chase calls."

She sensed him smiling in the darkness. "Don't tell me Chase is serious about this idiot who calls at two in the morning?"

She leaned down and kissed him. "I married the idiot who called at three."

He held her cupped hand against his bristly cheek. "I've been grateful ever since."

"Then why don't you tell me more often?"

"I'll try, Nola." He kissed her palm. "Is Kendall the young man from Oxford? The brainy one?"

No, that was another young man. Forgotten now, she thought. "Kendall is the American hopeful in this year's Tour de France."

"The cyclist? What is that girl of ours up to this time?"

"I don't know. At least she isn't in Prague."

"That's true, but she could have found herself a long-haired college professor in Prague with six degrees behind his name."

"Like Nigel Hampton at Oxford?"

"No," he grumbled. "Just my luck she'd find a protest marcher. Some whippersnapper who is politically minded, antigovernment, anti-nine-to-five hours, and definitely antiestablishment."

She drew back. "You make Chase out to be such a rebel."

"Isn't that what you like about her? She's her own person."

Nola's lips tightened. "That's why I think she might marry this cyclist. She's spent her whole life doing the unexpected."

"I expect Chase to finish her doctorate. I've invested enough money in it. Come to bed, Nola. Don't worry about her."

"You do. All the time."

"I worry about her not having a full-time job. I certainly don't worry about her marrying. She's too busy to settle down."

"She's busy trying to win your approval—trying to find some hard-working man just like you to marry."

"Like me? Why would she want to do that?"

"I wish I knew. It would only make her unhappy."

Exhaustion sapped him. He stretched on his back in the middle of their king-size bed. As he drifted toward sleep, his words grew muffled. "In her letter . . . she told us Kendall . . . was the last . . . person on earth she'd marry."

"That's why I'm afraid she's thinking about it."

Chase had used three pages in her letter to describe Ian Kendall. "He's spent his whole life racing," she had written, "and he's chalked up a number of good wins: second place in the Giro d'Italia, third in the Vuelta d'Espana." On the last page, Chase had underlined every word. "Don't worry, Mother. We're just friends. I'd never marry a man like him. I find him too arrogant. Cocky. Impulsive. But he's intelligent and handsome, too."

All of the things Nola had once said about Seymour.

"Seymour. Don't go to sleep on me. Help me figure this out."

"Honey, don't fret about Chase getting married. Not now."

"But I want her to marry the right person. She inherits a lot of money when she turns twenty-five. Seymour . . . what if Ian is a gold digger?"

He opened his eyes, but they drooped as he muttered, "Kendall has money of his own—big contract with Gainsborough. . . . I had him checked out after Chase's last letter."

"You didn't! She'll be furious. We'll have to apologize."

"I'll have . . . my secretary . . . tend to it . . . in the morning." His slurred words merged into a snore.

She shook him. "Seymour, you'll be gone all day. There'll be no chance to talk to you. And it's not like Chase to talk so much about some young man who doesn't have a college degree."

Seymour answered with a volcanic snort as he drifted into deeper sleep. Nola watched him in the moonlit darkness. In less than three hours he'd be off to work. She wouldn't see him again until dinner at seven. That was never the hour to bring up the children, unless they were talking about Tad and his latest business deal or Adele and the marvelous match she had made when she married a New York attorney. But dear Chase, as determined as Seymour himself, always made risky dinner conversation.

Nola grabbed the *Europe Magazine* from the bedside table and went down the spiral stairs to the spacious kitchen. Seymour had underlined several things in the magazine: the continuing IRA struggle, the latest on the young president in Poland, the pros and cons of the nuclear trade agreements in the European Union, and the EU's single currency. One small paragraph on the Tour de France had been double-scored: "Ignoring a series of bomb threats, the international cycling race will go on as scheduled."

Even as Nola poured milk in the sauce pan and turned the heat high, she couldn't get Ian Kendall out of her mind. She couldn't build an image of him either, except that he was handsome and tall. But was this handsome young man in danger? Chase's letter had been filled with his adventures—in England or Belgium one moment, in France the next. It seemed to Nola that Kendall's whole life was spent living out of a suitcase, expending his energy in a career that would be over by the time he was thirty-five. What kind of life could he offer her daughter?

Nola's heated milk boiled over. The fumes filled the room. She drank the scalded milk anyway, brooding over her grown children and wishing them to be little again so she could hold and comfort them. The last place in the world Nola wanted her youngest daughter to live was in Europe, an ocean away from them. She put her head down on the table and wept. Wept for the three o'clock call from Seymour so long ago when they still had their whole lives in front of them. Wept for the call moments ago from the young man in London who would have a rocky time pursuing Chase—that dreamy, idealistic daughter who wouldn't even recognize love if it knocked on her door.

Chapter 3

The countryside flew by as Ian did double time to London with his foot to the floorboard and his grandfather's fabulous Rolls Royce tested to the limit. Chase turned toward Ian and liked what she saw—a well-chiseled profile from the broad forehead to the firm set of his jaw and an athletic body crowned with sandy-red hair that brushed the headliner. "Slow down," she cautioned. "Your granddad won't thank us for wrecking his car."

He eased off for a second, and then his foot shoved hard against the gas pedal again, his freckled hands strong on the wheel. "I'm trying to outrun the man behind us."

She looked back, her hair sweeping against one cheek. "The Renault? Isn't he just part of the London traffic?"

"He's stayed with us ever since we hit the motorway."

"Why would he follow us?"

His jaw tightened. "I could pull over and ask him."

She picked up the newspaper on the seat between them and thumped the article on bomb threats against the American riders. "Maybe he has something to do with this."

"Rumors only. Besides, I ride with a British team."

"That doesn't change your American birth certificate. Bomb threats can't be laughed off. Why don't they cancel the race?"

His gaze slid back to the sideview mirror. "The French don't scare easily. Neither do I. I've spent too long preparing for the Tour to stay home on some bomb scare." He freed a hand from the wheel and touched her cheek, his eyes as blue as the summer sky on Long Island. "Let's talk about us. I want you at the race."

"You flatter me. Won't your family be there?"

"Dad and Grover always have an excuse, and my grandfather will wait out the race in Paris. That's why I want you there."

She glanced at the paper. "Terrorism scares me. Why doesn't the Tour go through England? I would go then."

"We did my first year on the Tour—straight from Calais to the Eurotunnel."

"You rode through the Chunnel on bikes?"

A smile tugged at his mouth. "We boarded trains for that. The Englishman Chris Boardman wanted to wear the yellow jersey into England, but it didn't work out that way."

"I'm sorry for him."

"He did better than I did. I dropped out in the mountains with a lung infection." His blue eyes were on her again. "The race starts in Holland this year and goes into Belgium close to where I live seven months of the year. Chase, will you come?"

"I'll think about it."

"I'll ask Basil's wife to make room for you. Just in case."

"For three weeks? Ian, I'm in Europe on a study program."

"*Et alors?*"

"So what? It's my whole life."

"Why don't you just marry me and get your degree in Belgium? You speak French and German as well as I do."

That idea was one of those crazy, wonderful things that her grandmother would have applauded. Still she argued, "You would grow tired of my academic world."

He sped past a line of cars, putting the stranger farther behind them. "I have two years' college credit in horticulture. But," he said, his jaw set, "professional cycling is my life for ten more years. After that, I'm going into the flower business."

With me or without me, she thought. Weeks ago he had placed well in the Giro d'Italia. Within days of the spin down the Champs Elysees, he'd be off for a one-day race in Belgium. After that, to one of the classics in Spain or Switzerland. "Ian, why punish your body for ten more years just for the glory of winning?"

"It's not just for that moment on the podium. When I finish my racing career, I want to be proud of the records I set."

She felt a tug of sadness for him. The end of Ian's cycling career at thirty or thirty-five would be like the autumn of his life. He'd be burned out. All this racing for autumn glory.

"Ian, the two of us—it wouldn't work. My roots are in New York, and yours are wherever you hang your helmet. If you kept on winning races, I'd have to share you with your fans."

"But I'd always come home to you." Ian's face clouded. "It's okay, Chase. Go back to Columbia and finish your degree. Just promise me you'll think about it while you're there."

She laughed and teased, "I'll go you one better. If you win the Tour de France for me, I'll reconsider your proposal."

"And I'll hold you to that promise."

As they neared London, she steeled herself against a sudden nameless darkness. She could never be content living Ian's simple lifestyle. She liked people, but not pressing crowds; the latest fashions, not sweat togs; concerts and skiing, not dusty biking trails. She would grow envious of watching him sign autographs for his fans while she stared blankly at her Ph.D. shingle.

Even if Ian wanted to take a risk, she didn't. It would be best if she flew back to New York before the Tour began. But would she be able to forget Ian Kendall so easily? Her thoughts flashed back to the Eagle's Nest and his lips on hers. Why was she suddenly remembering that tender, lingering kiss?

❀❀❀

In the American embassy in London, Drew Gregory stood in the doorway to his secretary's office, angrily gripping a steaming cup of cappuccino. Lennie glared back, struggling to focus on him out of her first pair of contact lenses. "Mr. Gregory, I most certainly did not leave a file on my desk."

The denial was worse than the act. He had found the folder there himself at 7:00 P.M. last evening. The hour—the exact moment of discovery—was as clear in his thinking as it had been last night when he wrestled the cuff of his shirt to note the time.

"Lennie, it was the Bosnia-Moscow report. I put it back in the locked cabinet myself. I covered for you."

Beneath the heavy makeup that she wore these days, he saw

her skin visibly blanch. Her voice tightened. "You know I never take chances with security, Mr. Gregory."

To keep his anger in check, he took a quick gulp of his coffee and sputtered at the sugary taste. "Lennie," he barked, "you know I like my coffee black."

"Oh, Mr. Gregory," she apologized, "Radburn likes cream and three sugar cubes. I guess I got mixed up this morning."

Radburn Parker, Lennie's new boyfriend. Her first beau as far as Drew knew. He could deal with the old Lennie; she didn't make mistakes. Lennie had always been a perfectionist, a prim and proper old maid in her dowdy clothes and rimless spectacles. Her work output had been flawless, and her manners and speech precise, British to the core. Drew had come back from his trip to Prague to find a fiftyish woman trying to look thirty-five with her new hairstyle and shorter skirt length. Only Lennie's sensible laced shoes still protruded from under the desk.

She appeared ready to rescue the offending cup, but he waved her back to her chair. "I'll have coffee with Vic Wilson. We have a nine o'clock meeting."

She frowned and ran her finger down his daily schedule. "I don't see anything listed here, Mr. Gregory. Not at nine."

He had slipped up there. The meeting was confidential. He cleared his throat, ready to confront her again with the security risk when the phone rang. She answered and covering the mouthpiece whispered, "It's the station-chief from Paris."

Troy Carwell. "I'll take it in my office." *And you'll stay on the line listening, the way you've been doing lately.* He kicked the door shut and raced to his desk. As he balanced the handset in the crook of his neck, he scrawled a memo on the scratch pad. It was time to ask for a new red phone, a line that even Lennie could not access. "Troy, it's Gregory."

"You took long enough," Carwell growled.

"I was in Lennie's room. Any word on Salvador Contoni?"

"Monique Dupree flew into Paris a few hours ago. Alone."

"Then she didn't find Contoni?"

"Find him? She just spent seven days with him, the last two cruising the Greek Islands on his yacht. She left him in Corfu."

"The island of Corfu," Drew mused, "and not in Milan?"

"That's the question mark. Everything went smoothly until their meeting with Vasille Golemis at his private villa."

Drew's spine stiffened. "Alekos Golemis's father?"

"The same. He's a member of the Parliament."

Golemis. The name tore at Drew's memory and quickly meshed with the senseless death of a young cyclist on the mountain near Sulzbach—a lad with strong Grecian features and eyes so dark they were almost black. He had been Ian Kendall's friend. The last time Drew saw Alekos, he was lying on a narrow metal table, his youthful body lifeless, those brilliant dark eyes closed. Dead. Murdered by a Russian agent. "Troy, why would Golemis meet with a man like Salvador Contoni?"

"We may know soon. Our agent shot pictures of their time together, including the Golemis villa. One agent nosing around was safer than alerting Greek Intelligence."

"So Monique couldn't persuade Contoni to come back?"

"We haven't heard from her, but the agent reports a rather cozy affair. It was your idea to use her, Drew. Never thought it would work. We got suckered in." Troy smacked his lips. "She took a taxi from Charles de Gaulle straight to her apartment on the Seine. Picked up her Renault and headed for Isigny."

"Her boys are there. Sorry, Troy. Thought she'd cooperate."

"Right now, there are more important things to deal with. Glenn Fairway—that old stickler for on-time appointments—will fill you in. How are things at the embassy?"

Drew thought of Lennie on the line, listening. "More priority files are missing. And, Troy, my secretary has become the scuttlebutt of the London embassy."

"Don't tell me your Miss Efficiency-plus has a beau?"

"Haven't met him yet, but he's turned my office life upside down." There was a faint click in Drew's ear. He switched to the scrambled line. "That was Lennie tuning out. She's one of the problems since I came back. Yesterday she was so anxious to meet Parker she left the Bosnia-Moscow file on her desk."

"If she's a security risk, get rid of her."

"I can't. I made the mistake of covering for her."

Embassy briefing room, 9:10 A.M. It was an odd gathering. Glenn Fairway, the London station-chief, sat at one end of the oval table flipping a pencil between his stubby fingers. The well-dressed American ambassador drummed his knuckles at the other end. Dudley Perkins was elbow-close to Fairway.

A meeting big enough to bring in MI5, Drew thought. *But who are the two strangers?* As Drew slipped into the chair beside Vic Wilson, Vic passed a hastily written note to him. "The man in tweeds is British, Fairway's latest asset. The thin man beside Perkins is Maurice Chambord, the new general secretary of the Societe du Tour de France."

The Frenchman's handshake was limp, the nameless Englishman's curt nod just as distasteful. Maurice Chambord was dark and wiry, his eye constantly on his watch. Drew let his gaze wander back to the big man in a tweed jacket and felt an immediate aversion to him. In contrast to Chambord, the Englishman was fair-skinned, his shrewd green eyes a shade lighter than his tie.

The ambassador nodded to Fairway. "Since this affects Intelligence, perhaps you could explain why we're here, Glenn."

Fairway relished taking over. There was little memorable about his face, just an ordinary, run-of-the mill appearance, but his voice commandeered the room. "It's those terrorist threats against the Tour de France—someone wants to stop the race."

"But France wants the race to go on," Chambord said.

"Too many French francs at stake?" Drew asked.

The Frenchman's look was censoring. "More is at stake than money, Monsieur Gregory. Lives are being threatened." His words spewed out sharp and angry. "They singled out an American—he wasn't in the original bomb threats. It could be an anti-American terrorist group going for an American hero. We don't know. We just have to take it seriously. That's why I'm here."

Dudley Perkins leaned forward, his face gloomy. "We're talking about your friend Ian Kendall, Drew."

"Not Ian!"

"Yes. He's a member of the British team, so it could be the work of the IRA aiming at the heart of Britain again."

"Then pull Kendall off the team."

Fairway shook his head. "What would that accomplish? You can't take a man's career away from him. The aim is to catch terrorists, not give in to their threats. And, Dudley, this is bigger than a threat against London's financial district."

Drew groaned. *Risk Kendall's life, and I won't be able to face his family again. I won't be able to face myself. And, Fairway, anger MI5, and we sit this one out alone.*

Drew didn't always agree with Perkins, but there was no point in aggravating him on his home turf. But Glenn was a cynical, self-centered man, too Company-minded to recognize that he was opposing a powerful man in the host country and quite possibly offending the Frenchman.

"Let's hear Chambord out," Drew suggested.

Chambord's smile was brief. "We can't lay the blame on any one terrorist group. No one has come forward and taken credit. But the threats have led us to believe—," he hesitated, "—that there is a Bosnia-Moscow connection."

"Impossible. Ian doesn't know anyone in Bosnia or Moscow."

Perkins's bushy brows scrunched together. "His grandfather knew people in both countries. Perhaps he has enemies there."

No, Uriah Kendall's ties with the past ended a long time ago. Drew thought of the file left on Lennie's desk. "If there is a Russian connection, then threatening the race could be a decoy to something bigger." *Or something as elusive as why Vasille Golemis would meet with a man like Salvador Contoni.*

An amused smile touched the Englishman's lips. "A problem in Moscow, Gregory? Must we blame everything on the Russians?"

Drew met the Englishman's arrogant gaze. He shrugged off his concern about Golemis and said, "The old desire for power is still there. Didn't they put a crack Russian unit in Bosnia as part of the NATO peacekeeping forces? Any problem with them?"

"Paratroopers. Good men," the Englishman countered.

The ambassador agreed. "We had nothing but praise for them."

Perkins sighed. "It's not the Russians who concern me, but a Serbian Intelligence officer is reportedly riding in the Tour—a Serbian war criminal with a contact here in London."

Fairway exploded, "You're usually up on those things, Dudley. If there's a known war criminal, turn him over to NATO."

Perkins rubbed his scrawny hands. "We only know the Serbian by his code name Roadrunner. And his English contact is called the Lily-trotter. But they slipped through our net."

The Englishman laughed. "A terrorist among the riders? Come now, Dudley, a Roadrunner and a Lily-trotter—that's absurd."

Chambord glanced at his watch again. "Gentlemen, the threats against the Tour are my immediate concern. France will understand if you withdraw your riders, but the race must go on."

"How can we help, Mr. Chambord?" the ambassador asked.

"By supporting the race. The Tour has its own police force, and our gendarmerie and French Intelligence are alerted." He glanced apologetically at Dudley Perkins. "Troy Carwell and the American ambassador in Paris are sending some men."

Drew turned to Fairway. "Me specifically?" he asked.

"You and Vic will ride in the caravan as inconspicuously as possible. You're there to protect the American riders. The French will cover the European teams."

Perkins said quietly, "I arranged for you and Mr. Wilson to ride with the Gainsborough team." He managed a sly smile. "I persuaded Jon—forced him actually—to allow you to ride in the team car as prospective sponsors for next year."

Drew nodded. "I'm sure Jon Gainsborough went for that idea."

Fairway grinned. "Like a hog snooting the mire. But the threats against the Tour are real. We can't ignore them. So we're with you, Chambord. We won't let anyone stop the Tour de France."

Chambord capped his pen and put it away. "I must leave now in order to make my plane on time."

"My deputy will drive you to Heathrow," the ambassador said.

Maurice Chambord smiled at last. "Thank you, gentlemen, for your time. And you, Mr. Ambassador, for your kindness." He turned to Dudley Perkins. "If there is a Bosnian war criminal riding in the Tour, we will find him."

"He won't be easily identified."

Chambord nodded. "That will make it more challenging."

Chapter 4

As the door closed behind the Frenchman, Drew massaged his temples. "What happens to Lennie while I'm gone?" he asked.

Fairway's smile did little more than twist his pointed nose and curl his lip. "If she's passing memos out of the embassy, we can't terminate her and risk her leaving the country. So, until we have proof, she goes into the secretarial pool with access to classified material."

"And under constant surveillance. Poor Lennie."

"Poor Parker," Fairway countered. "He's the one put to the task of dating her."

"Has anyone checked him out?"

"Parker isn't the problem, Gregory. He's part of our surveillance team."

"Lennie was doing her job until he came into her life. Why break her heart with a man who doesn't care one ounce for her?"

Across the table, the Englishman smiled. "It was the only way to win her confidence. Miss Applegate budded with red roses and evenings out on the town. She's turned into quite a love."

Fairway's gaze hardened. "Drew, why didn't you tell us Lennie had relatives in Bosnia?"

"That wasn't on her resumé."

"She failed to include it, but she comes from a clan of Russian Slavs."

If Drew told him he had reread Lennie's resumé two days ago, he would be admitting his own doubts about her. Annoyed, he said, "And I hail from the Irish Catholics. And Vic's mother was Hungarian or Polish. And you grew up in the Bronx, the Heinz variety. What difference does it make where we came from?"

Fairway's voice rose a notch. "She kept in touch with her relatives in Bosnia all through that long war and especially after NATO moved in."

"That doesn't make her a traitor."

The ambassador whipped out his handkerchief and swiped it across his glasses. "We're sorry, Gregory. Memos and files turned up missing at the embassy at an alarming rate while you were on your honeymoon. But the questions about Miss Applegate's loyalties came up while you were in Prague."

Drew turned to Vic. "And no one bothered to tell me."

"You were gone," Fairway said. "But we're telling you now. Everything points to Lennie."

"Thanks." His voice was so brittle that Fairway backed off.

Quietly the ambassador said, "In the last year she ran up some heavy debts and took out loans that she can't pay back."

"Maybe she needed money for the care of her sick parents."

"And for the transfer of funds to her family in Bosnia."

"From a London bank, Mr. Ambassador?"

"No, Gregory, through a Swiss account."

Drew knew that Lennie lived in a squeeze-box flat in a poor part of town, stretching her embassy salary beyond her limit. If she had just come to him and asked him for a loan. But Lennie had been tight-lipped about her private life and noncommunicative about her lifestyle. Now and then Drew had bought her tickets to a concert. Operas were her favorite. She had thanked him profusely and then gone off to the concert alone, a prim and proper lady in a drab suit and tied shoes, her hair pulled back into a bun. "Am I to ferret out my own secretary, Glenn?"

"It's our job to go after traitors."

"Unless you're working with her," the Englishman suggested.

He glanced at his watch and stood, a tall, distinguished forty-five-year-old with light hair and gray-blond brows who made ceremony of picking up his hat and gloves. "Fairway, I have a luncheon date. I'll report back to you in the morning."

Drew waited until he left and then asked, "Who is that man?"

"Radburn Parker," Fairway said. "He's working for us."

"Parker! He's a British asset? Since when, Glenn?"

"The last few weeks."

Drew's tongue turned acid. "You louse. You—"

A chill caught him between the shoulder blades. In the old days, he would have blasted Fairway with a string of expletives, but life had changed for Drew on the mountain slope in Sulzbach when he—a stubborn, willful man—had made contact with God. Still he raged inside. He could pray for Lennie, but he couldn't bring himself to pray for Parker or Fairway. Right now the blind spot in Drew's fury blocked out his sense of right and wrong. He fought against the admonition that a redeemed man should not let the sun go down on his wrath. He glanced out the window, arguing with himself on how to define sundown—when the sun slipped behind the mountain or when it was pitch dark outside? Regaining control, he asked, "Glenn, what do you know about Parker?"

"He's from a prominent London family."

The ambassador was more informative. "He was a minor secretary at the British embassy for a year. That's how Perkins and I met him. Some time back, he spent a number of years in Russia as a visiting history professor."

"It was a good relationship," Perkins said. "The whole time he was there, he fed intelligence information back to us—even sent some of the first information we had on the old Phoenix-40."

Disinformation, Drew thought. "And now?"

Perkins's grim expression lightened. "Thanks to the Parker Foundation, the Gainsborough cycling team can go to the race. Gainsborough keeps the team name, and Parker helps pay the bills."

"But whose idea was it for Parker to romance Lennie?"

There was a unanimous need to check their watches before Perkins said, "That was your idea, wasn't it, Mr. Ambassador?"

"No, Fairway's the one who came to me with it."

The London chief glared at Perkins. "It was Parker's idea."

As the meeting broke up, Drew latched onto Fairway's arm and whirled him around. "Why did you recruit Parker?"

Fairway brushed his sleeve. "With his steel plant tight on funds, Gainsborough needed money to keep the team from being pulled out of the Tour. As for me—I have odds on that American

rider. So Dudley and I had dinner with Parker to ask for money."
As if to further justify himself, he said, "Parker and I played polo
together—even played with Prince Charles a few times."

"Get to your point."

"After dinner and drinks, Radburn agreed to a loan from the
Parker Foundation. His word as much as guaranteed it happening."

"A loan had nothing to do with Lennie."

Fairway squirmed. "It had a lot to do with you, Drew. Parker
and I agreed on one thing. We want you out of the embassy."

"Why, Glenn? Are you still smarting over my working under
Carwell in Paris instead of your London station?"

"It is unusual. By the third drink Parker pledged his financial
support if we promised to check you out, Drew. It snowballed
after that, but Perkins here vouched for him. After all, the Parkers
are well respected in this country."

"And rich. That always counts with you, Fairway. So why
didn't Perkins hire him on at MI5? We don't need a man like
Radburn Parker in the American embassy."

Fairway stomped off, cutting his path out of the middle of the
corridor. In three quick strides Drew was at his side again. "How
did Parker get mixed up with Lennie?"

"He offered his services."

"You hired a rich playboy to ruin my secretary's name?"

"He didn't want money."

"Just access into the embassy? I bet you gave him top security
clearance without going through the usual channels."

"Time was important. We have a chance to win the Tour de
France, Drew." He rapped Drew's shoulder with his knuckles.
"And we can't risk a Deven or Ames showing up in the London
station."

"It sounds reasonable. Lennie is a British subject. Perkins is
internal security." His contempt aroused the old animosity
between them. "It was your chance for MI5 and the CIA to work
together—to better your relationships between the two countries.
So you agreed to run a smear campaign against Lennie."

"Lennie betrayed herself," he said hotly.

Fairway stalked off again, allowing Vic Wilson time to catch up with Drew. "Stay cool," Vic said. "Fairway has problems here at the embassy. The ambassador's on his neck—wants answers."

"I'm not the answer."

"Lennie may be—and she's your secretary; but if there's a smear campaign going on, it's against you, Drew. Fairway thinks you ruined it for the Agency when you took Porter Deven down."

"And he wishes I had gone down with him?" He ran his hands through his silver-streaked hair. "Fairway puts too much stock in Parker. We should have point men out observing his every move."

"What's the matter, Gregory? Are you just embarrassed that Lennie fooled you? She fooled all of us."

To Drew's silence, he said, "Until recently I thought Lennie was being set up, too. But everything blew apart when Radburn Parker showed up with photographs of Lennie meeting her foreign contact and passing embassy papers to him."

"Next you'll tell me I'm tied in with the whole mess."

Vic pulled him into an empty room. "You are involved, Drew."

"Make sense."

"You're trying to protect her—to cover for her. Fairway never took to your assignment to this embassy. My guess is he thought you came here because you wanted his job."

"Not for all the diamonds in Amsterdam," Drew told him. "Vic, have you seen those photographs of Lennie?"

"Yes. There's no mistaking it's Lennie Applegate. But all you can see of her contact is a man's hands taking the papers from her."

"Get me copies of Parker's pictures, Vic."

"You know Fairway's office is harder to crack than the Federal Reserve vault."

"Then charm his secretary."

"Fairway is busy doing that."

"Then blow up the vault. I want those pictures."

"Lennie isn't worth it."

The corner of Drew's mouth twitched. "She is to me."

Vic turned off at his own office with a low-tone parting. "Drew, if you have anything in those files of yours that you don't want found, clear them out today."

"Why?"

"Fairway plans a room search once you're gone. They'll fill your cabinet with substitute file folders. And—" He hesitated, and then said apologetically, "They plan to set the sprinklers off in Lennie's office."

"What if Lennie catches on?"

"Even if she gets back into the room after we're gone, her files will be waterlogged, nothing legible. She'll beeline out of there as fast as she entered, but the hidden cameras will capture everything she does."

Cameras that are already in place, he thought. *Recording my every move since I got back from Prague.* "Lennie is not the only one under surveillance, is she?"

"You, too, Drew, but I didn't dare warn you. I've checked out as loyal to the Company now. That's why I'm being sent with you to France as Fairway's eyes and ears."

"Good thing your friendship makes you half blind and deaf."

Vic grinned. "I was thinking the same thing."

◉◉◉

As Drew reached his office, Lennie stepped into the corridor. In spite of the warm weather she was wearing her lightweight Burberry belted tightly at her waist. She held one arm tight against her side, a purse clutched under the other.

"Oh, Mr. Gregory," she said, flustered, "I'm having lunch early. You don't mind, do you?"

Radburn Parker towered behind her, his eyes mocking as he looked at Drew. "Of course, he doesn't mind, my dear."

She met Drew's stern gaze, staring back at him reproachfully. "Mr. Gregory, Radburn tells me you are going on holiday again. I wish you had told me."

What else has Parker told you? "I just found out."

Parker tugged at her elbow and guided her toward the elevator, Lennie's shiny laced shoes tapping rhythmically beside him. She glanced back as they hurried away. "I didn't know you liked cycling. My nephew will be riding in the Tour, too."

A nephew? Did Lennie have a nephew? She never mentioned anyone except her ill parents. As the elevator doors slammed shut, Drew stormed into Lennie's office and stared around the empty room. *Lennie*, he thought miserably, *what is happening to you?*

He considered ransacking her desk, but it was exactly what Parker would expect him to do; and Parker, as far as Drew was concerned, was as unpredictable as a snake in the grass.

Back in his own office, he found the hidden cameras—because he knew where to look—and covered them. No one would come to check it out; that would be a dead giveaway that they were watching him. But in case the embassy really searched this room while he was gone, he wanted to retrieve the personal files that tied him in with Porter Deven and those trips to Prague and Sulzbach.

He went to the gunmetal gray cabinet. *Porter's file was gone.* Drew searched methodically; his perseverance paid off. The Prague file and Porter's were jammed together, the Aldrich Ames records squeezed between them. Lennie had no access to this cabinet, but someone did. He took out the Sulzbach report and the Bosnia-Moscow folder, thicker than he remembered it, and added them to his collection. Slapping the folders on top of the cabinet, he sent the drawer flying. It jammed on its rollers and took him another five minutes to get it closed and locked.

Back at his desk, Drew shed his coat and tried to focus on the opening line of the Bosnia-Moscow report, but he couldn't get Lennie out of his mind. Was Lennie being set up as Drew suspected, or had she willingly carried classified documents out of the embassy for a price? One persistent thought replayed itself. Why had Lennie never mentioned her Yugoslavian heritage?

Two years ago Lennie had been his last choice for a secretary, and she knew it. Shy and uncertain on her first day, she had said, "If you want to have someone else—"

"No. You'll do fine," he had told her. "Do you have children, Mrs. Applegate?"

"It's Miss, but please call me Lennie. I can stay overtime if you need. I'm a very good worker. You can ask Mr. Fairway."

"I already did." Looking at her troubled face, he had teased, "As long as you have a cup of cappuccino and the newspaper or a copy of the *U.S. News and World Report* on my desk every morning, we'll get on just fine."

The following morning she came into his office balancing a

brand-new mug spewing steam into the room, the *Evening Standard* under her arm. He had been too embarrassed to tell her he had already scoured the paper. Today's version wouldn't even be out until midafternoon, so he grinned and said, "Everything but the *U.S. News and World Report*."

"They didn't have one at the book stand," she apologized.

When she reported in on the fourth day, he was blessing his computer. It had just crashed, and he had no idea how to rally technology to his side. "You don't have to swear, Mr. Gregory," she had said. "I'll show you how to use it."

As predicted, she scored zero on personal relationships, but she knew how to run an office and to deal discreetly with classified material. She was, he had decided, the only good thing that came out of his assignment to the London embassy. Each morning began the same way: the coffee on a coaster so it wouldn't stain his desk; the newspaper opened for him, sometimes to the sports page; the computer booted up, ready to go. By the third week he found a book on British history on top of the *Evening Standard*, a gem from some secondhand bookstore.

"You mentioned this one last week," she said shyly. "No British history buff should be without it."

He tried to repay her kindnesses. Two theater tickets now and again. Once to the Royal Ballet at Covent Garden. Another to the *Mikado* at the Coliseum. Twice to the Royal Opera House. It took her weeks before she could tell him, "One ticket is really enough, Mr. Gregory. Oh, I'm grateful, of course, for two, but—it's difficult to get someone to go with me at the last minute."

It was as close as she ever came to admitting that she had few friends, if any. That first Christmas—after she'd told him she'd never been to Scotland—he had given her a three-day rail pass to Edinburgh with her hotel reservation covered. He felt secure with his generosity. Lennie never discussed her personal life with the other secretaries at the embassy.

It was months before he dragged out of her that she was responsible for elderly parents, and then he hated himself for the locker-room jokes. He had often chuckled over Lennie's laced shoes and dowdy suits, all four of them. "She's not the latest fashion," he admitted to the boys. "She even rotates her blouses, regular as clockwork. The pink one on Monday, the green one . . ."

Ever since that trip to the mountains of Sulzbach—ever since he had made that firm decision to put God at the top of his priority list—the old locker-room jokes came back to haunt him. That's when he told his colleagues, "Lennie is not the cream of society, but she's a woman of integrity." That elusive characteristic that Drew's mother had drummed into him from boyhood.

Now Fairway and the ambassador wanted him to eat his own words. Had he misjudged Lennie? Had she really fooled him? Or had she become the scapegoat for the missing embassy files? He spent the rest of the afternoon reading the Bosnia-Moscow report, one ear cocked for Lennie's return from her luncheon date with Parker. She never came back.

Bosnia. Croatia. Zagreb. Tuzla. The names touched the old sore spot that had landed him the desk job in London. He had been on a covert assignment in Sarajevo, a civil war exploding all around him. Everything went well until he met his Croatian contact. Even now his mind went back to Leopold Bolav, a burly man with a definite leaning toward vodka and communism. Twenty men recognized Leopold as the leader of their guerrilla unit, but Drew disliked Bolav. With a white Persian cat balancing on the shoulder of his faded fatigues and the laces of his muddy army boots loose at the top, he didn't give the appearance of a leader.

The day before Drew was to slip out of Sarajevo, Leopold had called an early morning meeting in the basement of a bombed-out shelter. When Bolav failed to join the unit, Drew walked across the underground room and pulled down a wall map. That's when the explosion flattened him against the wall. It was better than what it had done to the other twenty men. Drew was the only survivor in the room. His code name Crisscross was blown as well, bringing his covert career to a sudden halt. Sometimes his personal loss depressed him, but the loss of the men who hadn't lived long enough to see the end of that bloody war still tore at his gut.

Back in Paris, Drew had said, "I think Leopold infiltrated the ranks. Mark my word, he's a Serbian Intelligence officer. That's why my cover was blown."

Porter Deven, the station-chief in Paris then, had laughed at the idea. "Admit it, Drew. There's been a clerical blunder. That's all. Be glad you got out of Sarajevo alive." And with that, Deven had shipped him off to London to wait out a safe return to covert action. Drew was still rotting away at the embassy, ticking off too many birthdays. He rubbed his forehead, pressing his fingers into the scowl grooves to ease the miserable pain thumping there.

Everything at the embassy was buried under mountains of paperwork. Well, he'd add to the confusion. He switched on his computer—surprised that Lennie had not turned it on this morning—and began to revise the Bosnia-Moscow report. He filled it with disinformation that would infuriate Glenn Fairway if he caught wind of what Drew was doing. Disinformation that would trap Lennie if she leaked it into other hands. Deliberately, he filled in half-truths, new names—some that existed, others that formed in his mind as he typed.

He paused at his keyboard, then pulled more facts and figures from the air about the peacekeeping forces in Bosnia—some that had succeeded, others that had gone awry. He remembered the name of the Russian officer who had headed up the 1,500-man crack paratrooper unit. Drew had seen a picture of the man once, so he added a mustache and height for good measure. He suggested a possible tie between war criminals who had escaped the borders and the reported uprising of the Phoenix-40 in Russia.

Satisfied with the results, he made photocopies, and then with a flick of his hand, he deleted the file he had just created. *No record for you to find, Fairway. Not in my computer files. The computer and I are totally innocent.*

He turned off the computer. Click. Hum. Buzz. Flashing lights. The darkened screen appeared. He went into Lennie's office. Her copy of the Bosnia-Moscow report was right where he expected to find it, not in alphabetical order, but according to Lennie's own geographical placement. He smiled as he slipped the extra pages neatly into the folder and put it back into Lennie's drawer. On impulse, he decided to check out the Parisian Terrorist report. With his scheduled three weeks in France, he might as well have facts at his fingertips: known terrorist organizations and right-wing Parisians, the exact sites for bombings in the '90s, and their devastating statistics. *The Parisian folder was missing.*

Drew blinked against the image of Lennie's hasty exit for lunch, her arm held tight to her body. Tightly enough to conceal a file under her raincoat? Lennie could have walked out of the embassy with Parker's security clearance covering them both.

Drew's jaw locked; the pain jabbed beneath his ears and ran a rapid course down his jaw. *Lennie, Lennie. What happened to you?* He was still squinting with eye fatigue when his wife poked her head around the door, a visitor's pass pinned to her dress.

Miriam was elegant as always. Lights and shadows fell across her oval face like the vivid strokes of a Rembrandt painting, yet softened with the delicate touch of Renoir. Her mellow voice matched the image. "Drew, darling, you haven't forgotten about dinner with Ian and Chase?"

"Oh, *Liebling*, it totally slipped my mind."

"You'd better hurry. Ian can't miss his plane." Miriam glanced toward Lennie's door. "I was hoping to catch Lennie."

"She's been at lunch for four hours."

"And obviously without your blessing, dear. I wanted to invite her and her gentleman friend to dinner this weekend."

"Can you put that off until after the Tour de France?"

Her eyes searched his as she stepped to the side of the desk and gave him a quick peck on the cheek. "You're going away?"

"For three weeks. Fairway and Carwell volunteered my services at the cycling race. Go with me, Miriam."

"No, but you can drop me off in Paris for a shopping spree."

"I'll keep the credit card with me."

"I have my own. Drew, while you're away, work up some enthusiasm for my dinner guests. Lennie is a lonely woman. You told me that yourself. Besides, you agreed, my life in London would include lots of company."

"I didn't expect our guests to include Radburn Parker."

"Lennie's love? What a fancy name."

"For a scoundrel." He stood. "How did your day go?" he asked as he stuffed the file folders into his briefcase.

"I spent all morning at Sotheby's auction with Rupert Townsend."

"One of those auctioneers?"

"One of their department heads. An old friend. A dear man actually. He showed me some marvelous paintings. One by Rubens that I really liked."

"I trust you left the checkbook home."

She laughed. "Don't worry. We didn't have enough in our account for that one."

He swung the briefcase into his hand. "Would your *dear man* at Sotheby's keep something for me?"

Her eyes traveled slowly to his briefcase and back to Drew's face. "In his vault?"

"Yes."

"Well, I did pay for lunch today, so he does owe me a favor. And he won't ask questions."

Chapter 5

Chase watched Ian's British Airway plane climb until it was less than a dot in the London sky, and then she turned to the Gregorys. "Drew, what do you think happened to Coach Skobla? Ian is really worried about him."

"Ludvik Skobla is not Ian's problem. But give me a few minutes, and I'll make some phone calls."

Drew took off with a wink, not giving them a chance to ask questions. As he made his way toward a public phone, Chase said, "Miriam, Ian is getting too serious."

Miriam's deep-set eyes filled with pleasure. "I thought so. You couldn't find a nicer young man."

Chase saw her own sadness reflected in the window glass. "But, Miriam, how can I be in love with someone I barely know? We've never really dated, and he's already proposing."

"That sounds like Ian. He was never one to waste time."

"But I want a courtship with flowers and candlelight dinners and time to get acquainted."

"That's what I wanted, Chase, but Drew persuaded me to run off and get married six weeks after we met." The airport lighting could not diminish Miriam's beauty or darken her magnificent smile. Her reddish-brown hair was swept back from her face in a striking chignon that highlighted her remarkable cheekbones. "Most of my husband's roses came after we were married."

"It just wouldn't work for me. I have unfinished business back home, completing my Ph.D., for one."

Miriam squeezed her hand. "Dear Chase, you have a brilliant

mind. Use it. But you also have a tender heart. Listen to it. Make certain your unfinished business in New York is not an excuse. It just might be that you and Ian need each other. Drew and I do."

A few stragglers kept their faces pressed against the airport window, the pain of farewell still marring their expressions. "Miriam, when I marry—if I marry—it will be in Long Island in June when Mother's roses are the most lovely."

"Oh, Chase, everyone goes for a June wedding."

"Not everyone has a rose garden of her own."

"June wouldn't work. Didn't Ian tell you? He competes in the Giro d'Italia in June, and a month later it's the Tour de France."

"Maybe he could spare me a few days between races."

Miriam's brows drew into an arch. "A young man like Ian would want more time than that to take his bride on a honeymoon."

Miriam picked up a bridal magazine in the airport waiting room. The torn cover page showed a smiling wedding party at the altar with groomsmen in winter black tuxes and bridesmaids in long red velvet. "Why not wed off season—a late winter wedding?"

"I'll be hard at work on my Ph.D. by then."

"With me it was my love of art. I'm afraid with you, it's your love of learning. Make certain that's what you really want."

The closeness that she had felt to Miriam faded. "Marriage isn't all that important to me. My grandmother Callie used to say, 'You marry them, bury them, and then you spend their money.'"

"That's frightfully unkind. What sort of a woman was she?"

"She was wonderful, but my grandfather was always busy working on his next million. Callie had everything, but she would have given it all up just to spend more time with him."

"Chase, a man has to provide for his family."

"The Bartholomews were one of the richest families in New York. It's just that my grandfather was married to his job."

"Like Ian is glued to bicycling?" she asked. Foreboding filled her voice. "Chase, don't wait as long as I did to discover those golden moments of sharing someone's life."

They were the only two at the boarding gate now, but they could still see Drew at the pay phone, pounding his fist against the wall. "That has to be Vic Wilson on the line," Miriam said. "They always argue—Drew suggesting one plan, Vic another."

"I thought they were such good friends."

"They are. Who wouldn't be with Drew? They are as different as two beet tops, but they work well together, those two."

"Will Vic know where Coach Skobla is?"

"Oh, my, no, but he'll be on it the minute Drew hangs up."

They moved toward Drew as though Miriam sensed his need of her. "You're so alike," Chase said. "Ian and I are so different."

"No, dear, Drew and I are opposites. The art gallery is my whole world, but he endures the galleries for my sake. Don't be so afraid of Ian's career that you're afraid to look at Ian."

"He'd be gone so much of the time, like my grandfather."

"So was Drew. I fought Drew's career and lost sixteen good years with him." Her smile caressed Chase. "I have a funny feeling we're a lot alike, my dear," she said.

Don't I wish. You have the grace and sophistication that Callie had. The absolute confidence that you chose the right man.

"Chase, Ian is a lot like Drew—a man quick to know what he wants." Their steps slowed to a crawl as Miriam glanced at her. "There must be things you like about him."

"He's a challenge on the tennis court and like a gazelle at the Jungfrau in Switzerland. Even on the lower slopes the higher we climbed, the more determined I was to keep up with him." As they reached Drew, she said, "We both like England and Beatrice Thorpe." As she thought of Bea, darkness settled over her. "Bea's afraid something will happen to Ian during the race."

"Don't worry, Chase. Bruises heal," Drew told her as they joined him.

"Is everything all right, Drew?" Miriam asked.

Drew shook off Miriam's concern and winked at Chase. "Vic will have Coach Skobla located and on a plane back to France before we reach the house. Now about you and Ian—Ian thinks the world is on a crash course to oblivion and that you plan to right the wrongs before that happens."

"We do get in our worst rows arguing over politics."

"Ouch," Drew said. "So do Miriam and I."

"You do? Well, I don't like being several months older."

Miriam's laughter was contagious as she leaned her head against Drew's shoulder. "Chase! Dear child, Drew is eleven years older than I am. What is age if you really love someone?"

"You'd be financially secure," Drew said. "Ian has negotiated some profitable contracts during his cycling career."

"I don't need Ian's money. I come into a large inheritance on my twenty-fifth birthday." Embarrassed at her outburst, she asked, "Drew, does he really have a chance to win the Tour?"

"There are high odds on him. A couple hundred riders will start the race, but only five are contenders for the big win at the finish line. Ian is right up there."

"And the other four?"

"All older, some of them more experienced riders than Ian. The Swiss favorite for one. And he's racing against last summer's winner—that's never easy." He took their arms and propelled them down the corridor toward the exit. "Jon Gainsborough is demanding a win if they expect him to sponsor the team again next year."

As they fought the crowd, Chase mused, "Just a handful with the chance to win—then why do the rest of them kill themselves in such a grueling race?"

"Probably for personal glory," Miriam said.

"No, *Liebling.* It's more than that. For any man who ever wanted to conquer a mountain, this Tour is the ultimate test."

"And I thought it was all for a yellow jersey."

"No, Chase. I'm afraid the stakes are higher this time."

She stopped abruptly, causing a chain reaction at the exit door. "Drew, Ian pooh-poohs the bomb threats against the Tour."

He squeezed her arm. "So you know about those?"

"I know about the international repercussions."

"I'm more concerned about the death threats against Ian."

"Against Ian? Then I must go to him. He needs me."

Miriam's eyes danced. "Nice to be needed! Drew's going. Go with him. I have no intention of standing in the heat watching a bunch of young men pedal themselves into nervous exhaustion."

"Not even for Ian?" Drew teased. "You won't reconsider?"

"My darling, you told me women don't ride in the team cars."

"Neither does Central Intelligence, but I'm still scheduled to ride in the Gainsborough team car. Things are different this year, but they're mostly security precautions." When they reached the Rolls Royce, he said, "Chase, if I pull the right strings, they might make room for you as an American journalist assigned to the Kendall race. Do you know anything about journalism?"

"Enough to bluff my way. But what New York paper would I represent?" She grinned. "Samuel Abt reports for the *New York Times*."

"Just give me the name of a Long Island paper. I'll make certain that Langley gets you an official press card."

"Won't Mr. Gainsborough have a fit about that?"

"Let me worry about Gainsborough and Coach Skobla."

In the growing darkness as Drew helped them into the car, Chase saw a frown forming at the corners of Miriam's eyes. "Drew, don't let the Company trick you into telling the old lies."

"I won't, Miriam." His gaze slid past her to Chase. "Having Chase on board will be good for Ian. He'll take fewer risks."

"But, Drew, aren't you risking Chase's safety?"

He tapped the steering wheel. "I won't let anything happen to her, Miriam. She can be a real asset to us. Ian trusts her. He'll confide in her."

Miriam turned away, her voice strained as she said, "Then you and Chase can go running around the French countryside looking for terrorists if you want. I'll be safer shopping in Paris."

❦❦❦

On the other side of London, Jon Gainsborough checked the lock on his car door and rolled up the window as he turned his Audi A4 onto the narrow street. Night seemed darker here, the blackness broken only by old-fashioned lampposts and a flickering neon light on the corner pub. Jon was crunched in the compact car, the weight of his massive body pressed against his diaphragm. He mopped the back of his neck with his bare hand, hating himself for the fear that controlled him. An Opel Vectra had followed him for several kilometers—one of the boys from MI5 he was certain. Yet here in this back alley, when he would have been grateful for a tail, the Opel was no longer behind him.

Sweat formed on his temples and poured down the small of his back. He was on his own except for women traversing the sidewalks and two cars traveling slowly along the curb. This was not his part of town, not his way of life. He humped over the steering wheel, searching for the Maystead Inn, trying to imagine what kind of trouble Ludvik Skobla was in that demanded Jon's midnight ride to a seedy hotel with a thick packet of money in his pocket. If the London tabloids got wind of Coach Skobla's where-abouts, their chance at the Tour de France was over.

Jon couldn't handle more scandal. For weeks he had faced the accusations that he was involved in the sale of chemicals to Third World countries. Jarvoc, the steel plant near Prague, had already collapsed, his colleagues there held in custody. Now he worried about his own steel plant folding, a personal loss that would include his cycling team—the only joy that filled his life since his marriage had folded. He felt layered in humiliation, the latest one coming when the Parker Foundation pledged funds to keep the team solvent. He suspected that Dudley Perkins was behind the loan—Perkins, his old friend at MI5, his enemy now.

"Cheers, Jon," Perkins had said. "It's still the Gainsborough cycling team that Britain will root for. No one has to know that Radburn Parker is calling the shots now."

One humiliation after the other. And now this midnight run to bail the team's coach—the *directeur sportif*—out of trouble. At the first whiff of more scandal, Parker would back off and take his financial support with him. And that would be the demise of the Gainsborough team. Jon could never climb back from that dis-grace; the chance at winning the Tour was the only thing holding him together these days.

In the middle of the second block, he pulled into the Maystead's sparsely filled parking lot. The office in the two-story building was darkened. The venetian blinds hung crooked at the windows. A dog howled nearby. Tree branches swayed. A train whistled in the distance. He patted the money envelope inside his pocket and waited another three minutes. When no Opel pulled in beside him, he heaved his massive form from the driver's seat.

He was an enormous three-hundred-pounder, who tried to compensate for his short stature and thick-set body by wearing fancy Savile suits and decked heels on his Italian footwear. In the dead of night no one would appreciate his expensive attire or admire the speed and stealth with which he moved his hulking frame along the side of the building to the garbage pit.

His breath still came in short, tight gasps as he hurried past the shadows in the open terrace and climbed the narrow steps to the second floor. "The third door," Skobla had told him.

He counted them like a schoolboy, half expecting the wrong

door to open and cameras to flash, bringing even more scandal to his name. Sweat trickled down his fat jowls as he knocked. He jerked back as the door swung open. Across the dingy room, Ludvik Skobla sat in the wingback chair looking haggard and unkempt, his clothes slovenly, his feet bare.

"You're drunk. I should have fired you on the phone."

"You know I don't drink," Skobla said through swollen lips.

Jon adjusted his eyes to the fluorescent lighting. It was true. Skobla was a strict disciplinarian with himself and with the cycling team, a man intolerant of drinking or seedy living. He seldom spoke of his family back in the Czech Republic; but he was always the epitome of the sports world hero—from his spotless sweat togs with the team logo to his stark white running shoes.

Right now the Gainsborough sweat top was smudged with dirt.

The musty smell of stale cigar smoke filled Jon's nostrils as he stepped into the room. A streak of light beneath the door to the adjoining room blurred and lit again as though someone stood there listening. Jon's gaze strayed back to Ludvik. "What are you doing in London? You should be in France with the team."

"But you sent for me, Jon."

"I what?"

Jon realized as the door slammed behind him that there was a third person in the room. "Sorry," Jiri Benak said. "I sent the message to force both of you to meet me here."

"You!"

"Me, Jon," Benak said. "Alive and safely out of Jarvoc."

In the poorly lit room, it was difficult to distinguish Jiri's features or his snow-blond hair; even his blue eyes looked like dark circles in his narrow face. He was not unattractive, but a neatly dressed thirty-nine-year-old with cigars protruding from his shirt pocket and a pistol in his hand. His beige raincoat was noticeable now at the foot of the bed. He showed little emotion; his power lay wrapped in the mind games he played on others.

Gainsborough had silenced more than one man with his barbed glances, but as he stared at Jiri Benak, he felt like marshmallows inside. Benak, for all of his mild appearance, was a violent madman who designed destructive weapons.

"What do you want, Benak?" Gainsborough asked.

"Chemicals. Money. Your expertise. A job after the Tour de France. I expect you to help me."

"I no longer work for the steel mill in Jarvoc."

"Of course not," Benak agreed amiably. "The Russelmann family and the plant in the Czech Republic are shut down, but I have some of the records from there—ones that will prove that you worked for us and knew about the sale of chemicals."

"I *didn't* know."

"But you suspected. It's good you didn't fire Ludvik. It's too late to find another *directeur sportif* with the race just days away." His forced cheerfulness slipped as he waved the pistol. "Sit down over there, Jon. We need to discuss the race."

Gainsborough backed toward the bed and made a concave in the mattress as he sat down. "What happened, Ludvik?" he asked.

Skobla looked miserable. "He wants us to throw the race—to disqualify the boys with drugs if we have to."

Throw the race? Then Benak doesn't understand Skobla or cycling or steroids, Jon thought. *He doesn't understand the overall points that build during the race. Or how hard we've worked for this.* Whatever Skobla's background, he was not a man to cheat. He thought too highly of coaching, of winning.

"That's impossible," Jon said for both of them.

"I'll be there to make certain you do."

In spite of the pistol in Jiri's hand, Jon raged back, "We won't shame our team by throwing the race. The Tour de France has nothing to do with you, Jiri."

"But it does. I've bailed you out at the steel plant more than once, Jon, with my blueprints. And you, Ludvik, it was my recommendation that secured you the coaching job with the team."

"The race isn't played that way," Skobla said.

Jiri patted his gun. "Don't you want to live long enough to see who wins? Or must I turn to Moscow to stop this race? Believe me, Jon, I've already contacted the Russians."

Gainsborough couldn't conceive of a Muscovite willing to help Jiri, not with the whole world searching for him. Benak was playing his mind games. Was he behind the bomb threats, too? He was an expert with semiautomatics and Saran gas and homemade bombs. Jon kept his voice even. "Interpol is looking for you."

"For blowing up the Jarvoc tunnels? Didn't I die in that explosion?" Jiri's mouth hardened. "Or did Drew Gregory announce to the world that I was still alive?"

Jon wiped his sweaty face with the corner of the bedspread. Was the explosion in the tunnel all that Jiri remembered? He was mad, insane. Had he blocked out the gassing of some of the Russelmann family, the theft of chemicals?

In a flat voice, Jiri said, "If it hadn't been for Gregory and that Kendall family, I'd be running the Jarvoc plant now."

"Forget them."

"They ruined my chances. I saw Kendall. Our paths crossed at the top of Mt. Ventoux." Jiri blew down the barrel of his gun and aimed it at Jon again. "I left Kendall a message on the Simpson memorial. I dislike people who stand in my way."

A streak of light still shone beneath the adjoining room, the threat of someone's presence ominous. Jon's mind cleared. Jiri didn't know that Gregory would ride in the team car. But he must know that Kendall had a good shot at winning. If Ian won, Jon's dwindling finances would spring back. His hope soared. His only chance to escape was to agree with Benak—to talk himself safely out of this hotel and back to the car. One anonymous call to Scotland Yard on his cellular phone would guarantee Jiri's arrest.

He exchanged glances with Ludvik Skobla. "We'll have to throw the race, but it's your call. Coach?"

Skobla came to life. "We can't risk anything at the beginning of the Tour. It would be too obvious, Jon."

"When then?" Jiri insisted.

"When we reach the Pyrenees. Stage seventeen."

"No, Skobla. That's five days before the end of the race."

"Riders are exhausted by then," Gainsborough assured him. *And if you elude Scotland Yard tonight, we'll alert the French authorities to pick you up before we reach the mountains.*

"Jon is right," Ludvik said, rubbing his hands on his knees. "If our team fails to reach the summit, no one will be surprised. A lot of riders have to quit the race in the mountains. We'll make certain Kendall is one of them," he lied.

"Grant us that much time, Jiri," Jon said. "We need to reach the mountains. By then we can win a stage or two of the Tour. That way we save face with the racing world and won't be excluded from future races." In spite of the pistol still waving in his direction, he took the packet of marked bills from his pocket. "Ludvik, why did you ask me to bring money?" he asked, knowing.

"The money is for me," Jiri said. "I'm low on funds."

"Then it's yours." Gainsborough laid the envelope on top of Benak's raincoat. "This should cover you for three weeks." *By then you will be arrested. And Kendall may ride to the finish line in a yellow jersey in spite of you.*

Jiri looked at the lumpish, overweight man, with his abdomen stretched by overeating. But Jon's fleshy hands were well-groomed as he kettle-drummed his fingers on the money envelope, reluctant to let it go. "Is it all there?" Jiri asked.

Gainsborough's answer boomed across the dimly lit room, blasting Jiri's ears. "You can count it if you want." He shoved Skobla's shoes toward him. "Put those on, Ludvik. We've got to get you back to the team by morning."

Sweat formed on Ludvik's upper lip as he glanced from Jiri's face to the bedside clock. "I missed my plane, Jon."

"There are others," he said as he urged Ludvik to the door.

As Gainsborough's fingers wrapped around the doorknob, Jiri brought the butt of the pistol down across those fat knuckles. "Don't cross me, Gainsborough. Don't cross me."

He opened the door himself, smiling as they walked out. In spite of the problems at the steel plant, Gainsborough was useful enough for Jiri to let him live for now. As the two men descended the stairs, he dropped into the chair and counted the money. *Enough to buy more ammonia nitrate and copper wire. More than ample.* He slapped the bills on his bony knees as he glanced toward the adjoining room. *And Moscow will more than triple this once we can come to terms.*

He had no desire to live in Moscow—the offer had been made—but he was willing to sell his weapons for money, one intricate design at a time. If these didn't please the Kremlin, he knew enough about chemicals and nerve gases to pique their interest. Jiri had better plans than life in the frozen north. He would make his home in the English countryside among the rolling hills of the

Cotswolds, periodically leaving the safety of his thatched cottage to meet his Russian contact in Vienna.

The door to the next room opened and a solemn-faced cyclist in a hooded Gainsborough jacket came in with a brisk stride. His hair was wet from showering, dark strands of it damp against his forehead. He was a muscular twenty-eight-year-old with classical European features and eyes that had not laughed for a long time.

"They're gone?" he asked, his angry gaze fixed on Jiri.

"Yes, five minutes ago."

"Will they throw the race?" he asked.

"Perhaps. But Gainsborough is more crafty than I expected."

The cyclist was quick-footed and sturdy-legged as he paced the room, his shrewd eyes taking in every shadow. As a Serbian Intelligence officer, he had outfoxed his enemies during four years of war. He had escaped out of Bosnia when the NATO forces moved in, and both his name and his code name Roadrunner appeared on the war criminals' list of those charged with crimes against humanity.

Roadrunner talked as he moved. "So they are going to do exactly what I thought—nothing. Why did you let them go?"

"They agreed to stop the team by the last mountain stage."

"That's too late, Jiri."

"Jon's a foolish man. He won't let Skobla throw the race. They'd rather risk Kendall's life than give up their best chance of winning. The purse strings on the Champs Elysees are too tempting. But we don't need them."

"Then you must carry out the threats against Kendall."

"Against the world," Jiri said. "I will devise a way to stop this race, and you must help me, Roadrunner. Kendall's death is up to you."

"You've never killed a man, Benak?"

Jiri patted his pistol. "A few. But you are guilty of genocide—of ethnic cleansing," he mocked.

"Your victims did not die in a war, Jiri. Mine did. But killing hundreds of fans along the Tour is unnecessary."

"Then Kendall remains my personal responsibility," Jiri said.

"Yes. I will race Kendall—nothing more. And he knows that if I see a chance for a breakaway from the peloton, I'll take it."

"You're not on the team to win."

"The fans won't know that."

"It's an unnecessary risk. The Russians won't like it if the U.N. Security Council discovers your whereabouts."

"I am still Serbian Intelligence, not just a courier for the Bosnia-Moscow operation. Take care of your end, Benak, and I will handle mine."

Jiri shrugged, unwilling to argue any longer. "You plan to return to your own country, don't you?"

"Everything depends on this race. Once the Serbians take over again, I will go back with full honors, not with war crimes hanging over my head."

Jiri sensed his frustration. "Take my warning. Coach Skobla may claim residence in the Czech Republic, but he may have a direct phone line to Moscow. He may already know who you are."

Alarm registered on Roadrunner's face as he said, "Impossible."

"When you get to s'Hertogenbosch in the morning, how will you explain your absence to Coach Skobla?"

"My girl will vouch that I was with her." He zipped his hooded jacket. "What am I to tell my friends, Jiri?"

"The Russians or your British handler? Parkovitch, wasn't it? Tell them that my weapons expertise comes with a high price. Nerve gas is the poor man's atomic bomb. And I can supply that, but only if I deal directly with your man in Moscow."

"Professor Ivanski is more interested in what you do for us during the Tour de France."

Jiri's laugh turned brittle. "Reassure him that I am working with you. What's the life of a cyclist or a few hundred fans along the way to me?" *And Ian Kendall will blow with the others.* "So tell your friend Parkovitch that I'll create a hostage situation during the race that will please the professor and divert the world's attention away from Bosnia and Moscow. When can I meet with Parkovitch?"

"He'll be watching you, Jiri. If he trusts what he sees, he'll contact you during the Tour."

Jiri was losing control. He flushed his cigar ashes down the sink as the Roadrunner stalked across the room and tore off the bedspread, rumpled the bedding, and thumped the pillow.

"You make it look like I tossed and turned," Jiri said.

"Any other man with a history like yours, would have."

Chapter 6

In Russia, not forty miles from Moscow, Yuri Ryskov stepped from the bus three kilometers beyond his intended destination. He glanced around, his hooded eyes wary as he took in the half-dozen rundown shops that filled the cobbled square. Professor Boris Ivanski's country estate lay to the east beyond the village center and scattered farmhouses. Yuri would approach in a roundabout direction, circling the village and striking out through the woods to reach it.

Before he could take a step, the bus driver leaned out the window. "Make up your mind. I am leaving."

Yuri waved him on. "This is the place," he said.

The driver shifted gears and pulled away, leaving Yuri in a blinding dust cloud. As the dust settled, he stumbled to the water pump to wash sand particles from his burning eyes. His throat felt parched, his fetid breath tasting of garlic and onions. Ryskov was a dark-haired, wiry man in his mid-thirties with pasty skin and a nervous stomach that soured with every meal. Ever since Alekos Golemis's death in Sulzbach, Yuri slept and showered with his revolver close at hand. Even now it pressed against his ribs in a shoulder holster.

As the pump water dripped from his chin, he saw Boris Ivanski's housekeeper pushing her way to the head of the market line and waving a fistful of rubles that would guarantee her the best meat and vegetables in town. Few paid any attention to Yuri. Stranger or not, as long as he did not crowd in front of them, he could go about his business unhindered.

An old woman in a dark shawl sat on a stone bench, waiting her turn, her dark eyes turning curiously on him. In spite of the summer weather, she had tied a black head scarf beneath her sagging chin. Yuri pitied her. She was just another elderly pensioner with barely enough rubles to buy sugar, soap, and salt. As poorly dressed as she was, it was unlikely that she had money enough for vegetables and meat for a watered-down *borscht* soup for herself or for the listless grandson clinging to her side. Yuri pulled some fruit and hard candy from his pocket and went to them. Without a word, he put the fruit in her basket and the candy in the boy's hand. Impulsively, he touched the lines on her weathered face, and she shivered.

Almost July, Yuri thought, *and yet you are cold, as I am often cold, in this country of ours that never seems to be warm.*

Yuri moved on, afraid that her weary-worn smile would tear him apart. Inside, he wished her dead, but it was a merciful thought, for when he grew old, he would choose death, not the humiliation of poverty and scarcity. The woman couldn't know that Ivanski—the recluse in the estate outside her village—was ready to destroy the Tour de France so he could fuel and shape the Phoenix-40 into a powerful new regime in Moscow.

Ivanski had little concern for the poor. He wanted the old imperial leadership that would take them back to the days of the czars—to the old ways when only a few were rich. But what of the poor? Yuri hoped that in spite of the iron control of their lives, their stomachs might not seem as empty. But he knew that international cycling would be taboo and this woman and her grandson might well starve to death.

As he trudged through the woods of white birch trees, he snatched one of the bright green leaves and tore it into shreds. The heaviness in his gut was an unbearable knot. Fear. *Professor Ivanski would call it fear.* The professor had been his mentor, his friend. Six months ago Yuri had favored Ivanski's plan for a revolution; now he dreaded it. How could he still pretend to be heart and soul a part of the old Phoenix plan when all he wanted was a new life for himself in another country?

When he had last been here in the bleakness of winter, he had plowed through deep snow, the frozen crystals crunching beneath his boots. Now summer twigs snapped and bent beneath his weight, and fragrant wild flowers covered the rolling hills on Ivanski's property. Ivanski had guests, important guests, if Yuri could judge by the shiny vehicle parked by the house.

Yuri expected the housekeeper to answer when he knocked, but the professor opened the door himself. Curiosity filled Ivanski's dark, intelligent eyes as he greeted Yuri. "My housekeeper is upstairs—exhausted from pedaling her bicycle home so fast to warn me that you were in town. She doesn't know I sent for you."

He glanced beyond Yuri. "No one else saw you come?"

"No. No one."

"Come in. My other guests can wait."

He gave Yuri a welcoming thump on the arm, not the Muscovite embrace that he had always given during their years of friendship. With a wave of his smooth hand, he hurried Yuri into the library. A photograph of Ivanski's wife who had died in the bitter cold of a Moscow winter sat on the mantel, filling the room with her presence.

"Professor, your wife would have been proud of all your accomplishments, as Moscow is."

"Perhaps, but she did not live long enough to see them."

Long after her death, Yuri, a poor boy without rank or experience, found favor with the professor. Under his fatherly tutelage, Yuri became the youngest member of the Phoenix-40. The Phoenix rebellion had failed once, betrayed by one of their own, but the surviving revolutionaries were ready to strike again.

Ivanski waved his hand around the room. "Moscow expects me to spend the rest of my life completing a six-volume research work on Russian revolutions, dating back to the reign of the czars."

"A very great honor, Professor Ivanski."

There was no joy in Ivanski's face. He was brilliant, deeply respected in the intellectual circles of Moscow. He could quote Lenin, Stalin, Brezhnev, Gorbachev, and Nicholas Trotsky without displaying his utter dislike for them. Yet he was as fanatical and impassioned by revolutions as Vladimir Lenin had been.

Except for his full czarist beard, he was a plain sixty-four-year-old man in thick silver-rimmed glasses. His rumpled shirt sleeves were rolled up, his striped tie askew, and strands of his thinning umber hair unmanageable. As he sat down, a faint smile touched his lips. "What kept you so long when I sent for you? Are you still blaming yourself for the failed mission in Sulzbach?"

Yuri felt as though tart lemon juice had been poured on the raw lining of his stomach. Names came at him like darts: *Nicholas Trotsky. Alekos Golemis. Drew Gregory.* He hated thinking back to the dead Russian colonel, the murdered cyclist, the elusive CIA officer. "You sent me to find Colonel Trotsky's mother," he said.

"Oh—so I did." Absently, he stroked his beard. "You seem uneasy this morning, Yuri. Was this mission a failure, too?"

More acid burned Yuri's stomach. "The American CIA found her first, but she was already on a slab in the morgue."

"With no one willing to claim her body? Unfortunate, but these days families don't have enough rubles to bury their dead."

Yuri jammed his fists into his pockets. "How much worse will it get? In the old regime her pension would have been ample enough for a decent burial."

"Life changed with the collapse of communism," Boris reminded him. "Now our people have freedom of speech and empty stomachs. They are ready for another change, Yuri. Once we put the Phoenix plan into action, we will offer them a better life."

Will we? His dry mouth kept him from answering. He would end up like the old woman in the food line, just a hungry Muscovite waiting for a handout of runt potatoes and dark rye bread. He wanted more for himself—a land where he could lie down in a warm bed in the winters and fill his stomach with good food on a daily basis. Ever since he had tracked Drew Gregory in the mountains of Sulzbach, Yuri had contemplated defecting to America. He pictured himself slipping into an American embassy and seeking political asylum in exchange for—for what? He had nothing to barter with.

He fixed his eyes on the wood carving that hung on the wall beside the professor, Russian proverbs engraved on it. "Better to turn back than to lose your way. The tears of strangers are only water." *The professor believes he must turn the people back to the old ways,* Yuri thought, *before strangers in other nations overpower our land.*

Mentally, he ran down the list of Phoenix-40 names again: Jankowski, Kavin, Aleynik, Trotsky, Radbrazhensky, and

Parkovitch. Most of them were dead now. How had he and Professor Ivanski slipped through the net and gone undetected for so long? "Have you set a date for the revolution, Professor?"

"Soon." He tapped his hands together and rested his beard on the tips of his fingers. "History must reverse itself. It is time to bring back the days of the czars."

To that harsh, bloody rule of Nicholas I? Yuri wondered. He slumped into the chair across from Ivanski. *Or to Nicholas II, who was forced to abdicate?* "There are no royal descendants, sir."

"Then we will establish our own royalty. Some of our people have demonstrated in favor of going back to the monarchy. Why else would we still have a statue of our last czar? Why else do we sell pictures of Nicholas II in our marketplace?"

Because there are no meat or staples to buy, Yuri thought bitterly. *So we buy memories and worship a dead emperor.* "Not everyone is buying his picture, Professor."

"Imperial Russia must rise again. I plan a peaceful transfer of power. A diplomatic takeover. I am well-accepted, Yuri. The people will follow me back to the glory days of the past."

"Back to the palace in St. Petersburg?" Yuri asked.

"Yes, my grandfather was servant to the emperor there. Now I shall be the emperor." His voice grew curt. "But the men in the parlor believe a military takeover is the only answer."

"Ivar Noukov?"

"Yes. The general and his Serbian friend Leopold Bolav are here. They want me to step down so General Noukov can take my place." Ivanski's ghoulish laugh filled the room. "Bolav met with the president and the politburo to ask them to release an arsenal of weapons to them. He asked the Americans for money, but he comes to us for military aid."

"American money for weapons?" Yuri asked.

"No," the professor scoffed. "I don't know what excuse he used. Rebuilding perhaps. Or for agriculture. Yes, he asked the Americans for financial aid, but he comes to us for military aid. General Noukov insists that we help him."

"Let NATO help them again."

Ivanski's temples bulged. "Yuri, Mr. Bolav wants uranium. NATO won't supply that."

"Uranium? It would be five years or more before Bolav's people could come up with an atomic bomb."

"That's why I suggested nerve gas or biological warfare. I have a Czech supplier for this. Our hands would remain clean. For now," Ivanski said, "the availability of weapons or chemicals will serve Leopold's purpose. It will make the Bosnians and Muslims cautious. More importantly, it will take General Noukov out of Russia. I want the revolution to start in Moscow," the professor said calmly. "General Noukov and Leopold Bolav insist that we spread ourselves thin by striking in Bosnia first."

"With only one military unit there?"

"Noukov will delay the demobilization of our unit. The American president will protest—but he insisted on our being part of the peacekeeping forces in the first place."

Ivanski leaned back in his chair. "We will stage a chaotic disruption at the Tour de France. Within two hours—with the help of crack Russian troops and more planes, men, and equipment ready to go—there will be a Serbian coup in Bosnia." His eyes blazed. "While the NATO nations think that a Russian-Serbian rebellion has flared up in Bosnia—while the existing government in Moscow is condemned internationally for its involvement—the revived Phoenix-40 will march on Red Square and be firmly in control."

"It can only mean more bloodshed, Professor. The general will turn Bosnia and Red Square scarlet again."

Ivanski's confidence rose. "I do not care what happens in Bosnia, but I will offer our people here a peaceful solution—a return to the monarchy. Yuri, within hours of the tragedy at the Tour de France, Boris Ivanski will be the emperor. And you will serve with me."

Insane, Yuri thought. *His brilliant mind has snapped.*

Boris tapped his temple. "It is all worked out here. Once in power, I will demand an immediate withdrawal of our troops from Bosnia and bring General Noukov home in disgrace; he will be executed in Red Square." The professor glanced at his wife's picture again. "I want only what is best for my country."

Odd, Yuri thought. *I want nothing more than to leave it.*

The revival of the Phoenix plan would lead to death, and death was the one thing that Yuri feared more than failure. He yearned for the freedom that Colonel Trotsky had found in Sulzbach. Sixteen years ago Colonel Trotsky had been the mastermind behind the Phoenix-40, his leadership sound and calculated. In his own way, Professor Ivanski was as clever as Trotsky had been, another master of deceit, but was he brilliant enough to rule this country?

"The old Phoenix plan failed," Yuri warned.

"I will succeed because I know where Trotsky blundered."

No, Trotsky won, Yuri thought. *In the end, he won. He found his God there in Sulzbach and died a man at peace with himself. If only he had lived long enough to explain his God to me.*

A determined smile lit in Ivanski's eyes. "I know my plan will work. Noukov and Trotsky knew the strategies of war. I know the history of the Russian revolutions—the reasons why they succeeded or failed. I will not make the mistakes of other men."

Still Yuri argued, "Our people will not want another imperial Russia if it robs them of their religious freedom."

"What foolish nonsense, Comrade Ryskov."

Comrade to remind him of the old days and ways without God. Yuri snatched at courage. "Nicholas Trotsky believed in God."

"Comrade Trotsky is dead."

Granted. It was true. In the old days Colonel Trotsky had not believed in God, but Trotsky in the robes of a priest had spoken of peace, not just peace in the mountains of Sulzbach, but of an everlasting peace. The last time Yuri saw Trotsky, he was a dying man, but dying unafraid. Yuri said, "Our people can better die of starvation than to live without God again."

The professor gripped Yuri's knee. "I have lost General Noukov to my team. Am I losing you, too, Yuri? See me through this one. I need you as a courier one more time." He clapped his hands as though the matter were settled. "I have a man in London who will work with us. Do you remember Professor Parkovitch?"

"I thought he was dead, too."

"He has lived in England for years, supposedly as a Russian sleeper." Ivanski peered above the silver-rimmed glasses, past Yuri to a memory that rankled him. "Once Parkovitch was committed to helping us. I persuaded Colonel Trotsky to include him in the Phoenix-40, but I may have sent friends to their deaths because I trusted Parkovitch."

"If he was the British agent who betrayed the Phoenix-40, then why work with him again?"

Ivanski's eyes smiled. "According to my intelligence reports, he frequents the American embassy. That could be an advantage to us, Yuri. And he always had close ties with MI5. Once we saw that as a plus. Now—who knows?"

He seemed to be sifting his thoughts. "Parkovitch suggested that we use the Tour de France as a pivot point for passing messages. But I developed a better plan; a chaotic disturbance at the Tour will turn the world's eyes on France and away from Moscow. That's why I am sending you to Paris."

"To pass messages?"

"To check on Parkovitch. And to meet with a man called Jiri Benak. Benak is wanted by the International Police Force, another unsavory character who may be useful to us."

"But why use the Tour?"

"My dear Yuri, it adds a certain flare and style that no other revolution has had. A hundred years from now, we will be remembered for these glorious moments in history."

And you will be dead!

"We must test Benak. Not on our own soil, but there in France. If the Czechoslovakian proves himself worthy, then he will have a place in our new government—preparing weapons for us. He is a genius at that. And we have placed a cyclist on the British team. You will bring them all together, Yuri—Parkovitch, Benak, and the Serbian rider. You will test their loyalties to me. You will be my eyes and ears." A trace of a smile brightened his eyes. He tugged thoughtfully at his beard. "You won't mind going to Paris again, will you, Yuri?"

Paris! The taste in Yuri's mouth was suddenly sweet. He had walked past the American embassy on Avenue Gabriel more than once on his last trip to Paris, struggling to find the courage to ask for political asylum. If Yuri could get safely inside the embassy, he would refuse to answer any questions until they put him in contact with Drew Gregory, the American CIA officer.

Ivanski's words drew him back. "Find Parkovitch, Yuri. Play his cat-and-mouse game if you have to. If he betrayed us, he may not contact you, but he will be aware of your presence. You must be on guard." The mentor's eyes warmed for a millisecond. "The information you send back to me is crucial. Use coded information through the regular channels."

"The Moscow coup depends on me?"

"Yes, my young friend. Everything hinges on you. Imperial Russia will be grateful."

Yuri licked his parched lips. *And failure this time would be unforgivable.* The image of the American embassy on the Avenue Gabriel filled his mind again. Now he had something to barter with. What remained of the old Phoenix-40 definitely had plans to rise again in Bosnia and Moscow, and a British agent might be implicated. He could name names. Yuri had only to convince the French guards by the embassy gate to let him pass safely inside.

Boris swiveled in his chair and wrapped his thick hand around a bottle of Cognac. "Before we join General Noukov and his Serbian friend, Yuri, let us drink to our success and to the future when we rule from the old palace in St. Petersburg."

Yuri had no desire to celebrate a revolution. But he stood and lifted his glass. "Here's to that time when we have no rationing and we can bury our dead."

"And now, Yuri, let us go and deceive General Noukov and his friend. They believe we are working with them."

Yuri followed the professor into the modestly furnished sitting room. Something had amused Ivar Noukov as Yuri entered the room. A sneer still crinkled the general's ruddy features and tapered his dark eyes. He kept his hands on his lap, his thumbs spinning in perpetual twirls.

As Professor Ivanski took his seat behind the cluttered desk, his black cat sprang and landed on the other guest's shoulder. She pressed her fur against his cheek, purring. He scratched her neck, their potential for friendship obvious; but there was no welcome on his face for Yuri. "I'm Leopold Bolav," he said, not waiting to be introduced. "And you must be Yuri Ryskov. So, Professor, will he be joining us in Bosnia?"

"No, Paris has always been a city of intrigue, Leopold. I am sending him there to serve as your courier and perhaps to help negotiate a uranium transaction in the middle of the Tour de France. No one will be expecting that."

Leopold leaned forward, his cold black eyes shiny. "Then can you divert three or four hundred tons of uranium oxide my way?"

"I am certain we can help you. If not with uranium, then with Saran gas—or other useful weapons. We have contact with Jiri Benak, an expert in these areas. He assures me that he is in touch with a German chemical company that mines and processes uranium." The professor looked completely at ease as he said, "One of our British investors will determine whether Mr. Benak can help you without endangering our own security."

The Slav's cooperation wavered. He brushed the cat from his shoulder. "The fewer people aware—"

Ivanski cut him off. "If Mr. Benak and my British contact favor helping you, we will pass a message to you through the Serbian cyclist. I leave it to Yuri to work out the details."

"He is wearing the number 91 on his jersey. Do not forget that number, Mr. Ryskov, 91," Leopold repeated. Turning back to Ivanski, he asked, "What about General Noukov?"

"He can replace the general already there in Bosnia—"

Leopold cast a glance at Noukov. "It will be necessary to send the other man home in disgrace."

"A land mine would make a permanent exodus," Ivanski said. "And an acceptable reason for sending Noukov to replace him."

Noukov came out of his silence. "Leopold, I will be ready to leave as soon as you send back word—about the land mine. But, Professor, Paris is not a place for Yuri to meet Mr. Benak."

Ivanski's voice turned cold. "They will meet at Maxim's in Paris—out in the open, innocent fans at the Tour de France. And, Ivar, I will expect you to send word to me as soon as you secure a foothold in Tuzla or Sarajevo. Timing is essential. Send your messages through Paris. Yuri will make certain I get them."

The amusement in the professor's face never wavered. He was as certain of himself as Colonel Trotsky had been when he birthed the Phoenix plan. Once again the professor was in total charge.

Yuri pulled his chair to the desk and ran his hand over Ivanski's research notes on the Phoenix-40 and its failures. Parkovitch's name glared up at him. As the room emptied, leaving them alone, Yuri asked, "Why didn't you tell them that Parkovitch is your British investor?"

"There is no need for them to know."

"Professor, you have no intention of supplying the Serbians with uranium or Saran gas, do you?"

"Not if it risks my own security. But they are aware that Benak will set off a major bomb blast during the seventeenth stage of the race. Like I told them, timing is absolutely essential."

Ivanski walked briskly to a wall map and yanked it down, unveiling a well-marked world. London and Paris were boldly underscored. Small yellow flags outlined the Netherlands and France, each marking a stage in the Tour. He ran his hand clockwise. "This is the circuit that the Tour will take this year."

His hand stopped at the seventeenth stage. "I have been in touch with Jiri Benak and Parkovitch. Separately, of course."

Yuri waited, his eyes fixed on his mentor and the map.

"Benak is foolhardy, a madman no doubt. But we can depend on him to start a crisis situation at the seventeenth stage."

"While the whole world watches?" Yuri asked.

"Yes, while the whole world watches, Leopold can have his Serbian coup in Bosnia—and I will move into my palace. The people will follow me, Yuri. I know they will."

"What about Parkovitch and Benak?"

"If things go as I plan, they may eliminate each other."

He turned and smiled at Yuri, his finger still pointing to stage seventeen. "Yuri, this is what I want you to do. . . ."

Chapter 7

Grover Kendall left the District of Columbia and careened his Jaguar across the Maryland state line. As he sped toward his dad's construction site—an apartment complex this time—he knew he was destined for an argument. Ian, Grover concluded, had made a wise choice when he moved to Europe to avoid their father.

He parked unnoticed and sat in the convertible trying to interpret the mood on his father's sun-freckled face. Aubrey was taller than Grover and muscular, moving up and down the ladders with the agility of a bobcat. He expected hard work from his men, but no more than he was willing to do himself, which boiled over at 200 percent. For a man who seemed always at odds with himself, Aubrey Kendall had built an outstanding reputation. As advertised, Kendall construction jobs were done right and on schedule.

Aubrey's success had been a long time coming, delayed until wife number three appeared on the scene, stepmother number two for Grover. What blew Grover's mind was Jill's love for his father. Her love was reason enough for Aubrey to finally quit messing around and take the sobriety route. He had always pooh-poohed the twelve-step plan, but with Jill's support he would have gone for a fifty-step program. Jill had made a new man—a sober man— out of Grover's father.

But Aubrey struggled with other family relationships. He still harbored smoldering resentments against his mother for never being there when he needed her—for dying when he loved her. And he was bitter against his father for giving Olivia's grandson

Nedrick his rightful place in the family lineup. There had been little letup on Aubrey's violent fist-doubling against God—because
he couldn't blame anyone else for taking his first two wives.
Grover's mom with cancer and Ian's mother at childbirth. Lately
Aubrey's grudges were aimed at his youngest son. In Aubrey's
eyes, Ian's choice of cycling could never measure up to Grover's
junior partnership in a prestigious law firm.

Drumming the steering wheel with his car keys, Grover knew
he could put it off no longer. He eased from the car and picked
his way through the piles of lumber and steel rods and gravel to
the man barking orders—the man in the hard yellow hat with the
Kendall jawline and a surprised look on his face when he saw
Grover. "Son, watch your step," he called.

"How are you, Dad?"

Aubrey checked his watch. "Been dry six years, six weeks," he
said. He clapped Grover on the back. "What can I do for you?"

"I talked to Grandfather this morning."

"Uriah called from London? What did the old sot want?"

"The same thing."

"I've already told him—I'm not going to Europe. I can't leave
this construction project that long."

"I thought you sent for your passport."

"I changed my mind. I'm not going."

"But Gramps insists we back Ian as a family this time. The Tour
de France may be Ian's big win."

"It wasn't last year. I'll just catch the next one."

"Or the one after that?"

"Grover, if it's so all-fired important to you, go yourself. Maybe
Jill will fly to Paris with you."

"The timing is bad for me, Dad."

"Heavy date?"

"The firm asked me to represent them in Bosnia. One of the
congressmen is taking a group of investors to look over the eco-
nomic needs there. I'm to oversee the legal problems."

"What's wrong with the big boys? You lack experience in foreign law."

Grover kicked a mound of gravel. Aubrey always came up with
the downers, the negatives. "I guess the big boys don't want to
muddy their shoes," he said.

"Or get their feet blown off with a land mine."

"I was the logical choice. I'm good at Slavic languages." He risked reminding his father, "And I've been there before, Dad."

"When you were a kid."

And twice more after that, Grover thought. *During college, but you don't know about those two trips. You would have had my hide—called me a right-wing sympathizer.* "Dad, when I think of the Olympic Games in Sarajevo, I understand Ian and his international racing. It's a whole different, exciting world."

"Well, it's not my world."

"Sarajevo is one of my best memories. I'd just turned fourteen. And it was just Grams and me."

"I bet that was a first."

Grover's facial muscles tightened. "Ian couldn't tag along at the last minute. The flu or something."

"For months you talked about going back there to live."

"I still think about it sometimes."

"Maybe when one of those investors gets his business going over there, he can hire you on as his legal advisor."

No, Grover thought. *I made some bad moves there on my last visit—going in under the guise of a charitable organization to deliver food and bedding and coming out with propaganda pamphlets.* "I wouldn't be welcomed permanently," he said.

"Girl trouble?" his father asked.

"Yes, and I'd like to go back and find her." Five years was a long time to keep a pretty girl in his mind. She could well be one of those who died in that bitter conflict—fighting the war in her own way with an underground paper. He had handed her a wool blanket with the scratchy surface of army surplus.

"Charity," she had scoffed. "If you really want to do something, come back and fight alongside us."

He had mumbled something about finishing college. "All right," she had told him. "Then come once in a while and take my pamphlets back to America. Someone has to help us."

It had been the girl more than his own political views that had persuaded him to smuggle pamphlets out of the country with Serbian bombs exploding less than a mile away.

"Grover." His father's voice was sharp.

"Sorry, Dad. What were you saying?"

"I asked you to have dinner with Jill and me tonight."

Grover hated to say no. Aubrey would consider it a personal rejection. "Tonight is out, Dad. The firm signed me up for a refresher course in the Slavic languages."

"You expect to learn it overnight?"

"Enough to say 'hello,' 'good-bye,' 'how much?' And 'if my client here builds his business in your country, there will be no health benefits or retirement plan.' Legalese like that."

Aubrey surprised him and smiled. "You won't be a junior partner long. High school and college in three years each. The best law school—"

"Ian may have been Grandma's favorite, but she always provided for me, too. Her insistence on private tutors paid off."

Aubrey's smile vanished. "I suppose you think I let you down. It was always Olivia who was there for you while I hid behind my bottle. Is that it?"

"You said it, Dad. I didn't."

Aubrey shoved his hard hat back from his forehead. His eyes were as intensely blue as Ian's. It seemed to be all that the two men had in common.

"Dad, won't you reconsider going to the race?"

Aubrey shook his head. "It's not like Ian needed us. He's been on his own ever since he rode his first bicycle."

And the thing eating you is that Grandmother bought it for him. You were too stinking drunk to know that my brother wanted one.

But calmly he said, "Ian is going to win this one, Dad."

Aubrey wiped his palms on his jeans. "You always had a soft spot for that kid brother of yours."

Another jab at his father's old drinking days slipped from Grover's tongue. "We were both lonely growing up."

"How many times do I have to tell you I'm sorry? It was lonely for me, too. I buried two wives, remember?"

"That's over, Dad. Done with."

"Is it? You bring it up often enough. Either take me for who I am, Grover, or don't come around." Aubrey thumbed his sweatshirt. "I'm just an earthy sort of guy, son. Blue collar. That's me. At least you go to work in a business suit—smelling of Giorgio Armani for Men, Jill tells me. That's better than Ian has ever done." He almost spat the words on the ground. "Spending his life sweating in a cycling jersey and latex britches."

He flicked the lapel of Grover's designer suit, his mouth twisted into a crooked grin. "You're well-blended, Son, except for that mustard yellow tie. Better have Jill pick out your ties from now on."

"What about Europe, Dad? Gramps thinks we should go—"

"If Uriah wants to go, let him."

"He's not feeling well. The best he can do is be in Paris when the race ends."

"The rest is up to us? No. Have his stepgrandson go."

"Nedrick Russelmann isn't our problem, Dad."

"Sharing our inheritance with him is."

Jiri Benak stood alone in his rented house in the Basque village where he had found refuge. It lay on the French side of the Pyrenees; his window opened to a magnificent view of sheep grazing on the lower slopes with a craggy range of mountains rising behind them. He felt safe in this village, closed to outsiders. But it had opened to him—thanks to Ignasius.

Out on the slopes, Ignasius moved contentedly among the sheep. He wore dark knickers, knee-high wool socks, and a long-sleeved shirt-vest with bright multicolored designs on the lapel and cuffs. A royal-blue beret sat cocked on his head. Ignasius prodded his sheep with a staff as he herded them up one slope and down another; they disappeared into a valley, leaving only the mountains and sky for Jiri to enjoy.

Nature's beauty! And still Jiri could bring the face of Drew Gregory into focus at the snap of a finger, marring that beauty. He did so now, hating Gregory. Because of him, Jiri was a man without roots, without country, without money. All he had was his mind and his ability to design weapons of destruction.

The success of his mission depended on controlling his resentments. He fingered a piece of copper wire, carefully planning the bombs he would use on the Tour—homemade, not traceable to any company or location. Like his father and grandfather, Jiri was a designer of weapons. A brilliant man, he called himself. The key was fear. Strike fear into the thousands that lined the Tour route,

and he could cause total pandemonium, accomplishing what he
wanted with minimal deaths.

Abject fear. That was the key. Panic. He would create havoc,
utter confusion that would disperse the crowds in a frantic dash
for safety. First, he would continue the flow of typed notes to
threaten the riders, and then by stage eleven, he would use an
incendiary bomb to create a firestorm. Or a light-weight pipe
bomb designed for minimal destruction. Or better yet, a plastic
bomb to blow away the mountain. But he knew the invincible
French mind. Nothing would stop the race. And then stage seventeen! Jiri thrilled at the thought of the explosion that would
grab the world's attention and make what was happening simultaneously in Moscow and Bosnia seem small in comparison. Only
after he proved his worth to the Russians by destroying the Tour
de France could he plan the destruction of Drew Gregory.

The Basque village was a temporary solace—his invitation to
life in Moscow intolerable even to consider. What he wanted was
that cottage in the Cotswolds—a base from which he could work—
where he could return. For now, he must remain in this village
because of its proximity to stage seventeen on the Tour route.
From here he could safely transport his bomb. Everything
depended on an unhindered friendship with Ignasius.

They had met three years ago at a mercenary camp at the foot of
the Pyrenees, the two men as different as a glacier from a golden
wheat field. Jiri was a cold, cynical loner; Ignasius was warm and
friendly. Jiri, blond and blue-eyed, was German-born, German-
reared, an employee at the Jarvoc steel plant in the Czech Republic.
Ignasius was a farmer. His narrow face had been so dark that Jiri
thought him a Spaniard. He was of medium height, his prominent
nose so large that it formed stretch wrinkles between his brows and
across his forehead. An arrogant German and a swaggering Basque
peasant! They proved kindred spirits, blood brothers—distrustful of
authority, greedy for power and money.

In an unwritten pact with Ignasius, the villagers took Jiri in as
part of their isolated community, and once he was accepted, they
felt committed, obligated to protect him. That he came and went
freely—disappearing for days at a time—did not alarm them at first.
He was Ignasius's friend, a friend that must be protected from

Interpol and all outsiders. As long as Jiri danced with the people, drank with them, laughed with them, they found no fault in him.

He turned from the window and went back to his worktable, doing a mental rundown on the materials he had gathered. To his left stood the old battered typewriter with the faded ribbon and the packet of plain paper. To his right lay a spool of copper wire, a shoe box filled with new timers, and a rolled sheet of plastic. He toed the sack of silverware on the floor—the metal fragments that he needed when he built his bombs. A smirk narrowed his mouth as he thought about the locked shed behind the house where he had hidden bottles of ammonia nitrate and castor oil.

Not a week went by without his thoughts turning back to the steel plant in Jarvoc—and the explosion in the Jarvoc tunnels that had allowed him to put a safe distance between himself and Drew Gregory. He had never intended self-destruction, but the violence of that explosion had almost killed him. It had blown him against the shaft, sucking the wind from his lungs and blinding him with dust particles, cutting his face and hands with fragments. The whole horrendous experience had compelled him to hate Drew Gregory more.

Paris, 2 P.M. Drew Gregory and his wife stood outside the Hotel de Crillon at the Place de la Concorde, across the street from the American embassy. Drew glanced anxiously at his watch. "We're an hour later than I intended," he said.

"So why are we standing out here?"

"Carwell wants it to be a casual meeting and unrehearsed. And here they come, Maggie outrunning Troy as usual."

Maggie darted across the street from the embassy and pounced on them with a flourish, gushing, "Drew, dear, what a wonderful surprise! How nice to see you."

He accepted the kiss she planted on his cheek, grateful that it wasn't his lips. Their encounters had always been at the social level, mostly at embassy balls where she never sat out a dance. She had fought coming to Paris—had gone ballistic as Troy put it—but she had recovered enough to take on Paris with utter abandon. From her lovely, outrageous outfit, he could see that she had obviously found one of the wacky couture shops off the Champs Elysees.

Drew groaned. Troy's Agency salary could never cover Maggie's extravagance. And Miriam was going to be in Paris on a three-week shopping spree with Maggie Carwell! He'd be poverty-stricken the next time he saw Miriam.

As he turned to warn her, Miriam's head cocked slightly, amusement in those gorgeous eyes. She seemed braced for her own demonstrative greeting.

But Maggie said shyly, "I've so looked forward to meeting you, Miriam. I can hardly wait to hear about your art gallery in Beverly Hills." The ringed hands clasped. "Shopping and the galleries will be so much more fun with you here. Have you seen Paris before?"

She took a breath at last, waiting. Miriam obliged her and laughed. "On my honeymoon. Actually on both honeymoons."

"Then you don't know a thing about the city," Maggie told her. "We will have a perfectly marvelous time together."

"Not until I find a room."

"No reservation? Then you'll stay with us. No, I won't hear any arguments. There's plenty of room, isn't there, Troy, dear?"

He acquiesced, his brows arching. He gave Drew a brisk handshake, a nod to Miriam. Carwell was the CIA station-chief in Paris, a proper man groomed this morning in English tweeds and smelling of Tiffany cologne. His wife chose his wardrobe, but she could not hide the emerging bald spot in his thinning gray hair.

"Miriam will be comfortable with us," he agreed pleasantly.

Miriam will be exhausted, Drew thought, *but safe.*

Maggie glanced at her jeweled watch, another of Troy's bribes to keep her happy in France. "There's a fashion show in another hour. We mustn't miss it." She looked up at her husband. "Troy, love, be a dear. Have Drew transfer Miriam's luggage to the embassy limo. You can bring it home when you get there—at midnight." She turned a scolding glance on Drew. "I hope you don't detain my husband any longer than that."

So Maggie thinks I arranged this meeting, Drew thought. *Wrong!* He was here on Troy's orders for another behind-closed-doors meeting with Maurice Chambord, a time-gobbler that Troy had insisted upon. "We have more information," Troy had said on the phone. "Best discussed in person."

Drew slipped his arm around Miriam. "I was going to treat my wife to the Hotel de Crillon, but I'll feel better about her staying with friends. I didn't like the idea of her wandering around Paris alone for three weeks."

"Oh, we'll be together the whole time," Maggie promised.

"But what about you, Drew?" Miriam asked.

Troy was quick to avoid another invitation. "We'll get him a room here at the de Crillon. He leaves early in the morning."

By three at the latest, Drew thought. Tonight, if Troy's meeting ends sooner than planned.

Miriam squeezed his hand. "You haven't forgotten dinner with Robyn and Pierre this evening?"

Embarrassed at his memory lapse, he said, "I wish they hadn't insisted on flying over to Paris just for dinner."

"Pierre is here on business, a medical supply conference of some sort. Robyn came with him. Besides, Robyn has to see you, Drew, just to make certain you're all right."

"Nothing's going to happen to me."

"She's afraid for you. For herself actually."

He turned his face away from the Carwells and said, "Miriam, I'll never walk out of your lives again."

She whispered back, "Robyn knows that, but the fear of losing you is never far from her thoughts. She hates what you do for a living." She flashed him a warm smile. "Robyn said they have something important to tell us. Something that can't wait."

He gripped her shoulders. "They're all right?"

"Of course. They've never been happier." She turned to Troy. "Could Drew leave the meetings early? Say around seven."

Troy nodded. "It will give us an excuse to break early."

"That's settled then," Drew said. "I'll make reservations."

"Pierre made them at Maxim's. Meet us there at seven, Drew."

Carwell checked his Gucci watch. "Maggie and I will pick Miriam up at the restaurant at eleven. Is that late enough?"

"Ample time," Drew said. He glanced down at his suit. "I won't have time to change before dinner, Miriam."

"The children won't even notice, not with their good news."

She tilted her face toward him. Dismissing his own dislike of public affection, he kissed her with growing intensity at the thought of their three weeks apart.

With a quick wave to Troy, the women were off to the fashion show, Maggie talking at avalanche speed. Troy shook his head. "I hope your wife can keep up with Maggie's constant chatter."

"She'll keep you young, Troy."

"Or put me in an early grave. My sons warned me that I should think twice about marrying a woman so much younger, but Maggie is the joy of my life, Drew. I'd be lost without her."

As the pedestrian crowd thinned in front of the Hotel de Crillon, Drew asked, "Are we meeting at the embassy?"

"No, I wanted our meeting to be casual." He nodded behind them. "The Societe du Tour director agreed. Chambord and the other gentlemen are waiting for us in the private tearoom."

Drew whistled. "Not on my expense account."

"No. On the Agency's. Drew, before we go in—the less you tell your daughter about the problems at the Tour, the better."

"I won't lie to Robyn. I'll abbreviate the truth—but that's as much as I can promise." He restrained Troy as he moved toward the de Crillon. "Now you tell me—why did I make this unnecessary trip to Paris? What's wrong with using the phone?"

"Chambord is not too sure of you, Drew. He's afraid you'll go off and run things on your own during the race."

"Is that how you described me to him?"

"I guess something I said gave him that impression. Chambord thought your coming to Paris would give you a good view of the Champs Elysees."

They were steps from the boulevard. "I've seen it before."

He pulled Drew against the store front. "We wanted you to see it again so you could picture the avenue in your mind lined with half a million fans. It's up to you to make certain Kendall makes it all the way to the Arc de Triomphe."

His fingers pressed against Drew's arm. "I don't want any surprises in the meeting."

"Meaning?"

"Did Kendall tell you about the latest threat?" Drew raised one eyebrow. "At Mount Ventoux? He glazed over it. He didn't seem alarmed enough to warrant notifying Chambord."

"Or me. I still had to hear it from Chambord. That should have come from you, Drew. Kendall denied it, of course, so we're forced to go on the word of Basil Millard, one of his teammates."

"Maybe Millard wants Ian off the team," Drew said.

"No, they're friends. He photographed a chalk message at Mount Ventoux, the second or third threat against Kendall. Millard notified MI5; they notified Chambord. Without Millard's help we would be unaware that the problem was ongoing. Most of the threats are against the Tour. Now it's narrowed down to one team. One rider."

"We discussed it before—it could be someone with a personal grudge against the Kendall family."

"We've compared all the warnings. Some are typed. Others scrawled in ink. The signatures differ. After comparing the bomb threats and the warnings to Kendall, we're convinced that the problem is not limited to one organization or one man. We may be dealing with two separate terrorist groups, Drew."

"Tell Chambord to call off the race."

"The French don't bow down to threats."

"So no extremist group has taken credit?" Drew asked.

"They won't unless the bombs go off. The Palestinians and the IRA like to take credit after the fact. Or send a warning thirty minutes in advance." Carwell paused. "We've been checking, but young Kendall has no ties with any of these organizations, no political interests in them. His whole life is cycling."

"I could have told you that, Troy."

As people hurried by them, Carwell retreated into the hotel entryway. "I think the terrorist organization is using the international race to speak out politically, but we still don't know their terms or why they are targeting Kendall. Kendall's record comes up clean. Doesn't drink or carouse. Probably doesn't even vote absentee ballot." Carwell kept running at the mouth. "His grandfather hasn't been active in MI5 for years, and his grandmother's politics died with her."

"You've got to look beyond the family, Troy."

"We have." Carwell cleared his throat. "Chambord and I have discussed every terrorist group that has attacked France in the last twenty years. We turned over every name we could think of to Interpol. French Intelligence has increased security threefold."

"What about Coach Skobla? Maybe he's involved."

"What earthly reason would he have to stop the race, Drew? There's money in winning." He lowered his voice as he opened the hotel doors. "We don't have answers yet, but Chambord still insists there could be a Russian connection."

"Any specific reason?"

"None that makes sense unless you count the possibility of a political uprising that we're not onto yet. I lived in Moscow, Drew. Chambord's right. You can never outguess them."

Drew grimaced as they stepped inside the lobby. "It might be as simple as the Russians not having more cyclists in the race."

Troy's tired eyes darkened. "To pacify Chambord, we brought in a Russian handwriting expert, a rather likable chap."

As they walked over the glittering marble lobby floor in the luxurious eighteenth-century hotel, Troy said, "We've arranged for a team doctor to ride with you. Dr. Raunsted. He's French, knows the language. Spent years in sports medicine."

"Jon Gainsborough won't go for that added expense."

"We didn't ask him, and, based on your concerns, we didn't notify Radburn Parker either. The doctor has worked for us before, Drew. He'll be there to keep a close watch on Kendall and the team. And on you, too."

He put on a smile as they entered the private garden room, empty now except for a table of three. The man with the handlebar mustache grinned as they approached. Drew recognized Francois Pellier, the French commandant who had helped him on a previous assignment in Paris. Out of uniform, Pellier was casually dressed, yet a polite, articulate man as he rose to meet them. "Monsieur Gregory, how good to see you," he said with a warmth that twisted the whiskery ruffle on his upper lip.

The man to Commandant Pellier's right had fiery red hair; shocks of it stood straight out from his temples. He was thirty perhaps, certainly not more than thirty-five. This had to be the handwriting expert, the analyzer of an open *o*, an uncrossed *t*, the undotted *i*, or a poorly looped *l*. Drew didn't trust their theories, but then his own handwriting was nothing to brag about.

The expert's shoulders were stooped, either from long hours at the desk, Drew concluded, or as compensation for his gangly six-foot-four frame. He had a pleasant look on his face, a noted relief to Drew when he saw Maurice Chambord scowling up at him. Drew took the Frenchman's proffered hand in his, skin brushing against skin, Chambord's distance carefully maintained with the limp handshake.

Chapter 8

Drew arrived at 3 Rue Royale fifteen minutes late and passed under the awning into Maxim's legendary opulence. The interior of the restaurant glowed with mahogany and copper and full wall paintings—stylish enough to delight Miriam, masculine enough to please Drew. He strolled to the reservation desk. "I'm with the Courtland party," he said, glancing around.

The maitre d' led him through the crowded restaurant toward a secluded corner. Drew had anticipated a quiet dinner with his family, but he was bombarded with a steady hum of foreign languages as he wound around the tables. French. German. Spanish. Italian. The high-spirited clientele was as mixed as its one-hundred-year-old history, with tourists chattering nonstop and fashionable Parisian celebrities demanding attention. He sidestepped a chair as a diner stumbled to his feet, mumbling in Russian. Casting a preoccupied glance at the man, Drew turned his attention to his family, waving as he approached them.

"Don't get up, Pierre," he told his son-in-law as he placed a hurried kiss on Miriam's cheek. "Sorry, I'm late, *Liebling*."

"I'm used to it. It's your daughter who's been fretting."

He leaned down and whispered in Robyn's ear. "I've missed you, Princess." As he sat down between Miriam and Robyn, he asked, "Shall we go ahead and order? I'm starving."

"I gave the order," Pierre told him. "But I asked the waiter to hold off serving us so we could visit awhile."

"Oh! Guess the majority rules. What shall we talk about?"

"You, Daddy."

His guard went up. "You first, Princess. You're the one with the good news."

Her smile turned impish. "You remember the Prescotts?"

"You know I do. If it hadn't been for Andrea and Sherm, I never would have found you and your mother again."

"Sherm rang us up yesterday—with a birth announcement."

Drew felt disappointment. All through the meeting with Chambord and Troy Carwell, he had tried to guess Robyn's news. It had all gone back to the possibility of having a grandchild of his own. He managed a cheerful, "They've had a baby? A boy?"

"No."

"A girl then?"

"Well, not exactly."

Drew's face clouded. "What then? Has something gone wrong?"

"They had twin girls, Dad," she said excitedly. "Katrina and Kathryn. Katrina was named for Andrea's grandmother."

Drew tossed Robyn a wry smile. "I guessed as much. I met Katrina York. She was married to my superior officer in my army days." He fought off deep emotion. "I spoke with the captain's wife a few times before she died, and I'll never forget her."

"And the name Kathryn?" Miriam prompted, taking his hand.

"That would be for Ryan Ebsworth's aunt."

His thoughts spun back to Andrea York's flight to Canada after witnessing the assassination of the American ambassador in Paris. Andrea had sat in the jet a few rows in front of him, a beautiful girl in her chic Italian suit with Ryan, the spindly Canadian terrorist sitting beside her. Drew had followed them to Lake Harrison under orders to protect Andrea, but Sherm Prescott had complicated everything by falling in love with her.

As Miriam squeezed his hand, he said, "Ryan's aunt was a godly woman. She raised Ryan as her own son and loved him, but he broke her heart with the choices he made. He drowned in Hell's Gate Canyon with Andrea looking on."

Robyn's sea-blue eyes held his. "Were you involved, Dad?"

He twirled his glass and watched the lemon wedge swim around the rim. "I tried to capture him, but Ebsworth chose suicide."

"Dad, I didn't mean to upset you."

"It just brought back memories—not all of them bad." He watched his daughter in a detached mood as she blew against the wisps of auburn hair tumbling across her forehead. "Robyn, I thought Andrea might have told you about those days in Canada."

"A little bit, but not about Kathryn or Ryan."

"The Prescotts are good people. How like them to allow Kathryn to be a grandmother by proxy."

Robyn's fingers touched his, the wedding band and diamond on her finger still sparkling with newness. "Pierre is wiring flowers to them tomorrow—when we get back to Geneva."

"I can send them from Paris," Pierre offered. "Should we add your names, Drew?"

"Would you? Mother's and mine. And double whatever you plan to spend on baby gifts. Something really feminine," Drew suggested. "Katrina and Kathryn were both stylish women."

"Dad, will you be as excited when you're a grandfather?"

His neck snapped as he turned to her. "I'd be the proudest man on earth—except for Pierre here. I missed so much of your childhood, Princess. I want to be around for my grandchildren."

"How? You're always away on another assignment." Her finger locked around his. "Dad, don't get involved in the cycling tour."

"Has your mother been upsetting you?"

"She hasn't said much. It's what the news media say about the bomb threats that worries me. Why don't you just stick to tennis matches at the embassy, Dad? You'd stay safe that way."

"There's nothing to worry about, Princess. They have the Tour de France every year."

"Except for World War I and World War II," Pierre reminded him. "This is another time when they ought to cancel out."

"And give the terrorists a victory?" Drew's jaw clamped. "I'll be safe. Vic Wilson and Chase Evans are going with me."

"Ian Kendall's girlfriend?"

"Robbie, they're just friends," Miriam said. "Ian wishes for more, but he'll ride better knowing Chase is there for him." She ran her finger over Drew's wrist. "If anything happens during the race, your dad is counting on Ian confiding in Chase."

"The old theory that a woman keeps a man more focused?"

"It works for me, Princess." Drew groped for words to reassure

Robyn. "Honey, security is tight. We're just working with the Tour organizers to make certain the race runs smoothly."

Pierre leaned forward, hands clasped. "If they expect a smooth race, then why invite intelligence agents to ride along?"

Drew matched Pierre's cynical gaze. "Dealing with the threat of terrorism anywhere is part of our job."

Pierre's dislike of intelligence agencies showed in his sunbronzed face; his gaze challenged Drew to defend Company honor. For a man with Swiss blood running in his veins, Pierre was good with statistics that defaulted the intelligence system. He could spew off the Agency history from Donavan to Colby almost as well as Drew could, and throw in Woolsey, Webster, and Deutch as though he kept a personal dossier on each one.

"You're a marksman, Drew. Is this what it's all about—the assassination of some foreign leader attending the Tour?"

Not some foreign leader, Drew thought, *but the assassination of a cyclist.* He sat stoically, determined to quell any argument that could put a wedge between his daughter and his son-in-law.

"What about it?" Pierre asked. "It's not up to me to explain your job to your daughter. She gets upset whenever I suggest your Company has a long history of questionable operations. This Tour business is just getting you involved again."

Drew didn't like locking horns with Pierre or risking their tenuous truce right here in Maxim's. He'd come to appreciate Pierre over the months—a young executive in his early thirties who loved Robyn more than anything else in life. He had a pleasant face—angry at the moment—strongly chiseled, honest, direct. But he wasn't budging an inch this time.

"Well, Drew? Is the Company up to its old tricks?"

Fortunately, Drew thought, *you only know what you read or hear.* The history was tainted, Drew had to admit. Bill Colby and men like him spilled the Company history into books; Ames and Porter Deven had sold its secrets, but the record wasn't all bad.

"Daddy?"

Miriam maintained her calm, her hand still resting on his. "Pierre—Robyn, dear, that's enough. This was supposed to be a family celebration. A happy time. Let's not quarrel."

"But Drew's job makes my wife unhappy."

"It doesn't have to, Pierre." She faced her daughter. "Robyn, dear, your father's life is a world unlike our own."

One beyond your comprehension, he thought ruefully. *A Company still trying to live down its assassination teams and government takeovers. A Company still tainted by the old days, the Cold War ways. But must I always apologize to my family?*

Miriam smiled, the half-smile that Drew dreaded. He knew that his Company loyalties still prickled her skin.

"Robbie," she said, "come to the powder room with me. Please."

In her own gentle way, Miriam would squelch the questions so that their dinner together could be special. *Colby's honorable men,* Drew thought as they walked away. The code of silence that Miriam had always hated. Drew's miserable world of intrigue left so little room for those who meant the most to him. Again he met the scathing in Pierre's eyes. "Truce," he suggested.

"Good idea—but how serious are the threats against the Tour? In Robyn's condition—"

"Is something wrong with my daughter?"

"Only with her worrying about you. I met this Maurice Chambord at a company dinner recently. He was our guest speaker, drumming up enthusiasm and funding for this year's Tour." Pierre paused and then said, "He was an impressive, well-dressed man, but not my kind of person. If you're working with him, Drew, it could mean trouble."

Tongue-in-cheek, Drew said, "Chambord did suggest an assassin to take out the man or organization threatening the Tour. He looked directly at me when he said it."

Pierre's face filled with disappointment. "I counted on your experience on the Sulzbach mountain to change your old tactics."

"I didn't take Chambord seriously, and I certainly didn't agree." Drew touched his chest. "Don't judge me too severely, Pierre. That moment on the mountain changed me in here. It didn't change Company policy. I'm needed. The terrorists are targeting Ian Kendall."

"Kendall? Let the British handle it. He's riding for them."

"He's an American, Pierre, and a personal friend."

"Stay out of it, Drew. A death at the race could put a shroud on the Tour for years to come."

"The Munich massacre didn't stop the Olympics." From the corner of Drew's eye, he saw the girls coming back. "Even when the militia threatened to disrupt the last games, they just beefed up security. That's what this is all about. Security."

Protection for Kendall and those other fine young men.

"You have enemies, Drew. Be careful—" Pierre's words hung in the air unfinished as Miriam and Robyn took their seats again.

Drew checked his watch. "Pierre, what happened to that meal you ordered? Did you ask them to roast a whole lamb?"

Pierre lifted his hand and a waiter stepped from the shadows, a massive tray balanced in his palm. He grinned as he served them bowls of creamed mussel soup with onions and parsley swimming on top. He turned to Drew, "Ground pepper, monsieur?"

"Please."

"Drew, we're having breaded Sole Albert for the main course," Miriam said as she tasted her soup. "That should please you."

"Did you remember the torte Tatins for dessert?"

"Exactly like our honeymoon."

"Even to the glasses of vermouth, *Liebling?*"

"We'll do what we did then—leave them."

"More lemon Evian?" the waiter asked. "Or anything else?"

As Pierre shook his linen napkin, Drew said, "I don't seem to have any silverware—or napkin."

The waiter turned to his tray and swung around again, placing a service setting by Drew's hand. He grinned as he waited.

"Did you run out of Maxim's napkins?" Drew grumbled.

"Oh, Daddy, don't make a fuss. Use what he brought you."

Drew unraveled the rough terry cloth and caught the silverware in his hand. The waiter hadn't moved. Miriam nudged closer to Drew. Robyn slipped her hand into Pierre's. Four pairs of eyes focused on him, the waiter's bulging with anticipation.

"What? It's not linen." He shook the terry cloth open and glanced at the waiter. "I don't understand."

The waiter shrugged, palms extended. "The monsieur, the madame want to surprise you."

At a signal from Miriam, the waiter lifted the cloth and tucked it around Drew's neck. "A bib for you, monsieur. I read it. 'I love my *grandpere.*' That's you, Mr. Gregory."

"It's true?" Drew asked, his grin matching the waiter's.

Robyn nodded, her face glowing. "I'm—we're—Pierre and I are going to have a baby. You're going to be a grandfather."

"And if you're going to be around as promised," Pierre said, "you had best plan on retirement by the end of March."

"March! You mean—"

"That's what she means, Drew. Our daughter is pregnant. That's why our kids insisted on dinner together this evening."

"You already knew, *Liebling*?"

"I guessed."

So did I, he thought, *but that Prescott news threw me.*

"Are you pleased?" Robyn asked anxiously.

With the bib still tucked beneath his chin, he pulled Robyn to her feet and into his arms. Across the top of her head, he winked at Pierre. "I'm pleased for you both, Princess. I can't believe you flew to Paris just to tell me."

"We thought you'd be more cautious during the Tour de France if you knew. You will be, won't you, Dad?" she asked as their dinner plates were served.

"I'll just be gone three weeks. I promise."

Promises! He was always making promises to Robyn. He had promised to climb Heidi's mountain with her a long time ago. "Princess, I guess we have to put off our trip to Heidi's mountain a little longer."

"I'm not crippled—just pregnant. You are happy for me?"

"As thrilled as I was the day I learned about you. I can still see your mother coming out of the doctor's office, saying, 'Yes. Yes. Yes.'"

"Then why do you look so worried?"

"I want everything to go right for you."

Miriam's pregnancy had not gone well. Toxemia. Swollen hands and feet. Periodic bed rest. Just as violent was the emotional upheaval as they fought about Drew's overseas assignment. They had agreed on the name Wallace for a boy, but the whole time Drew had wanted a girl, a girl baby as pretty as Miriam. He smiled at this grown daughter of his who favored the Gregory side of the family. No child had been more wanted. No child was missed more during those long years of separation from Miriam.

Pierre pushed back his dinner plate and slipped his arm

around Robyn. "Drew, if we have a son, we plan to name him Drew Wallace after you. Robyn's idea, but I concur."

Miriam's face glowed in the candlelight as she leaned over and kissed Drew's cheek. "Darling, we'd better pray for a little girl. I could never handle another Drew."

Drew Wallace! Wallace for the dad that Drew had loved and admired. "Wallace! Then my grandson will be a giant of a man. My father was."

Outside of Maxim's, as the Carwells pulled up to the curb, Drew hugged his daughter. "Princess, boy or girl, Mother and I will be pleased as long as the baby is healthy."

He kissed her on the forehead and released her. "March." He glanced at the Carwells standing politely by their car. "By then I should be retired." *The Tour will be over. And the trouble at the embassy—the trouble with Lennie—should be settled by then.*

Carwell frowned as Robyn asked, "Will you retire nearby?"

"I planned on Scotland until your mother came back into my life, but your mother wants to stay in London or Switzerland, close enough to be with you and Pierre now and then."

"And to bounce your grandchild on your knee." She leaned against him. "I'm so glad you two are back together again."

"I never wanted your mother to go away in the first place."

"Any more than I want you to go away now? I'm afraid you won't come back. Why don't you tell Mr. Carwell you can't go?"

Pierre stood by the open taxi door, waiting for Robyn. "I have no choice, Princess," Drew said. "I'm just doing my job."

۞ ۞ ۞

Yuri Ryskov sat alone in the corner of Maxim's, unobserved by Drew and his family. The herbed sole still lay on his plate, half-eaten, bits of unfamiliar stringy greens beside it. He had drained a second glass of vermouth, and now the pain in his stomach rose to a new pitch, gnawing and tearing at his innards.

He had seen Gregory arrive—his good fortune unbelievable as he recognized the American CIA officer from Sulzbach. For a fleeting moment, hope rose in Yuri's breast. He stumbled to his feet as the waiter led Gregory past his table, intent on begging him for asylum. He cried out in Russian, but in the blaring cacophony of the foreign voices all around him, Gregory did not hear his cry for help.

He sank back down to his chair, defeated, the taste of mussels and onions filling his mouth. He yearned for someone to speak his native Russian so he could ask for the English words that would grant him entry into the American embassy.

He tried to sort out the discord of sounds that pressed all around him. Deep voices. Soft voices. No one turned his way. No one offered to sit at his table. Now the orchestra was playing "The Merry Widow," the notes of the song familiar to his ear.

Yuri watched Gregory slip his arm around the stunning woman beside him and saw the faces of the young couple animated and smiling as they spoke with Drew. Suddenly Gregory was on his feet, a strange piece of cloth tucked around his neck, his arms open to the young woman who looked so much like him.

Longing gripped Yuri as he watched Drew Gregory. Yuri had never known the love of a woman, never felt the touch of his own child's hand, never slept in Paris without fear of a gendarme knocking on his door. Perhaps in America he would no longer be alone, no longer be afraid. Peace. Yuri wanted peace.

But could there be any peace in the bronze glow of this room? Fear wrapped its tentacles around him. Here in Paris, he was following Professor Ivanski's orders. Somewhere in the shadows of Maxim's, Yuri's contact from the Czech Republic was surely aware of his presence. Why had he not made himself known?

Chapter 9

As the airliner stopped at the Schiphol terminal, Salvador Contoni vaulted from his seat and grabbed his luggage from the overhead rack. By the time the cabin door swung open, he was by the attendant's elbow winking. "Sorry, I'm in a hurry," he said.

She glanced at his suitcase. "You travel light."

"It avoids delays at the roundabout." *And the risk of the* politie *noticing me,* he thought. If he needed clothes, he would buy new ones, or when the race neared Isigny, he'd go to the farm and pick up the suits he had left at Monique's in March.

The flight attendant's dark eyes looked like brilliant saucers as she said, "Thanks for flying with us, but I thought you were going to show me Amsterdam this evening."

"Next time." He knuckled her cheek and deplaned while the other passengers still crowded the aisle.

First class had accommodated his last-minute arrival and now allowed for this quick departure. The moving walkways swept him through the terminal, past shops and car rentals; then with long strides he was out of the airport and boarding a hotel bus for the fifteen-kilometer ride into Amsterdam. For convenience he took a room at the Seven Bridges, grateful that at the peak of summer there was still space available. Monique preferred to stay at the elegant nineteenth-century Amstel that overlooked the river, but the Seven Bridges was more to Salvador's liking—not even a dozen rooms, but his had been tastefully furnished. The owners frowned upon credit cards, so there would be no surprise when he paid cash for his lodging. The bountiful breakfast would be served in his room, giving him the privacy he needed.

Once settled, he struck out for the diamond center to keep his appointment with Willem Christofels. When Sal reached the Singel Canal, he lingered on the bridge to take in the lights and shadows that might have inspired a Rembrandt painting—or the mystery of a Ruisdael landscape. He loved this hearty city. She was a capital of trade and finance that appealed to his love of money, a network of waterways and flower markets that delighted him, a unique metropolis filled with businessmen pedaling their one-speed bicycles to work. He wished Monique were by his side so she could enjoy these faces of Amsterdam set against a delft blue sky one moment and then darkened by the shifting clouds the next.

His mood swept to the gray of the clouds as the bells of the Westerkerk tower rang out the notes of "John Brown's Body." This was Amsterdam as Sal knew it—full of the unexpected, a city of carillon bells and gifted artists—a city tolerant of those with goals less noble than the painters. Ignoble was how Monique described his plans to find Ian Kendall. Did she not understand? It was not Kendall that he wanted to destroy, but Drew Gregory.

He pounded his anger against the pavement as he walked rapidly toward the diamond center. Any other man would be going there to buy a diamond for the woman he loved. Sal had other plans. He reached the glittering shop in ten minutes. A gloved attendant held the glass door open for him. Once inside, Sal gazed around and did a visual recheck. The grinding and polishing of diamonds was done in the rear of the store with a few professionals out front to impress the tourists and the potential buyers. Willem Christofels could usually be found front and center, overseeing his customers and his profitable business. This morning he was noticeably absent.

"*Goedemorgen.*" The pleasant voice belonged to the elegantly dressed receptionist, the pretty face and figure to someone in her early twenties. Christofels's daughter? The oldest one?

"Brunhilda?" he gambled.

Her curious eyes settled on him. Her voice lowered. "I didn't recognize you, Mr. Contoni."

"It's been four years—but your father is expecting me."

Her gaze shifted uneasily. "He left early."

"But we have an appointment."

She scanned the calendar. "*Gisteren*," she told him.

"No. It was not yesterday. This morning." He made a point of glancing at his watch. "Precisely at eleven, and I am on time."

"Perhaps you can reach him tomorrow, Mr. Contoni. If it is diamonds you want, I can—"

He left her still making excuses. The doorman swung the door back for him, preventing an enraged thrust of Sal's bare fist against the glass. Outside he looked back. She had picked up the telephone. *Go ahead. Warn your papa,* he thought.

It took him a fraction of a second to picture Christofels's home in his mind; it was just two or three blocks from the store beyond the ring of canals. No, he remembered. It was one of the charming canal houses off of Keizersgracht or Prinsengracht. The look-alike houses sat flush against a sidewalk lined with elm trees, typically Dutch, spotlessly clean, and tippy with age. They clung to their seventeenth-century charm, existing without benefit of yards or porches, yet having the glistening waters of the canal and the flowered houseboats in easy view from their front windows.

Salvador recognized Christofels's gabled home when he saw it—a narrow three-story house of stucco and brick leaning into its neighbor. The shutter-windows were open, and a flat portion of the red roof served as a hideaway for the potted geraniums. Sal strolled into the gift shop filled with curios and books, nodded briskly at Christofels's wife, and slipped past the lace curtain into the living quarters before she could stop him.

At the foot of the narrow, twisting stairs, he called, "Willem, it's Contoni. I must see you."

An unwelcoming grunt erupted as Willem filled the top of the stairwell. "Why did you come here, Contoni?"

"You didn't keep your appointment."

Christofels looked thirty pounds heavier. He was a hardworking family man, visibly unhappy with his unwanted guest. As Sal climbed the steep steps, he imagined Willem's bulging hips brushing the walls. He stopped two steps from the man's doubled fists, not risking a confrontation.

"Don't come here haunting me with past mistakes, Contoni."

"Relax, Christofels. No one knows that your polished diamonds helped fund the mercenary camp in the Pyrenees."

"Harland Smith lied to me about my investments."

"No, he fed into your right-wing sympathies."

"I thought we were running guns to help the Bosnians."

Sal shook his head. "You should have realized Harland had no political loyalties. He sold arms to anyone that wanted them."

"What a fool I was."

"That's over now and the camp shut down. But I still need your help, Willem. I need to borrow a bicycle."

Christofels visibly relaxed. "That's all? Your visit has nothing to do with—my old political views?"

"I don't care how a man votes," Sal said. "My whole association with Harland Smith was for money." *No, that's a lie,* he thought. *I stayed on, waiting for the day when something happened to Smith, and Monique was free to be mine.*

Christofels's glance strayed to his wife at the foot of the stairs. He turned abruptly and led Sal into the tidy sitting room. "Why bother me? I cannot risk loaning you a bike. The International Police Force is looking for you, Salvador."

"The black kettle speaks. What about you, my friend?"

Christofels overlapped the chair as he sat in it. "I have nothing to do with politics anymore."

"Nor do I. But, Willem, I need your bike and your car."

"You can rent them elsewhere. Don't involve my family."

"A privately owned Volkswagen will be safer—your wife's car perhaps—with a bike rack on top." He leaned forward. "And I need two cycling jerseys—one identical to what the British team is wearing, the other a duplicate of one of the Dutch team jerseys."

"How can I do that?" Christofels whined.

"How is your problem. Your contacts in s'Hertogenbosch will know where those teams are staying. Steal them if you have to."

"What are you into now, Contoni?" Alarm darkened the pouches beneath his eyes. "Are you involved in the bomb threats against the Tour de France?"

"Bomb threats?" Contoni asked. "Of course not. I'm not a fool. But I am attending the race, and I do need transportation."

Sal grew anxious as he heard footsteps on the stairs. "It's just for three weeks, Willem. After that, you won't see me again unless I come to buy a diamond for Harland Smith's widow."

Willem's jaw cracked. His mouth twitched involuntarily. "You always took a fancy to that woman. Get out. I can't help you. I won't—"

Christofels turned, startled, as his daughter ran into the room. "Mother is frightened, Father. Tell him to leave."

Salvador smiled at Brunhilda. "He just did, but I am not going until your father promises to help me."

"I can't do what he asks, Brunhilda." The whine twisted his mouth. "He wants shirts like the cycling teams are using."

Her eyes narrowed. "I'll help you get them."

"But I will not loan him your mother's car."

"Then let him have mine," she said.

Salvador welcomed his unexpected ally. "I will return it in three weeks, Brunhilda. With not a dent in it."

"Just leave before my mother's heart gives out again."

"I will trust you and your father to have everything ready for me by morning. . . . And no police—for your own good."

Christofels was too polite to ignore Dutch courtesy. He extended his hand. "*Dag meneer*, Mr. Contoni."

"Good day to you, too, sir." Contoni barely let their hands touch, and then he pulled out the press card that he would wear at the Tour de France. "Everything is legitimate this time."

"You're a journalist now?" Christofels asked.

"And why not? A man has to make an honest living."

🌀🌀🌀

At three Salvador spotted Monique slipping into one of the brown cafes not far from the art museums. She was seated at a wooden table by the time Sal reached her. "Where have you been, Monique? I waited for you at the Rijksmuseum for two hours."

"I thought you said the van Gogh gallery."

He let the excuse slip by. She was lying, but there was no need to confront her. Not now. Not yet. "There are 250 rooms in that place! I searched everywhere for you."

"I am sorry. I hope you saw Rembrandt's *Night Watch*."

"I stared at it so long I know every stroke on that canvas."

His fury abated as he saw her long-lashed eyes brim with tears. Even so, she was lovely to look at with that gentle softness to her mouth and her shiny dark hair brushed to a sheen. "It's all right, Monique. I'm just glad I found you."

She tried a smile, but it only pushed her tears to the edge.

"Are you hungry? Thirsty?" He rubbed the back of her hand. "Of course. Why else would you have come here? What will it be? Hot chocolate? The Amsterdammers smother it in whipped cream."

She wrinkled her nose. "Just coffee with milk."

He ordered *koffie verkeerd* for her and a glass of iced *jenever* for himself. He wanted to keep his mind clear; the juniper berries would give his drink a fruity taste without being intoxicating. "And ham and cheese *broodjes* for both of us," he told the waitress. "You can add liver sausage to mine."

While they waited, he said, "I took a room at the Seven Bridges. I want you to stay there with me."

"No." Her response was firm, a denial that there had ever been anything between them. "I already have a room, Salvador."

"At the Amstel?"

"Yes."

He glanced away, unable to laugh as the locals were doing. They were a happy lot, sitting on the plain, wooden furnishings, enjoying the congeniality of their companions as much as the drinks in their hands. The dark wood-paneled walls of the cafe had turned yellow from centuries of tobacco smoke; the fresh haze from smoke stung Sal's eyes—and yet it was a cozy atmosphere with the old prints hanging on the wall.

He faced her again. "Monique, did you bring the cycling helmet and placards with the number 190 and number 191 inscribed on them?"

She pointed to the sack beside her. "The fans will know there are only 189 riders," she said miserably.

"Few, if any, will notice."

She picked at her sandwich. "Salvador, I'm cold. Maybe I should try that hot chocolate after all."

Moments later he leaned over and blotted the whipped cream mustache that had formed on her upper lip. "There. That's better. Now—did you find us a room in s'Hertogenbosch?"

"Yes, in a private home a block from Kendall's hotel. You can walk to the starting point of the race from there."

He smiled. "If we can get through the crowds."

"I'm not going back there with you."

"What? When did you decide that?"

"When I visited the Anne Frank house this morning."

"No wonder you've been so depressed."

"She was so young, Salvador—like my sons. I cried when I saw that room where she spent two years of her childhood locked away with nothing to do but pin magazine pictures to her wall."

He wedged her hands free from the cup and held them. "When I build our home in Italy on my father's villa, there will be plenty of room for the boys. They will never feel locked away."

"But my boys are happy on the farm where they are."

"And you?"

"What makes them happy is enough for me."

"Monique, when the Tour leaves Belgium, I'll drive over to see you and the boys."

"No, Salvador, I don't want to see you again."

He glared at her. "But I promised Anzel that I would come."

She stopped arguing. She would never stand in the way of a promise to Anzel. Anzel with his dark eyes and thick black hair looked like his mother, but his face was chiseled in stone. He still struggled to come to grips with watching his father die—knowing that he had held the rifle and pulled the trigger.

"How much longer will he go on condemning himself for his father's death, Monique? Doesn't he realize it was an accident?"

"No," she said sadly. "Anzel knew what he was doing. But what choice did he have? Harland would have killed Gregory."

"Perhaps even his own son."

She shuddered. "Yes, I believe he would have. But I can't tell Anzel that."

"I'd like to spend time with Anzel. Let me take him to the race with me. I know he'd enjoy the excitement."

"That's madness. As crazy as my parents telling me that Anzel needs God's forgiveness to make everything right again."

He reflected. "Perhaps."

She chewed her lower lip. "How can I tell him about God's for-giveness? The truth is, I haven't forgiven my own son for killing his father. Poor Anzel. He is just beginning to take to his music again. Other than that, he has nothing left."

"Anzel has you, Monique. That is more than I have."

◎◎◎

Chase Evans stood by the hotel window in s'Hertogenbosch and stared down at the ancient moat that ran along the old town wall. She was too excited to sleep. The first stages of the Tour de France would be played out in this city. As she tried to calm the erratic thudding of her heart, she kept her face to the window, fearful that Vic Wilson would read something in her expression and ask, "Are you that excited at seeing Ian Kendall again?"

Was she? *Focus on the town,* she told herself. *On anything but Ian.* The town lay little more than a leisurely drive from Amsterdam, but Vic had made it seem like a steeplechase run, allowing them only glimpses of the flat countryside that lay between the airport and this second-story hotel window. Her images of the Netherlands had been little snatches: a modern airport, the sparkling canals in Amsterdam, and small dairy farms with those unused windmills in the distance. As they drove into town, the carillon bells in the cathedral rang on the morning air.

Vic had grinned and said, "Someone knew you were coming."

She turned from the window as Vic slammed his suitcase on the bed.

"It's lovely here in Den Bosch, Vic."

"Thought you'd like it. But you can thank the Duke of Brabant, not me." He grabbed his shaving gear. "It all started with Brabant's twelfth-century hunting lodge and a bunch of sheep. I had nothing to do with it."

"And now all of this! Canals. Cathedrals. Ancient crumbling walls. Narrow three-story houses. It's all so charming."

"That's right," he said, picking up his bath towel. "It's twentieth-century people living in thirteenth-century houses."

"Vic, if you're going to take a shower, I'll go on down to the lobby and wait for Ian. I'll be safe there."

"No." His voice sharpened. "I'll take a quick shower, and then we'll go down together. Drew's orders! You're not to be out of my sight until he gets here."

"That could be midnight."

"Or six in the morning, but he'll be here." As he picked up a clean shirt and undershorts, he said, "Stay put. Don't even go to your own room."

As the bathroom door slammed, Vic's clutter tumbled from the mattress, spilling black-and-white photographs on the rug. She scooped up the mess and tossed it back on the bed, all except the pictures of a woman. These she scrutinized with growing interest as Vic whistled in the shower. At last the water was turned off, and Vic came back into the room, still whistling.

She held up the pictures. "Is this a friend of yours, Vic? Honest, you do make a lousy photographer."

"What are you doing with those?" He snatched them from her and dropped them in the suitcase along with his dirty clothes.

"Well, did you take them?"

"No."

"Then you are not the lousy photographer. I thought maybe she was your girl—so you cut off your competition."

"Lennie is not my girl. I don't have a girl anymore."

She heard the longing in his voice and remembered that he had sworn off dating since being diagnosed as HIV-positive. Embarrassed for them both, she glanced down at the photos again. "Are they surveillance?"

"Again, not mine. Lennie Applegate works at the embassy. She's Radburn Parker's lady friend. And before you ask, he's a Londoner, a thorn in the flesh to Drew. So don't press Drew for answers, and don't worry your pretty head about Lennie."

Vic was overcompensating. His attempt to kill her curiosity had aroused it. "What's wrong? Is her husband having her tailed?"

"There's no husband."

Chase took the risk of picking the pictures up again. "This Lennie is obviously with a man. The photographer cut him off."

"I told you. I am not a camera freak."

"Her companion is a big man."

He pivoted around, still tucking his fresh shirt in. "What makes you say that?"

"His hand is in the picture—and it's big. And this Miss Applegate of yours seems to be looking up at him."

"Observant, aren't you?"

"I had plenty of time. You took a long shower. So why is Drew having her photographed on so many different days?" To his frown, she said, "I think these were made from a video camera. Day and date provided."

He grabbed them from her and shuffled them like a deck of cards. "Any other information from that pretty head of yours?"

"Yes, it's the same man in each picture."

Again his brows shot up. "Go on with your rundown."

"He always wears the same jewelry—an expensive watch and diamond cuff links."

That seemed to surprise him. "I thought you would zero in on the onyx ring on the man's finger."

"That, too," she agreed. "But you wear one just like it."

As Vic shuffled the pictures for the third time, she said, "You've come up with something. I see it in your eyes, Vic."

"Those cuff links look familiar, but I can't quite get a grasp on why." Vic's face twisted with displeasure. "I think I'd better hold off showing these to Drew until I figure it out. Okay?"

"Okay." She eased them from his hand and placed them on the bed. "We'd better go," she urged. "I don't want to miss Ian."

An hour later—after repeated trips to the desk—Chase sank deeper into the chair in the hotel lobby, determined to wait out Ian's arrival. Vic dozed in the chair across from her. Sleep distorted his angular features. The sagging jaw line and gawking mouth made him seem vulnerable and older. She wondered how much of it was ill health or just physical exhaustion. With rumors of Vic's HIV status surfacing at the embassy, it seemed that Drew was Vic's only friend—unless they counted Miriam and herself.

They found Vic likable, but they worried about him. He had brushed off the bronchitis of a month ago and insisted that the unrelenting low-grade fever of the last few days would go away. It seemed to Chase that Drew Gregory lived under the pretense that Vic would live forever, at least until he was ninety. She tried to form an image of Vic a year ago—before she knew him—with an array of girlfriends at his beck and call. Somewhere along the way, one of them had given him more than a night of pleasure. She didn't know the girl—Vic didn't either—but Chase resented her for giving Vic the virus that could take his life.

He stirred and cast a sleepy eye her way. "No Kendall yet?"

"Not through that front door. Should I tell him about Drew?"

"Just enough."

She drummed her fingers on the arms of the cushioned chair. "I don't even know why Drew went to Paris."

"More high-level meetings. Just tell Ian Drew will be here when the race begins. Guaranteed." His words caught in a yawn. "Kendall is a smart boy. Once he knows we're riding in the team car, he'll figure out why."

Chase glanced toward the lobby doors again. "Vic, I wonder if Ian's staying at another hotel tonight."

"No, his team checked in here, and it's against the rules to overnight away from them. Otherwise the rider is disqualified."

"Really?"

"Really." He yawned again. "Let's give it another half hour and then call it quits. Tomorrow's a big day, Chase."

She fingered the press card in her pocket. "And I will be a blubbering novice with all those journalists."

"You'll do okay. Wake me when Kendall comes."

Six minutes later three cyclists charged through the lobby door—Ian, the fair-skinned Basil Millard, and the dark-eyed Orlando Gioceppi. Her eyes and smile focused on Ian. Damp strands of shiny red hair peeked out from beneath his cycling helmet. She stumbled from the chair, her numb legs almost toppling her.

"Ian!"

"Chase!"

She willed her feet to run to Ian as he bolted toward her. And then she was in his arms, pressed against his sticky jersey. He tilted her chin up and kissed her urgently.

"I wasn't expecting you," he said, still holding her.

"You invited me. Did your dad and brother come?"

"I told you—they never come." He nuzzled her hair, blowing softly through it. "Basil's wife can make room for you."

"Don't bother," Vic said, joining them. "We're booked here at the hotel. Let's go up to the room and fill you in on what's happening."

Pleasure drained from Ian's face. Jealousy rose in its place. "Sorry, " he said, releasing Chase. "I'd better turn in."

"Keep a cool head, Ian. You'll need it." Vic shot a warning glance toward the cyclist coming through the door. "Who's that?"

"Marcus Nash. Nash has been gone all day, off on his own."

"Ian, isn't that the man who followed us to London the other day?"

"He can't be, Chase. I would have recognized him."

"Not if he was wearing dark glasses and a wig," Vic said. "Let's get out of this lobby. Chase is here at great sacrifice. We don't want the two of you seen together very long. And, like it or not, Gregory and I are riding in the team car for your protection."

"Over Jon Gainsborough's dead body."

"We have his permission. We're to make sure you live through this race, Kendall. Now let's go up to the room and talk things over."

Chapter 10

Drew Gregory stood in the doorway to the press room looking down at Chase's angry face. The gold in her blouse heightened the sizzling luster in her wide brown eyes. Officially Chase was on her own now, name tag and all, one of the few female sports writers on hand for the outset of the Tour de France. But some of her spunk was gone this morning, that do-or-dare smile that he liked cut off by the stubborn tilt of her chin. Behind her came the clicking of computers, the murmur of voices, the flashing glare on the television screen as the Dutch commentator predicted more rain when the cyclists rolled down the ramp and started on their 2,495-mile journey toward Paris.

"Say something, Chase," Drew said.

Her expression remained as gloomy as the weather report as she stared beyond him toward the lively crowd outside.

"Listen to me, Chase. Thanks to Langley, you are here as a journalist. That means being in the press room."

She swept a strand of her burnished chestnut hair behind her ear. "It's not fair, Drew. I want to be out there by the starting ramp to see Ian off."

"Not today. You don't want to be caught in a thunderstorm."

Her gaze riveted on him now. "I've been in the rain before."

Did he dare argue with her? She was accustomed to having her own way, to making her own decisions. "You're my eyes in the press room, Chase. Keep a lookout."

"Do you expect me to find a terrorist in the press room?"

"I don't know where we'll find him. But stick close to some of the seasoned journalists. They'll be quick to spot a problem."

Drew wanted Chase out of harm's way as the 189 cyclists left the enclosed *Brabanthallen* and rolled down the ramp, a minute apart, one right after the other, racing against the clock in a time trial that would leave only milliseconds between the winner and the man in second place. He dreaded the moment when Kendall would be on the starter's ramp in full view of the cheering crowd and that lone terrorist determined to take him out.

He left Chase sulking in the newsroom and headed back to find Vic Wilson. Outside, grayness filled the Saturday sky. Trees along the boulevard still dripped from a midnight rain, leaving the pavements slick from the dampness. News commentators kept announcing their gloomy weather forecasts, but the rest of the citizens of s'Hertogenbosch were eager to show off their city to the riders and their fans with a *van harte welkom*.

Drew shared their excitement but more from the urgency of getting the race underway. As far as he was concerned, the sun and the hot stickiness of a summer morning would surely break through the thunderclouds.

Fans crammed the streets, closing in on a bigger guest list than s'Hertogenbosch had seen in decades. They were up to the task. The city sparkled with preparation, its clean and spotless streets scrubbed even cleaner, its shops that normally didn't open their doors until later in the morning already opened. Flowers in a rainbow of colors filled the windows. On one side of the street, vendors had set up a table of Indonesian *rijsttafel*, but the smell of currant and rye breads and sweet bakery goods that permeated the air broke down Drew's resistance. He bought pancakes for Vic and a tart stuffed with apples and cinnamon for himself. Everything was for sale. Tour trinkets and hats, *koffie* and tea, wine of French and German vintages, and one ingenious young man was selling thick slices of ham and cheese.

Drew leaped back as Maurice Chambord's official red car bounced over the sidewalk and back into the street, screeching to a stop near the starting ramp. Chambord stepped out and strutted about in his forest-green blazer and dark gray trousers. He seemed as nervous and jittery as the riders, but he managed a broad smile as he mingled among the neophytes who had never ridden a Tour. He offered a handshake to the cyclist standing beside his Lotus bike and a pat on the shoulder to the rider slumped on a chair waiting for that final medical clearance.

Chambord stopped short of greeting last year's winner. The Spaniard was aloof and confident, his most vocal competition two bikes from him and his strongest French rival with his back to the crowd. Despair swamped Drew's usual optimism. Ian Kendall was a superb cyclist. Hadn't he proved that in the Giro d'Italia? But what were Ian's chances against these other world champions?

Chambord's quick movements caught Drew's attention as the Frenchman brushed shoulders with the crowd and pushed his way to the nearest gendarme. *So that was what the stroll was all about—a final word to the constable in charge.* Chambord's gaze strayed slowly over the people, coming to a stop when he spotted Drew. Drew swallowed the last of the apple tart and went reluctantly to the Frenchman.

"Where's Vic Wilson?" Drew asked.

"Waiting for you in the team car. That gives him access to a cellular phone and small TV monitor."

"And Ian Kendall?"

Maurice nodded toward a square tent near the start-line. "In there warming up."

"Is he with Coach Skobla?"

Chambord shook his head. "That is one man I want you to watch closely. I don't trust him."

"And Jon Gainsborough?"

"They are two of a kind. It's good that you and Wilson will be riding with them."

"Any problem?"

"Nothing but this," Maurice said. He took an envelope from his blazer and handed it to Drew. It had been addressed to Chambord at the Societe du Tour de France and postmarked from Gascony days ago. *I'm waiting for the race to begin,* it said.

To Drew's arched brow, Maurice said, "Our handwriting expert checked it out. It was written on the same typewriter. Signed by the same man. He's somewhere in the crowd, Monsieur Gregory."

Inside the wind-trainer tent, the wheels hummed and spun. The stifling acrid air smelled of sweat as another twenty riders sat on stationary bikes and pedaled with all fury.

Pearls of perspiration rolled down Ian's face. He brushed them away with his shoulder. The dampness made ringlets of his wavy hair and sent rivulets of water down his bare arms. His thoughts pedaled faster than his legs. Unlike many contenders in the race, Ian didn't seek a solo win in the prologue. That had been his strategy last year—win the prologue and stay on top of the overall standings for the first three stages.

It had been a dreamer's scenario, out of reach for a rider still new to the Tour. He laughed to himself. Young riders always felt invincible. Was that just a year ago? He had been twenty-two then, a man ready to take on the Tour de France. He was a mountain climber—had been even then, but he wanted a good show. The whole race or nothing at all. For his grandmother?

Yes, it had always been for his grandmother. He hadn't even made it into Paris and didn't know now whether he would have had the strength to run the full course, even if the crash hadn't put him out of the race. He'd done well, exceptionally well according to the *L'Equipe* write-ups the day after the race ended for him.

A year made a man wiser and older, old at twenty-three, going on twenty-four. He made his legs go faster, enjoying the exhilaration and safety of the wind-trainer. His helmet hung from the shoulder strap on the handlebars, swaying as he pedaled, his grandmother's message taped inside. He tried to focus on his grandmother so he could push Alekos Golemis from his memories. Alekos should be on the wind-trainer beside him. That big, grinning Greek should be alive, not buried on Corfu.

Once Ian left the tent—once he lined up on the ramp and started his time trial—he would give it his best, but he wasn't set on a win. With the shaky weather conditions outside, he knew better than to start out the long journey risking a win in the prologue and breaking an ankle like Chris Boardman had done in '95 on a slick, wet curve. Ian would settle for coming in with a good standing—top ten maybe. Or at least the top twenty-five. He'd make up time with wins in the Alps and Pyrenees. He was ready. He was an endurance man. This was his year. His race. With all due respect for last year's winner, Ian knew he had a chance for a place on the Paris podium. First place if he had his way.

His grandmother kept tapping his memory, pressing into his thoughts. *I'm still riding for you, Grandma,* he told her.

But I'm riding for Alekos Golemis, too. I owe him one, Grams. He wanted to be here riding with me. I should be riding for the team, but I'm riding for you and Alekos.

And, Grams, I'm riding for Chase Evans.

Here in this stinking tent he could almost see his grandmother as he had last seen her ten years ago sitting across from him in the Fox Hunt Restaurant in London, elegantly dressed, with her wide eyes full of love for him; and then hours later lying dead in the street outside of No. 10 Downing, her dress splattered with blood and her body motionless. As the sweat blinded him—or were they tears?—he knew that she would be pleased with Chase Evans.

Chase was his grandmother's kind of gal.

He saw someone coming through the tent flap and recognized Gainsborough's *directeur sportif,* a serious coach who believed in the team, a man who switched to his native Czech tongue when he was excited. Ian didn't break his rhythm as Ludvik Skobla approached. At forty-five, the coach kept his body trim, but this morning he looked tired, stressed out as he came slowly across the room in his stark white running shoes. Fringes of his hair had grayed at the temples, with the lines on his face adding a dozen years to his age.

"Something wrong, Coach?" Ian asked.

"Kendall, you're to get out there and take the race today."

"That wasn't the game plan."

"It is now. Jon Gainsborough wants you to win the prologue."

"It's not worth the risk in these poor weather conditions."

"Those are your orders, Ian."

Ian cast a glance down the row of riders. "Talk to Orlando, Coach. He's the one super motivated to win the prologue."

"You're the team leader—our best chance in this Tour."

"I can't waste my energy on the first day. I'm a mountain rider. That's where I can gain overall points and move ahead."

"You're a sprinter, too, Ian. The best all-around rider I have. Just ride hard for those seven kilometers."

Resentment took over. "Coach, there are eighteen turns—a couple of sharp curves to negotiate. No way am I going to risk my safety with a fast ride over wet roads."

Ludvik flexed his arms, his fists doubled. For a moment Ian was certain the coach would pull him bodily from the cycle. "Ride to win today or don't ride at all."

"Crash today and I'm out. . . . Or don't you and Gainsborough want me to finish this race?"

The vessels in Ludvik's neck throbbed. "I want you to live through it. God helping me, Ian, I want nothing more than for you to stand on the victor's podium in Paris. That's why I've worked so hard with this team. You're a good rider. I'm proud of you."

"As long as I beat everyone else's time trials today?"

"It's for the best." The haggard lines on Skobla's face deepened. "Ian, how are you getting along with Orlando now?"

"He still blames me for Alekos's death."

"Gregory talked to him about that this morning."

"It was none of Gregory's business."

"He seemed to think it was." Ludvik glanced across the tent at Orlando. "I think you and Orlando will be friends again now."

"Any fast cures for getting on with Marcus Nash? That man can never take Alekos's place with the team."

"Give him a chance."

"You should have given us a choice!"

"We needed the Parker Foundation funds. Nash riding with the team was part of the agreement."

The whir of the trainer-wheels screeched in protest as Ian braked. "I didn't know."

"You weren't supposed to know. But if he gets out of hand—"

"I can handle Nash."

"Stay away from him. That's our best advice. We're concerned about your safety." He moved closer and gripped Ian's handlebar. "If you see anything out of the ordinary today or anytime during the next three weeks, drop back to the team car and tell us."

"I don't go backwards in a race, Coach."

"Then send one of your support riders. We'll whip you into the security of the team car as quickly as possible."

"If you think you're trying to reassure me, Coach, you're doing the opposite. You are scaring me spitless."

"Then talk to your friend Gregory. He has his own way of dealing with fear. He insisted on us having prayer together before we left the room this morning. That's an experience I haven't had since I was in knee britches."

As he swung Ian's helmet, he fingered the paper taped inside. "Is that your rabbit's foot?" he asked.

"No, just some words I live by."

Skobla read aloud, "'Run with patience the race that is set before you.' Nice words—a quote from some Scottish poet?"

"No. Days before my grandmother died, she underlined those words in her Bible and wrote my name beside them."

Skobla's gaze mellowed. "Then run that race of yours well."

An hour later Ian sat at the top of the starting ramp, his feet on the bike pedals, the strap of his riding helmet tight beneath his chin. The tower of St. Janskathedral loomed above the city, shrouded in a faint gray mist; but the clouds were lifting, the streets drier than when the first cyclists set off.

Only 7.3 kilometers to go, he told himself. *You can do it, man. You can do it.*

He waited for the signal to go and then rolled down the ramp into the sultry morning. Gripping the straight-up handlebars and bent in a tight aerodynamic tuck, he sped toward the center of s'Hertogenbosch. The faces in the crowd became a blur as people leaned over the steel barricades and urged him on.

He wiped Chase and his grandmother from his mind as he rode south along the seventeenth-century town wall into the suburbs. Zooming past more cafes and narrow three-story houses, he careened around the circuit in an explosive burst of speed. Negotiating the first of a dozen curves at seventy-six kilometers per hour, he passed the man who had left the starting ramp a minute ahead of him.

Fans held up placards. *Five kilometers to go. Four.* The last three rose on a slight incline. He pedaled hard as he swept back into the town square to the music of a noisy jazz band and the distinctive smell of the locally brewed beer tickling his nostrils. As he free-wheeled across the finish line in his sweat-soaked jersey, Ian slumped over the handlebars.

Minutes later, his head shot back, his eyes glued to the clock as the remaining riders came racing across the finish line. Orlando was beside him now, pouring a glass of water over Ian's head and shoving a bottle of juice into his hand. "The prologue favorite crashed halfway through the race," Orlando told him.

"In the rain?" Ian asked.

"He skidded out on the wet pavement."

There was no time to ask about last year's winner. Ian's name came over the loudspeaker. A deafening roar erupted. He had just a seventeen-second lead, but enough to make him the overall leader as the day's prologue ended.

From the large television screen in the press room, Chase watched Ian mount the podium and felt both pride and sympathy for him as he tugged the yellow jersey over his head. He looked so serious, handsome actually. He was no longer disheveled from the race, his face no longer sweaty. Somewhere after crossing the finish line and dismounting the bike, he had found time to splash his face and comb that thick red hair. *Smile,* she thought. *Your grandfather and Beatrice Thorpe are watching you on television.*

Ian had won the individual trials from a well-fought race, but the news commentator negated his victory, saying, "The last thirty racers had a distinct advantage riding over drier roads."

His voice droned on as he announced that the Netherlands champion racer had crashed when he skidded on the rain-slick street. "The American Ian Kendall won," he said, "by sheer luck."

As Chase's fist hit the table, the man beside her winked. "You must be covering the young American," he said.

He was a good-looking man, casually dressed in slacks and a white polo shirt, his mocking gray eyes laughing at her. "There's more than one American racing," she reminded him.

"But only one with the chance of holding on to the yellow jersey all the way to Paris."

"Do you really think Kendall will win?" Chase asked.

"I don't think much about it. I cheer the Italians myself."

She glanced at his thick blond hair. "The Italians?"

He grinned. "Born and reared in the vineyards near Milan."

"But I thought—"

"That all Italians had dark hair? Wrong."

She smothered her embarrassment. "Lesson number one," she said, smiling up at him.

His eyes and voice danced at the same time. "I'm Salvador Salatori—but just call me Sal."

"Chase. Chase Evans." Her hand seemed lost in his, his release of it taking longer than pleased her. She pulled free. "My hometown paper wants Ian Kendall to win. So do I."

He gave her a sly wink. "No matter who wears the yellow jersey, the long racing history of the Tour belongs to France."

"And today the glory belonged to s'Hertogenbosch."

"They did pay thousands for the privilege of being the host city—many more lire than I'd invest."

The stirring notes of the "Star Spangled Banner" on the TV drew Chase back to the screen. Ian looked relaxed now, and shy, as he held the bouquet of flowers and took the perfunctory kiss on both cheeks. He lifted the flowers and waved them. His smile started at the corners of his mouth, little indentations that added to his boyish confidence. Then the twinkle lines by his eyes deepened. *Now he will pour on all his charm,* she thought. She was beginning to know him, and the realization surprised her.

Her flesh prickled with pride as he tucked an American flag in with the flowers and waved them again. She squeezed her arms against her chest. "I love being an American," she said.

As Ian stepped from the podium, Sal's eyes narrowed. "Odd that they did not play the British anthem for the Gainsborough team, but it doesn't matter to me who wins the Tour. Like you, I cheer for my countrymen. But if we do not win, at least I hope it will not be the British team—or that American cyclist."

"Why do you dislike Americans?"

Salvador shoved his hands deep into his pockets. "I don't. Only a few of them."

Chase picked up her laptop computer and swung the strap over her shoulder. "I think I'd better go."

"Will I see you tomorrow?" he asked.

"I plan to be here."

"Then I will save you a work spot next to mine."

"Why bother? I'm still going to cheer for Ian Kendall." She left the press room, working her way gradually through the crowd back to the hotel where Drew and Wilson waited for her.

"Well," Vic asked when she came in view, "are you pleased with the outcome?"

"With Ian's win? Of course. But I didn't like being cooped up in the press room all day."

"Did you meet any seasoned journalists?" Drew asked.

"Just one pompous Italian who doesn't want an American to win."

Chapter 11

tage two, day three—the Netherlands. Like the prologue, stage one had started and ended in Den Bosch. Tight curves on the slippery roads and traffic islands in the town had caused several crashes, ending the Tour for more than one rider as he looped through the countryside past gigantic windmills and winding streams. But nothing had slowed the sprinters or dampened the spirit of the cheering crowds in s'Hertogenbosch.

Now as Drew waited for the second stage to begin, his mood was as gloomy as the dark misty weather. He checked his Gucci watch for time and date, accurate as always: July, Monday—thirty minutes before the peloton rolled out of Holland and headed for Belgium. Ian still held a marginal lead, giving him a second day in the *maillot jaune* as the overall leader. As far as Drew was concerned, the yellow jersey put the spotlight on Ian, making him a vulnerable target for the madman determined to eliminate him.

Drew searched the pre-race crowd. The fans were eager to see the riders set out, yet reluctant to let them go. Journalists were catching last-minute interviews with the Tour favorites. Kids crawled under the barriers for autographs with the police looking the other way. The last rider stepped up to the sign-in chart, looking tired and jittery.

Drew didn't envy today's schedule—a 228-mile ride over narrow roads with torrential rains predicted before they rode up a steep, cobbled hill and finally reached Wasquehal. For Vic Wilson it meant breakfast in Holland, lunch at a sidewalk cafe in Belgium, and dinner in a historical setting in France. But as the peloton rode off, Drew planned to head to a small airfield outside Den Bosch where a private plane would whisk him off to Normandy.

As Drew looked over the crowd, a tall man in stone-washed denims sauntered toward him with a come-a-day, go-a-day bounce to his steps. His worn baseball cap sat backwards on his head, and a mammoth grease rag dangled from his hip pocket— a good cover for Brad O'Malloy, one of Troy Carwell's casually dressed bright boys from Paris.

O'Malloy stuck out his hand and flashed a brash grin. "I'm here for the duration of the race," he said, pointing to his I.D. badge. "I'm replacing one of the Gainsborough mechanics."

"It looks like you're replacing me."

"Just for a day or two. I'll keep Kendall's bike in good working order."

Brad was a ten-year man with the Agency, spoke French fluently, and in spite of his sleepy eyes, his alert mind clicked in every happening in his mental notebook. He hooked his thumbs in his belt and yanked his jeans a notch higher. "You can fly off to Isigny without giving security a second thought. But let me warn you before you see Madame Dupree—Salvador Contoni may be back in France planning rough moves against the Tour."

"I thought she came back from Italy without him."

His eyelids drooped at half mast. "Just go peacefully and check it out. The latest intelligence reports have them both here."

Drew balked. "Why don't you go in my place?"

"You'll recognize Contoni." He thumped Drew on the shoulder. "We've got things covered here, Drew. Vic's in the team car. I'm riding in that one with the bike rack on top."

"And Ian Kendall is riding out there in a yellow jersey."

His gloom deepened; the prayer that he tried to pray for Ian's safety drifted with the clouds. "Have you met Ian yet?" he asked.

"Over a flat tire. He thinks I'm a replacement for Nick who went down with the flu yesterday."

"Kendall isn't that trusting."

"Then we'll both be on the alert. I gave his cycle a once-over this morning. That way it passed safely from my hands to his." He gave another yank to his jeans. "Don't worry. I strip down car engines for relaxation. It's good for my stress level."

Drew had no doubt that O'Malloy could strip down a damaged cycle or fix a flat with equal efficiency and have it back running within seconds. Brad's office at the embassy in Paris was a clutter, but not his thought process and not those strong hands of his, greasy at the moment.

O'Malloy whipped the rag from his pocket and wiped his hands. "Carwell suggests that you bypass Nogent-sur-Oise and meet up with us in Soissons."

"Two days with Monique Dupree? I'd wear out my welcome."

"Just stay cool, Drew. One of the bomb warnings came from Soissons. French Intelligence is checking stores against the sale of timing devices and plastic explosives."

"That's like finding a pebble at the top of the Alps."

O'Malloy shrugged indifferently. "Carwell wants you to check out each day's route ahead of time."

"I'd need a bomb disposal unit for that."

"The French have one of those ROB devices. That robot's like a one-man bomb squad."

"You have your head in a turnip patch, Brad."

"No joke. It's a remote control unit built from spare parts." He wiped rain from his face with his grease rag, smearing the side of his cheek. "Even works on rainy days like this."

"What do you want to do—terrify the fans along the way?"

"Someone else plans to terrify them," he argued. "A bomb disposal unit was your idea. If you don't like a made-in-France label, ask the White House to send one of those state-of-the-art jobs from the air base in Turkey. Langley could check on it."

"The Tour will be over before we'd get through all that Washington red tape."

"We have Americans in the race, don't we?"

"Six of them, counting Kendall. All on different teams."

O'Malloy's sleepy eyes narrowed. "So we'll get you your bomb unit. Langley can speed things up. That or anger the White House because some American rider got himself killed in the Tour."

As the riders lined up at the start-line, Brad went back to his car, leaving Drew pressed against the steel barrier with rain washing over the bridge of his nose. The riders pedaled toward him, shoulder to shoulder. The streamlined bicycles glimmered in the rain, the many colors of their team uniforms brilliant in spite of the mist. As riders bent forward over the handlebars, helmets and dark goggles masked their faces, but Drew saw Ian toward the front of the pack. He gave Ian a thumbs up and then made his way through the crowd to the waiting taxi.

Thirty minutes later Drew was airborne, the pilot lapsing into silence after three aborted attempts at conversation. Still he pointed down to the peloton riding over the winding hills below them. Then he lifted the plane higher, swooping above the windmills and marshes of Holland as they headed into the strong winds above the Belgian countryside.

The wind currents snapped at the plane, bouncing them mercilessly into an air pocket as they crossed the border into France. They rode the French coast, speeding along the windswept beaches above the chalky cliffs, and came in for a rough landing in a lush pastoral region on the edge of Isigny.

Again Carwell had a car waiting for him.

Beech trees broke the heady winds as he drove past the high-hedged fields and half-timbered farmhouses. Finally, turning into the Duprees' driveway, he parked beside another car rental. The familiar weather-beaten house was set back from the rural road; brown-and-white Norman cattle grazed lazily in the rain. He welcomed the raindrops on his face and listened for the shouts of the boys' voices as he walked over the cobbled path toward the house. He saw no movement at the windows, heard no sounds, yet he sensed that someone was watching him. Before he could wrap his fingers around the old brass knocker, the thick wooden door swung wide. Monique Dupree's curious brown eyes were as dark as her shiny hair. The smile around her sensuous lips was forced, her eyes full of mistrust.

"I was in the area," he said, and then remembering his new covenant to be up front and honest, he added, "Actually I left the Tour de France to see you, Madame Dupree."

She stepped back, visibly shaken, and beckoned him in. "You should have called. I haven't much time to visit now."

He stopped in the middle of the room to glance around and then turned and faced her. There was an elegance to the way Monique stood there looking up at him, a delicate grace that seemed out of sync in this aged farmhouse with its stone fireplace and frayed throw rugs. Only the nervous twitch of her eyelid marred her outer beauty. She was uneasy in his presence, overly anxious to show him the way back to his car.

"Are the boys out?" he asked.

"They are down by the river with a friend."

A friend with a car rental. Contoni? Contoni and a boat. Salvador always left room for escape. "And your parents—are they here?"

Monique nodded toward the back of the house. "Just *Maman*."

He glanced up in time to see Monique's mother—a buxom, wide-hipped woman—escaping down the narrow hall to the safety of her blue-tiled kitchen with its cast-iron range and old-fashioned water pump. As the tantalizing smell of beef and vegetables reached the parlor, he felt an urgency to state his business, leave, and find the nearest cafe en route back to the plane.

"Your father?" Drew pressed.

"Working the fields."

Berger Dupree, as his name implied, was a tiller of the soil, a man who made his living off the land. Monique's parents were religious people, but they withheld their pleasantries with Drew, blaming him for the death of their son-in-law. Or was it their utter dislike for intelligence officers that made them so cold toward him?

She made no effort to offer him a chair. He held his ground. "Madame Dupree, I haven't heard from you since you came back from Italy. We had an agreement. You were to bring Contoni back to France with you."

She avoided his eyes, hesitating long enough for him to know that she was lying. "I never found him."

"But my Company kept their part of the bargain. The settling of your husband's estate is moving rapidly through the courts."

"Yes. I will soon be the sole owner of Harland's houses and land. Small comfort to my sons," she said. She folded her arms tightly against her chest. "I told you, I didn't find Sal."

Drew smiled patiently as he took some pictures from his pocket and spread the prints on the arm of the sofa. "These are proof of your times together. This one was taken in Milan—and this one from a helicopter above Contoni's yacht. And this on the island of Corfu—willingly in the arms of Salvador Contoni."

Her hands curled into tiny glacier-white balls as she sank into the safety of the cushioned sofa and stared down at the pictures. "Sal—Mr. Contoni would not come back with me."

"But you must have made some arrangement with him?"

"None." Her answer was too quick, too sharp.

He looked at the bowed head and gently lifted her chin. "Are you certain that Contoni is not here in France again, perhaps at the Tour de France? Or perhaps with your boys even now."

Her dark eyes blazed. "I told you—they're with a friend."

"He is a poor companion for young boys, Monique."

As she winced, Drew pressed his advantage. "Contoni shot a friend of mine—at your castle at the foot of the Pyrenees."

"Salvador never carries a gun."

Even in her anger, she was beautiful, desperately trying to protect Contoni. Drew knew the signs. Monique Dupree was in love with Contoni, involved in the one way that would destroy her.

"I was there, Monique. When my friend Jacques tried to escape, Contoni killed him."

"No, never. I've been with him. I know how kind he can be."

"To you, but he's not good company for your sons."

She bit her lip. He surprised himself with gentleness, saying, "Contoni always carries a gun, Monique."

She dabbed at the blood forming on her lip. "No. On his yacht—he carries a weapon for protection, but he knows there are to be no guns around my sons." She glanced toward the black cavernous fireplace. "Have you never killed a man, Mr. Gregory?"

In the army, he thought. *And on covert action with the Agency.* His gaze shifted to her clasped hands, the transparent skin tight enough to tear. Yes, he had killed men, but always in the line of duty. But he was redeemed now, forgiven for the past.

"Well, Mr. Gregory, have you ever killed anyone?"

His jaw slackened, then went taut again. "Yes."

He saw the triumph in her gaze and wondered if the blue-gray of his own eyes had turned to steel. "Contoni is a wanted man," he said. "Interpol, French Intelligence. We must stop him before he kills again. For your safety and the safety of your boys."

She turned toward the wide farm window. As she looked out over the fields, she chewed at her lip again. "He won't hurt my children. He is fond of them."

And more than fond of you.

Her face was easy to read. Anger. Fear. Motherly love. He pitied her for the loneliness that she must feel. Her husband had been twice her age—a powerful, secretive man. Contoni was younger, vibrant, perhaps genuinely in love with her. Drew picked up the snapshots from the chair, placing the one of Monique and Contoni on the island of Corfu on top. They were standing on the deck of his yacht, Contoni wearing his skipper's cap, Monique's dark head pressed against his broad chest.

"I'm sorry," Drew said. "If I had known there was anything between you, I would not have asked you to go to Milan for us."

He put the snapshots in her hands, the picture of Salvador and Monique on top. She folded her fingers around them. "I don't have a picture of us together," she said. "Thank you."

Outside the two car rentals were still parked side by side. Birds chattered in the tree by the window. Down the hall they could hear Monique's mother bustling about in the kitchen. "Are the boys with Salvador?" he asked.

"Their grandfather is out there."

But not with them, Drew thought. "I'm going after them."

"You must not hurt my boys."

He placed his broad hand over hers. "I would never hurt your sons. Anzel saved my life."

"I was afraid you'd forgotten."

"A man doesn't forget a sacrifice like that."

"Mr. Gregory, when Sal saw you coming, he forced the boys to go with him. Oh—they went willingly enough. He's good to them."

Tears washed over her high cheekbones. "Promise me you won't hurt any of them, Mr. Gregory. Promise me you won't take Sal on my father's land—not with the boys watching."

Drew glanced at the rental cars again.

"He didn't come that way," she said.

Was she lying? Or was she hiding another guest? "Contoni can't get too far." Drew reached for the phone.

"Don't bring the gendarmes here. Anzel is still terrified of the police. I'm certain Sal is gone by now."

"Then we need your help to find him."

"He's following the race—I know that much. But I won't help you find him, not when Salvador is my friend."

Down the hall, the back door closed. Drew moved swiftly to the window in time to see Monique's mother hurrying toward the barn. "So your *maman* goes to warn him?"

"She goes to protect her grandsons."

He spun around and caught her off guard. "Monique, what does Contoni have against Ian Kendall?"

The color drained from her face. "Ian Kendall?"

He had the urge to cross the room and shake those narrow shoulders. "Kendall is riding with the British team in the Tour de France with a good chance to take the prize on the Champs Elysees. But someone is trying to stop him. We've received several threats against Ian, even bomb threats against the Tour."

"Sal wouldn't do that. He wouldn't risk his own safety. Not that way. . . . And he doesn't even know Kendall," she whispered.

"Then why is he sending death threats?"

"Why would he do that? When we were in Corfu, someone paid him to stop Kendall from winning—but not to kill him."

Drew stared at her. Ian's friend Alekos Golemis came from the island of Corfu—was buried there. Alekos's father lived there and had met with Salvador at the family villa. "Someone in Corfu paid Contoni to go after Kendall?"

"Yes. A large amount of money."

And Vasille Golemis has money. "And you were there when he hired Contoni? You can identify him."

"I won't. I can't. He is a powerful man."

He glared down at her. She would never willingly help the Agency. She had spent too many years living with her husband's twisted thinking. "I don't need his name, Monique. I am certain I know it already." To confirm his suspicions, he added, "I knew his son. The boy was a friend of Ian Kendall's."

Her chin lifted defiantly. "Sal has nothing against Ian Kendall. It's you he hates, Mr. Gregory. Not the young cyclist."

As Drew walked back to his car, the boys ran across the fields toward him, Giles's short, stubby legs pumping. Drew held out his arms. Giles would arrive first, eager for the candy treats that Drew carried in his pocket. Anzel would come shyly behind his younger brother, asking for nothing, expecting nothing. They were just yards from him when rifle shots exploded, the bullets zinging over their heads.

"Get down," Drew shouted.

Anzel dropped flat on the ground with his arm around Giles. As Drew crawled to them, another round of bullets whizzed above them, lower this time. He lifted his head as he reached the boys and saw Monique start out the door toward them. She was yanked back inside. *Salvador Contoni? He's in there with her.*

A third volley split the air to the right of him. Drew wrapped his arms around the boys, keeping their faces to the gravel. "Who's out there, Anzel?"

"My grandfather."

"Not Salvador Contoni?"

"He left, Monsieur Gregory. An hour ago."

Drew lifted his head higher. Fifty yards from them, Berger Dupree stood in the open, his rifle aimed on Drew. An AK-47? Or one of those French jobs that would be just as deadly? Berger was a nationalist, apt to sport a French MAS service rifle even if it dated back to World War II.

As Berger moved steadily toward them, Anzel turned his head, a grass stain showing on his hollow cheek. "Grandfather will kill you if you don't leave," he said.

Giles's body quivered beneath Drew's arm. "Put the gun down, Berger," Drew called. "Your grandsons are here."

"I know," the stony voice called back. The old man was less than twenty yards away now. He was still handsome in spite of his seventy-plus years, but there was fire in those enormous mahogany eyes.

As Berger closed in, Anzel said tearfully, "He won't hurt you, Mr. Gregory, if you go away."

Drew touched Anzel's upturned face. "Put the rifle down, Berger," he shouted again. "You're frightening your grandsons."

Wisps of Berger's snow-white hair tumbled over his forehead; the bushy brows arched. His skin had been leathered by the sun and wind storms and by long hours in the fields. He was tall, bent slightly, his work pants tucked into high boots, his hands steady as a bar of steel as he kept his sights on Drew.

"Those were just warning shots," he thundered.

"I came here for Salvador Contoni."

"Didn't the boys tell you? He's gone. And I have another round to go. So get off my farm, Monsieur Gregory. I will not let you stand in the way of my daughter's happiness."

※※※

Inside the house Monique screamed as Thymous Golemis yanked her back into the entryway. She fought against his manacling grip.

"So that was Drew Gregory?" he fumed.

"Yes."

"He never even guessed that I was here."

"You stayed well hidden, but he parked beside your rented car. . . . Now, let me go, Thymous," she cried out. "Before something happens to my sons."

Thymous kept her in his grip as he leaned against the wall and stared out the window. He was breathing hard, wheezing. "Your boys are all right. The man with the rifle will not hurt them."

"My father?"

"Yes."

"Not Salvador?"

"Gone, I think."

"Did you hear everything we said, Thymous?"

"Enough to know that Gregory can ruin my father's career unless I can stop Contoni from carrying out my father's plan."

She stopped squirming, her thick lashes wet with tears. "I don't want you to find Sal," she whimpered. "I don't want anyone to find him."

His black eyes filled with pain. "You are so foolish. So foolish." Thymous relaxed his grip and lifted Monique's chin with the back of his hand until their eyes met. "You can't have both worlds, Monique. Someday you will have to choose. Salvador Contoni can only bring you unhappiness."

"And you, Thymous?"

"I would be good to both you and your boys."

Chapter 12

Jiri Benak left the Basque village at sunup and caught the nearest high-speed train to Paris for his meeting with the Russian agent. After deliberately delaying the meeting, Jiri felt pleased with himself. He could imagine Yuri Ryskov waiting for him at Maxim's five days in a row. But Jiri was following his own agenda, not Professor Ivanski's.

For Jiri, the deaths of Drew Gregory and Ian Kendall were priority; that it would cost the lives of fans and other young cyclists was of little concern to him. Within days he would strike against the Tour de France—before the riders even reached the Pyrenees. He smiled at the headlines of the newspaper in the hands of the man in front of him. Soon the eyes of the world would turn, not to the young riders racing toward Paris, but to Jiri—to what he would do along the way.

In Paris he stepped from the train as rested as when he had boarded. The depot was swarming with gendarmes. Approaching one of them, he boldly asked the way to Notre Dame. Then he sauntered to the curb, cocksure and smug, and hailed a taxi in the opposite direction. Wanted as he was by French Intelligence and Interpol, why could he move about so freely?

You will never find me, he thought. *I am too visible.*

Danger nurtured Jiri, satisfying him like morsels of a thick, rare steak. He chewed on danger, survived by it. Yet taking Ivanski's warning, Jiri hired three separate taxis, riding switchback across both banks of the Seine as unhurried as he had been when he laid his plans for this day. He had given himself ample time for his noon appointment. If the French taxi drivers remembered him at all, it would be as that fare whose face had been masked by thick, dark glasses and a wide ash-blond mustache.

Benak left the third taxi a block from the Arc de Triomphe, and as the driver merged with the traffic, he pocketed the glasses and removed the false mustache that irritated his upper lip. From here it was an easy walk up the Champs Elysees to Maxim's. If today's meeting with Yuri Ryskov turned sour—if Ryskov had set a trap for him—Jiri would outsmart the Russian.

Paris was too crowded for Jiri, too filled with antiquity and historical buildings. But now as he made his way through the heart of the city, he found himself acutely aware of the Arc de Triomphe, viewing it as little more than a crumbling war memorial in need of repair. Even the modern Pompidou Center annoyed him with its ducts and cables. He shaded his eyes for the same critical gaze toward the city's most famous landmark; to Jiri the distant Eiffel Tower was a mass of scrap iron. Except at night. Illuminated at night, the tower was as eye-catching as the floodlit domes of the Sacre-Coeur, brilliant against the night sky. For a moment his eyes went back to the distant tower. He wondered what size bomb he would need to destroy it and then shrugged. No, he had no real desire to destroy these remarkable structures—these landmarks. Let the Parisians have their city. Jiri's sights were set on the Cotswolds and a peaceful thatched cottage of his own.

Halfway down the boulevard, he slid into the empty chair at a sidewalk cafe, grateful for the bright red umbrella that shaded him from the glaring sun. As he quenched his thirst with a lager, he watched the maddening throng of tourists, wondering if Yuri Ryskov or Parkovitch walked among them. Work with these men? Why should he? Create weapons for them? At the right price, yes. What did it matter to Jiri if Ryskov and Parkovitch came into disfavor with the professor? Jiri did not like dealing with little men.

And you, Professor Ivanski, you remain an elusive leader, a shrewd man that I already despise. Refuse to meet me personally? he thought. *Belittle me, will you? No, not for long.*

Help Ivanski in the Tour and what guarantee did Jiri have that his Russian connection would work to his advantage afterwards? He must go slowly and not bow to the professor's demands, no matter how well Ryskov presented them. He wiped the lager foam from his lips, then pushed back the cuff of his sleeve with his finger. Just ten minutes to reach the far end of the tree-lined Champs Elysees.

For hours Yuri Ryskov wandered around Paris, finally reaching the Hotel de Crillon for the third time that morning. Across the narrow street lay the ghostlike embassy with the American flag flapping atop the building. Yuri passed the entrance to the hotel and stopped at the corner to light his last cigarette. He puffed nervously, his shrewd eyes wary of the strangers shoving past him. Yuri had only to cross the narrow street to speak to the American Drew Gregory.

A block from him lay the Rue Royale, the way to the Church of the Madeleine and Maxim's restaurant. To his left a nineteenth-century fountain spewed its waters on the Place de la Concorde. He had sat there for an hour this morning with the sound of traffic throbbing in his ears and his thoughts on the reign of terror that had once filled the square. Two hundred years ago, Louis XVI had been executed in almost the very spot where the sun now filtered through the fountain waters.

The French Revolution. Yuri wanted no part in any revolution. Not here in this picturesque square, nor in Moscow. Professor Ivanski's plans would lead to another reign of terror. The stub of the cigarette burned against his fingers. He flicked it into the air and watched the ashes form tiny gray specks. *Ashes. Nothingness. Like my life.* He wanted to be free. He wanted to know the deep peace that Nicholas Trotsky had known. Trotsky, dead now, was once a revolutionary, but in the end he was a man at peace. Yuri must find Drew Gregory, for surely all Americans knew about this God whom Trotsky worshiped. Or was Yuri's mentor, Professor Ivanski, right? God did not exist.

Thoughts of immortality haunted him. The tragic deaths of Nicholas Trotsky and the young cyclist Alekos Golemis hung like a canopy of black clouds over him. To contemplate the destruction of other riders seemed hideous. These were innocent young men who had no interest in the old glory days of Russia.

Yuri's mouth went dry; the sour taste of garlic and onions and stale cigarettes coated his tongue. He must break with Professor Ivanski and disappear as Trotsky had done. But he dreaded the consequences, feared the cowardice of dying without peace and facing that unknown tomorrow. Across the street lay his one hope for freedom, for answers. He took a step toward the curb, the tips of his shoes dipping precariously. He tried another step. Thoughts of his mentor in Russia sent cold sweat running the full length of his spine. Dare he betray Ivanski? Dare he seek political asylum?

Somewhere behind him, cathedral chimes began to ring. The Church of the Madeleine? He could not be sure. The ringing that surely brought joy to others pierced his ears. *Twelve noon. Maxim's.* Time to meet with the Czechoslovakian and finalize the plans that would disrupt the Tour de France and quite possibly set off another revolution in Moscow. Ivanski longed to go back to the old Imperial Russia, but Yuri knew there could be no going back, no bloodless coup. No, his people—and they were still his people—would die by the thousands in a bloody massacre that would start in Red Square. He lifted his eyes toward the embassy once more, his throat so constricted he could hardly breathe.

Move, he told himself. *Run. Seek freedom.*

Above his own strangled cry, he heard the voice of his mentor saying, *Yuri, am I losing you, too? See me through this one, Yuri. The people will follow me.*

Radburn Parker moved briskly through the city of Paris with total disregard for others. He cut a straight path, his large frame forcing the Parisians to break rank and go around him. His sense of superior worth—if currently not in his thoughts—was visible in his strides. When he took the time, as he did now, he admired his reflection in the store windows. He was a man of great height, as ramrod straight as any Burmese Army Ranger.

His father had been a British ranger in the 1940s, sowing his wild oats abroad and living out much of his life on the northeast frontier far from the family residence in London. On one of his infrequent trips home, he had married unexpectedly. Forty-five at the time, he soon grew restless to go back to the Far East. Radburn was born in his absence. Memories of his father were sparse and bitter—a stranger on brief leaves, an authoritative figure with his Burmese walking stick coming down hard on Radburn's knuckles or stinging across his buttocks at the slightest provocation; but his father was an impressive man, tall and striking in his uniform, with a raucous laugh and sunburned skin. The Parker Foundation money would have been his if he had not chosen a military career. Instead, it had passed down to Radburn.

They had never liked each other, yet Radburn had his father's sense of pride, his gift for languages, his hidden cruelty in dealing with others. And he had something his father never had—outward charm. The very words caused Radburn to stop and smile at the store window. The reflection came back as that of a happy, pleasant-faced man. He lifted his hand to brush down a few wild strands of his thick crowning glory. He considered himself handsome, a gentleman, gratefully rid of his wife—thanks to the British courts—and free now even of Lennie Applegate.

Thoughts of his family seldom pressed him. They did now. He considered it prophetic, a warning of trouble ahead or a premonition of danger. He rarely carried a weapon, depending on his own ingenuity to protect himself. He set out again with quick strides, his mind unwillingly turning back to his father's swagger stick. "The perfect weapon," his father had called it.

On impulse, Radburn made his way to the back streets of Paris to a quaint specialty shop where he had twice found relics of war for his son's collection. "Monsieur Parker," the owner greeted him, "you've come back. How can I help you?"

Parker moved slowly along the aisles. "Just browsing."

"For that boy of yours?"

Radburn smiled. "Hardly a boy. He's seventeen now."

"And still interested in military school?"

"Unless I find him suitable employment at the Parker Foundation."

"You should bring your son with you sometime."

Radburn cared not a wit about any of his children, but he said, "I'll do that. But I warn you, he leans heavily toward John Major's political views."

"That should please you."

No, Radburn thought. *It has set us at odds.* From his own Cambridge days on, Radburn never wavered from his communistic convictions: universal power, universal control. His roots of dissatisfaction had smoldered in his boyhood, but it was his forced education at his father's schools that had spurred his sudden interest in the writings of Karl Marx, a philosophy that was nurtured during his days in Moscow.

He found the counter he wanted toward the back of the store, a marvelous display of solid canes and sharp-pointed walking sticks. "My son would like one of these."

The shopkeeper grabbed up the gold-handled one and raised it toward Radburn. "What about this trekking stick?" he asked.

Radburn winced as he had done when his father came down hard against his knuckles. "That's a Burmese Army stick, isn't it?"

"Just a good imitation," the owner admitted. "The original was issued exclusively to the Burmese Army Rangers."

"I know. My father owned one."

He took it in his hand now, noting the sturdy construction and solid rowboat handle. Like the original, it was made from baby bamboo. It had possibilities. A man like Jiri Benak could use it to take Kendall down in stage seventeen. He ran his fingers down the hollow stick, feeling for the bolt and nut mechanism that allowed the cane to fold in two. *The perfect weapon.*

"Does your boy mountain hike?" the man asked.

"Around London? Hardly."

"It rains there. This would be good for fording streams."

Parker chuckled. "That was one of the purposes for it when Sir Jeffery Hillpig Smyth designed it. I'll take it."

Carrying the parcel under his arm, he reached the Champs Elysees without even noticing the turns he had taken. He stopped mid-boulevard and went inside a sidewalk cafe. He was sitting there sipping coffee when Jiri Benak took up a table outside, the red patio umbrella casting an odd tinge on his snow-blond hair. In less than three weeks the street in front of them would be blocked off for the final day of the Tour de France when the cyclists rode into Paris, if they rode in. They were counting on Benak, but Parker had misgivings. He held little hope for the meeting between Yuri Ryskov and this Czechoslovakian madman.

He sat back in his chair as Benak lifted a second lager. Until recently, life had been dull, too routine, Radburn's every need met through the Parker Foundation. He had become bored living as a sleeper in London for a dozen years or more, constantly waiting for someone to pick up the reins of the old Phoenix-40. But

Ivanski as a leader with his wild imperialistic dreams? His plan was mad, but because of the uncertain state of the Russian leadership, it held the possibility for success. And then Lennie Applegate had come his way feeding American secrets to him, documents that assured his position once again with Ivanski and the old Phoenix-40.

Parker had the best of both worlds—the intriguing possibility of working both sides as a double agent. He had his high social status in London and his close ties with British Intelligence that had swung the doors wide open at the American embassy. And now he would be an active participant in the most unexpected coup in Moscow. But if the need arose to protect himself, intelligence agencies around the world would pay him well just to know what Ivanski planned.

Benak stood and left the cafe. Radburn followed him at a safe distance up the Champs Elysees, down through the underground passage beneath the Place de la Concorde and back up into the sun, still heading toward his appointment at Maxim's.

As Radburn paused to shift his package to his other arm, he noticed Yuri Ryskov walking alone, walking unsteadily. *He didn't even see me. Drunk?* Parker wondered. *At noon? No, Ryskov is having trouble with his stomach and is staying away from hard liquor.*

Something was wrong. He switched surveillance and lagged behind Ryskov, expecting him to turn right on the Rue Royale. He walked straight on. At the corner near the Hotel de Crillon, Yuri hesitated at the curb, waiting to cross the narrow alley in the direction of the Avenue Gabriel. Across the street lay the somber-looking American embassy. "Ryskov," Parker called softly.

Yuri turned, startled. He licked his lips as their eyes met. Seconds passed and then recognition. "Parkovitch!" he said.

Parker pulled Yuri back from the curb and glanced at the embassy. He kept his voice low, calm. "That's the wrong way, Yuri. We still need you. You have a meeting with Benak."

"I know. About the Tour." His eyes looked sunken, his sallow skin tight against his cheeks.

He's sick, Parker thought. He edged Yuri away from the pressing crowd to the side of the colonnaded building. "Have you talked to Professor Ivanski lately?" he asked.

Yuri nodded. The cold stone wall against his back seemed to rally him. "Yesterday. I tried to warn him that our plans won't work unless Benak cooperates with us. And there's a girl," he said. "Ian Kendall has a girlfriend. She could cause trouble for us—she's one of the journalists at the Tour. Her family has political connections."

"Yuri, we know about the girl." The wary eyes turned back at the sharpness in Parker's voice. "Yuri," Parker continued, "our plans are set in motion. Forget Miss Evans. Everything depends on you getting the message to Ivanski at exactly the right moment."

"I know. Trust me. Stage seventeen," Yuri said. He pushed his shoulders hard against the wall and sighed. "But can we trust Jiri Benak?" he asked.

Can we depend on you? Parker wondered. It was too late to move another agent into position. "You know your way to Maxim's. You're late. You'd better hurry."

"Are you not meeting with us, Parkovitch?"

"Not yet. It is best that Benak not be able to identify me. You size him up. Report back to me." *And in the meantime, I will decide your fate, Yuri Ryskov. I will not allow you to ruin it for all of us. For me.*

Yuri's gaze strayed back toward the Avenue Gabriel. For a moment, Parker was impressed with the short distance to the embassy. He had only to cross the narrow alleyway himself. Perhaps it was safer to bow out now before Ryskov did something foolish. Americans would pay Radburn well for any information that would stop the threats against the Tour de France.

On a whim, he said, "Give Benak this package for me. . . . Here, Yuri, do as I say. Take this to Benak."

Ryskov took it. "It's light."

"It's a Burmese walking stick. It may prove valuable for stage seventeen. . . . He will know what to do with it."

"Do I promise Benak anything if he succeeds?"

"Tell him I have our tickets to Moscow. We're booked on a flight the day after the race."

"What happens if the plan fails—if our timing is off?"

He gripped Ryskov's shoulder. "We won't fail."

But if we do, you will have nowhere to go, Radburn thought. *But I will tear up my ticket to Moscow and go back to London and call British Intelligence.*

There was only one thing wrong with going back to London. Lennie Applegate would be there.

Chapter 13

C hase waited until Ian's roommate left the room, and then
she winked at Drew. "Thanks, Drew. I won't be long."
"Good. Anyone catching you coming out of Ian's room
might misunderstand."

"You won't. That's what matters." She paused, her cheeks
flushing. "I want Ian to know I miss him when I don't see him."

"Get going. I'll hang around until you leave."

Chase hurried down the hall, turned the knob, and slipped in.
"Ian," she whispered. "It's Chase."

He propped himself up on his elbow, looking groggy, his chest
bare, his sheet tucked against his waist. One bare foot poked out
at the end of the bedding. "You shouldn't be here," he warned.
"It's against the rules."

"I had to see you. Are you all right?"

"I'm fine." With his gaze still on her, he shoved a crumpled
sheet of paper under his pillow. "You look nice." He eyed her curiously. "What's wrong, Chase?"

"I don't know why I came on this Tour. I never see you."

"I didn't want it to be this way. But the rest day is coming
before we ride into the Pyrenees. We'll spend that day together. I
promise." He struggled with the sheet to free his other foot. "I feel
like I'm under house arrest. This is the first morning I didn't have
Vic or Drew standing guard at the bathroom door."

"Is it that bad?"

"Worse," he grumbled, "now that this O'Malloy fellow is sniffing around like a third hound dog."

"I thought he was the new Gainsborough mechanic."

"You think they'd pull in some unknown with security as tight as it is? He knows the mechanic's jargon, but ten-to-one, he's with the CIA." His voice deepened. "Come here, Chase."

She crossed the room and sat on the edge of his bed, suddenly shy at their nearness. Embarrassed, she thought, *If I marry him, this is what I will awaken to for the rest of my life: that quizzical boyishness that is creeping into his expression, that unrelenting gaze in those blue eyes, tender as he looks at me now. That curly mop of sleeptousled hair.*

"I love you, Chase," he said.

"Please don't, Ian. I have to be sure."

His shoulders were strong and muscular, but his upper torso was lean, the thumping beat in his chest visible as he searched her face. "I forgot," he said. "I have to win the race before you can make up your mind about marrying me."

"Oh, Ian, I was only teasing when I said that." An overnight growth of beard had formed a shadow on his face. The reddish bristles felt rough to her fingers as she traced his jawbone. "I don't just champion winners," she said. "I've been interviewing the exhausted riders who abandoned the race. To me, it counts that they started—that they gave it everything they had."

He grinned slowly. "No street corners here. You'll have to do your political campaigning from the mountaintop. What will it be this time—the riders who don't make it to Paris?"

"No—my same old soap box. AIDS victims and the elderly."

He sobered. "You're a funny girl. Sophisticated one moment. Out to conquer the world the next."

"Just my small part of the world." Her throat tightened. "My mother called me last evening. My friend Jeff is dead."

"The young man with AIDS?"

"Yes. I really liked him, Ian. Jeff's nurse called asking for me, so Mother went in my place."

"Your mom sounds like a great lady."

"She is, Ian. The greatest. But I think it's the only time in her marriage when Daddy threatened to leave her. Mom's visit to Halverson House made the society page. So she won't go back."

"To keep your father happy?"

"No, because it was so depressing. But she's asking her bridge club to send care packages to the residents there."

"Nice gesture."

"It's more than that. Mother saw beyond the illness to the person dying. That's what happened to me when I visited Jeff. I really wanted to see him again. I didn't want him to die."

"We all have to die sometime, Chase."

"But not that way, with his body wasted and his life snuffed out before his time."

Ian's mouth twisted. "How then?"

"Jeff's brother said he'd understand if Jeff had died in a war. Even an accident would have been better—"

"We'd know how that way," Ian agreed. "But not why. I don't think we ever understand why a young person has to die."

"Whatever you do, Ian Kendall, don't you leave me."

"Wouldn't think of it. Now—you'd better go and give me time to get dressed and signed in before the race."

She reached under his pillow and snatched the crumpled sheet of paper from its hiding place. "Tell me about this first."

"It's not from another girl, if that's what you think."

She spread the embossed hotel stationery out on the bed and read: *Remember Simpson, Kendall. You will never make it to the top of your mountain.*

"Oh, not another threat on your life. I can't bear it."

For an instant, he forgot the covers he was clutching and wrapped his broad hand around hers. "I'll be all right."

"But he's here in the hotel."

"We don't know that for certain." He eased the paper from her fist. "Someone slipped it under the door this morning."

She glanced toward Marcus Nash's side of the room. "I suppose Marcus found it?"

"Come on, Chase. He's my roommate."

"I don't trust him. And Drew definitely doesn't."

"If it makes you feel better, neither do I. But I'm stuck with him until we reach the Pyrenees. Then we switch again."

If you reach the Pyrenees Mountains without being hurt, she thought. "What do you know about him, Ian?"

"Not much. He was a last-minute replacement for our team."

"I'll do a profile on him and see what I can find out."

"Stay out of trouble, Chase."

"You, too."

"I fight my own battles. You stick to your old folks and sick boys." She stood. "I'm going before the coach finds me here."

"Or worse, Drew or Vic. Chase, what do you do with your spare time?"

"I spend it with a journalist. He's thirtyish. Italian. And frightfully attractive," she teased. "It gets me out of that hotel room full of women."

"I thought you liked rooming with Basil Millard's wife."

"I do. I did. But her baby is fretful, and Marcus Nash's fiancée—who is prying and curious—gets dibs on the bathroom first, blares the TV at all hours, and takes the best bed."

"She sounds like Marcus. Considerate and kindly." As she backed away, he pursed his lips. "You've forgotten something."

She started to laugh and then in spite of herself leaned down and kissed him soundly on the lips.

When she reached the door, he called across the room, "Have you told your folks about you and me yet?"

"Bits and pieces. We talk on the phone every day. Mom says they are actually printing my articles in the town paper. Imagine, I'm making it big-time back in Long Island."

"Great!"

"Well, the editor and Dad are good friends. But Mom doesn't think it's just that. She thinks I'm good."

"You are."

She flushed happily. "I'm doing profiles on the riders."

"What about me?"

"I'm saving you for the grand finale." She blew him another kiss. "I'll write you up when you win."

"Don't wait that long, Chase."

Salvador Contoni had learned long ago never to sneak around but to go boldly to his task. He did so on Friday morning under the canopy of a charcoal-gray sky, whistling cheerfully in spite of the weather and the weight in his knapsack. If anyone stopped him, he would cockily point to his I.D. badge clearly labeling him as a journalist. But if the search went further, they would find he was carrying a laptop computer, some wire, and a few hand tools. A hollowed log—fifteen inches long—lay at the bottom of his knapsack, completely concealing the Contoni Interceptor.

Without breaking his stride, he stepped from the major walkway and eased alongside the thirty-foot TV Mobile unit. He could hear muffled voices coming from inside the truck where the communications equipment with its control panels and a row of television monitors were being manned. In another thirty to forty minutes, there would be bedlam inside the truck when their monitors went blank.

Sal stepped carefully around the satellite dish and over the numerous cables that fed into the TV screen in the press room. He moved more cautiously now toward the rear wheels where he slipped his knapsack to the sodden ground and emptied the contents: the intercept box, wire, his tools. He worked quickly—no longer whistling—as he tapped into the main line that ran directly into the press tent. Placing the black intercept box against the trunk of a tree, he secured it to the side of the cables with gleaming bolts. Deftly he connected the wires, the frequencies already modified to French television. Back in the press room, he would activate the switch with a remote control; the click of a second button on the keyboard would send the warning over the huge screen, a message for Maurice Chambord and the world to read. Sal would have five seconds, ten at most, to neutralize the main lines, blackening the truck monitors. It was all the time he needed to block out the regular Tour transmissions. A third click of a button, and the startled journalists and the world would be forced to remember Bottecchia. Ottavio Bottecchia—the man who could have become the greatest Italian rider.

Chase was crossing the street, helping a stranger find her way in the rain, when she saw Sal come from behind the cable truck and hurry toward the press room. She pointed the woman toward the hotel and then darted inside, hesitating just past the doorway, wondering where Sal could have gone. Images flashed across the huge television screen. Hundreds of journalists occupied the folding chairs. Long tables were cluttered with paperwork, blinking monitors, laptops, and computers with cellular phones attached. Phone cubicles stood on the sides of the room; with their constant audiovisual linkups, journalists could spin their transmissions around the world within seconds.

From where Chase stood, the summer drizzle sounded like the pelting of a violent storm against the thick canvas tent. She shook the rain from her blouse and hand-wiped her damp hair. The journalist beside her rubbed his bifocals with his handkerchief and grinned. "Love, you look lost," he said. "Can I help you?"

"Cycling journalism is still all new to me."

"Can't be timid in this business." Putting his glasses on, he peered at the press card pinned to her blouse. "Evans, eh? I'm Galleger. You haven't seen Samuel Abt this morning, have you?"

She shook her head. "I don't know him."

"Right. You're a novice then. Better get acquainted with Abt. He's one of the seasoned journalists at these Tours. Writes for the *Herald Tribune* and the *New York Times*." He brushed some more rain from his sleeve. "But I got my start in Tour journalism with a Belgian writer, Harry Van den Bremt. Ever hear of him?"

"I'm a novice, remember?"

"Big name to Tour journalism. Bronzed. Overweight. Always smoking. A wide grin that showed the gap between his front teeth. But I liked the chap. Harry always said the only way to taste the race was to be out there watching up close."

She thought of Drew's opposition. "I'd like to do that."

"Then take a day on the sidelines. Sometimes I think the monitors give us distorted images. We never see the pain and courage of the riders up close." He glanced at his waterlogged shoes. "But this is one time I'm glad for an indoor press room."

"But it's not the same as being on hand at the finish line."

"You sound like Harry. This is different from the early days of Tour journalism, Miss Evans, but that's what the big tele screen is all about. It lets us know what's happening and gives us the official results without us drowning in a rainstorm. Well, cheers! Gotta run." He gave her a comradely thump on the arm. "See you about town, love. And if not again this year, then next. Cycling events are my permanent beat until I cash in."

As she watched him make his way to the back of the room, she saw Salvador and waved. He pointed to the empty chair beside him.

"Nice to see a familiar face," she said as she reached him.

"Especially when it's yours. Where were you last evening?"

"Interviewing the young man who rode in the Broom Wagon."

"That's like leaving the race in a hearse, Chase. Why waste your time with a quitter? What's he hanging around for?"

"His doctor's clearance. He was hurt when he hit that wall."

Sal booted up his computer. "Chase, stick with the winners."

She thought of Ian. "I am."

The computer buzzed like a turbojet warming up. Now Sal seemed preoccupied. Checking his watch and the monitor. Running the mouse over the pad. Glancing furtively at the screen. Chase kicked his sodden knapsack, questions rising in her mind.

"Sal, I saw you out by the television truck climbing around all those cables. Can't you read signs?"

"Not if they're not in Italian. Tell me, what did they say?"

Her gaze went from his face to his hand as he clicked the mouse again. "It said, 'no trespassing,' Salvador."

His voice came back sharp. "Who was the old lady you helped across the street?"

"She wasn't an old woman, Salvador. She was my grand-mother's age. Still rational. Still able to get around. She just needed directions to the hotel. She reminded me of the Willowglen."

"The what?"

"A senior residence—a place for the elderly in my hometown. I have several friends there."

"What are you—some kind of a crusader?"

"I just like to help people."

"Then help me." His eyes were cold as he glanced at the wall clock and said with a hint of irony, "Help me find a way to stop the American from winning, and then maybe one of my coun-trymen will come in first."

As the screen saver danced with rainbows, she ran her hand over Sal's cellular phone.

His hand clamped hers. "Don't use that."

She winced at the pressure on her wrist. "Sorry. I wasn't plan-ning to use it, Sal. Can't you be a bit more pleasant?"

"It's too early," he said irritably. "Sit down, Chase. Turn on your own computer."

She slumped into her chair, determined to lash back. Before she could say more, there was a flashing light in the front of the room as the giant screen went blank. Laptop computers crashed. A rumble of discontent filled the room. A technician ran toward the light switch. . . . expletives . . . grumbling journalists.

"What's going on?" Sal asked, clicking his mouse again.

And then a warning flashed across the big screen: *Remember Bottecchia! It will happen again this year.*

🔱🔱🔱

Vic fell into step with Drew as they walked along the road. "Did you hear about the glitch in the computer system?"

"I didn't like it. What's this Bottecchia business?"

"Ottavio Bottecchia. A rider back in the twenties. Won the Tour twice. The Italians pinned their hopes on him. Found him dead along the side of the road three years later."

Drew frowned. "And the computer hacker was sending a message that we'd find one of our riders the same way? This Bottecchia fellow, was he killed in a race?"

"Who knows? Chase can ask her Italian journalist friend. From what I hear, Bottecchia died of a skull fracture. His bike was intact. None of his clothing ripped. Political maybe. He was anti-Fascist. Not popular back then perhaps."

"Then ask Chase to check some more."

Vic rubbed his angular jaw. "She did tell me she saw this Sal—Salatori—whatever his name is—prowling around the cable truck shortly before the glitch showed up."

"Is she connecting him to the problem?"

"If she is, she's not saying." Vic's jaw rub had reached beneath his chin, his hand resting now against his Adam's apple. "Chambord's boys found an intercept box out by the cable lines."

"Did it cause the malfunction?"

"Could have. Some journalists lost everything on their hard drives. All it needed was someone pushing a remote control and whamo—a five-second interruption to the regular transmission."

Drew groaned. "And all Chambord will do is call it a small problem in the electrical system."

❀❀❀

On Saturday Drew sat sideways in Maurice Chambord's official red car wishing in a month of Sundays that he had stayed in England. He missed Miriam, worried about her shopping spree in Paris, and longed simply to sit down with her and talk about the baby that would make them grandparents.

"I'm anxious to get home," he had said in their last phone call, and Miriam had replied, "Take all the time you want, darling. Maggie and I are having a marvelous time shopping."

The voice thundering in his ears now didn't belong to Miriam. "No security measures take place in the Tour without my approval," Chambord said. "Do you understand, Monsieur Gregory?"

What Drew understood was that he was running interference for Troy Carwell. Carwell had stepped out of line by contacting Langley about a bomb disposal unit without going through Chambord. Drew controlled his own anger and waited for the showdown, his lanky legs cramped as he faced the Frenchman. Working for Chambord was difficult, taking his orders unbearable.

Chambord's narrow lips were tight, bloodless. "We do not want Washington involved in this." A tremor vibrated his words. "Washington contacted President Chirac—"

He tented his fingers—the nail beds turning blue—as though by the very act he could keep his fury in check. "We have a thousand international journalists at the race, Mr. Gregory. If they get wind of this, the public outcry would be worse than the bomb threats. Panic worldwide. Bedlam. It would ruin us."

Drew could guess the rest. Global acceptance mattered to Jacques Chirac's presidency. Chirac would have chewed out the Tour leaders. And now it was Drew's turn. "You didn't think you could get the French robot," Drew reminded him.

"I didn't want that robot unit. I have my reputation to consider. The entire Tour is my responsibility." He leaned forward. "I have called off my order for the robot bomb unit."

"It's not available?"

"We have no need for it."

"Mr. Chambord, we have another twelve days in the race."

"I know. I know. But we're halfway through. Our internal security is good. Nothing has happened." He recanted that with, "Except for some injuries and ruffled feathers among the riders. These bomb threats have all been a hoax. Don't you agree?"

Drew didn't agree, never had. But he held his tongue.

In spite of the weather reports and the contest that loomed ahead in the Alps, Maurice Chambord's confidence had grown with each passing stage. The bomb threats had become routine for him. Excitedly, he said, "As President Chirac pointed out, the only real problem we've had is bad weather."

And plenty of that, Drew thought. He'd quit many a picnic for less rain than they'd suffered in the Tour. Bolts of lightning and thunderstorms with torrential rains. Streets and villages awash with rain water. Temperatures dipping until they wondered whether they were hitting an early fall in July. The cyclists had been constantly buffeted by head winds as they raced over the narrow winding roads and past windblown wheat fields.

Drew waited for the ax to split the heavy air between them. Days ago he had tried to force a confrontation with Chambord, insisting on an all-out search for Salvador Contoni; his concern fell on deaf ears. But Interpol and Drew's old friend Pellier, that polite, articulate police commander in the city of Paris, welcomed the latest news on Contoni.

Within hours, Pellier had distributed a police sketch, a good likeness of the handsome Italian. "He's ours now," the commandant had said, twisting the tip of his handlebar mustache. "What do you Americans call it—a feather in my cap?"

Drew was certain that Chambord had managed forty seconds of silence before the ax fell again. Chambord's eyes were shiny pinpoints when he said, "Mr. Gregory, you were absent from the Tour for two days without permission."

Drew shrugged. "I didn't cherish riding the flatlands of Belgium in a torrential rain. Thought it might make me car sick."

"So you settled for a choppy ride in a chartered plane."

"I guess I did. Had a friend to see in Normandy."

"A wealthy widow," Chambord snapped.

"The wealthy widow who informed on Salvador Contoni."

Drew reached for the door handle, unraveled his long legs, and stepped from the shiny car. He turned and leaned into the open door. "I have a report to make to Troy Carwell in Paris. Should I make reference to this little exchange?"

"I tell you, everything is under control, Mr. Gregory, except you. Tell him that! The person behind these threats is just some crackpot who gets his fancy by frightening others."

"I still think the threats are real, Monsieur Chambord."

Chambord looked at Drew as though he were a schoolboy failing to comprehend his lessons. "Every race has had its threats," he said. "Don't you see, Mr. Gregory? We went across the flatlands of Belgium. Where was our terrorist? Up those magnificent streets of Antwerp. No problems. Soissons and Chambery—nothing happened. We are safe."

"Safe because we've taken precautions," Drew argued.

Chambord tapped the steering wheel. "Here we are at the foot of the Col de la Madeleine ready for our first alpine climb. Where could a terrorist hide along these mountain ridges?"

Just behind the parapet wall, Drew thought.

Chambord's forced smile eased his facial muscles. "Gregory, we will get you safely up to the Alpine Ski resort. Such beauty. And over the Galibier Pass. Have you ever been there?"

"Never."

"Two or three days in the Alps, my friend—that's where the race begins. You will see some of the greatest riders ever. Even you will forget about the terrorists up there."

But Maurice Chambord's optimism was premature. On the eve of stage eleven, the first bomb exploded.

Chapter 14

Drew pushed his morning coffee aside and came out from behind the newspaper as Ian joined him. Ian was ready for the race, right on down to the helmet strap secured snugly beneath his chin. His thigh-hugging shorts bore the Gainsborough logo. The stem of his riding goggles was tucked at the top of his jersey. It struck Drew again that Ian had grown from a lanky, awkward kid into a handsome, athletic young man, with his grandmother's sensitivities and Uriah Kendall's stubborn jaw. He had, after all, known Ian all his life, but he felt closer to him now, more like an uncle to his favorite nephew.

If Drew could bypass Troy Carwell's orders, he'd have Ian on the first flight back to the Cotswolds. As far as Drew was concerned, there wasn't a cycling race in the world worth losing your life over.

"You wanted to see me," Ian said.

"Just to wish you well on today's ride."

"It's an easy one. We head east for a while over some rolling hills. We should have a good tailwind to speed us along."

"What're your chances, Ian?"

"I'm going to pace myself. I have my eyes on stage eleven."

"Climbing in the mountains? That's where you shine."

"Expect to." He slid into the chair across from Drew and removed his head gear. "So don't ask me to quit now."

"And risk disfavor with your grandfather? It crossed my mind." Drew flattened the newsprint. "You look good, Ian."

"I felt good until I saw the headlines. How do you tolerate a daily diet of coffee and news? It's the same old thing. Bomb threats. The assassination of prime ministers. Nuclear power. Train derailments. Intelligence communities blowing it again."

Drew checked his irritation. "Don't remind me about Aldrich Ames and Porter Deven. Granted—the world's a mess. But it's nothing more than a warning, a trumpet call from a coming King."

"You sound like my grandmother and Beatrice Thorpe."

Drew gave him a reluctant morning grin. "For the first time in my life, I'm beginning to think like them."

"I run on my grandmother's steam. She taught me to run my race well. Got her challenge taped inside my helmet here."

Drew pointed to Ian's chest, heart-level. "Make sure that truth gets inside. Wow! I really do sound like your grandmother."

"I've got it stowed away. I wouldn't be out riding in that pack today if I didn't believe God rode with me."

Vic sauntered up to their table, his face looking gaunt as he sat down uninvited. "You two solving the world's problems?"

Drew nodded. "Been talking about the King's business."

Vic held up both hands. "Hold off, Drew. I'd rather talk about the race. What do you say, Ian? Is it still your burning ambition to ride up the Champs Elysees in the winner's jersey?"

"Right on. For me, July is meant for Paris with half a million fans cheering me on."

"I thought you just wanted to impress Chase."

"I want to marry her, but it's not what she has in mind."

"Just another 1,000 miles to go. If you win, maybe you can pick up a bride as well as the torch from Greg LeMond."

"I'm not picking up anyone's torch, Vic. I'm riding my own race." His face clouded as he turned to meet Drew's gaze. "The threats are coming against me. At least put me in the picture."

Drew refolded the newspaper, the edges even, and laid it on the table. "We've made little progress. Each time we lay out our strategy for stopping the terrorist, Chambord insists that it is simply a madman out there angered over unemployment."

"Thanks, Drew. That's really comforting."

"Chambord won't hear it, but a man named Salvador Contoni may be out there in that sea of faces along the Tour route." Drew slid Contoni's police sketch across the table. "It's a long shot, Ian, but I'm convinced that this man was hired by a Greek millionaire to stop you from winning."

The effect was explosive. "Alekos's father?" he blurted. "He still blames me for his son's death? Alekos and I were friends."

His mouth opened, then clamped shut. "Does Mr. Golemis hate me that much?" The words were too repugnant for Ian. He snatched up the police photo and his helmet and stalked from the room.

"Was that wise to tell him about Golemis?" Vic asked.

"I can't worry him with unconfirmed reports about a Bosnia-Moscow connection or a Serbian war criminal riding beside him."

"He ought to know all the risks."

"He's too close to them. He could be rooming with the Serbian. . . . Yes, that's right. Marcus Nash may be Dudley Perkins's Road-runner. We've sent Nash's fingerprints to Paris."

"And they're bunking together night after night?"

"The coach arranged it for me. We have to know the truth. If Carwell is right, Nash is quite possibly a Serbian Intelligence officer. If he is, then he knows every move we're making."

"You'd do better checking out Coach Skobla, not some poor rider who made the team at the last minute."

"His name never appeared on any major race this year, yet he qualified for the biggest race of all. Nash is clever, too interested in self-preservation to harm Ian in the room. Vic, whatever happens will be along the Tour route."

"And we're in trouble if we picked the wrong man. Let's just pull Ian out of the race and be safe."

"Troy Carwell said no! The Serbian's London contact is here in the crowd, too. Sooner or later Nash will make a mistake."

"If we haven't made the mistake—"

Drew ignored Vic. "If we're right, we can deliver the Lily-Trotter right back into Dudley Perkins's hands—some double agent who's sitting right under our noses."

"Drew, you're not trying to finger Fairway? That stinks."

"So does treason."

⊛⊛⊛

Four hours later Maurice Chambord's shiny red car pulled alongside the Gainsborough vehicle. Drew rolled down the rear window as straggling cyclists pedaled past them.

"Morning," Drew said.

"It is afternoon," Chambord grumbled. "We had reports that someone was riding Kendall's rear wheel wearing placard number 190."

Drew grabbed his list. "What's his name?"

"How would I know?" Chambord shot back. "There's no rider registered with that number."

"Is Kendall all right?"

"He is now. But number 190 ran him into a brick wall. Cost Kendall a few seconds, so he'll lose points in today's stage."

"Pick the man up, Chambord."

"Impossible. It's every fan's fantasy to ride in the Tour. When the gendarmes rushed him, the cheering crowds just opened a path and let the man slip away. Then they closed ranks again. Happens like this every year. Some fan taking a glory ride."

"It's the wrong year for jokes, Chambord."

In southwest France, Jiri Benak hiked through the fields toward his friend tending sheep on the hillside. Ignasius was wearing his patched knickers and knee-high socks, a red beret cocked on his head, and boots laced tightly against his ankles. He turned as Jiri approached, his face wreathed in smiles.

"My friend," Ignasius said, "you are back."

"In from Paris late last night."

"I thought you might sleep the morning away."

"I have always been an early riser, Ignasius."

The man leaned against the crook of his staff. "More so when you are troubled. You should be as I am. The past is put away. I am back where I belong—with my people, with my land."

"I have no people," Jiri said. He envied Ignasius for that unearthly calm, that simplicity of life.

"Did everything go well?" Ignasius asked. "Did you keep your appointment?"

"As planned. I left before the Tour reached Paris."

Ignasius grinned slyly. "But it comes our way soon. I think you knew this. That's why you came here a few weeks ago—so you would be here when the cyclists climbed the Pyrenees."

You have been in my cabin, Jiri thought. *Seen my equipment. Sifted through the box of timers and nails. Found the copper wires and bottles of ammonium nitrate hidden in the shed. And guessed my purpose.* "I will move on in another month," he said.

The weather wrinkles in Ignasius's face deepened. "Some of my people are anxious for you to go on now. But what of the race, my friend? Will you see it with me? We have a young rider who makes his home in one of the Basque villages."

"You want him to win?"

A raucous laugh rose from his belly. "It makes no matter to me who wins. But you, my friend, I think it matters to you."

"And does that shock you?"

"You never shock me, Jiri. We no longer think alike. Someday perhaps you will find a village like this and settle down."

"But not in this one?"

Jiri's thoughts traversed the continent, winging to the Cotswolds and the stone cottage that would be his one day. He was yanked back by Ignasius's next words. "I think not. A Basque way of life is too basic, too modest for you."

Ignasius stooped down by the lamb nibbling grass by his feet and ran his rough hand behind the woolly ear. "We would do better to part as friends," he said.

"Will you help me once more before I go?"

The black eyes met Jiri's, guardedly, amusement beginning to creep in. "And what do you have in mind?"

"You've used avalaunchers—blown away rock slides."

"And you want me to create a rock slide? No," he said flatly. "The cyclists will ride through my village peacefully."

"Before that—before they get here."

"Then you will move on?"

"As soon as the race is over."

"And where is this mountain that you want to blow away?"

"At the beginning of stage eleven—and I want only to block the roadway. To send a warning."

"I know you well. To destroy it is more likely, my friend."

He no longer trusts me, Jiri thought. *That part of our friendship is dead, gone.* The nostalgia of the loss dug at him. "Just go with me. Carry one of the knapsacks. Help me."

"So the launch site looks like the work of a peasant?"

"Show me how to pack the plastic explosives against the rocks. I will set the timer. I will blow the mountain."

"A moment ago it was nothing but the road. No lives lost."

"None. We must leave soon. I can hire a private plane."

The peasant's face brightened. "I have never flown before."

"Then you will tonight. And you will be back here on your land and with your people by morning."

"Perhaps you could be gone from our village by then?"

"Not until after the race."

Ignasius shifted uneasily. "What purpose is all of this?"

For a flash, the thought of Drew Gregory blurred Jiri's rugged features. "I am trying to stop an old enemy," Jiri said.

"Was he once a friend?"

"No, you are my only friend." He spoke confidently now. "There's a steep place along the mountain curve. The slope has been stripped of timber. Or an old avalanche left it barren. There are massive boulders and tree stumps left. We can bring them down and dam up the route."

"You are quite mad, Benak," Ignasius said. "Quite mad." But he smiled, a curious mischief awakening in those dark eyes.

He turned and prodded his sheep with his staff as he swaggered off to climb his beloved hills. Jiri watched him go.

I am not mad, Ignasius, he thought.

Jiri was driven by anger. Drew Gregory had robbed him of his livelihood at the steel factory in Jarvoc. Even Boris Ivanski's offer of opportunities in Russia or his own obsession with the illegal sale of weapons meant nothing to Jiri as long as Drew Gregory lived. Yet, in a strange, compelling way he knew that killing Gregory would not satisfy him. He could inflict a far greater wound on Gregory by exploding a bomb along stage eleven and sending the warning message direct to Gregory: *Your friend Ian Kendall will never stand on the winner's podium in Paris.*

When Jiri looked again, Ignasius and his sheep had dipped below the crest of the first hill. He gazed higher to the craggy mountains above him where the gigantic peaks of the Pyrenees were snow-capped and the lower slopes stripped of their timber.

🏺🏺🏺

Wednesday, 9 P.M. Jiri and Ignasius balanced the heavy ruck-
sacks on their backs and climbed three kilometers up the mountain, their shadowy movements like part of the rock formation.
Ignasius stayed in the lead, Benak behind him. A lone figure in a
hooded Gainsborough jacket followed them, his steps so stealthy
that only Ignasius had heard him. Ignasius rounded a boulder
and held up his hand. When the third man came around the boulder, the shepherd secured him with a choke hold.

As the two struggled, Benak demanded, "What are you doing
here?"

With reluctance, Ignasius released him. The young man
rubbed his neck, saying, "Benak, I came to ask you the same
thing."

"Then come with us, Roadrunner. And watch us blow away the
mountain."

Ignasius led the way again around the rock wall. Five minutes
later, he reached the area of an old rock slide where a whole section of mountain lay bare. He struck out straight up the cliff, losing his footing on the stones as he went, clawing to keep from
tumbling back to the road. Finally, he signaled to the others and
set down his rucksack.

They worked deftly, silently. Across the road, there was no barrier—just a straight drop-off down into the valley. Some of the
tumbling mountain would soar off the cliff. Jiri found a V-shaped
recess that pleased him, one that was set against gnarled tree
roots. They worked quickly, piling layers of rocks around on the
ground. They positioned two cone-shaped cylinders filled with
explosives at the base of the rocks, leaving part of the charges
exposed. Jiri took over now, inserting a detonating cap into one
end of each cartridge. Wires were attached. Screws tightened. The
delayed timers set. Five minutes apart.

It will work, Ignasius told himself. *It will blow part of this mountain away. It will create another avalanche.*

He bent down again to pile more rocks and earth around the
cylinders. And then as stealthily as they had come, they slid back
to the road, creating a small rock slide as they went. "We separate
here," Ignasius said. "It will be safer that way."

◉◉◉

Long after Sal and Chase left the press room, the sun plunged behind the mountain, leaving only darkness and a hazy moon. Case studied the Italian as he capped his pen and stared out the cafe window.

"Are you all right, Salvador?" she asked.

He sighed as he turned back to her. He was a handsome, moody man, talkative one moment, sullen the next. He seemed to brood more as darkness set in. "Well, are you?"

"I should be content. Good meal. Good company. You didn't even give me your usual excuse about getting back to your friends."

"They were busy," she admitted.

"That was to my advantage. Thank you for having dinner with me, Chase. I hate eating alone—and my hotel accommodations get worse."

She laughed. "Mine get more crowded—and Millard's baby cries constantly. But I really must go so they don't worry about me."

"I have a better idea. Why don't we cycle up the mountain a short distance and check out tomorrow's route?"

"In the dark? I don't think it's a good idea, Sal."

He gave her his cocky grin as they left the restaurant. "You're not afraid of me?"

She wasn't really afraid, but she didn't want to be alone with him on the mountainside—and Drew Gregory would have fits. But she said, "Of course not. But without streetlights, we'd ride right off the mountain."

"At least we could stretch our legs and walk a bit. I will have you back at your hotel in an hour."

"I'll hold you to that."

She struck out guardedly, afraid that he might attempt to take her hand. Half an hour up the slope, Salvador said, "Chase, I keep seeing you with that American rider."

"Ian Kendall? We're friends."

"I thought *we* were friends."

She laughed uneasily. "Can't I have more than one friend?"

"You should have told me. You know what I think of him."

"You don't even know him. He's special to me. Don't you have someone really important to you, Sal? You never mention your wife and family. Aren't you married?"

"I'd like to be."

"Does she have a name?"

"Monique."

"That's pretty."

"So is she."

"Sal, where were you this morning? You missed that crazy fan who rode in the Tour today."

"Did I?" he asked.

"He wore number 190 pinned to his jersey. He forced Ian into a brick wall; it could have cost Ian the race."

"Probably an accident," Sal said indifferently.

In the moonlight she noticed his bandaged fingers, and her suspicions rose again. And then like the dawn breaking, realization came. She said, "Sal, you know there's no rider registered with that number."

"Are you suggesting that I wore that number?" he teased.

"It could have been you, Sal. You never showed up in the press room. And you have a bike. . . . You didn't, did you?"

"Ride into Kendall? What do you think?"

She didn't like what she was thinking. Not Sal. Not her friend. "What did Ian ever do to you?"

"Nothing," he admitted. "But if he wins the race, he gets rich. If he loses, I do."

She shivered. The implication of Sal's words chilled her. Or maybe it was the mountain air putting goose bumps on her arms. Then they saw a young man in a hooded jacket coming toward them from higher up on the slope. When he spotted them, he hesitated, and then slipped over the edge of the road, scrambling into the darkness.

Chase went another step or two, then felt the earth tremble beneath her feet. As she tried to steady herself, a shock wave rocked the mountain. A split-second stillness followed before the mountain rumbled like a gigantic earthquake.

The groan turned into a deafening roar as the hillside exploded. Sal threw Chase to the ground and covered her with his own body. Sand and gravel began to fall, building momentum until it roared down the slopes like a waterfall. Rocks and tree stumps soared and plunged to earth. Metal fragments from the explosives broke into jagged pieces, scattering with a tremendous force, the metal shards cutting Chase's cheek and hands. And then the massive boulders broke free, pitching and lurching as they tumbled down, twisting and somersaulting like cannon-balls, forming craters in the road as they landed. A quarter of a mile away, the swoosh of fire cut the brush along the side of the road. The flames threaded their way across the road, over the cliff, and down toward the valley. They danced and snaked along the ravine and over the gutted path of an old avalanche where they would burn out. In the semidarkness an eerie gray funnel of smoke rose from the mountain. And then utter stillness as the rock dust choked them.

Chapter 15

Thursday, 8 P.M. Outside the restaurant window, dusk chased away the pink and gold streamers in the night sky, leaving the snowcaps at the top of the Alps draped in darkness—as silent and mute as Drew had been with Vic sitting across from him. Drew couldn't sleep—hadn't slept—for twenty-four hours. Last night's explosion at the foot of the mountains kept playing in his mind. The smoke cloud rising in the night sky. The second detonation. The rocks and boulders soaring like war missiles. Somebody had set that explosion. Somebody had gotten away with it.

He tried to block out their frantic search for Chase, but it kept flashing back. As well, he recalled the utter relief when they found her. She had been sitting alone, terrified that the mountain might explode again. Her hands like ice. A cut on her cheek. Even in the darkness, her eyes looked like saucers. Aftershocks shook the foundation beneath them. Then the procession came—trucks and people on foot. Walking. Running. Climbing. Shovels and picks in their hands. Dogs barking by their sides. Women carrying buckets. And singing. The people were singing.

"They're singing," Chase had said.

"Yeah, off-key." He squeezed her hand and said lightly, "Maybe they're just scaring the terrorists away."

"Then they didn't find them?"

"Not yet. But the terrorists didn't defeat the people in this village. They're fighting back. Everything is going to be okay, Chase."

They had stumbled down the mountain together, leaving the

townspeople with their torches and lanterns, their picks and shovels, an all-night crew determined to clear a narrow path in that rubble so the cyclists could ride up their mountain.

The Italian journalist had been nowhere in sight, but Drew hadn't thought about that last night. He thought about it now, realizing how gladly he could strangle the man for deserting Chase. Now he allowed himself to question why the man had fled into the darkness without her. Drew's mind stayed on standby, too numb to rehash the events even with Vic Wilson.

"I still want Chase to go back to London," he said aloud.

"She refuses. Insists on going back to the press room to make sure her friend is all right."

"It's more than he did. Leaving her alone like that."

"But, Gregory, he stayed with her until he saw help coming." As Drew rubbed his eyes, Vic reached across the table and poked him with a fork. "Don't look, but trouble is on its way."

"Chase and the Italian journalist?" Drew asked.

"No, Chase was turning in early. Marcus Nash just came in." Vic frowned, his dusky face hard like granite. "That was quick. He's already leaving. Stopped at the reception desk, turned around, and walked out."

"Did he leave anything?"

"Can't tell. Want me to check it out?"

"Too obvious. I'm just glad he left. Brad O'Malloy is on it. I told him to keep an eye on Nash."

"Cancel that one. Jon Gainsborough ordered his mechanics to keep a twenty-four-hour vigil on the equipment."

"So Nash is out there wandering around on his own."

"So is Salvador Contoni. When are you going to show Chase that police sketch?" Vic stretched his vision beyond Drew, and a smirky grin twisted his mouth to the left. "Brace yourself, Drew. You aren't going to like this one bit."

Drew flattened Vic's hand. "No games tonight, Wilson. I'm dog-tired."

"Edgy is more like it. Radburn Parker just walked in, looking sporty in his London tweeds and hiking boots."

"Is Lennie with him?"

"No, but he sure put on the charm for the receptionist."

Drew hid his displeasure when Parker walked up to them. The

man's thick, wavy hair appeared more wheat-colored than blond, the skin of his squared face pocked in the flickering candlelight.

"Gentlemen, Jon Gainsborough told me I'd find you here."

"What are you doing up here, Parker?"

He put his handkerchief to his runny nose and said, "I have a personal interest in the British team. Or have you forgotten?"

"Oh," Drew said. "I try to keep that on the back burner."

Parker remained unshakable like a miserable cold, his bullish-eyed gaze unblinking. He twisted the band on his Zodiac watch. "I have an hour to spare. May I join you for dinner?"

"The chair's empty. Take it."

Even sitting, he looked massive, composed. He flung his ruck-sack on top of the tablecloth—barely missing Vic's elbow—and pulled out some photographs. "Obviously Glenn Fairway didn't tell you I was coming, Gregory."

"I haven't been in touch with him."

"Which displeases Fairway."

"Nothing to report. So far the race is going well."

Parker's sharklike smile deepened. "Are you discounting last evening's mishap? Plastic explosives, wasn't it?"

"The gendarmerie handled it."

"But I thought half the mountain came down."

"Only part of it. What's happening at the embassy?"

"Nothing but stolen memorandums. Fairway ordered a twenty-four hour surveillance on Lennie. She won't get very far."

"Does she know you're in France?"

"She knows I'm away on a business trip. I had to leave. I couldn't face what was happening to her. It's been difficult for me, Gregory. I am quite fond of her."

I bet, Drew thought.

Parker pointed to the photos. "Fairway asked me to deliver these to you, Gregory."

Drew slid his hand across the linen and spread them out. "These are all of you and Lennie."

"We have had some great times together. The opera. The theater. She is well-informed about literature and music."

One by one Drew picked up the pictures—seeing, yet not seeing the old Lennie in fashionable clothes, a love-sick expression on her face as she looked up at Parker. His broad hand rested on hers. Involuntarily, Drew glanced at Parker and was startled to see a wedding band on his finger.

No, Drew thought. *You didn't go that far! You didn't marry Lennie.* "You're married?" he asked.

"The ring? I wear it when I travel. My wife and I are divorced— long before Lennie," he volunteered.

"Why bring these to me? I'm not interested in your affair with Lennie—if you two have a problem, let Fairway handle it."

"He wants to avoid your arguments on your return to London. No surprises that way. He insisted on these surveillance photos. I agreed—but all of that was before she meant so much to me."

You lie well, Drew thought. He pulled his pen from his shirt pocket, uncapped and recapped it. These were places that would have delighted Lennie. St. James Park, the Victorian Room at Geffrye's Museum, the two of them strolling arm in arm by the docklands, a close-up one on the steps at 16 Oakley Street, and a fifth one of them browsing at Vanbrugh's Rare Book Store.

"None of these prove her guilt," Drew said.

Parker's smile was condescending. "But when we dated, she insisted on taking the tube home alone. Sometimes it would take her hours to get home after that. I'd keep calling and calling—"

Maybe she just didn't answer her phone after midnight. But traveling alone—well, why not? Drew wondered. Lennie was too timid to arouse questions in the minds of neighbors by arriving home in the company of a man. Drew's aggravation mounted as Parker shoved a second set of photos across the table.

"Fairway persuaded me to follow Lennie," Parker said. "Once to Gabriel's Wharf, another time to Waterloo Station. These are the result."

Drew frowned. *Waterloo Station! Isn't that the route she took to her parents' residence?*

Parker's tone became urgent. "The woman in both sets of photographs is the same person, Gregory. There is no mistaking that this is your Lennie Applegate. Those computer disks in her hands were taken from the embassy and passed to her handler."

"What kind of a fool photographer are you? You left out the man's face."

Parker's wide lips sealed for a moment and then opened again.

"There is another problem, Gregory. Fairway insisted that I tell you. . . . Lennie has a brain tumor. Inoperable by now."

Drew felt as if a cold wind had swept in off the Alps and engulfed him. "Lennie ill?" His fists clenched around the uncapped pen. "You're talking a tumor—a brain tumor?"

"Right on. It is terminal, old man," he said, his gunmetal gaze steady. "Gregory, surely you knew about her headaches?"

"She was squinting a lot lately," Drew admitted, "but I thought it was her new contact lenses."

"Then your lack of concern may have cost Lennie her life."

Drew had the urge to plow his fist straight into Parker's Roman nose. "She's dying? My secretary is dying?"

"That's what the doctors say."

"Parker, if Lennie has a brain tumor, no wonder she got into this mess. She's confused—not thinking clearly."

Across the table, anger flared in Vic's eyes. "A terminal illness doesn't mean a person's not in charge of her faculties."

"What—"

"Drew, you know I'm a walking time bomb, a body waiting to test positive to AIDS this year, next year. But I can still think. The medical odds are against Lennie and me, but we're still responsible for our actions." Vic shuffled through the pictures. "Face it, Drew. Lennie knew what she was doing. She was well paid for every memo, every secret that left the embassy."

Drew couldn't equate the mousy, shy Lennie with a shrewd spy who could walk boldly out of the embassy with American secrets. "She wasn't after Jaguars and mansions, Vic. She just wanted to help her parents. They're old and ill."

"There are government agencies for that," Parker said.

Vic shook Drew's arm. "Don't let your loyalty blind you."

No, Parker and Fairway are trying to take Lennie down, and it's up to me to stop them. He brushed Vic's hand away. "I'm okay."

Parker's thick brows lowered, forming dark awnings above his eyes. "I admit, in the beginning, dating Lennie was part of the surveillance. I never expected to care about her." He drew his shirt cuff over his watch band. "But it was all over between us before we discovered that Lennie had helped the Serbian cause."

Another lie, Drew thought.

"According to Fairway, she sent money every month—a pittance to be sure—but what she intended for her family was used by the rebels. The truth is Lennie helped in the barbaric war effort without knowing it. That didn't sit well with Fairway nor with me. We both felt that with Lennie's employment at the embassy, we should have been informed about her personal ties with Serbia."

"What about the brain tumor, Parker? Surely this has something to do with what's happened."

"I've urged Lennie to consent to the surgery. She refused. So I convinced the doctors to increase her medications to help her get through the rough spots. What else can I do, Gregory?"

You're a good actor, Drew thought as Parker's voice wavered. "Why doesn't Fairway detain her—and insist on medical care?"

"Fairway feels that the important thing is to catch her taking a classified document from the embassy. And that's it. She's ours."

"And where will you be, Parker, when that happens?"

"I fly back to London in the morning. I will want to stand by her, of course."

Of course.

The smirk on Parker's face tightened the lines around his mouth. "Gregory, do you question Glenn Fairway's time frame? Ah! I see that you do. But you Americans took a long time tracking Porter Deven and Aldrich Ames."

Drew winced. "I don't feel much like dinner, Parker. I think I'll ask the waiter to send a tray up to my room."

"I'll join you, Drew," Vic offered. "You don't mind eating alone, do you, Radburn?"

"Under the circumstances, no." He ran his hand over his burlap skin, barely controlling the twitch at the corner of his mouth. "I don't like this any better than you do, Gregory. Neither does Fairway."

Back in their hotel room, Drew paced back and forth, pounding his fist against his palm. "Why this pictorial sham? Parker doesn't care about Lennie any more than Fairway does."

Vic loosened his tie. "Parker seems genuinely fond of her."

"As attached as a Siamese cat befriending a bulldog."

Drew covered his eyes, hoping to shut the miserable pictures from his mind. Why was he so uneasy about Parker? They were on the same side, weren't they? He was helping them, wasn't he?

"It's not Parker we're after, Drew. This is takedown time for

Lennie. She's played a high-stakes chess game and lost." He tossed Parker's pictures on the bed and dropped another set beside them. "Here are the photos from Glenn Fairway's vault."

"And you're just now giving them to me?"

"I held off—I've been trying to put it all together myself, but there's nothing we can do about them until we get back to London. They're just like Parker's photos."

Drew spread them out. The old Lennie with the new look was clearly evident, but again the camera had caught only a man's arm, a cuff link visible on his sleeve, an expensive ring on his finger, a computer disk in his hand. What kind of a dud was Parker with a camera? A schoolboy would have had enough smarts to include the man's face. "Vic, what if Parker faked these pictures on Fairway's orders?"

"Then we're about to hang Lennie on Parker's photography."

Drew scrutinized the photo where Lennie's fingers rested on the man's broad wrist. Mousy Lennie overtly touching someone? "That's it," Drew said. "There's a blue Zodiac watch like the one Parker wears. I saw it on his wrist again this evening."

Vic's shrill whistle blasted through the room. "That's it then. Lennie gave Parker a watch like that for his birthday. But how? She couldn't afford an expense like that on her embassy salary."

"She could if she's selling embassy secrets." Drew leaned over the bed and with a wild brush of his hand swept the pictures onto the floor. "If Parker didn't take these pictures, maybe Glenn Fairway did. They're in it together, Vic. Mark my word."

Parker glanced at his watch and cursed himself for wearing it. He had removed his Cambridge ring before leaving London and even remembered to leave his favorite diamond cuff links at home. But automatically he had worn the Zodiac—Lennie's birthday gift to him. He had in truth been flattered by her gift, but wearing the watch this evening had been a careless mistake.

He knew it the moment Drew Gregory thumped one of the photos, his finger actually pointing at the Zodiac. "What kind of a photographer are you, Parker? You left out the man's face." Parker had felt the heat rise in his neck, yet Gregory made no mention of the watch. Would he, once he studied the photos again?

Parker swallowed his drink. Gregory and Wilson would be in their room by now. He shouldered his empty rucksack and left the restaurant without ordering dinner. Outside, he glanced around. Even at night the chateau was as gleaming white as the snow-covered glaciers above him. He strolled over the cobblestone path and disappeared into the shadowed darkness of the evergreens that climbed the mountain slopes. As he inched deeper into the foliage, he smothered a sneeze with his handkerchief.

He moved more cautiously now, avoiding the marked trails and listening for sounds of snapping twigs behind him. He felt the rawness of the mountain air against his cheeks. His nose ran from the annoying scent of the wild alpine blooms that clung to the granite rocks. It had to be their pollen or the last of the Martagon lilies giving him fits; they were beautiful in the chateau gardens, disastrous for his allergies. The shadows grew longer, darker, with only fading streaks of light from the chateau windows to guide his steps. He kept his handkerchief to his face and muffled another sneeze.

"Over here. What kept you so long, Parkovitch? I left word with the receptionist."

He stopped, waited. The shadowy figure remained hidden among trees, forcing Parker to take the first step. "Roadrunner?"

The cyclist stepped forward, sullen and dark like the night, his handsome features partly hidden behind the hooded jacket. Parker saw the glint of the knife in the young man's hand and felt contempt as he faced him. "Put that away," he said.

"I had to be certain it was you. Jiri Benak must be somewhere nearby. Did he contact you?"

Parker took the handkerchief from his face long enough to answer. "I don't intend for him to identify me. Not yet. But I've been watching him. Benak is a clever man, most useful to us."

"What's wrong with you, Parkovitch?"

"Flowers make me sneeze."

With a throaty laugh he said, "You must be allergic to the lilies or thistledown."

"I'll live," Parker told him. "But I need to get back inside the chateau. And you should be resting for tomorrow's race."

"I had to see you first."

"Risky with Gregory and Wilson staying in the same hotel."

"Did they tell you about last night's bombing?"

"It made the news. A bloody good show."

"You call a botched job successful? Benak is running his own timetable. I don't think we can trust him."

"You worry too much. We can still use him."

"The villagers spent all night clearing the debris, forming a path for us to ride over. It slowed the race considerably. Two of the riders dropped out—refused to ride the stage."

"I know. I know. And there was destruction in the valley along the burned hillsides. But no deaths. Few injuries."

"You knew about it, didn't you, Parkovitch? Knew it was going to happen. You and Benak should keep me better informed."

No, I didn't know. He said, "You're safe. Nothing happened to you. The major plan is still the same. Stage seventeen."

"Are there any more bombings before that? The timing has to be perfect. When do I alert my people in Bosnia, Parkovitch?"

You won't live to do that, Parker thought. *Professor Ivanski has no lasting interest in Bosnia or a Serbian uprising. You are useful and expendable, Roadrunner—my job, according to Ivanski—but I will arrange to have someone else take care of it.*

He blew his nose and with a nasal twang said, "It's all arranged. Benak sets off the bombs. You create an accident for Kendall—a pileup of cyclists that will plow into the bystanders. Ryskov contacts Ivanski. And Ivanski notifies the Serbs."

"So everything hinges on Ryskov getting his message through to Moscow. Let me take care of Kendall before then."

"Ivanski insists that everything must happen at once."

Roadrunner shrank deep into his jacket, his resistance as dark as the night. Parker pitied him. He was young, but he was accustomed to giving orders, not obeying them.

"Nothing will go wrong," Parker assured him.

"Ivanski will end up with a bloodbath in Moscow."

"What would it matter? The rich Mafia will still be wealthy. The elderly poor still hungry. It's time for the Russian people to do more than just dream of the past." *Time,* he thought, *for the remnants of the Phoenix-40 to rise to power.*

"You seem more Russian than British, Parkovitch."

Yes. His pulse quickened; he sensed excitement in his own voice. "The present Kremlin regime is unpopular. The last elections didn't solve a thing. Many men still covet the presidency. Yavlinsky. Zyuganov. Zhirinovsky. Even Gorbachev still yearns for a comeback. All of them former party members," Parker scoffed. "Only Ivanski has the answers."

"The blood in Red Square will turn a deep purple before this is over."

"Unless Ivanski's plans for an Imperial Russia are put into play. It will be a bloodless coup, but once in office, he will disband nuclear disarmament and build a strong military backup."

"A strange mix of peace and power. And you believe he will succeed?" The young man bent his head back, his face to the starless sky. "If everything goes wrong—for you, for all of us—where will you go, Parkovitch? Back to London?"

"I can always go to Moscow. Ivanski has promised me a position in the new leadership—as second in command."

"With your British ties? You are as crazy as the professor." He started to slip away along the unmarked trail.

"You haven't asked about your aunt," Parker called.

As Nash faced Parker again, a patch of light from the chateau windows fell across his high cheekbone. "Aunt Lennie?" he asked sadly. "Poor woman. Does she really believe I am her nephew?"

"The longer she does, the safer it is for you."

⚜⚜⚜

At midnight Drew patched a phone call through to Glenn Fairway in London. "Sorry to call you so late, Glenn. I'm worried about Lennie Applegate. How is she?"

Drew heard Fairway tapping his fingers on his desk before he said, "You know her. Never misses a day at work."

"In spite of the brain tumor?"

"What tumor? No one told me she's sick."

"Fairway, she gets headaches a lot lately."

The finger tapping grew louder. "Not since you've been gone. The only thing strange about Lennie is the portable radio on her desk. She keeps it tuned low to the BBC reports on the Tour."

Drew tried to sort it out, but he said, "Is she that interested in the race?"

"She is since Radburn Parker left."

"I saw Parker this evening up here at the Alpine Ski resort. We— almost had dinner together."

"He's there already? I'm surprised. He had a business appointment in Paris. Something to do with the Parker Foundation. . . . I didn't realize he was joining the Tour so quickly."

"He's the one who told me about Lennie."

Fairway sounded disgruntled. "Well, he should have told me."

"About those pictures—"

"What pictures?"

Didn't Parker show them to Fairway? Wait. He remembered Parker's exact words, *"Fairway asked me to deliver these to you, Gregory."*

"Look, have Parker call me. He said he was heading back to London tomorrow."

"No, he took a two-week holiday to the continent."

"Switch to scramble. I need to know what's going on with Lennie. What evidence—"

Fairway's tone sharpened. "That's not the thing to discuss over the phone." The switch hollowed the sound of Fairway's voice as he said, "The last couple of days, nothing has turned up missing. She's back to her old routine. Comes to work. Goes home. Never leaves the apartment except to visit her parents."

"I have to get in touch with Parker, Glenn."

Fairway chortled. "If he's not staying at your hotel, scan the fans. He'll be there somewhere. He's sticking with the Tour until Paris. He's quite a cycling fan. Been following it for years. Now with a team of his own—"

Drew wanted to yank the phone from the wall and toss it across the room. Parker had lied to him. Or was Fairway doing the snow job? "Doesn't Lennie have a nephew in the race, Glenn?"

"You've got me. Never heard that."

Surely Fairway knew. Drew allowed the memories to flash back to Lennie's loyalties right on down to a cup of steaming cappuccino on his desk first thing in the morning. Had he ever thanked her for her efficiency or that impossible filing system of hers that never failed? His thoughts raced from the dowdy suits to a grateful Lennie with an opera ticket in her hand and her shy way of telling him about her parents, yet never asking for sympathy. But he didn't like recalling his own wedding, with Lennie sobbing and dabbing her eyes during the ceremony.

Where had it gone wrong? Where had he missed Lennie's cry for help? Everything pointed back to Parker coming into Lennie's life. Drew pictured clearly that last moment with her—Lennie going off to lunch with Parker, her shiny laced shoes tapping rhythmically down the embassy corridor. She had turned and called back, "My nephew will be riding in the Tour, too, Mr. Gregory."

"You're running up the phone charges, Gregory. If you have something else to say, say it, or let's cut this exchange short."

"Glenn, Lennie has a nephew riding in the Tour. Check it out for me in the morning. Name. Team. I have to find him."

Drew sensed Fairway's resistance and hated his hard-nosed way of not answering. "You can reach me tomorrow night at the Reims Couette, a bed and breakfast just outside of Gap. Try the name Marcus Nash on her. He's on the Gainsborough team."

"Should I tell Lennie you need the information, Drew?"

"Not yet. She still trusts me. Let's leave it that way. But squeeze the information out of her. Parker would."

Drew slammed the handset down and disentangled his fingers from the cord as he dropped into the chair. Lennie Applegate was walking a thin line at the London embassy. Her health was threatened if he could believe Radburn Parker, and her safety in London was endangered by a station-chief whom Drew no longer trusted.

Chapter 16

Greece. On the island of Corfu, Vasille Golemis stood on the edge of the cliff overlooking the tranquil sea. Far below the vertical drop-off, the waters were radiant, peaceful. Inside, he felt nothing but turmoil. He stepped closer to the precipice, his toes flush with the overhanging cliff. Life seemed so empty, the villa too quiet, the ache in his chest unbearable. He was due back in Athens in a week, his extended leave over. But still he grieved. Still he longed to see the face of his son again. Vasille wanted to die. He wanted to be done with Parliament and politics; he wanted to see his son—wanted to tell him that he loved him.

These days he kept wondering whether he had ever told his son how much he loved him. Or had he left those words for Olympia to convey to their children? There was a rustle behind him, the thud of familiar footsteps on the path as the gardener came through the rose arbor to stand beside him.

"Are you all right, sir?" he asked.

Golemis turned his head, a faint smile on his lips. "I was thinking about my son," he said.

"Thymous?"

"No, Alekos."

Andreas Savo fingered his hoe like a flute, as though the melody had eluded him. He was an old man—with the family for thirty years now. Deep facial ridges were sun-baked into his skin, his hands callused from long years in the gardens. His dark eyes were scolding. "Try to remember the good things, my friend," he admonished. "You can never bring Alekos back."

Vasille would have word-whipped his political opponents for less than that, but he considered Andreas a trustworthy friend. "Andreas, I miss him."

The caretaker patted Vasille's arm and gently pulled him back from the rocky ledge. Vasille glanced at the rippling bay again. "It is so peaceful down there, Andreas."

"But you have your wife. Let her comfort you."

"My wife does not understand. All she does is pray."

"Your wife prays because she understands."

"Where is she, Andreas?"

"Cutting back the grass and weeds from Alekos's grave and polishing his tombstone."

"Olympia does that every week." Vasille's voice filled with despair. "That won't bring Alekos back. Our son is gone."

"But it comforts her, sir."

"And my other children? What comfort are they? Thymous and Zoe have been gone for days."

Andreas removed his straw hat and brushed the garden dirt from his trouser leg. The wrinkled face was filled with concern, the eyes still reproving.

He is growing old, Vasille thought. *I cannot bear to lose him, too.* "Do you know where Thymous and Zoe are?" he asked.

"They have gone to France." He covered his sun-toasted bald head again. "They had promised Alekos they would go to the race."

Golemis felt no surprise. "Then they have betrayed me by going. Do they intend to cheer Mr. Kendall on to victory?"

"No, they love you. They want only to stop Mr. Contoni before something worse happens."

"So you know about him? Did Thymous tell you? He always confided in you even as a child."

"No, I overheard you speaking to Mr. Contoni in the library. Forgive me, sir, but what you asked him to do broke Zoe's heart."

"Ah! I had forgotten. Zoe has always liked young Kendall. But he is wrong for her. She will get over him."

"That is not why she went to France."

Vasille looked at the bay again. "So Zoe confides in you, too."

"Only when her father is unaware that she is hurting."

His mouth twisted as he asked, "Have I been so neglectful?"

Andreas nodded. "You are sad. Your children understand."

"There was an accident at the Tour de France yesterday, Andreas. Do you think my children understood that?"

The old man shook his head. "A bombing," he said. "How could they understand that?"

"Surely they know that is not what I asked Contoni to do. He was to stop Ian Kendall from winning." Slowly he turned again and met the old man's watery gaze. "Was I wrong when I hired him, Andreas? Have I done the wrong thing?"

⓪⓪⓪

In Russia Boris Ivanski unlocked the top desk drawer and took out Yuri Ryskov's last transmission. He shoved pencils and the Phoenix-40 papers aside and smoothed it out against the desktop. Running his finger under each word, he read it again: "Lunched at Maxim's. Met an acquaintance of yours. His next planned events: eleventh and seventeenth. Unable to change plans. Major competitor uncooperative. Advise friends."

An acquaintance? The Czechoslovakian? Ivanski wondered. *Or Parkovitch? Or both?*

His housekeeper stood in the center of the room gripping a coffee tray. She was a square-faced woman with sulky features and black unfeeling eyes who had come to his employ after his wife's death. He tried to recall the occasion for employing her and could not—tried to remember who had recommended her, but that memory was lost too.

"Do you want something?" he asked.

"Do you? Something to eat? More coffee?"

"Nothing. Has Ryskov called?" he asked.

"There have been no phone calls, Professor. You were here all morning—"

She cut her words short. She seemed to look straight through him—seemed to be severing the phone cord with her gaze. It was as though at this moment she hated him. But she had not hated General Noukov. She had respected him. Was it Ivar Noukov who had recommended her? Or Yuri? No, Yuri had never trusted her.

"That will be all," he said curtly.

For an instant, she stayed unmoving, her big scrubbed hands

balancing the tray. Then she turned abruptly and left him to his misery. He folded his hand over Yuri's coded message. He faced the truth now. The Czech was following his own agenda with no concern for the original plans. Without Jiri Benak's cooperation, the planned coup in Moscow could fail.

"Competitor uncooperative." In opposition to them all, Benak had chosen the dates with a plan of his own. He had tried to blow away a portion of a mountain in some unknown French village. Was he trying to stop the race before it even reached the Pyrenees?

"Unable to change plans." Yuri had lost contact with the Czech. "Advise friends." Advise Noukov and Leopold Bolav, and all of Ivanski's plans would crumble. He reached for the phone. Pulled away. Reached again. His fingers caught in the cord. Noukov would be waiting for his report. How could he tell the general that something had gone drastically wrong in France? Or warn him that something worse could happen before the seventeenth?

❀❀❀

In Bosnia that morning, two men sat high on the hillside overlooking the shelled city, the Serbian with a stray cat purring in his lap and the Russian general with a half-filled vodka glass at his feet.

"What do you see?" Leopold asked, brushing the cat's fur.

General Noukov peered through his binoculars. "Soldiers."

"The French? Americans?"

"Here. See for yourself." He handed the binoculars to the other man, the cat hissing at the intrusion.

He grunted, his voice gravelly. "Will they ever leave?"

"Some have." Ivar Noukov wiped his hand across his bushy mustache and reached for his glass. "If they all do—if even the covering forces leave—then the Russian contingency goes as well. I would have no reason for keeping them on."

"Our time is running short then. And no word from Ivanski."

"It will come. He never admits defeat." Noukov smiled. "He will call. If he doesn't, his housekeeper will get word to me."

"Can we trust her?"

"I don't," the general said. "But I trust her more than the professor. Ivanski is brilliant, but I question his methods."

"His methods no longer include you, do they, General? Is that why you chose to come to my country?"

"A man obtains his freedom in any way he can. Ivanski and I covet the same position. His was a mad scheme from the beginning. And now—" He palmed the sky and shrugged. "Stage eleven has gone sour, and the professor will see it as my strategy gone wrong."

"But nothing unusual has happened since then."

"Except some nails on the road that caused a number of flats. A few stiff hills to climb. A photographer with a broken leg. And at least another dozen men have abandoned the race."

"None of Mr. Benak's doings. Nor yours."

He chortled. "How can you be so certain, Leopold?"

"My men watch you closely, and Benak—he takes pride in destruction. According to Marcus Nash, Benak still has plans for stage seventeen. I just trust they agree with our own."

"And if they don't?"

Leopold sighed. "My country was at war so long that I felt defensive when the peacekeeping forces came. And now I am remembering how it was six years ago. Living in peace. I'm not certain I want to go back to killing my neighbors again."

"Then will you go back to your village and your work?"

"As an engineer? It is all that I know except soldiering. But to go back is no longer my choice. I am on the wanted list."

The general studied the man beside him. "And Marcus Nash was one of your men—the only one who could betray you?"

"Yes, that is why I made certain he left Bosnia. War criminals, they call us. Poor lad! He was simply carrying out my orders. But, Ivar, if only one of us survives, I intend for it to be me. Nash can only return here if Ivanski's plan works."

"Do you plan to betray me as well, Leopold?"

"Survival is a strong instinct. We expect more American businessmen to grapple for the rights to rebuild this land. I could probably get more help from them than from Ivanski."

"You are fortunate. The Americans will need engineers who can speak the language."

"And you, General, what will you do if our plans fail?"

"Stay on with you," he said, smiling. "It would never do to go back to Moscow. Ivanski can turn on a man very quickly."

۞۞۞

At the onset of stage fourteen, four cups of steaming black coffee and the sports page did little to alleviate Drew's black mood. He had not seen Radburn Parker since that evening in the Alps. If Parker was riding with the Tour, he was keeping out of sight, a strange disappearing act since he had such a heavy investment in the Gainsborough team. Drew poked at the rubbery scrambled eggs and scowled up at Vic as he joined him for a late breakfast.

"Where have you been, Wilson?" he asked.

"Seeing Chase safely to the press room. Either she starts taking a hotel room alone or she's packing it in."

"Back to London? Doesn't she like her accommodations?"

Vic chuckled. "I would, but it's a problem for Chase. She has five women in one room. She's sick of climbing over suitcases and listening to Millard's little girl cry half the night."

"I thought she liked Millard's wife and daughter. Chase can't go first class all her life. Sharing a room is good for her."

"You're in your usual morning grouch. Here, have some more coffee." Vic filled Drew's cup. "Sugar?"

"Black. Just black."

"That's how Chase feels. She caught Marcus Nash's fiancée going through her luggage last evening. I'm telling you, Chase is out of here unless we find her another place to stay."

"Brigette is just jealous of Chase's fine luggage."

"I don't buy that—not the way you mistrust Nash."

"So keep them both under surveillance. And let's give up our hotel reservation to Chase and sleep in the lobby."

"I'll scout around and see what else we can do. But when Ian finds out about Brigette's luggage inspection, he'll have a cow."

"Let's send them all home!" Drew tossed a crumpled note across the table. "Chambord got this an hour ago. Read it."

Vic smoothed out the note and read: *Take care in stage seventeen. Next time it won't be a bomb.*

"Wow! This accounts for your foul mood."

Drew wrapped his fist around the warning note. "Chambord brought us here because of the threat of terrorism. Now he insists that we've been mistaken; no terrorist group has taken credit—so none exists. Just a crackpot out there. Logical, eh?"

"Ian doesn't put much stock in the threats either."

"None that he's admitting. He says if we force him to quit the race, we may lose our terrorists. He's right, of course."

"Ian checked out okay this morning, Drew. He's not talking ter-rorists—just grumbling about another bowl of muesli mixed with yogurt. He'd eat steak for breakfast if they'd let him."

Drew poked his cold eggs again. "Smart boy."

"Last night in the therapy room, Ian looked wiped out even with his head pillowed on that yellow jersey, but Kendall recov-ers quickly. These last few days would have done me in."

"That's why Carwell has you riding in the team car."

"Guess so. After the beating he took in the Alps, what does Ian do today? Holds on to the jersey for one more day."

"I hope he can hold on to his life." Drew swallowed hard and went back to burying his face in the sports page. He had started the Belgian reporter's article three times and still found his thoughts drifting back to London. To Glenn Fairway and Lennie.

Drew gave up on the article and signaled for more coffee. "Vic, I can't keep my mind on the race; all I can think about are the problems back at the embassy."

"You usually lay out the puzzle pieces."

"They don't fit together this time."

"Name them."

"Here in a public dining room?"

"Someone could bug our room and report back to Fairway. But no one knew we'd eat here at this table at this precise hour."

Drew glanced down at the sports page again and mumbled, "Troy Carwell delayed my retirement because of a problem at the London embassy. And suddenly Fairway wanted me out of London, and Carwell wanted me back in France."

"Monsieur Chambord asked for your services."

"At Carwell's suggestion." Drew kept his voice low-key. "Chambord didn't know I existed. With the problem with Lennie, the logical thing would have been to keep me in London."

"The threats here are greater."

"Greater than national security?"

"This one has an international twist. Besides, Ian Kendall is your friend."

"So was Lennie."

"You suggesting a connection, Drew?"

"No, they don't even know each other." He smashed the paper together and dropped it on an empty chair. "We're dealing with two separate problems. Lennie possibly turning traitor. Ian trying to do the ride of his career."

"And someone trying to stop them both."

"Vic, maybe I'm being set up. These are people close to me—my secretary and the grandson of a good friend. And the more lies Parker and Fairway throw at me, the more convinced I am that Lennie and Ian are nothing but scapegoats, a couple of innocents taking the blame for something I did."

"Possible," Vic said. "But not likely. If you were the target, you'd be dead by now. Let's just stick with the two scapegoats—but two separate problems? I can help you with one problem, Drew. If we believe Parker, Lennie is sick and dying. If we believe Fairway, she never misses a day of work. Do you want my cousin Brianna to check it out?"

"How?"

"Do we have a doctor's name? A clinic? The hospital?"

"Brianna can't just walk in and take medical records."

"I don't question Brianna's methods. She knows her way around a hospital better than the nurses do." Vic gave his tongue-in-cheek grin. "When they wouldn't be up front with her about my case, she put on a volunteer's smock and marched right down to the records department. Made copies of all my papers. Even ordered copies of my X-rays before they caught on."

"Sounds like Brianna."

"Great gal. My best friend." As Vic tried to glide over the catch in his voice, he wiped the back of his hand across his mouth. "Brianna will fall apart when I check out. We go back to our preschool days—throwing sand at each other one minute and best pals the next. Been that way all our lives. Drew . . . when the time comes, if this AIDS thing takes me out, will you stand with Brianna for me?"

"Miriam and I will be there. Count on us."

Vic made a quick comeback. "If Parker's story about Lennie's brain tumor is a hoax, Brianna will be on top of it right away."

"Glenn Fairway won't thank us for getting your cousin mixed up in this."

"Brianna likes taking chances."

"Warn her. Lennie's under twenty-four-hour surveillance. That's one thing Parker said that I believe."

"Lennie takes the tube home each night, doesn't she, Drew?"

"Catches the Bakerloo Underground."

"Brianna can post herself at the ticket window until Lennie pops up. It won't matter who's following her, Brianna will make a good show. She'll have the information we want by the time they reach Lennie's station."

"Too risky. What if it's a short run? Someone is bound to recognize Brianna—she's been at the embassy enough."

Vic snapped his fingers. "Brianna will have to quiz Lennie the first time out. She'll make like a ventriloquist and fool anyone watching her. If it's standing room only, she can stand beside Lennie. If there's a seat, she'll grab it. Trust Brianna. She loves playing cat-and-mouse. We did it all through our childhood." Vic's eyes sparked with the memory. "If she has to, she'll play nurse or doctor and ask some pertinent questions."

"Tell her to be careful. Lennie could turn on her."

"Trust Brianna. She'll get the answers we need with the surveillance team totally in the dark. We'd better go, Drew," Vic said. "Gainsborough has fits when we're late. But Ian would ride off happier if Chase were in the team car under our care."

Drew checked the bill and counted out the French francs, leaving in spite of his gloom, a sizable tip. "Ian should be happy just having her nearby."

Vic grinned. "He didn't like that Italian journalist paying so much attention to Chase. Ian likes to protect his own territory."

As they reached the crowded sidewalk, Drew said, "The press room would have been a perfect place for Contoni to hide out. He's clever enough to have developed that intercept box that threw the glitch in the television system. And maybe even clever enough to have set the explosions on the mountain."

"You're wrong on that one, Drew, if you're still trying to line up Contoni and the Italian journalist. The journalist was with Chase when the hillside exploded. He protected her with his own body."

"But why the sudden disappearing act right afterwards? Check it out for me, will you, Vic?"

"I did. He didn't show up in the press room. Hasn't for the last five days. His computer—everything gone, his spot beside Chase cleared off."

Drew thrust his hands into his trouser pockets and struck out for the hotel. "We have to find him, Vic. Chase's safety depends on it."

Chapter 17

ondon. Lennie Applegate peered into the cracked mirror in her desk drawer. Her eyes and face looked as peaked and dull as her gray linen suit. She fluffed the sides of her hair, but they felt limp and lifeless in her fingers. *Lipstick! I need lipstick.*

Her hand trembled as she applied it. What was the use? Radburn was gone. On a business trip, he had said.

Radburn had walked out of her life. Had he ever been in it? *Gone. Gone. Everything gone. It's only a matter of time before they arrest me.* But Radburn Parker would go free. Were the ambassador and Mr. Fairway so blind—so unwilling to see what a deceiver Radburn really was? Like the Third Man, he had wedged himself into the embassy life and secrets. And still they trusted him. Was she the only one who knew the truth?

Lennie tidied the clutter on the desktop and stood. She left the room and walked slowly down the embassy corridor, taking petite steps as she passed her old office still ribboned off for redecorating. She could see the painters in Mr. Gregory's room, whistling as they rolled the fresh cream paint over the walls. She wondered if Mr. Gregory would like that color—he was so particular about satisfying his wife's aesthetic tastes.

Her eyes downcast, she counted her own steps.

One. Two. Three.

They will arrest me now. She stole a glance down the long corridor. *That young marine ahead—perhaps he will stop me, handcuff me, search me. Go ahead,* she thought. *I want to be caught. Do you hear that, Mr. Gregory? I want to be punished. I'm guilty, but I am not a*

traitor. She licked her lips and tasted the ruby red lipstick. *My loyalties are to Britain, Mr. Gregory, but I did not betray the Americans.*
Four-five. Six-seven.

Other secretaries—other employees—hurried around her. A girl from the ambassador's secretarial pool smiled, a friendly smile. *Oh, Mr. Gregory, did you see that? Someone just smiled at me.* Her forehead felt damp. And why not? It was July and hot even in this air-conditioned hallway. *Radburn said that I would ruin your career, but I would never hurt you, Mr. Gregory. You are my friend. I wanted you to notice me. To like me.*

Mechanically, she moved down the corridor, one step at a time. Muted. Frightened. *Eight*—that was her left foot.
Nine-ten . . . twelve-thirteen.

Tears brushed at her lashes. She wiped them away with her gloved hand. *You are a traitor, Lennie Applegate. You are a traitor.* The words thundering in her mind sounded like Mr. Gregory's voice; the iron-gripping vise set off a sudden violent headache, churning her stomach until she felt her insides would spew out on the embassy floor.

Yes, I have sold secrets to the enemy. I did it for my nephew, Mr. Gregory. You will understand, won't you? I did it for my nephew—and for my beloved Radburn. But, Mr. Gregory, I am not a traitor. I am not a spy. I am Lennie Applegate, remember? I am not an undercover agent like the Countess of Romanones.

A broad shoulder bumped hers. "Good night, Miss Applegate."
She looked up, stunned. "Good evening, Mr. Fairway."

Her steps dragged behind his. *Fifteen-sixteen. Seventeen. Eighteen.* Mr. Fairway stopped and glanced back her way as he spoke to the marine. She could see the marine's facial features now—so young, so handsome in his uniform, his profile rigid beneath that visor. *He sees me now. And I am afraid. I must prove to him that I am not carrying secrets from the embassy.*

She slid her right foot forward. *Nineteen . . . twenty.* Several steps from the exit Lennie pitched forward, her purse and its contents spilling on the floor. The marine was at her side at once, kneeling beside her, his hand firm at her elbow. "Are you all right, Miss Applegate?"

So you know my name? She nodded up into his handsome face and fought the tears pricking behind her eyelids. He was young enough to be her son with a wash of freckles across the bridge of his narrow nose and a crew cut so stubby that it barely showed its flaming red. *See,* she thought as he helped scoop the articles back into her purse, *I have nothing more than my wallet. My comb. My lipstick—the ruby red that Radburn likes. My vial of perfume.*

"Oh, no," she cried. "The lens in my sunglasses popped out."

He tried to replace it. Their eyes met, his sparkling with youth. "I'm sorry, Miss Applegate." He ran his hand over the floor. "You'll have to have them repaired. The screw is missing."

As a tear made its way down her cheek, she brushed it away. Always, she had wanted a son, a boy named Michael with red hair and blue eyes, like this young man had. He was on his feet, pulling her gently up beside him. "Be careful, hear."

She saw the microphone wire attached behind his ear and knew he would report the incident the minute she left the embassy. She could imagine him saying, "1700. Miss Applegate leaving embassy. Fell deliberately. Purse contents normal. No computer disks."

She marched stiffly through the door, out into the glaring light of a summer day, a brilliance that could not touch the utter midnight of her soul. Down the steps she lurched, past two London bobbies who tipped their hats to her. One of them steadied her on the last step. She smiled back, wondering if he was aware of who she was. Of course. For the first time in her life, her every move was under scrutiny. She, a Miss Nobody for so long, had become important enough to follow twenty-four hours a day.

Don't you understand? I did it all for Radburn.

As she squinted against the glare of the late afternoon sun, the rolling waves of her visual migraine forced her to grope blindly for her dark glasses. She fumbled with the broken lens, but could not attach it. It remained clutched in her hand as she wound around the stone barricades and through the iron gate to the sidewalk. *See, I am in no hurry tonight. I have nothing to hide. See, I am going one step at a time.*

As she put her left laced shoe on the rough pavement, the terrible pain in her head struck with pounding intensity. She stopped again without looking back. Was the man who had followed her yesterday and the day before and the day before that in position to follow her again? Was he British or American? A friend of Radburn's or an acquaintance of Mr. Gregory? She had resigned herself to the final outcome. They would arrest her, but when would the police car pull up and an officer invite her inside? Would she have her wrists shackled behind her? Tonight when she reached her flat, would she find it ransacked?

That day would come as surely as Radburn Parker had walked into her life and out of it. She had loved him, but he had used her, and she had let him. She hated his vain promises now: freedom for her nephew, her nephew's name removed from the war criminal list in Bosnia, her parents well cared for. She had trusted Radburn and had been thrilled at the arrival of her nephew—the young man she had not seen since he was a baby. Handsome. Dark. So frightening with his black moods. So unlike what she had expected.

"We must help him. He's our blood," her father had said.

And she had obeyed. What had it mattered to her father that she must betray the Americans? Family was what mattered to him.

Footsteps behind her pounded like the beat of drums between her temples. She fumbled for her change purse at the train ticket window. "My money," she cried. "It's back on the embassy floor."

Tears streaked her makeup. A young woman's hand reached out. "Here," she said. "Take my travel card. I have two." Her voice was kind, her face blurred by the exploding stars in Lennie's eye. The girl lagged behind, lost in the crowd again, but the sweet fragrance of her Arpege lingered.

Down the steps to the underground Lennie went, gripping the iron railing because the rolling waves in her left eye would not go away. If she could reach her flat, she would lie down with cold packs on her face and pray that the awful pain would let up. It would take another hour before the waving pattern would stop altogether. She must not vomit in the underground this time. She must control that terrible feeling. *Get home. Get home. Everything will be all right if you can only reach the flat.*

Lennie ran for the train, stumbling in her haste. She shoved her way through the crowd and collapsed on a seat. As she closed her eyes, the visual waves changed to deep purples and black; the subway car spun around her. A passenger climbed over her legs and sat down beside her. The smell of Arpege was strong again.

As the young woman flipped open her newspaper, she said, "I'm Brianna. I'm a friend of Drew Gregory and Vic Wilson."

Lennie's eyes flew open. The woman was pretty, coolly dressed in a sleeveless frock. She wore a narrow gold band on her wrist, another around her ankle. There was a deep gloss to her lips and a high sheen to her shoulder-length hair. The newspaper rattled as the girl turned the pages. Softly, she said, "Don't look at me, Lennie. Just listen. I'm here to help you."

"No, don't. I'm being followed."

"I know. He's an attractive brute, but he found standing room only. He can't hear what we're saying." Brianna folded the paper in half. "Drew is worried about your tumor, Lennie."

Lennie's spine seemed to fuse. If she turned squarely and looked at this stranger, surely her ribs would crack. Her voice was as rigid as her back. "I have no tumor," she whispered.

"But Mr. Parker—"

"Radburn? What does he know? Lies. All he tells are lies."

The newspaper rattled as the girl turned to the theater page. "He told Drew about the CAT scan and the X-rays. When are you going to have the brain surgery, Lennie?"

"I refuse to have surgery."

"But the doctor said . . ."

The tube roared to another stop. The standing passengers swayed with the car, scrambling to keep their balance. The man who had followed Lennie took a seat two rows behind them. Lennie clutched her purse. "Are you from the doctor's office?"

"I told you. I'm Brianna—Drew's friend. Vic's cousin."

Lennie did not remember Brianna, but she had smelled the sweet fragrance of Arpege in Mr. Wilson's office once, moments after his cousin had been there. Could she trust her? If only the terrible headache would go away so she could think more clearly.

"Are you all right, Lennie?"

"I'm in pain. And the vision in my left eye is blurred."

"Then let me see you home."

"No. That man has been following me for days. And when he disappears, someone else takes his place." She feigned interest in Brianna's newspaper and pointed to the second column, her eyes too blurred to see the words. "Tell Mr. Gregory I don't have a tumor—but the wall of an artery in my brain is wearing thin."

"An aneurysm?"

She heard alarm and sympathy in Brianna's voice and felt a strange sense of comfort in finally telling someone what was happening to her. "Yes, when it breaks—"

"Lennie, you could bleed to death."

Brianna faced Lennie. "Lennie, I know my way around hospitals and doctor's offices. Let me go with you to your next appointment. If you need surgery, I can be there for you."

"No. No surgery. It could be a slow bleed, even weeks before something happens, but when it explodes, I will be free."

"You'll be dead. Drew Gregory won't like that."

"Radburn will."

"Whose side is Radburn Parker on?" Brianna asked.

"I thought he was on my side. And no one at the embassy is really sure which side I'm on." The London tube was pulling into Lennie's station. "Don't follow me," she begged. "I only have a short way to go."

"Give me your doctor's name, Lennie. Perhaps Drew can help."

Lennie fumbled in her purse and took out a business card. She dropped it on the seat between them. Brianna kept her eyes on the paper as she palmed the card and slipped it into her pocket.

"Don't follow me, Brianna. I won't be alone." She nodded toward the man already making his way toward the exit doors.

"I'll run interference for you so you can go home in peace."

🌀🌀🌀

On the platform, Brianna made straight for the stranger. He was a muscular hunk, attractive in a tough sort of way with his sharp jawline and eyes that looked right through her. She barreled into him and groaned as her narrow shoulder collided against his rock-hard chest.

"Get out of my way," he demanded, his gaze on the crowd heading for the stairs.

She massaged her shoulder. "You almost knocked me down, and now you're going to be rude on top of it?"

He tried to step around her, his broad shoulders pushing against her. "Move," he ordered.

She blocked his way again, thinking, *You're just one of the hot-*

shots from the embassy, too bullish to do anything but frighten peo-ple. You're doing a good job on me. She brushed her long hair back from her face. "I expect an apology."

"Apologize to you? Look what you've gone and done."

"What?" she asked innocently.

"I was trying to catch up with a friend."

Brianna glanced around, praying that Lennie had the needed head start. The crowd on the stairs had thinned, but Lennie had just now dragged herself to the top step. Brianna looked back at the stranger just as his elbow slammed against her.

She stumbled backward, grabbing at his arm. "What about your apology, mister?" she insisted.

"I'm sorry." His gray eyes hardened. "I've seen you before."

"In your dreams maybe."

"No, at the embassy."

"What embassy?"

He seemed unsure now. "Are you with security?" he asked.

"Obviously, I don't know what you're talking about."

He took off running, taking the steps two at a time. She sashayed up the steps behind him and lingered on top for twenty minutes wondering which direction Lennie and the man had taken. At last she went back down the steps, through the turnstile and boarded the train headed back to the heart of London. Easing into the first unoccupied seat, she swung one slender leg over the other and took refuge in staring out the murky window.

Only when the train picked up speed and roared along the track did she take the business card from her pocket and read it: "Dr. Kirk Hammerill, Neurology."

It was an appointment card from the outpatient desk of a char-ity hospital for 7 A.M. the following day. *Okay, Lennie. I'll see you there.* She leaned back in her seat, lulled by the swaying of the train. *And now, my sweet cousin Victor, I'll see if I can get through to your hotel room.*

She had nothing but bad news regarding Lennie, but they had to know the truth. A brain tumor? No. An aneurysm? Quite pos-sibly. The outlook for Lennie was grave either way. But there was one more thing. Brianna wanted the whole truth from Vic. The embassy wouldn't put someone under surveillance for ill health. No, Lennie Applegate was in trouble. Deep, serious trouble.

Chapter 18

The next afternoon while Brianna Wilson waited for her, Lennie sat in Glenn Fairway's private office in an uncomfortable straight-back chair, her hands folded tightly on her lap, the toes of her laced shoes turned inward. She pressed her knees together to keep her legs from shaking.

Fairway's stubby fingers tapped impatiently against the desktop. His eyes—gray or blue, she couldn't tell—looked directly at her. His movements were deliberate. He tilted his head, avoiding the glare from the window. The tapping stopped long enough for him to take a thick manila folder from his desk.

This is it, she thought. *I am not to be arrested on the streets of London, nor to be handcuffed and torn from my apartment with my neighbors watching. I am to be detained by security before I leave the embassy this evening.* She shuddered, dreading the words he would use. Spy. Traitor. Foreign agent.

But I did it all for Radburn.

She allowed her gaze to stray over Fairway's spacious mahogany desk with the latest state-of-the-art computer to the rich brown swivel chair where he sat. Veiled sunlight from the window marked a clear path to his bookcase lined with thick leather-bound volumes. In one corner, two Queen Anne chairs faced the aquarium with its colorful squirrel and butterfly fish. The walls of the room were crowded with diplomas and awards and two framed mountain scenes, one of Mont Blanc at dawn. But everything came back to the man who controlled this room—back to her own portable radio centered on his desk so she could see it.

Mr. Fairway was solidly built. A lock of curly gray hair hung down on his bony forehead. Other than that, his features—pleasant enough—were nondescript. No aquiline nose nor moles, no scars nor laugh wrinkles to remember. He was someone who had wormed his way through the crowds unnoticed, yet noticing everything himself. Still his silver hair and well-cut suit gave him an air of dignity, but Lennie knew he was greedy for power. Even a slight insult could spark his anger.

He seemed to be waiting for her to speak, to confess. She avoided his eyes and focused on the bridge of his nose. Fairway was charming to women, a quick-witted man who wanted to possess the good-looking ones who worked for him and to consign the less attractive to out-of-the-way cubicles in the embassy.

Two years ago he had dumped her back into the secretarial pool. If Mr. Gregory had not taken her as his assistant, she would have been jobless. Jobless and fiftyish. She never quite admitted to her real age, but to be tossed out into London to tread the rain-soaked pavements in search of another job had been terrifying. She was too uncertain of her own abilities. Mr. Gregory had been a godsend—a formidable boss to be sure, but he proved to be a kind man. A single man back then. She blushed at the remembered fantasies that had gripped her those first months.

When Fairway finally broke their silence, his voice was stern. "Miss Applegate, my secretary tells me that Brianna Wilson is waiting for you."

"Yes. We're having tea together before I go home." To cover her concern, she added, "She's Mr. Wilson's cousin."

"I'm aware of that, but I didn't know you knew each other."

He was forcing her to make an excuse.

"She's been to the embassy many times, Mr. Fairway."

"Has she?" He scowled as he said, "Miss Applegate, I understand your nephew is riding in the Tour. I need to know his name—and the team he's riding for."

Her stomach muscles tightened. *You sent for me to ask my nephew's name?* She wanted to laugh out loud. Radburn knew his name. Radburn had placed him on the Gainsborough team. "My nephew, Mr. Fairway?" she asked.

"Is your nephew's name Marcus Nash, Miss Applegate?"

Give that away and they could trace her heritage back to Bosnia. She risked lying. "I have no nephew, Mr. Fairway."

He reached out, flicked on her radio, and twirled the dial. "You have followed the Tour de France quite closely," he said.

You took my radio. "So has half of London," she countered.

"Very well." He turned back to the folder and opened it. "Lennie, are you planning to go away with Mr. Parker?"

Involuntarily her head jerked back until she met his gaze. His eyes seemed green now, the gleaming glow of a Balinese cat. In silence, he shouted at her, *Traitor. Traitor.*

She wanted to scream. "Radburn—Mr. Parker is out of town."

"And you don't have plans to go somewhere together?"

He was confusing her—accusing her of a romantic getaway.

"Mr. Parker is in Paris on business, Mr. Fairway."

"Are you to meet him there after the race, Miss Applegate?"

"No," she said faintly.

"Speak up."

"No, Mr. Fairway, I don't expect to see him again. Ever."

"Then you knew he was going away for good when he left London?"

If he left the prominent social and familial position that was his in London, where would he go? He would never forsake the wealth and pleasurable life that the Parker Foundation provided. Mr. Fairway was mistaken. "He never told me he was moving away, if that is what you mean."

"But you suspected?"

"He talked of visiting Moscow again. On holiday, I think. He taught there, you know. Some years ago."

"The historical philosophies of ancient leaders, if I recall correctly. A modern Plato."

"Radburn was a history or science professor," she corrected. "There on an exchange professorship."

"A rare invitation."

Had Fairway discovered the truth about Radburn's past? About his plans for the future? Fairway's catlike eyes demanded an answer. "He was friends with one of the university professors," she said.

"Which university, Miss Applegate?"

"Radburn never said. I never asked. It never seemed important. . . . It was such a long time ago."

Fairway thumped the folder. And now she wondered whose folder was on his desk. Hers? Radburn's? Or was Fairway trying to corner her? She could never betray Radburn. He had warned her against it. "I wouldn't want something to happen to your parents," he had said. "Or to your nephew."

"Miss Applegate, how long have you been working for Radburn Parker?" Fairway asked.

Meekly, she said, "I thought he was working for you."

Fairway's eyes blazed. As his neck vessels bulged, he wedged his finger into his shirt collar and tugged. "It would seem that he has deceived us both."

She rubbed her eyes, trying to block out the tension headache that was building. "Why are you asking me about Radburn?"

"Because I need answers." His chin pressed against his folded hands. He looked like a man betrayed.

Arrest me, she thought. *Don't taunt me like this. Don't force me to say things that I dare not tell you. I can't let anything happen to my parents. They are old–*

"I have your medical reports here," he said, his eyes not unsympathetic. "You are ill."

"I am seeing a doctor for my headaches."

"Yes, we know. Your reports are all here."

Brianna! Brianna had betrayed her. Or Radburn. Anger gave her courage. "How dare you look into my personal life," she said.

"When it involves our security, we have no choice."

She gazed down at her clasped hands and watched her knuckles turn a chalky white. *It is coming now. He will arrest me. He will speak of the secrets I have taken from the embassy.*

She felt a sharp jabbing in her eye, intense heat and pain as a black speck swam in her visual path. Her eyelids fluttered as the speck spread like spilled ink, its dark, weblike tentacles clouding her vision. The headache broke, acute, piercing like a sharp spike driven through her temples.

"Miss Applegate."

She opened her eyes. The room spun, the desk and chairs riding in pinwheels around the ceiling. Fairway's face blurred. He tilted with the room.

"Are you all right?" He was standing over her now. Touching her. She flinched, but his hand remained firm on her wrist.

The aneurysm? No, she would have already drifted into unconsciousness. She was in pain, but she could still reason. "I must go home, Mr. Fairway," she whispered.

"I need your answer first. Give me your nephew's name."

"Please. I am ill."

She was aware of him leaning back across the desk and striking the intercom button. He spoke urgently, but his words were meaningless to her. Silence. And then his fingers were tapping again—the back of her chair this time.

"Take a deep breath, Miss Applegate," he told her.

Behind them his office door opened, and light steps came tripping across the carpet. "Miss Wilson," he said, "Miss Applegate is ill."

Brianna knelt beside Lennie and gently took her clammy hand. "Hi," she said. "We've sent for the ambulance, Lennie."

"No . . ."

"You're not well."

"I can't see you with my left eye, Brianna."

"One of the hemorrhages that the doctor warned us about." Lightly she added, "Besides, I'm not worth looking at."

Brianna—attractive, fun-loving. Fragrant with Arpege perfume. Casual and carefree. "You're young. Pretty."

Brianna pushed a lock of her shiny hair from her face and smiled. "I'm older than you think. Thirtyish like my cousin Vic."

"But better looking," Lennie whispered.

"I'd better not tell him that."

The pain came fierce again. "Am I dying, Brianna?"

"Shhh!" Brianna patted her arm. "Don't say that."

"She can't leave the embassy yet," Fairway announced. "I have questions to ask her."

About the missing disks? Lennie wondered. *And the bank accounts?*

"Ask her tomorrow," Brianna snapped, "when she can think more clearly."

"Now," Fairway demanded, "before the ambulance comes."

"If I have to call the ambassador, I will," Brianna warned. "Miss Applegate is too sick to question right now."

"I have to know what she did with the embassy disks."

"She's not going far, Mr. Fairway. Can't you see? She's ill. If she lives long enough, you can question her again. Tomorrow maybe. I'll take full responsibility—"

"You'll take more than that if she escapes."

Commotion filled the office as a stretcher was rolled into the room. Ambulance attendants. A marine guard. The ambassador's secretary who had smiled at Lennie. Lennie felt herself lifted from the chair, her body limp as they laid her on the hard surface. The leather strap tightened around her, securing her arms against her body. "My purse," she cried.

Through her blurred vision, she saw Brianna snatch it from Fairway's hand.

"I'll keep that," Fairway said.

Brianna outshouted him. "We'll need her medical cards."

Someone was listening to Lennie's chest. Someone else was ripping the sleeve of her new gray suit and placing a cuff there. She squirmed against the pressure and heard the attendant whistle. "The diastolic and systolic are about to converge."

She thrashed, frightened. *My blood pressure is running wild,* she thought.

"Forget that IV," Fairway ordered. "Just get that woman out of here."

As they rolled Lennie from the room with the IV running, she heard Fairway on the phone. "Get me a full report on Parker—everything you can on his background, especially his years in Russia," he demanded, his tone razor-sharp. "I want to know who his chief contacts were when he lived there."

You won't like what you learn, Lennie thought. She strained to hear Fairway's words as the stretcher jammed in the doorway. His voice seemed distant now, but still she was certain he said, "Call Dudley Perkins over at MI5 and tell him to get over here. And get the station-chief in Paris on the line. . . . Of course, I mean Troy Carwell, you idiot. I want to ask him about his old posting in Moscow."

Brianna leaned over the stretcher as they hurried down the corridor. "I'm here, Lennie. I'll ride in the ambulance with you."

"That's not allowed, miss."

"It is this time," Brianna told the attendant.

Lennie tried to pull away as Brianna squeezed her arm. Brianna Wilson was not her friend. She was working for Fairway.

🏺🏺🏺

An hour later Fairway's rage was under control, his outright suspicions of Parker hidden, when he met with Dudley Perkins. As they sat in the Queen Anne chairs facing the aquarium, he made his inquiries sound casual. "We are wondering whether Radburn Parker could be passing information to old friends from his Moscow days. Innocently. Do you think that's possible, Dudley?"

"Mr. Parker comes from a well-established family, Glenn."

"So did Kim Philby—and Anthony Blunt, the queen's art historian."

"Let's not do battle," the Englishman said. "You Americans have your shameful history, too."

"Yes, Porter Deven and Aldrich Ames. And now we have Harold Nicholson's betrayal to contend with."

"Not easy," Perkins said quietly. He was a gaunt, spindly man with a pinched face and thin smile. Fairway knew him to be uncompromising, inflexible, a strong defender of his country and countrymen. His pale, inquisitive eyes focused on the aquarium as a brown-spotted eel slithered around the coral, causing the Yellow Tang to swim in the opposite direction.

"You've added a Trigger Blue Throat since I was last here."

"Yes, that one with the yellow-tipped fins. And the calico—that one's new, too."

"Colorful," Perkins said, his voice passive.

"Dudley, we have a problem at the American embassy."

"I am aware of that. The young woman, Gregory's secretary."

Fairway smiled. "She's fiftyish, middle-aged. And she's been in the company of Radburn Parker a lot lately."

"We agreed to that, Glenn."

"But we were lax in our security check on Parker. He slipped in without a thorough investigation on our part."

"We've been over that, too. What are you suggesting?"

Fairway soft-pedaled the blow. "We need your help over at MI5. Parker was quite political in his youth, wasn't he?"

The grave smile was discerning. "So was I."

"Dudley, it is quite possible that Parker made serious friend-
ships in Russia that might be useful to us now. That's all we're asking for—a bit of background on his time in Moscow."

"I know you too well, Fairway. Your implications are more serious. You're not accusing Parker of espionage within these sacred
American halls? Parker and Miss Applegate—I won't hear of it."

"Someone has been her handler, her contact person."

With controlled rage, Dudley said, "Is that what this is all
about—throwing suspicion on a member of a prominent British
family?"

"His social status is not the issue, Dudley."

"The Parkers are friends of the queen. They were her guests at
the Royal Ascot races recently. Don't bring scandal to the Parkers."

"I saw it all on TV—the Parkers riding in an open landau behind
the queen's carriage. Radburn seemed a bit tipsy."

"Probably embarrassed in the company of Miss Applegate. It
did take it a bit far. There's just so much fancy fixing you can do
with a woman like Applegate. But she wore a stunning hat."

"Quite impressive," Fairway agreed, chuckling to himself.

Perkins refused to be humored. "If what you are suggesting
reaches the news media, the tabloids will tear the Parkers apart."

"What if Parker is not really on a holiday? Perhaps he had
another reason for going away—like catching the Red Express to
Moscow," suggested Fairway.

"You won't let up, will you? What do you want from me,
Fairway?"

"A full report on Radburn Parker's time in Russia."

"Those records belong to MI6."

Perkins sat quietly for several minutes, blotting his face with a
starched white handkerchief, a scowl forming between his bushy
brows. Without conviction, he said, "I think you are wrong,
Fairway."

"Prove it."

At last Perkins said, "At the risk of the boy's safety—at the risk
of my own position—MI6 has a contact person studying in
Moscow. Vladimir Wecker was born in London of Russian immi-
grant parents and speaks the language fluently."

"Studying at the University of Moscow?"

"No, at the Academy of Sciences. He majors in earth sciences—geology and mining. It allows him a number of field trips throughout Russia. For a while he sent my wife postcards."

"Have him look into Parker for me."

"MI6 won't thank me for interfering. Wecker is a touchy subject with them. Three months ago they contacted my wife and advised her not to write to him again."

"Hard to do for an organization that doesn't exist."

He laughed dryly. "Molly thought that if they wanted to be so secretive about their existence, she could ignore them. But they paid us a midnight visit in our home, warning us that Wecker's safety was at stake. It was a shame—Molly and the boy have always been close, especially since Joel's death." He blotted his face again. "Wecker's mother worked for my wife's family for years. You will go carefully?"

Dudley seemed intrigued with the fish again, his gangly fingers tapping the glass. "But I must warn you—Wecker tends to make friends with political dissidents."

"Risky."

"That's the business we're in, Fairway. MI6 has no real ties to Wecker. He's on his own with no official contacts with our people in Moscow. He's just a student abroad who sends reports at irregular intervals at prearranged drop points. That's the only way they know he's still alive. But I will see what I can do—if for no other reason than to clear Parker's name. If you ruin Parker's reputation, the queen will have my job."

"When we searched Parker's flat this morning, we found a number of scholarly articles by the Russian Boris Ivanski."

"The Nobel prize winner? He's quite a controversial figure, well-known in Moscow. Parker would find his writings most interesting."

"Have Wecker check on Professor Ivanski, will you? Just in case Parker knew him personally."

Dudley stood—a tall and distinguished English gentleman. "Wecker reminds me of my son. Fearless. Adventuresome. Molly worries about him. If anything happened—"

Fairway shrugged. "Dudley, why don't you and your wife have dinner with me soon? My treat. Your wife likes the Le Gavroche's or The Connaught, doesn't she?"

"My wife is still in the Greek Islands." He tipped his hat, his smile somber. "If M16 agrees to help, I will get back to you in the morning, Glenn."

No reconciliation yet, Fairway thought as Perkins left the room. Perkins's social position had come through his marriage to Molly, a gracious woman who had too often taken second place in Perkins's life. Sadly, their only son was one of the casualties of the Falklands crisis. He was dead—the same direction in which their marriage seemed to be heading.

As Fairway tapped the aquarium, the fish shimmied to the top. "Hungry little critters, aren't you?" he asked.

He teased them, delighting in their playful cavorting. Then he sprinkled food into their tank, laughing at the marvelous blend of colors as they swam hungrily to the water's surface. He sobered as he watched the shimmering fish gulp down the confetti-like morsels. Was he being duped, suckered in as fair game by Perkins? With the rivalry that still existed between MI6 and MI5, would there be any chance of Dudley unraveling Parker's days in Moscow? If not, Fairway was dependent on Troy Carwell pulling strings with his old associates in Moscow. But it was easier on a man's pride to turn to Perkins—to take his chances with the Englishman.

Chapter 19

For two days Professor Ivanski stayed at his research work and took light meals in his study, barely going inches from his desk lest the phone ring and he miss Yuri Ryskov's call. His calendar was clearly marked: "July 17, Stage 17." He dozed in his chair, his mood deteriorating with the weather and the silent phone. He wanted action, but today dragged as the riders took a rest day at the foot of the Pyrenees. But in twenty-four hours he could march triumphantly into Red Square with the people chanting his name as he returned them to the golden days of imperialism. But everything depended on Yuri Ryskov's signal, his phone call.

Ivanski spun in his swivel chair and gazed at the picture of his dead wife on the mantel, her presence as real to him as if she had just gone from the room. "Have I trusted the wrong man?" he asked her.

He wondered how she would have looked in the palace as the wife of an emperor or whether she would have approved of his deep desire to rule this land. He pictured her in a long sequined gown, her delicate hands held out to him. If only she had lived to share the days ahead with him. As he mused, a sound disturbed his reverie. A stone thrown against the house? Company? No, his housekeeper would tell him if guests had come to the door.

He spun his chair until he faced the open window. Soon dusk would settle over the forest behind his property. He demanded privacy, thrived on it. It had not taken the villagers long to know that they were unwelcome on his estate; yet at the edge of the woods he saw a young man limping toward the farmhouse. The man met Ivanski's stare, making no effort to be secretive. Perhaps he was lost, simply in need of direction back to the village.

Ivanski opened the window and called out in Russian, "Get off my property!"

The stranger hesitated, his weight on his good leg. In fluent Russian he said, "I would if I could walk, sir."

It was a friendly voice. He limped forward, obviously in pain, his empty hands hanging limply at his side now. *No weapon!* Then he paused again, recognition on his face. "You're Professor Ivanski," he said pleasantly. "Imagine finding you out here."

"This is my home. What are *you* doing here?"

"I was on a field trip. Came alone." He had limped another yard closer. "I'm majoring in earth sciences." He pointed toward the mountains. "I've been in the old mine shaft."

"And you injured yourself?"

"I slid in the loose gravel. I sprained my ankle, I'm sure."

"You are not from the village."

"No. Moscow. I am Vladimir Wecker," he volunteered. "I missed the late afternoon bus. It left early."

Ivanski reflected. Yes, he had heard the bus for Moscow grinding up the road ten minutes off schedule. He looked down into the guileless, unblinking eyes, daring the young man to come closer. "You must go. I am busy."

Wecker shrugged, running one dirt-smudged hand through his thick hair. The rucksack on his back was as caked with dust as the shoes on his feet. "If I could just rest first, Professor."

Without invitation he traversed the last three yards to the side porch, sat on the bottom step, and rubbed his swollen ankle. "I heard you lecture at the Academy of Sciences a few months ago," he said. "It was marvelous."

"The lecture on intercontinental missiles?" he challenged.

Wecker twisted his neck to glance sharply back at the professor. "No, sir. You spoke on the history of Russian imperialism and the revolutions against our country. The Phoenix-30 or -40—something like that."

Russian imperialism and the revolutions had been his topic; they always were. But he was certain that he had never mentioned the Phoenix-40. And strangers never came this way unless someone sent them. Someone like Parkovitch. Sheltered by the forest, the farmhouse was not even visible from the main road. No, Wecker had come deliberately, but was it safe to let him leave?

The young man's eyes sparked with curiosity. "You seem to know all about the old Russia, Professor."

"Yes," Ivanski admitted, not without pride.

"My grandfather thinks the revolutions in our country date back to the Decembrist. He called it the seedbed of Marxism."

"Did he?" Ivanski asked. Marxists, Bolsheviks, Bloody Sunday—what did it matter? They were part of the past; Ivanski was about to make history by restoring the old imperialistic days of the czars. "Vladimir, I must get back to my work," he said.

"If I could just use your phone first—to call a friend. There's not another bus back to Moscow for hours."

For a flicker of a second, he wondered if the young man had strayed from the trail and stumbled on his property accidentally. He scoped the forest with his sharp eyes and detected nothing, not even the flutter of leaves as dusk crept in. Could Wecker be an innocent Muscovite, as he claimed? But why would he have left the bus stop on an injured leg? No, he must lure Wecker inside and into the basement before the call from Ryskov came through.

Wecker no longer rubbed his swollen ankle. He was balancing on his good leg, looking wary. "I better go before it gets dark."

Ivanski's housekeeper peered around his shoulder. "He's hurt, Professor. He can't walk on that leg. I can help him."

She has guessed my plan and will not allow me to harm this stranger. Reluctantly he stepped back from the window. "Bring him in then and tend to that ankle. And allow him one phone call."

"But you are expecting—"

He silenced her with a scowl. "Help him, and then I want him out of here as quickly as possible." *I want him silenced.*

🏺🏺🏺

All Vladimir Wecker could think about was beating it back to the safety of the village even if he had to crawl. But there was no turning back. The door was open. He followed the housekeeper inside. She led him down the hall past the professor's library. He had only a second to glance inside. No time to check it out.

She was urging him to hurry as she led him into the kitchen. She was a strange woman, her shifty eyes never meeting his, and yet she gave him a scalding cup of black coffee before going off and bustling about her stove.

As he watched her, he tried to decide where he had gone wrong. When he had approached the farm, he sensed no danger. It was a well-kept house, isolated and shuttered and nestled against the forest. He found no stone or wire fence high enough to keep strangers out. No armed guards stopped him. No attack dogs snarled and nipped at his heels.

The MI6 request from London had been urgent. Wecker was to report back on Boris Ivanski and his possible association with the Englishman, Radburn Parker. And wasn't that Wecker's whole purpose in living in Moscow—of actually studying at the Academy of Sciences—to be available for the good of England? He had felt supercharged when the assignment came. He didn't mention his sprained ankle—just packed up his knapsack and caught the bus out of Moscow. Professor Ivanski! He knew the man's reputation. What could be so important that he had sparked MI6's interest?

Even as he had limped across the grounds, he was certain that Ivanski was just an eccentric recluse who liked his privacy. But he knew he had misjudged the professor the minute he said the words "Phoenix-40." He had blown it.

The housekeeper was back now with a steaming basin of water, smelling medicinal. In spite of her gruff appearance, she bent down and eased off his shoe and stocking, her eyes finally meeting his. "You should not be here," she told him. "Professor Ivanski does not like company."

Gently she turned Vladimir's discolored foot in her hand, examining it. Alarm filled her dark eyes. "This is an old injury," she whispered.

He could taste the fear. "I know. I thought it was healing—but I twisted it again out in the mine."

"But you injured it even more by coming out here."

She plunged his foot into the basin and held it there until he felt his skin burning, but he bit his tongue and held on, and moments later she seemed grieved for what she had done. "Do you still want to make that call?" she asked.

Vladimir nodded. As his foot soaked, she pulled the cord free and dragged the kitchen phone to him. He knew now that the chance of leaving the farm was minimal. He had overstepped his boundary and, feeling cocky and sure of himself, had gone beyond the MI6 orders to check out the farm. Slowly, as though he were trying to retrieve the number by memory, he dialed a pre-arranged number.

The cheerful operator stationed in a small wing of the British embassy said, "Academy of Sciences."

Good so far, he thought, *especially with the professor listening on the other end.* "This is Vladimir Wecker." He spoke distinctly, willing himself to think clearly. To use his ingenuity to leave this farmhouse alive. "I need to get a message to my housemate, Sergei Glass."

Both names were traceable, registered students at the academy. Authentic right on down to biographies that would pass Professor Ivanski's scrutiny. "Tell him I missed the bus back, and I'm out with a bad ankle." *Deliberately missed it.*

Surely Sergei would read into his words and know that Vladimir was out on a limb. In trouble.

"No," he told the operator. "It was a field trip."

"And was it worth it?" she asked.

"I found what I wanted," he said. *Are you listening? Are you writing down what I'm saying? I found what Sergei expected me to find—trouble at the Ivanski farm.* Did the operator hear the professor's heavy breathing on the other end of the phone? Or did she think it was Vladimir?

"My location? A farmhouse forty miles from Moscow." He glanced at the housekeeper. "Boris Ivanski's place, right?"

She frowned.

"No, I believe he lives alone—except for his housekeeper." The operator was a trained agent, taught to pick up bits and pieces from his words. *Are you reading me right?* he wondered. *Are you understanding that there is no visible security?*

"His housekeeper is helping me. My foot is really bad." He winced as she dragged his ankle from the basin and wrapped it snugly. As he said, "The farm is isolated, but I'm sure Sergei can find it," she gave another severe tug to the bandage.

The woman on the other end came back apologetically. "Sergei is gone for the evening. Is there anyone else?"

"No, Sergei's the only one with a car." A double meaning. Transportation out was urgent. The message for Sergei's ears only. That would put it straight through to British Intelligence. Straight to London maybe.

"When he comes back—"

The housekeeper was glaring at him now. "I guess I'd better go back to the village. I've worn out my welcome here."

Did you understand me? he wondered. *I've got problems here.*

His words had reached her. "Wecker," she said, "you should never have gone so far on that bad ankle of yours."

It was a gentle reprimand. "It will be easier for Sergei to find you in the village, so go there as quickly as you dare."

You don't think you are going to see me again, he thought. He cradled the phone, setting it down as though it were china.

"Go," the housekeeper said. "Go while you have the chance."

"Thank you," he told her. He risked one final remark. "I thought Radburn Parker lived here with the professor."

"Professor Parkovitch?" She winced. "Go," she said. "Now."

He had sent the message to the embassy as clearly as he dared, using the right words to alert the others, a message that might even now be going out in an embassy pouch to London. He had found Ivanski, and he was unwelcome. If the place was secured, he had seen no one. He was going back to the village for his own safety. And he needed transportation out of here as quickly as they could get it to him. Something was going on. And, yes, the well-known Professor Ivanski bore watching. But he had not been able to convey the housekeeper's reaction to the name Parker.

His foot barely fit into the shoe, but he forced it on and made his way down the steps. He didn't look back but limped steadily toward the forest, determined to beat the race against total darkness, to distance himself from Ivanski.

He had just reached the edge of the forest when he heard the footsteps tracking across the moss-covered ground behind him. There was no time to dive for safety, not even a second to spare to spin around and face his assailant.

It was a single shot at close range, the sound and the pain hitting Vladimir at the same time as the bullet pierced between his shoulder blades. He pitched forward without even a cry.

At noon Glenn Fairway found Dudley Perkins strolling in St. James Park. Perkins was carrying his umbrella like a walking stick, tapping along the path, deep in thought. He was a rangy chap, a somber man with languid eyes, his homely face and thick skin giving him a morose appearance. Yet he was highly respected, a member of the British think-tank. He had worked himself up through the intelligence ranks, a man committed to his job and country.

Fairway didn't relish the job at hand. He was about to tell him that Vladimir Wecker was dead. He signaled Perkins off the walkway to the nearest empty bench and sat down beside him. He was startled at the pinched gauntness in Perkins's face. Dudley never required more than five hours sleep, but the deep half moons under his eyes suggested that he was going on less than that now.

"Glenn, have you heard from Vladimir?" Perkins asked.

"Indirectly. We had a call from MI6."

"About Vladimir? They didn't call me."

"I know. It's bad news. Vladimir Wecker is dead."

"He can't be!"

Perkins's eyes closed. Fairway gave the man another five minutes to recover. "His friend Sergei Glass found him in the mine shaft several miles from Professor Ivanski's place."

"Then Wecker never reached the Ivanski farm?"

"He found Ivanski's place all right. Even managed a phone call from the farmhouse."

"But you said Wecker died in the mine shaft."

"His body was dumped there. He was shot. I'm sorry, Dudley."

"What have we accomplished?" he asked. "A young man wasted."

"He went beyond what he was instructed to do. He confronted Ivanski face to face. But we have no proof, of course. So it's still a waiting game. We do know that Radburn Parker and Boris

Ivanski taught at the same university. Parker often dined in the Ivanski home and may have shared the man's ideology."

Perkins dug the ground with his shiny black shoe. "I can hardly believe that Vladimir sent you that kind of information. Parker and Ivanski may have been working colleagues but not conspirators. Have you told this nonsense to Drew Gregory?"

"There's no need to yet. Personally, I don't think this has anything to do with the Tour de France—apart from the fact that Radburn is in partnership with the Gainsborough team. This is embassy business. And Lennie Applegate is right in the thick of it." Fairway rested his arm on the back of the bench and glanced at the swans in the pond. "The information is based on our own intelligence reports. The possibility exists that Ivanski was part of the old Phoenix-40. We are working under the assumption that they both held membership. We can't pick them up on guesses, but we're keeping surveillance."

"That's outrageous. Parker is the British citizen who first exposed the Phoenix-40 rebellion."

"Before or after some of their leaders were executed?"

"Before, I think. Keep in mind that Ivanski is a Russian historian. Of course, he would be well versed on the Phoenix-40."

"Dudley, Parker is supposedly on holiday, yet when we examined his flat here in London, we found no personal papers. No canceled checks left behind. No letters. No receipts or files. His books are packed away."

Not a muscle twitched. "So he isn't coming back to London?"

"If he senses danger, he may catch a Red Eye to Moscow."

"And leave Miss Applegate behind? Embarrassing for your reputation, Fairway."

"We have all been quite duped, Miss Applegate most of all. For now, we sit tight. We've arranged for Parker to ride in Maurice Chambord's official car. That way we know where he is." He shrugged. "The Russian, of course, is not our responsibility."

For an instant his attention riveted on the swans again, and then he said, quite kindly, "I'm sorry about Wecker." They stood at the same time. "Dudley, when is your wife coming home?"

"I'm afraid to ask her. But it will be a while yet. Her hostess persuaded her to spend a few days on the island of Corfu. Seems that the woman has an old school friend living there. Lost her son a few months ago." His face was reflective. "Molly thought she might be able to help the woman."

"Believe me, Dudley, I hate adding to Molly's pain. Will you tell her about Vladimir?"

"No. It would be like losing our son all over again. She was fond of Vladimir Wecker."

"How can you keep the news from her?"

"If I say nothing, she will think of him as alive. She won't grieve that way—not until his family gets in touch with her."

❀❀❀

The villa at Corfu. Even on the veranda where she sat, Molly Perkins could see the portrait of Alekos Golemis—a handsome young man, his features dark and striking, and those marvelous hooded eyes full of life. She could not have endured seeing the likeness of her own son staring down from the barren wall—and be forced to grieve as the woman across from her was still doing.

Molly crossed her long legs and sipped the light wine that Olympia Golemis had offered her. She swallowed but did not taste it. She wondered now why she had allowed Marcella to persuade her to fly to Corfu. "We'll just spend a couple of days with my dear friend, Olympia and her husband. They have only recently lost their son. Oh, darling Molly, you will do them so much good."

How? Molly wondered now. *Do I tell her about my own grief, my own loss so many years ago? Do I tell her about Joel? Joel as a little boy and the shared disappointment that there never was a brother for him to play with? The wretched way I felt when he went off to boarding school, my secret fears as he learned to fly, and my thoughts of suicide when I knew he was dead? Do I tell her that the girl Joel was going to marry married somebody else? Do I tell her how Dudley packed away every picture of Joel in the house, taking even that small comfort from me?*

She groped for words and found them in the spectacular Grecian setting. "Olympia, you have a lovely view here."

"Didn't I tell you?" Marcella asked. "Absolutely gorgeous view. Why do you ever go back to Athens, Olympia?"

"We haven't, not since Alekos died. His father insists on being here . . . with Alekos."

Molly shivered. She could not have borne having her son's grave on the family estate as this dear woman had done. This morning she had stood in the guest room watching from the window. She saw Olympia down on her knees. *Praying,* she had thought. Then she had realized that Olympia was cutting back the weeds and polishing her son's tombstone. Molly had slipped into her shorts and pink tunic and gone out to her, extending her hands without a word.

It had been no easy task to help Olympia to her feet. She was a heavyset woman, not the once-glamorous schoolgirl that Marcella had described. But her hostess had a very gentle face, even with the grief lines around her eyes and mouth. Olympia had put the tools in the large pocket of her wraparound skirt and dusted the dirt from her fingers. And then they had linked arms and walked back to the house without speaking.

"Marcella tells me that you lost your son, too," Olympia said as she rocked her empty glass.

"Yes. In the Falklands. Joel was a pilot. He crashed at the San Carlos bridgehead." She sounded like a schoolgirl again, answering a question in history class. The more facts she could give, the better the grade. Barren rocks. An isolated mass of land off the coast of Argentina. In defense of the queen. Dead Brits. Dead Argentines. Her beloved son. Her only son.

"Afterwards, Joel's wing commander came to tell us what he could. Mercifully, Joel died quickly." *Mercifully.*

"He was young," Olympia said.

"Older than your son. Joel always wanted a younger brother."

Marcella had brought her to Corfu to comfort Olympia. Instead they were both about to dissolve into tears, the death of their sons as raw as the day they had occurred. "I'm sorry," Molly said, "I didn't mean to burden you with my own sorrows."

"On the contrary, we need each other. Was he an only child?"

Molly nodded and felt the tears prick her eyes, the way they had the day the news came. She thought of Joel's childhood and said out loud, "We spent long hours together, Joel and I."

"Where was Mr. Perkins?" Olympia asked gently.

"Building his career." Her words were sharp, bitter. She set her wine glass down, fearful that Olymbia would see her trembling fingers. Fearful that she would ask again, *Where is Mr. Perkins?* She couldn't bear to admit that she had left Dudley—that she did not know when she would go back to him because she waited for the impossible. She waited for Dudley to beg her to come home again.

"I would never have survived Alekos's death without Vasille."

"Seems to me," Marcella protested, "it's the other way around. Vasille would utterly fall apart without you."

"Vasille needs me. That's why I will never leave him."

I will never leave him. Molly choked at the words. She had run out on Dudley, and yet she knew he still needed her. Across the veranda their eyes met and held, Olymbia's kind and sympathetic. "Will you holiday much longer?" Olymbia asked. "Or will you be going home again soon?"

Marcella opened her mouth to comment, but Molly quickly said, "I suppose you're right. It is time to think about going home again. But Dudley rarely misses me. He's so busy."

"Marcella tells me your husband is in politics, like Vasille. Vasille's whole life was politics until Alekos died."

Marcella was on her second glass of wine. "Vasille is in Parliament," she said. "Dudley can't match that one, can he?"

Molly smiled at them both over the brim of her glass. She did not want Olymbia to know—any more than Marcella knew—that Dudley was in intelligence work. She looked beyond the porch railing over the vast Golemis property. The gated land swept down over the verdant hillside to the magnificent bay below. "I thought this lovely olive orchard was your husband's job."

"A family business," Olymbia said. "Handed down for generations. Vasille feels obligated to keep it going."

"And he has," Marcella chirped, "quite successfully." Her expression did not change, but envy colored her words. "Vasille hoped that one of his sons would take it over."

"I'd forgotten about your other children, Olymbia," Molly said apologetically. "Older? Younger?"

"Older. Our son Thymous and our daughter Zoe."

"And a handsome pair they are," Marcella said. "If I were a younger woman, I would give that Thymous a run for his money."

And it would be for his money, Molly thought. As wealthy as

Marcella was, rich after two divorces, she would never have enough.

Olympia smiled, and now the sweetness of her face unveiled her beauty. "Someday he will meet the right woman, Marcella."

Marcella put her hand to her chest. "If only I were younger. And Zoe—does she still carry the torch for the young American?"

As swiftly as Olympia's smile had come, it disappeared, the lines on her face anguished over something. "Marcella, don't mention him in front of Vasille. He despises that young man."

"Whatever for? Such a nice young man and so eligible."

Molly wanted to kick Marcella, to warn her away from troubled waters, but Marcella plunged on. "A cyclist, wasn't he? A friend of—"

Her words caught up with her. "I am sorry. I never meant—"

"They were friends." Olympia turned to face Molly. "Alekos and the American rode on the same cycling team. And now Zoe and Thymous—in spite of their father's objection—have gone to France to watch the Tour de France."

"How heavenly!" Marcella exclaimed, trying for lightness again. "So Zoe's flame grows brighter?"

Tears brimmed in Olympia's eyes, one tear slipping over her rounded cheek. "They went to keep their promise to Alekos."

Chapter 20

I an came out of his troubled sleep with a start, grasping at the dream already slipping from his mind. Someone had been waving at him. Chase? No, the dream was coming back now—fading, coming back: a pileup on the mountain curve and his grandmother dressed in white smiling down on him, her blue eyes brilliant beneath the dark velvet lashes. She waved, beckoning him to follow. The same premonition of tragedy that had come to Ian on the day of her death stalked him now like an alarm that couldn't be turned off.

He groaned and tossed on his narrow hotel bed, the top sheet twisted and knotted around his bare legs, the flimsy floral spread spilling onto the floor. His upper torso was covered with sweat, his innards cramping violently.

It has to be last night's upset stomach, he reasoned.

Miserable abdominal cramps had accompanied him to bed and had driven him to the bathroom every hour. His gaze wandered across the room, returning to the makeshift IV pole in the corner. He remembered now—Chase coming to his room shortly before midnight just to say good night.

Alarm registered on her face when she saw him. "I'm getting Drew," she said.

"Don't. Vic and Drew slipped out of the hotel hours ago to scout around."

"Scouting for what?"

He didn't know. He was too worried about the cramps that

were tearing at his gut, threatening his chances in the Tour. He tried to grip Chase's hand and felt too weak even to do that.

"I think someone poisoned me."

"The cook," she said. "You're not the only one ill."

He actually smiled at her. "Thank God," he said, meaning it.

Her eyes grew misty. "Well, according to Drew and Beatrice Thorpe, that's the right person to thank."

"Can you just sit with me for a while, Chase?"

"No. If anyone catches me here, they'll disqualify you. You know Gainsborough's rules. No wives. No girls. No fraternizing."

And no illicit affairs, he thought. That was always Gainsborough's final word to the team before every race. In the middle of the conversation with Chase, he had to make a beeline for the bathroom. The cramps were getting worse. Embarrassed, he said, "You'd better go, Chase."

"I'll go, but I'm going to wake the doctor. You're sick."

�884

Dr. Raunsted made his appearance moments later, barely thrown together with his shirt hanging free, his black bag in his hand and his hairy toes jammed into ill-fitting sandals. The doctor reached out and steadied Ian as he groped his way back to bed.

"I think I have the stomach flu, doc."

"Half the guests in the hotel do."

The doctor's examination was quick and precise, Ian wincing as Raunsted palpated his stomach. Then Raunsted chuckled. "After tonight's meal, a number of you are crying for mercy. I'd say the cook added a bit of bacteria to his stew."

Ian doubled his legs to his chest. "The pain is terrible."

"You have ridden more than 2,900 kilometers. You've worn your immune system down."

The doctor was a good man, into athletics, a runner himself. In his jeans and rumpled shirt, he didn't look much like a doctor, but Ian was grateful to have him on board.

"Am I washed up?" he asked.

"It's your call, Ian. You have today to rest up. I will check you tonight and again in the morning. You will live. Gregory insists on it. You're just dehydrated, Kendall."

"I've got to keep racing, doctor, but I'll never make it the way I feel now."

"Kendall, if anyone can be back on that bike in twenty-four hours, you can. If you're lucky, this is just the twenty-four hour bug. You have that long to recover. The rest day will help."

He ignored Ian's arguments as he strung up the makeshift IV pole. "You need a glucose drip."

"No drugs, doc. They'll disqualify me."

"If the food poisoning doesn't."

As Raunsted uncapped the needle, Ian practically backed into the wall. "No medicine."

"It's not a steroid. It's okay. We have to settle your stomach so you can ride again. Everything is legitimate, Kendall. We just have to get some fluids in you."

❦❦❦

That had been hours ago. Now Ian's gaze went from the pole in the corner to the door. He willed Chase to reappear, to be up and about like the dawn. From the corner of his eye, he caught a glimpse of a sheet of paper sliding under the door. The sour taste in his mouth turned to fear. He forced himself to sit up and fought the dizziness as he calculated the steps. Six? Seven? Could he make it? He was sweating, weak as a newborn kitten as he stood. He risked one step and fell back against the pillows.

The doorknob turned. Basil Millard poked his head into the room. "Morning, old top. How are you?"

"I've felt better. But how will I ever ride today?"

"You won't have to, except for our training run. It's a rest day, remember?" As Basil stepped into the room, his foot crushed the sheet of paper. Their eyes met.

"Bring it to me, will you, Basil?"

Millard hesitated. "Wait until the doctor gets here. He's with Drew Gregory right now."

"Is Drew sick, too?"

"He cut himself."

"Shaving?"

"Out scouting, he called it. Tracking Nash probably. Drew has a nasty gash in his arm. He will explain when he sees you."

Ian held out his clammy hand for the paper. "Is it another warning?" he asked.

"Just like the one at Mount Ventoux. It's the only kind of mail you've been getting this trip."

Ian's thoughts raced back to the Tom Simpson memorial. *You will never make it to the summit, Kendall.*

"I'm going to turn this over to Drew. You have enough on your mind." Basil's freshly scrubbed face was full of concern. "You're sick, and you need the rest. So enjoy it."

Ian swung his legs to the side of the bed again, his head spinning as he did so. "I promised to spend today with Chase."

Millard pushed him back down. "You are not going anywhere until the doctor checks you out." He tucked the warning in his pocket. "Ian, the team and I have been talking. You have to drop out of the race. A win isn't worth your life."

Ian glanced out the window at the Pyrenees, the mountain chain that rose like an impassable barrier to his dreams. Rangy peaks and barren rocks awakened him to the challenge of the climb. Or, after all his training, was this remote terrain that towered above the lush hills out of reach for him?

"Are you listening?" Basil asked. "We want you to abandon the race. You have a stomach upset. It's a good excuse."

"I'm not looking for excuses—just for the chance to climb that mountain."

"Don't push yourself too far. Tom Simpson did."

They both knew that the lonely ride toward the crest of Mount Ventoux had been a final mountain climb for Simpson, his heart unable to take any more physical beating in the blistering hot sun. "This is not Ventoux," Ian reminded Basil. "I won't quit."

Millard's breathing sounded as labored as Ian's as he thumped the warning in his pocket. "You do not have a choice."

"You've met my grandfather, Basil?"

"Good man. I admire him."

"In his younger days, he served with British Intelligence. Did you know that?" Without waiting for Millard's answer, he said, "Gramps never gave in to terrorists. I won't either."

Millard's jaw locked. "I wonder what drove Simpson?"

"Maybe he rode for the glory of it, like the rest of us. Summer glory! Autumn glory!" Ian's fist struck the damp mattress. "Call it what you want, but I have to finish this race."

Millard's eyes were sympathetic. "Simpson's grasp for the top left a young widow and two little girls who didn't have their dad around as they grew up. Is that the legacy you want to leave behind, Ian?"

"My legacy is wrapped up in winning."

Basil took the note from his pocket and shook it in Ian's face. "If this were addressed to me, I'd take my wife and child and fly back to Birmingham today."

"You're not me. And I don't have a wife and child."

"You have Chase."

Ian looked away, unwilling to voice his fears. If he missed the top of the mountain as the threats warned, only Chase and his grandfather Uriah would grieve if something happened to him. And Drew and Miriam. It all boiled down to having nothing to leave behind except a handful of mourners. *Chase, Chase,* he thought miserably, *I love you. Will you ever know how much you mean to me?*

"Ian," Basil said, "you won't make it up the mountain unless you do a conditional run today."

"My poor body says no, but maybe we can go later."

"I'll check back after lunch to see how you're doing." Millard slapped the paper in his palm. "I'm going to turn this over to Gregory. Why don't you talk with him about it?"

"I don't want to bother Drew again."

"You better talk to someone—and Gregory seems to have a direct line with heaven."

Ian managed a smile. "I think they call that praying."

☙☙☙

When Basil reached Raunsted's room, Gregory was ready to leave. "You okay, Mr. Gregory?" Basil asked.

"Just tripped in the dark. Nasty cut, that's all."

"Then could I talk to you two?" Millard asked as he stepped into the room. He unfolded the paper and handed it to Drew. "The team wants Ian to go home."

Raunsted's eyes were as dark as his hair. He rubbed his jaw and said, "That's Ian's decision. How is he this morning?"

"Weak."

"Still vomiting?"

"Not while I was there."

"He may not get his strength back to ride the mountains. But he'll make the first twenty kilometers from sheer determination."

"And after that?" Drew asked.

"I won't destroy the man's spirit. I don't know why winning is so important to him, but Kendall has to make the decision." He gave them a wry smile. "But in my mind he will never make it to Paris. The boy is knackered with fatigue. He'll have to abandon somewhere along the way. I'll go by and give him another slow glucose drip. That will keep him resting for the morning. After that it's up to Ian's body to recover."

"That's your medical opinion?" Drew asked.

"Are you questioning my training, Gregory?"

"You came on board for the Tour at the invitation of Troy Carwell. I wasn't sure you even had a medical degree."

He smiled. "You thought all I did was collect blood and urine samples and report in to Carwell?" Raunsted's smile turned into a deep chuckle. "No, I come with full credentials. I did my medical training in France and graduate study in sports medicine. That's when I discovered my first love—the value of exercise physiology on team sports. I even throw in a bit of fatherly counsel now and then."

"You're only a dozen years older than the team."

"Old enough. And you, Basil, you need to get some rest yourself before tomorrow. Your red blood cells are down, your iron store depleted. You need your strength if you're going to ride support for Ian all the way."

"But you don't think he'll go all the way?"

"No, but you will."

"Doctor, can you have someone stay with Ian so he rests?"

"Are you volunteering someone?"

"If you give the order, Chase Evans could be there."

"I'll arrange it as soon as I see Kendall."

He smiled at Drew as Millard left the room. "I'm glad Carwell asked me to come. These threats have affected the whole

Gainsborough team. They race hard. Orlando Gioceppi's toxins are high, his liver overworked. Robbie has the start of an infection that could take him out of the race. I ordered Ramon back on the exercise bike for another thirty minutes to clear up the lactic excess. The team is plagued with exhaustion."

"And Kendall?"

"I expected him to break under the stress. But he's a tough one. Stubborn. The stomach bug might do what nothing else could."

"Put him out of commission?"

"I'd rather see him go out that way than risk another tragedy in the mountains. We've had enough of those in the past."

۞۞۞

It was just past noon when Ian awakened again. He stretched and felt better. He reached out for his water glass and saw Chase curled in a chair near his bedside, reading. She lowered the book and smiled. "Hi, sleepyhead," she said.

"Chase!" he said groggily. "What time is it?"

"Almost one."

"I've been asleep for four hours?"

"Your body needed the rest."

"But I promised to spend the whole day with you."

"You did. You just didn't know it. The doctor insisted that someone stay with you. Millard volunteered me. How do you feel?"

"I think I'm better."

She felt as surprised as he looked. "Then my praying really worked."

"What do you mean by that?"

She was embarrassed. "Well, Drew told me we should pray for you to get better."

Ian laughed at her. "Did you?"

"Did I what?"

"Pray."

"I'm not really sure. I don't have any experience in it."

"Drew didn't either until recently. My grandfather always said Drew was not a very religious fellow. Oh, he was an altar boy—but he outgrew all of that."

"Well, he talks about heaven like he's going to be there some-day."

"He is. He did a turnaround in the mountains at Sulzbach, ran the whole nine yards, from there to eternity."

She curled a strand of hair behind her ear. "My family never talks about things like that. We only pray at weddings and funerals, and I can't even be sure about that."

"You should talk to Drew."

"And not to you?"

"I believe all that stuff. I just don't know how to put it into words. About all I can do is hand you my grandmother's Bible. Other than that, I never know what to say. But you could talk to Beatrice Thorpe when we get back to England."

"But, Ian, she's confused."

"Not about things that matter. She's a straight-shooter then."

"Then go with me—as soon as we get back to London."

"I'll do that. I'll even hold your hand while we're there. Right now, I'm trying to decide whether I feel strong enough to take you to dinner. But I don't think I'd better go that far."

"What about the patio gardens? It's restful out there. We could have tea. I could go down and get a table for us."

He sat up. Slowly. "Okay so far," he said. He wet his lips with the water and began to whistle.

"I don't recognize the song," she said.

"It was a favorite with my grandmother. 'I've Got a Date with an Angel.'"

She flushed, pleased.

He grabbed his robe and slipped into it. "So far so good," he said. "Now if I can take nourishment."

"Just take it easy," she warned.

"I will. I'll shower and dress. And if I'm not down there in the patio in twenty minutes, come looking for me."

He pressed his cheek against hers, and she pushed him away. "Oh, Ian, make that thirty minutes. You need to shave."

She waited until he crossed the room to the bathroom and disappeared behind the closed door. *So far, so good,* she thought. *At least you're still standing.*

Still she lingered, waiting for the sound of the shower running. When she heard it, she fluffed her hair in the mirror, applied fresh makeup, and left. Above the running water she could still hear him whistling "I've Got a Date with an Angel."

🝗🝗🝗

The infusion of light and color in the scented chateaux gardens was like surveying a Thomas Kinkade painting. Striking red flowers grew against the stone wall, their brilliance softened by the delicate hues of blue and pink flowers. A family of ducks waddled around the flower pots and under the white iron benches. Sun rays cut through the high trees and across the rippling pond. Nearby a string quartet played softly.

The maitre d' led her to an empty table. She was seated facing the chateaux, waiting for Ian, when she noticed the guests at a table for two. Sal had dropped from the Tour since the night of the bombing, but there he was, as ruggedly good-looking as ever, caressing the hand of a beautiful, young woman. The girl's dark red-brown hair was swept back from her face, silken strands of it falling softly over her left shoulder.

For a moment, Chase wanted to rush over and demand answers from Sal. How dare he disappear as he had done without a word to her! But then perhaps the girl was the reason he had gone away. He was smiling, but the girl looked near tears, those wide eyes reproachful. She looked up and caught Chase staring.

At a nod from the girl, Sal turned. He recovered quickly and beckoned Chase over. He stood when she reached them and gave her a quick hug. "I missed you, Chase."

"You are the one who went away."

"And I'm leaving again this afternoon," he said with a wink. "For Nordlune this time." He turned back to his companion. "Zoe, this is Chase Evans, a journalist friend of mine. Zoe Golemis. Chase reports on the Tour for her hometown paper."

"Sal and I met in the press room."

Zoe seemed surprised. "In the press room?"

"They have a special place for journalists," Chase said.

"Then it is no place for Salvador. For all I know, he is the one responsible for the bombing on stage eleven."

Shocked, Chase said, "He couldn't be. He was with me. Actually, I think he saved my life."

At closer inspection, Chase saw that the girl had been crying. Her complexion was dark, her skin lovely, and now her long lashes brimmed with more tears.

"The two of you will like each other," Sal said. "You are both rooting for the American."

Zoe turned back to Chase. "You know Ian Kendall?"

"She knows him quite well," Sal announced.

Again Chase saw pain cross the girl's face. Gently she said, "I know the Kendall family, Zoe."

"The whole family? You didn't tell me that." Salvador's voice danced, but his eyes had turned cynical. "I have just been telling Zoe that I am still against the American winning."

"Mr. Contoni, please go," Zoe begged. "Please."

Mr. Contoni? Not Salatori. She was about to ask him when he said, "Zoe, I thought we were going to have lunch together."

"I'm not hungry, Sal, but if you change your mind—"

"I do not want your money. Your father already paid me."

Zoe flinched as he touched her cheek, her expression angry enough to push him away. Sal took no notice, his tone arrogant as he turned to Chase. "Her brother was a friend of Kendall's. They rode together once—but her father dislikes Ian intensely."

Was a friend. Golemis. Chase felt sick. *Alekos Golemis.*

"I'm sorry, Zoe," she said as Salvador left them. "How can you bear to be here at the race?"

"You know who I am?" She dabbed her eyes. "I promised my brother Alekos that I would be here for him."

"You called Sal Contoni, not Salatori, the name he gave me."

"Salvador Contoni—that's his real name, and, Chase, he is not a journalist. He never has been."

Zoe was looking beyond her, and Chase knew without looking up that Ian was making his way slowly to them. He was cleanly shaven, casually dressed, and scented with French cologne. His eyes were bright, or had they brightened when he saw Zoe Golemis?

"Zoe," he said—and there was affection in his voice, "why are you here? This is too painful for you."

"I promised Alekos I would be here for him. You are riding very well, Ian. He would be proud of you."

"I never got to tell you how sorry I was."

"My father wouldn't let you. It was shameful for him to send you away. But you mustn't stay at the race. You must go home."

"I have to ride to the finish line."

"Oh, Ian, you were always a bird in flight. I thought nothing would ever bring you down to earth. But I think maybe Miss Evans has done that for you." She stood hastily.

"Don't go," he begged. "Have tea with Chase and me."

Zoe reached up and kissed Ian on the cheek. "Some other time," she said.

Ian was quiet long after Zoe walked away. Finally, when their tea was served, Chase asked, "Were you with Alekos when he had his accident in the Sulzbach mountains?"

His eyes glazed over. "That was no accident, Chase. Alekos was strangled by a Russian agent."

"Killed? . . . Murdered! How awful—for all of you. But why didn't you go to his funeral? Orlando and Basil did."

He gave her a ghost of a smile. "I tried. But Zoe's dad told me to get off the island of Corfu." He reached across the table and took her hand. "I've come to terms with that, Chase."

"Have you come to terms about Zoe?"

His hand tightened over hers. "Alekos wanted Zoe and me to get together. Permanently."

"And what did you want?"

"For a while I thought the chemistry was there. The spark. But that was all. The only person I really want is you. You're all I think about."

"If you're going to win, you can't be thinking about me."

"I can't stop thinking about you."

Chapter 21

tage seventeen. Ian Kendall awakened to the challenge of the Pyrenees. This was the day he had waited for, a climber's dream. He felt better, refreshed, unwilling to quit. Downing his muesli and yogurt, he felt confident that it would stay down. He eyed the fruit and unbuttered pasta and omelet more cautiously. The omelet only reminded him of the misery of the last twenty-four hours. He grinned to himself and voted for his grandmother's challenge: *You can steel your mind to anything.*

He stuffed the pasta in, swallowed, prayed, and kept his thoughts on the race. Day after day, six to seven hours each day, Ian and the other cyclists had ridden the roller-coaster roads and cobbled streets of France, dipping into Italy and until yesterday racing through rainstorms or tiny villages in 90-degree heat. Ian had sweated up the steep mountain slopes of the Alps with the world's best riders and cruised over the lower lands to the Pyrenees. The 189 racers had dropped in number, ill and exhausted. Two days ago one Spaniard had raced to his physical limit and been carried away on a stretcher. One Italian had crashed out. The Australian had slipped from his sweaty saddle and dropped by the wayside in a heat stroke. Franz, the square-jawed German on the Gainsborough team, abandoned the Tour in tears, a respiratory infection wracking his body. The rest of the pack rode on, too goal-oriented to notice their fallen competitors or to see the medieval castles or golden fields of sunflowers. They were guilty of seeing only the riders in front of them or the road beneath them and always waiting for the red kite that would signal a kilometer to the finish line or listening eagerly for the roar of the fans cheering them on.

As he reached the sign-in podium, Ian looked around for Chase and saw her running toward him. He held out his arms, and she allowed herself to be swept up in them. He twirled her around once and knew that a second turn around would send him spinning.

"I love you," he said, setting her down.

"Is that all you can say?"

"It's all I can think about. How come you're not in the press tent?" he asked.

"Drew insisted that I stay with him today after showing me the police sketch of Salvador Contoni. I don't like thinking about my friend Salatori deceiving me—"

Ian touched her lips. "Just think about me."

She nodded. "We borrowed a car for the drive to Nordlune."

"That's the third mountain pass—at least four hours into today's stage. So you're on official business?"

"The helicopter will check the race course from the sky."

"The helicopters are part of the press corps every day."

"There's an extra one today," she whispered. "Sal Contoni drove up to Nordlune last evening. That's why we're going."

"So you can take any bomb meant for me?"

"Drew wouldn't take me if he thought it wasn't safe."

"Funny girl, how could he stop you once you made up your mind to ride with him?"

Chase touched his cheek. "Ian, nothing will go wrong. I will be there when you come over the crest of your mountain."

For an instant he rubbed his eye, feigning a visual irritation. In his recurrent dream, his grandmother was always at the top of the ridge beckoning to him. "You'll miss my starting out," he said. "This is my big day."

This rugged mountain was his challenge. His foe. His dream. A single summit could determine the outcome of the race and the man who would wear the yellow jersey in Paris. He wanted to be that man. Ian flattened his jersey against his muscled stomach. Yesterday's pains were gone. He felt strong. This was his chance to grab a piece of glory for himself. He didn't dare dwell on the warning: *You'll never make it to the top of your mountain.*

Chase ran her finger over his wrist. "Be careful today."

He felt her shudder and said quickly, "I'll be fine. After the Pyrenees, the roads are flat along the Garonne River. And after the rolling hills of the wine country, we head straight on to Paris. We're going to make it."

"Oh, no," she said, "I think Chambord is heading our way."

He strutted toward them in his forest-green blazer and dark gray trousers, the level of his mood hidden behind dark glasses. But his voice was pleasant. "*Bonjour*, Kendall." His smile broadened to include Chase. "Beautiful day. Beautiful day. Don't worry about a thing. Our gendarmes and escort motorcycles will protect your young man the whole way."

His gaze remained on Chase. "Gregory tells me you're chasing the wind to Nordlune. Lovely Basque village. Used to be a way station for pilgrims, but hardly a place for terrorists." He rattled on. "If you stand down the hill from the Chateau de Arceson, you will have an excellent view of the race."

Chambord stared off at the towering Pyrenees with their craggy, snow-capped peaks. "It's a formidable challenge, my boy. I dreamed of being a cycling champion once. Rode with Eddy Merckx back in the seventies."

"I didn't know that," Chase told him.

"Glad you didn't. I had the humiliation of riding the Broom Wagon when I abandoned the race. I was never a winner, Miss Evans, but I can recognize a champion when I see one. I saw this young man of yours ride four years ago—just a young man then."

Chase smiled back. "That's when you turned professional, wasn't it, Ian—just before your nineteenth birthday?"

"You'd better go," Ian cautioned. "Drew hates waiting."

Yuri Ryskov had to warn the Serbian rider that Jiri Benak was quite possibly following his own agenda. Stage eleven had been proof of that. Yuri had no idea what the Serbian looked like, only that he wore a Gainsborough jersey. *Number 19. Or was it number 91?* He tried to remember back to the meeting at Professor Ivanski's farm with Leopold Bolav and General Noukov. "Remember that number," they had told him.

Number 19? Or 91?

He pushed his way through the crowds toward the host of riders gathering around the start-ramp. Team uniforms in every color. Endless numbers—139 riders left, 139 numbers . . . 6 . . . 30 . . . 88 . . . 99 . . . 111. He kept searching, more frantic now as the twenty-one teams mounted their bikes. His message—blocked out in a childlike scrawl—was burned in his mind:

> *Benak foiled plans. Moscow alerted. Advise General Noukov. Will attempt to salvage project in Paris. Meet Parkovitch there.*

Yuri studied the faces again, finally recognizing three Gainsborough riders. One with a bushy blond mustache. The darker one called Orlando—Orlando Gioceppi, if he remembered correctly. And the cyclist with strands of red hair poking out beneath his helmet and wearing the placard number 19.

A gendarme yanked Yuri back, but Yuri pulled free and ran. He was short of breath when he reached the rider with 19 on his bike and jersey. He shoved his message at the startled man.

"Take it," he ordered in broken English.

A broad hand wrapped around it. "What's this?" the young man asked.

"Read it. Be careful," Yuri warned.

Before he could explain, Yuri was pulled back behind the yellow barrier, the gendarme cursing him in French. But he smiled complacently. The red-headed Serbian was reading the message, a frown cutting across his youthful face.

Number 19 folded the note, tucked it into his headgear, and looked around. Across the yellow barricade their eyes met. And then the whistle blew. It was time to ride into the Pyrenees.

❁❁❁

As Ian rode off, Chase thought, *He's recovered. He'll make it.* She was still smiling when she reached Drew. Even Drew's usual morning grumpiness failed to squelch her happiness. She didn't quite understand what was happening, but she knew deep inside that Ian Kendall—number 19—was part of her future plans.

Chase and Drew barely spoke on their drive to Nordlune. She

preferred thinking about Ian and how important he had become to her. But when they reached the Basque village at high noon, even Drew had to come out of his sour morning mood. Nordlune was like stepping into the last remaining wilderness in the mountains. What had once been a way station for pilgrims had emerged as a flourishing spa town, serviced by people in Basque costumes and black berets. Sheep grazed the lush hillsides beneath the remote terrain and jagged peaks of the Pyrenees range.

Drew and Chase wandered through the seventeenth-century chateau with its beamed dining room, enjoying the delicate aroma of Basque cuisine coming from the kitchen. But later, when Drew came out of the loo, she startled him by grabbing his arm, her face ashen. "I—I just saw Jiri Benak walk through the lobby," she gasped.

"Don't joke, Chase. It had to be someone who looked like him. Benak would never attend a sporting event like this."

Her tears brimmed over. "But, Drew, I will never forget Jiri's face. Remember, he tried to take my life in the tunnels of Jarvoc."

He took her hands in his and rubbed the warmth back into them. "Leave him to Interpol."

"But, Drew, how can I? I have nightmares about him still." She pulled away from him. "That man really did look like Benak."

He nodded. "Don't think about those days in Prague, Chase. We're to keep our eyes open for Salvador Contoni."

"Well, maybe I was mistaken." She began to relax.

"Now let's find ourselves a spot on the mountain to wait for Ian," Drew suggested.

Beyond the chateau lay the scented garden and a gushing mountain stream, and farther down the hillside the turbulent, fast-flowing river. The town was filled with whitewashed houses with red-tiled roofs and a lone twin-steepled cathedral. Standing with Drew just below the crest of the mountain, Chase felt peaceful, content, Jiri Benak all but forgotten. She felt invigorated by the mountain air, fascinated by the jagged mountains. She couldn't imagine a more lovely setting to wait for Ian.

Jiri Benak left his three homemade plastic bombs and the bottles of ammonium nitrate hidden in the trunk of his car, and then he took up his post on the ascending side of the mountain with Yuri Ryskov standing begrudgingly beside him. Benak had already taken notice of the beautiful young Athenian in the crowd on his other side, a stunning dresser who wouldn't even give him the eye. But it was all right. He was too preoccupied thinking about his friend Ignasius. They had quarreled as he left the village.

"Go," Ignasius had told him. "And don't come back."

A wise move, as he considered it, for if by some small chance he were traced back to Ignasius's village, they could deny his presence or at best deny knowledge of where he had gone.

The girl finger-brushed her dark hair behind her ear, a quick feminine gesture. Still she would not look at him. He tossed his beige raincoat over his other shoulder, feeling miserable with the sun beating down on him. He would be grateful when the cyclists rode by and he could make his way safely out of Nordlune—without Yuri Ryskov. Let Ryskov send whatever signal he must; Jiri was not interested in the planned coup in Moscow. He would take refuge in the Cotswolds. Still he worried. What about the bombs hidden in the car? Nordlune was an isolated town with only one main road for an escape route. No, he would not set them off here. His own safety came first. He would save them for Paris. The tighter his chest felt, the more grateful he was for the cane. He leaned on it, his trigger finger going automatically to the nut-and-bolt mechanism that would allow him to fire at Kendall as he crested the mountain pass. But it was up to Marcus Nash to edge Kendall toward the crowd, putting Kendall within firing range.

He gave a hint of a smile to the girl and then turned to Ryskov. "You were late arriving, Yuri," he said. "What kept you?"

"I made certain that Kendall was well enough to ride today."

The fractional smile cut at the corners of Benak's mouth again. "It won't be long now, Yuri."

"What if something goes wrong? Marcus Nash may not be able to keep up with Kendall. He's never ridden in a race before."

"He's riding well in this one. He spent years riding a bike in the mountains in Bosnia with mortar equipment on his back."

Benak looked down in disgust at the Russian, wondering what cowardice drove him. Or was it fear? He was a reluctant revolutionary. The girl seemed to be listening now. Jiri kept his voice low, confidential. "Once Kendall crashes, it is up to you to call the professor."

"I will use the phone at the chateau."

And while you place your call, Jiri thought, *I will drive away, and you will not see me again. And if you cross me, Ryskov, there is a second pellet in my cane, and I will use it.*

In the broiling heat, the stranger beside Zoe Golemis had chosen to carry a beige trench coat and a walking stick. Zoe had paid little attention to him until she heard him mention the name Ian Kendall. He spoke in an unfamiliar dialect. *Slavic,* she guessed. But the name Kendall came across clear, distinct.

He was attractive, but far too serious, like her brother Thymous. Unlike Thymous, this man's hair was so blond that it looked snow-white; his eyes—whatever their color—were shaded by dark glasses. He was much older than Thymous but still too young to be carrying the Burmese walking stick with its handsome gold handle. He must have sensed her studying him, for he turned now and looked down at her; in spite of the sunglasses, she could see that his eyes were cold and disdainful. As he tossed his trench coat over his shoulder, she felt a hard bulge in its pocket and cringed.

A gun. She was certain the man was carrying a gun.

She inched away, glancing around for a gendarme, but saw Thymous instead pushing his way through the crowd toward her. She tried to tell him about the gun, but Thymous distracted her.

"Have you seen Salvador Contoni?" he asked.

"No, he probably didn't come to this village after all."

"Town," Thymous corrected wearily. "And I don't even know why we came."

Zoe didn't risk telling him that it was Salvador who told her about Nordlune. And she still hadn't found the courage to tell Thymous about her meeting with Ian. Talking about Ian would only open old wounds for her, as seeing him had done.

"Yesterday when I lunched in the gardens, I overheard someone mention Nordlune. I'm glad we came. It's lovely up here, Thymous, so please don't fuss. Don't be disagreeable—"

"I won't," he promised, "but we don't have to stand in the sun. I rented a room in the chateau with a balcony and a coffee urn. It will be an hour or two before the riders reach the pass."

"Long enough for you to call Monique Dupree?" she asked.

His dark eyes flashed. "She refuses to take my calls, Zoe."

She linked her arm with his. "Does she matter to you?"

"A little," he admitted. He squeezed her fingers. "But coming here to France has been harder on you, Zoe. I should never have let you come."

"There was no way to stop me."

As they ran up the steps of the chateau, she looked up at him and realized afresh how handsome he was. Yet his dark eyes were sad—and had been ever since their brother's death. These days Thymous never smiled. She feared he would never smile again.

Salvador Contoni stood behind the steel barricade, his press I.D. badge visible on his lapel. As he waited for the riders to come around that last curve and scale the hill, he opened the box of nails in his hands, his muscles flexing in anticipation as he wrapped his fingers around them. He would throw them. There was nothing to it. It would be like tossing a ball to Anzel Dupree. Sal felt powerful, invincible, like the craggy Pyrenees that rose before him. The mountains were majestic, but to Sal they didn't begin to match the Italian Alps. No, the mountain ranges of his homeland were far more spectacular, the terrain more fierce.

Idly he studied the faces of the Frenchmen and foreigners around him, some of them tipsy with wine after a chilling overnight in the mountains. The Chateau de Arceson lay directly behind them, situated near a fast-flowing river with the mountain road beside it as the only way out of town.

Again his gaze swept the people around him, and he was struck by two men—one a towhead like himself, with a manacle grip on a hand-carved cane; the other gentleman was pasty-skinned, his eyes sunken in a gaunt face. They stood in silence, like strangers, but Sal was certain that they traveled together. His attention had been drawn to them because Zoe Golemis had been standing there beside them. At the sight of Zoe, he shrank behind other spectators. Sal saw no need to strike up yesterday's argument. Zoe had humiliated him in front of the American journalist.

"For all I know," Zoe had said, "he is the one responsible for the bombing on stage eleven."

But he remembered with pleasure Chase Evans's quick defense. "He couldn't be. He was with me."

Because of Chase's loyalty, he no longer wanted to harm Ian Kendall, but he would stop him from winning by filling the narrow road with nails. It didn't matter how many young riders piled up on the mountain curve. Nothing mattered as long as he could puncture Kendall's tires and rob him of that marginal lead that he was clinging to so desperately. Delay him on this stage of the race, and Kendall would lose the chance to ride into Paris in a yellow jersey. Once the loudspeaker announced that the riders were almost to the summit, Salvador would toss his sharp nails on the road and walk away whistling.

What did it matter if Zoe Golemis saw him? She had made a fool of him—and no one ever made a fool of Salvador Contoni.

🕉️ 🕉️ 🕉️

As Ian rode the flat section of the high valley, he battled through his pain, calculating each kilometer in the steep climb to the third mountain pass. He was driven by Chase's promise, "I'll be there when you come over the crest of the mountain."

The blistering sun made him sweat. Or was his feverish body still reaping the toll of twenty-four hours of illness? The sun seemed to melt the tar on the roads and the rubber on his wheels. And yet the mountain air chilled him, sucking at his already blowtorched lungs. His throat felt dry and raw like sandpaper, his legs threatening to cramp.

The first ascent had taken little more than an hour, the wild descent less than twenty minutes. The second summit was another well-fought battle, won in segments with its 6,000 feet of vertical climb; but this legendary pass in front of him towered much higher, with twenty-nine hairpin turns to the top. He did not allow his thoughts to wander toward the finish line nor to think about quitting. Twice he found himself humming "I've Got a Date with an Angel." Even this distracted him, so he pushed the song from his mind, forcing himself to count one kilometer at a time.

❀❀❀

Salvador Contoni's mouth soured. The nails stuck to his clammy palm as the riders winged around that last hairpin turn and hit a straight course toward the peak. There were two Gainsborough riders, Ian Kendall in the lead. Or was it three of them ascending the steep hill as though they were one?

Now, Salvador told himself. *Throw the nails and then split. Get out of here.*

Sal saw the agony on Ian's face, the strain of the ride visible in his eyes. Sweat poured down the athlete's face. The muscles in his legs and arms were wired tight as he pedaled against the wind. The greater the pain, the harder he rode, swaying and lurching his bike to keep his balance.

The cheers were deafening. Flags waved. Bottles were emptied in celebration. Little children screamed without knowing why. Sal dropped the nails back into the box and brushed his damp palm against his trouser leg. He was sweating like the riders.

Something was wrong! One rider pushed hard against Ian, shoving him toward the crowd. The shouting turned to cries of dismay as Kendall grasped his neck and began to ride erratically. Alerted now and Argus-eyed, Sal saw the man with the gold-handled cane lower it to his side. For an instant, his gaze locked contemptuously with Sal's, and then the two men were swallowed up in the crowd. They were leaving. Escaping! The box of nails dropped from Sal's hand and clattered at his ankles. He knew with the instinct of a man bent on survival that he would be blamed for whatever was happening.

❀❀❀

To Ian's left lay the rock wall and a steep drop-off. Every part of his body ached, each breath filled with pain. He drove himself forward, his eyes barely focused on the crest of the mountain. Today's eight-hour stage was too long to have nothing but a thin layer of spandex between his skin and the saddle. He accelerated, riding out of the saddle to relieve the pressure; and then for the last of the long climb he sat toward the back of the seat and pedaled, his arms spread wide to ease his breathing.

Behind him, the peloton rode together along the narrow road; in minutes some of the pack would launch an attack and try to sprint past him. Marcus Nash rode on Ian's wheel, forcing Ian to take the brunt of the wind. Ian flew over the cobbles, trying to out-distance him; finally in sheer exhaustion he dropped to twenty-five kilometers per hour at the steepest incline.

Just ahead he saw the top of the mountain pass, the three rid-ers ahead of him mounting it even now. The crowds were elec-trifying. He accelerated again, borne on by their cheering. Still Nash kept doggedly at his back wheel. He tried to warn Nash off as they sped toward the top, wheel to wheel.

"Get back," he shouted.

Nash kept coming. Suddenly, he swerved toward Kendall, forc-ing Ian toward the crowd.

The jab struck Ian's neck. Stunned him. A violent pain that came from nowhere. The numbing rode down his arm. Tingled his fingers. Cut off his windpipe. He grasped his neck. Nothing. A small welt. Only a drop or two of blood. Sweat poured over his eyes, fogging his wraparound goggles, blurring his vision.

Ian tried to warn Nash off again. Now he could no longer form words. They were descending the mountain, the momentum building. His body crouched over the handlebars, his knees locked in a fixed position. His head spun. He was drifting into darkness. Lurching. Swaying. Veering across the path of the oncoming peloton. And then he saw his grandmother. She seemed to be part of the fleecy clouds, but the face was her own, the radiant smile the one he remembered. She said nothing but simply beckoned to him. And then he was catapulting over the stone wall, soaring like a bird in flight, his body twisting, spin-ning, plunging, his legs and arms flailing like broken wings. He felt his body lurch forward, shudder on impact, and then the light dwindled to darkness, emptiness.

Just before the accident, Drew and Chase had stood in the swel-tering sun, jammed in the flag-waving crowd. Drew knew from "Tour Radio" that a Banesto rider and two men from the Telekom team were in the lead. A six-man breakaway had launched an attack on their wheels, Ian Kendall and Marcus Nash among them. According to the commentator, the men rode with only seconds dividing them.

The roar of the crowd turned boisterous. The deafening shout of the fans came simultaneously with the riders scaling the top of the pass. Drew raised his fist in a triumphant thrust toward the sky and said, "Here they come, Chase."

For an instant the cycles skimmed above the surface of the narrow mountain road, bounced, and were riding rubber to rubber again, building momentum as they raced down the mountain. Drew recognized the lead riders: Mario wearing the polka dot jersey in this stage of the journey; Nicholas the Greek riding in his first Tour de France; and Conan, the Irishman, expressionless as he rode by. Behind them came Ian and Marcus Nash and, surprisingly, Orlando Gioceppi, the Italian whose friendship with Ian was back into full swing. The rest of the Gainsborough team were nowhere to be seen, struggling no doubt in the pack not yet coming over the hill. Nash was like a wild card, a last-minute selection to the team, still riding Ian's back wheel, laughing, jeering. Now they rode side by side, shoulder to shoulder.

"Drew," Chase cried, "he's forcing Ian into the crowd."

Drew was still beating the air with his fist when Ian's bike jerked out of control. He stifled the soundless, sickening fear in his throat as bike and rider veered erratically across the road in front of the oncoming peloton. Ian tugged at Nash's hand before his own bike slammed wildly into the stone wall.

For an instant it remained airborne, and then bike and rider disappeared down the sun-splashed cliff. Silence. Dead silence before the screams erupted around Drew, Chase's cry jarring, earsplitting. More cries meshed with hers as a pileup of young bodies and bikes scraped the gravel. Photographers emerged from among the fans. Bulbs flashed. Video cameras rolled.

Nash smashed his bare hand into one of the cameras as he waited for the team mechanic to replace his cycle. Then he rode off, not even giving a fragmented glance at the cliff where the medical staff was already scrambling down the slope toward Ian.

"We're family," Drew told the gendarme as he and Chase broke through the police barrier and dashed across the road. He kept his hand tight on her icy fingers as they vaulted over the stone wall.

They could see Ian's twisted body lying down the mountainside, his bike in ruins a few yards from him.

"Wait here, Chase," Drew told her.

But she kept stumbling down the rocky cliff behind him. Midway down, she grabbed an overhanging tree limb and hung on. "I can't go," she cried. "I'm frightened."

He knuckled her chin and stumbled on, slipping and sliding over the rocks and bracing his own fall with the heels of his hands. Ian's body was battered, his face bloody. Thatches of red hair poked out from his high-tech cycling helmet and fell across his forehead. The bloody bare fingers of his hands lay limp. Brad O'Malloy and Dr. Raunsted were already kneeling beside Ian, Raunsted with a stethoscope in his ears. O'Malloy offered a sympathetic nod to Drew.

As Drew called Ian's name, Ian gasped and lay still.

Raunsted yanked the helmet free, exposing a raw red gash beneath Ian's chin—and a round two-millimeter puncture mark on his neck. As Raunsted initiated CPR, the rescue helicopter hovered above them.

Drew didn't even try to forestall the tears as a flood of memories swept over him. A scrawny kid on a swing. An awkward schoolboy dropping ice cream on the red leather seat of Drew's car. Ian with his beloved grandmother. Ian with Uriah. Ian and Chase and the dreams that were ending. And now this. Drew couldn't watch. He stared down instead at the Giro helmet and the white sheet of paper that had fallen beside it. He picked it up, startled at the frightening message it contained:

> Benak foiled plans. Moscow alerted. Advise General Noukov. Will attempt to salvage project in Paris. Meet Parkovitch there.

He caught O'Malloy's eye and handed the note to him. "Go with Ian—and get this to Carwell in Paris."

"Is it important?"

"It may have cost Ian his life. Awhile ago Chase told me she thought she saw Jiri Benak in the crowd, and I brushed it off."

As the helicopter lowered, Drew bent down and touched Ian's limp hand once more. Drew turned and brushed shoulders with

Radburn Parker. As their eyes held, Drew calculated, remembered, condemned—and wondered. Within inches from where Parker stood, Drew saw the fingerless glove caught beneath the rear wheel of the twisted bike, a different-colored glove than the ones Ian wore. It had been torn, ripped from its rider's hand. Drew stowed it in his pocket and dug his way back up the cliff to Chase.

She was still clinging to the overhanging limb. Frozen. Frightened. "I must go with Ian," she said.

Drew pressed her head against his shoulder. "Don't look anymore," he told her gently. "Just remember Ian the way you saw him yesterday. That's the way he'd want you to remember him."

Chapter 22

Only seconds, moments, an eternity for Salvador Contoni. He stood transfixed, detached, riveted to the mountain as though he had been impaled on the slopes of Nordlune by the very nails he had intended to throw across Ian Kendall's path. Confusion! Hysteria! The crowd was breaking up, many surging toward the descending side of the mountain. Their frenzy startled Sal. He was galvanized, electrified. Driven by his own need to escape, he bolted toward the chateau in pursuit of the two strangers—the pasty-skinned man and the one with the golden hand-carved cane.

As he ran, someone cried above the din, "Stop him."

Hands reached out ripping the sleeve of Sal's jacket, tearing at his polo shirt, grabbing at his skipper's cap. He wrestled for his freedom. "You idiots," he said in Italian. "You have the wrong man."

An angry woman tore the press card from his lapel. What did it matter? Salvador Salatori did not exist! A muscled young man jumped him, tugging Sal to the ground. In the brief time since he had dropped the nails, the shouting on the other side of the mountain had turned to piercing cries. Sal was forgotten, the hold on his shoulders loosened.

He ran toward the chateau parking lot, determined to be on the narrow mountain road before someone else attacked him. *Paris. Freedom. Monique.* As he reached in his pocket for the car keys, he saw the stranger—the taller one with the gold-handled cane aimed at him. The man was like marble standing there, his expression cold like the rocks around them.

Salvador ducked down and crawled like a child on his belly, his heart pumping wildly. He tried to reach up with his hand to unlock the car door, but he sensed the man creeping closer.

"Jiri." The call came from the chateau. "Jiri!"

The cane lowered. The steps that had dogged Sal retreated as the man sprinted toward his friend. Salvador lay motionless on the ground. Their car accelerated, wheels screeching as the driver put distance between them. Then came another cry, the same despairing voice by the chateau. "Jiri, don't go without me."

Salvador rolled over, facedown, and used the palms of his hands to push himself cautiously to a standing position. Stark fear gnawed at his gut. He needed a drink, needed something to steady himself before he faced that drive down the mountain. But did he dare follow so closely behind the stranger? The man could be waiting for Salvador on the next hairpin curve, waiting with his finger on the firing mechanism. Sal leaned down and retrieved his skipper's cap and dusted himself off. *The drink.* He would go inside the chateau and calmly order a drink. He cocked his cap on his head and forced himself to assume his usual jaunty stride as he entered the chateau and made his way briskly into the bar.

"Did you hear?" the bartender asked. "They just lifted one of the riders out by helicopter." He pointed to the radio wedged in among the rows of glasses. "Dead, they say."

"Ian Kendall?"

"No name released yet. But there is more than one rider down. Big pileup."

Sal ordered a whiskey and took it straight down. He plunked the glass on the counter and without a word between them, the bartender filled two whiskey glasses, and they drank in silence.

Sal feared that whatever had happened out there would be blamed on him. He shrank back from the icy tentacles clawing at his gut. He felt trapped with nowhere to run, nowhere to hide. He would go back to Milan, home to Mama as he had done as a small boy and find comfort in those strong arms—and he would ask Monique to go with him. But would Monique condemn him for the accident here on the mountain without ever knowing the truth?

He feared the Golemis family as well. They would read the

headlines and see the accident on television with news reporters blowing everything out of proportion. If Golemis had stooped to hiring Sal to stop Kendall from winning the Tour de France, what would prevent Golemis from hiring someone else to eliminate Salvador?

He wanted to phone Monique. "I have to make a phone call," he told the bartender, and his words were calm, decisive.

The bartender went on polishing a glass to a crystal-clear shine. "Phone on the wall," he said, "if that man over there is through with it."

Sal allowed a sweeping glance of the room over the brim of his glass. The man with the pasty skin sat at a corner table, staring down at the wine goblet in his hand. When Sal reached the phone, the receiver was off the hook, the cord dangling.

He snatched it up and heard an angry voice on the other end demanding, "Yuri Ryskov. Yuri Ryskov, are you there?"

An odd accent, Sal thought, *and the crackling, wavering sounds of a poor connection. Not French, definitely not French.* The words were shouted this time, "Yuri Ryskov."

Sal hung the receiver in place, silencing the growing fury of the man on the other end. He walked slowly to the corner table. "Yuri Ryskov?" he asked as he took the seat across from him. He could see that Ryskov was carrying a weapon, a Russian model 9mm, but he was too distraught to aim it. "My name is Salvador Contoni," Sal said. "I believe we can help each other."

Ryskov's eyes looked like sunken holes in his gaunt face; the skin stretched too tightly over the bony cheeks. An empty goblet and a half bottle of wine sat on the table in front of him, but he was not drunk. Ryskov belched without apology, and the stench of garlic and onions blew across the table at Sal.

You are not just frightened, Sal thought, *you are ill.*

"What do you want?" Ryskov asked.

"I saw your friend in the crowd—the one with the gold-handled cane. Perhaps we should have a drink together," Sal suggested.

Ryskov winced, blinked, and filled his glass again. "Shall we drink to bombs?" he asked. "And Red Square bathed in blood? The death of fans and riders won't stop."

The man's accent was Russian. He rambled on. "My friend went off without me. . . . Are you American?"

"No," Sal said. "Italian."

"Benak won't stop. He'll meet the others in Paris."

"Someone wanted you on the phone, Ryskov."

Ryskov's gaze veered away. "Is Professor Ivanski still waiting?" he asked.

Ivanski. Sal tucked the name away. "I severed the connection."

Ryskov tilted his third glass of wine. "Professor Ivanski. Bombs. Death. Paris. Red Square. It won't stop."

If Ryskov was joking, Salvador wasn't laughing. Sal stood. "I'm leaving," he said.

"Take me with you," Ryskov begged. "I need to get to Paris."

So do I, Sal thought. *To Monique's condominium on the River Seine.* But he would stay out of sight for a day or two in Bordeaux. Rest. Wait. Have the car checked. Once the Tour passed through Bordeaux, he would move on. "I'm driving toward Paris in a day or two," he said. "Would that help?"

Yuri Ryskov wiped his mouth and shoved his goblet aside. "I want to go to the American embassy."

So Sal had a defector on his hands. The man was crazy. Beside himself. "To the Avenue Gabriel? Why there?" Sal asked.

A glint of hope lit the dark eyes. "I want to be free," Ryskov told him.

🏺🏺🏺

As the helicopter airlifted Ian Kendall's battered body above the slopes of Nordlune, Radburn Parker made his way back up the sheer cliff behind Gregory. He allowed a safe distance between them, unwilling to face the man head-on. Silently, Parker was counting his losses, chalking up his advantages.

As Parker mounted the stone wall, Maurice Chambord met him. "I think we lost him, Chambord," Parker said.

The Frenchman's mouth twitched. He turned and led the way to his official red car. For three days, Parker had ridden in style with Chambord, sitting beside the tour director and hearing first-hand reports on the race and its riders. He had become the confidant to Chambord, commiserating with him on the terrorist threats and advising Chambord to keep a sharp eye on Gregory.

Now they rode in silence for miles, Chambord drumming his fingers on the window—waiting for the cellular phone to ring.

"Maurice, what happens if—"

"If he dies?" Chambord asked coldly. "I will have to announce it over the 'Radio Tour.'"

"It has happened before," Parker said.

"Does that make it any easier? They were all good men. Francesco Cepeda sixty years ago. And Tom Simpson and Fabio Casartelli. I was there for that one."

"What about Ottavio Bottecchia?" Parker asked.

"His death was different. And there have always been the accidents. Men missing the twists and turns on the road. Some plunging over the cliffs in the mist—one paralyzed for life."

"There was no mist today, Chambord."

"I know. I know."

Parker lapsed into another silence, calculating, recalculating. He was safest in the car with Chambord, the shiny red car like a wall of protection for him. Always before, Parker had used humor to work his way through difficult situations. But this was no time to joke, not with Kendall's life hanging in the balance. But the truth was, Radburn wanted Kendall dead. It would be one less worry when he reached Paris. For now he fretted, wondering whether Yuri Ryskov had sent the signal to Moscow. He kept hoping that the commentator on "Radio Tour" would interrupt the program with the announcement of a successful coup in Moscow—and Professor Ivanski's triumphant entry into Red Square.

At dawn Parker had placed a long distance call to Ivanski's residence. A stranger had answered, not the professor. And not that housekeeper of his. Perhaps just a friend, but it had been a brusque, authoritative voice, saying, "The professor is not in."

Radburn closed his eyes as he pressed his head against the cushioned seat. *Had the professor fled?* he wondered. He must know. Otherwise, he dared not risk flying to Moscow to join him. He still had two tickets for the morning after the race, first class out of Charles de Gaulle. One for himself. One for Benak. But where was the Czechoslovakian at this moment? Other than Ivanski, only three men knew that Radburn was part of the uprising. If Ryskov or the Czechoslovakian or the Serbian rider on the Gainsborough team betrayed him, he would execute them.

Radburn Parker! A good name. A well-established reputation in London. A man acquainted with the royal family and some of the hierarchy in British Intelligence. He would maintain these privileges at all costs, suppressing his own political views if he had to. Yes, if their plan failed, Parkovitch would slip into anonymity, but Radburn Parker could still go back to London and hold his head high. He might even get back in time to see Lennie Applegate arrested and put on trial. And he would most certainly soak up the sympathy extended to him as the financial arm behind the Gainsborough team and its lost rider.

The cellular phone rang. Chambord didn't move. *Answer it, you fool,* Parker thought. *It might be good news.* Yes, the death of Ian Kendall would be good news to Parker.

Chapter 23

Washington, D.C. As Grover Kendall crossed the Maryland line into Washington, his cellular phone rang. He put his coffee cup down and answered it. The hysterical voice on the other end had to be calmed. "Jill, what is it?" he asked sharply.

"We've got to get to Aubrey," she cried. "Before someone else tells him."

"Tells him what, Jill?"

"There's been a horrible accident at the Tour. Oh, Grover, the news commentator said—"

"What, Jill? Tell me."

"Ian is dead."

Grover's car swerved, spilling his coffee over the leather seat. He gripped the wheel, struggling to steady himself. Cradling the phone, he groped for the knob, trying to tune in the news station. Static. Nothing. Music. Everything. Everything but what he wanted.

"Grover, say something."

"You're certain?" he demanded of his stepmother.

"I'm not sure of anything. I pray there's been a mistake. Oh, Grover, your father left for work at dawn. We've got to get to him before he hears it from someone else."

"It won't change his work schedule," Grover said bitterly.

"Don't say that. You know this will break your father's heart. Are you going to help me or aren't you?"

"I'm on my way."

"I'll shower and dress and come, too."

"Drive carefully," he admonished as he roared down the off-ramp and rerouted his vehicle back toward Maryland.

He was sweating, speeding when the news station repeated the story. "Tragedy has struck the Tour de France again. . . . The American cyclist Ian Kendall is believed dead. . . ."

Grover worked out the time difference between the Pyrenees and Maryland. The accident had occurred hours ago. Why hadn't they been notified? Why the delay? Dead. His brother. That kid brother who lived for cycling. *No, Ian,* he cried. *This was to be your big win.*

For the second time in two weeks, he pulled the Jaguar into his dad's construction site. His hands felt frozen to the steering wheel. July, and he felt cold inside, lifeless, sick—the way he did the time he fell into the Delaware River in the middle of winter. Ian had screamed from the riverbank, "Don't die, Grover. Dad will be mad at you."

"Don't die, Ian," he cried. "Dad will be mad at you."

Grover felt dead inside, dead like his brother. He parked by the edge of the yellow ribbon.

"Move on," a worker warned. "This spot ain't for parking."

"Where's Mr. Kendall?"

There was a generalized wave of the man's hand. Grover stepped defiantly from the car and plunged forward—past the piles of lumber, the gravel hills, the rows of iron rods.

He found Aubrey high on the scaffolding, fearlessly balancing on a two-foot plank. The sun had freckled his father's face even more, its blistering rays turning that full mustache to a golden hue. Without benefit of a hard hat, Grover shaded his eyes and called, "Dad, I need to talk to you."

"It's a busy time, son. Call me this evening."

A man sauntered by with a crackling portable radio. He turned toward Grover. "Did you hear the news? The boss's son—"

Grover tore the radio from the worker's hand and snapped it off. "I'll tell him," he said.

"Okay. Okay. Have it your own way."

Grover squinted up at his dad again. Aubrey stood on the edge of the plank, youthful in spite of his forty-six years, one hand in his jeans pocket, the company name Kendall Construction emblazoned on his polo shirt.

"Dad, it's important," Grover said.

Aubrey saluted him with an empty coffee cup. "Then climb up here and get it off your chest."

Grover calculated the distance between the scaffolding and the mounds of gravel on the ground. He couldn't risk his father falling if he told him now. Behind him a car door slammed, and Jill's soft voice asked, "Grover, have you told him yet?"

"Not yet."

"Jill. Jill, what are you doing here?" Aubrey stared down at them, his face beneath his hard hat visibly shaken. "It's Dad, isn't it?" he asked.

He began working his way down, one hand on the ladder, the other on his cup. His muscular body moved with the speed of a bobcat on a reverse run. As his feet hit the ground, he turned and faced them, his probing eyes an intense blue like Ian's. As he searched their faces, the coffee cup slipped from his hand and shattered on the rock pile. His red-freckled face turned ashen. "Has something happened to Dad?" he asked.

Jill fell into his arms weeping before Grover had time to whisper, "It's not Gramps, Dad. It's Ian."

Long Island, New York. Ten minutes after Nola Evans fell asleep, Seymour's snoring awakened her. She came to with a start, her body in a cold sweat in spite of the summer heat wave that had hit the east coast. She poked Seymour. For a moment the room went quiet, terrifying her even more as she thought of the children. Shivering, she slipped out of bed and into her robe and went into her dressing room to phone.

"Tad, are you all right?" she asked as her son answered.

"Mom, it's midnight. Of course, I'm all right."

"I called earlier this evening."

He laughed. "Checking up on me? I had a heavy date. Nice blonde. Just got in—haven't even showered yet."

Nola could hear the water running. "Are you alone, Tad?"

"Not lately."

"I think I'll call Adele."

"Talked to that old thing a couple hours ago about a legal matter. She's her old self. Almost bit my head off. So your little flock is just fine. How's Chase?"

"I was hoping she had written to you."

"Chase and me? We don't keep in touch. She's probably cooped up in some library corner. That's not my style."

"No, Tad. She went to the Tour de France." She hesitated. "As a journalist."

"That's a laugh. Didn't think she could get her head out of the books long enough for something practical and fun."

Nola went limp. Would the children never come to terms? Never speak kindly of each other? The sound of running water in Tad's bathroom ceased. She knew that Tad was not alone.

"Good night, son," she said.

"Hey, Mom. Tell the old man I'd like to go sailing this Saturday. Hope he doesn't need the boat."

"Your father is not an old man."

"Sorry, sweetheart."

"Tad, make your own arrangements with your father."

Nola went back to the bedroom and paced, finally stopping by the wall where the portraits of the children hung. She couldn't see their faces in the darkness, but she knew they had been happy, spoiled children. Seymour had always demanded more of them than they could give. She had never demanded enough. Three spoiled children. Three self-centered adults. What kind of selfish monsters had they reared? Adele haughty and thoughtless, never calling. Tad slipping from one unstable relationship to another with no regrets over a failed marriage. And sweet, caring Chase traipsing around the world chasing after the wind—this time chasing a young cyclist born with the wind against him. Her sigh was so deep it felt like a chest pain. Dear, dear Chase. She would always be special to Nola and worth defending.

The bedside clock glowed in the darkness, its hands moving toward 3:15. Nola felt lightheaded, exhausted from lack of sleep. Pacing back to the window, she stared into the night sky, willing it to streak with dawn. She wanted morning to come and disperse the shadows—wanted the alarm to awaken Seymour. She needed him. She knew that something had happened to Chase.

It was 3:30 when Seymour's own snoring awakened him. "Nola," he said groggily, "what are you doing over there?"

"Praying that you'd wake up so I wouldn't feel so alone."

"I'm here. What's wrong? Is it your hot flashes again?"

"It's Chase. Something has happened to Chase."

He practically fell out of bed trying to reach her. As his arms went around her, she cried, "Oh, Seymour, I've been awake all night just worrying about her. I know she's in trouble."

He pulled back and laughed. "Nola, she's always in trouble."

"That's not true."

He stood there in his rumpled pajamas and bare feet, his uncombed hair making him look boyish. In the youthfulness she saw Chase. The two of them were so much alike, so often at odds.

Amusement replaced his grogginess. "By now she's marching in Piccadilly Circus on behalf of a British labor union. No, that wouldn't be right. This month she's tooting around France." His chest vibrated with his chuckle. "Give her time, Nola dear, and she'll hook a ride with one of those cyclists right into Paris."

He led Nola to the bed and turned on the bedside lamp. "Sit down, honey. I'm going to make us a pot of tea."

"I'm not thirsty."

"I am. I need a drink before I call the American ambassador in Paris. I'm going to tell him you need to get back to sleep."

"You can't get the ambassador out of bed at this hour."

"Why not? We're friends. I met him at the White House on his last trip to Washington. Besides, there's a time difference. Four here. At least mid-morning there. He'll know where the Tour is." He knuckled her chin. "Chase will be all right."

As Nola waited, the room felt suffocating. Still she shivered. Her bloodshot eyes burned from the winds blowing in from the Long Island Sound. She hugged her body trying to calm herself as Seymour came back to the room.

He framed the doorway, suddenly unable to come across the room to her. "I forgot your tea," he said.

For a second she thought her heart had quit beating. Now it raced uncontrollably. "Seymour, what did the ambassador say?"

It didn't look like Seymour standing there. It didn't sound like him when he spoke. "Chase's young man—that cyclist—has just met with a tragic accident. He was killed . . . yesterday . . . today. I don't know exactly with the time change."

Nola gripped her pillow and rocked on the edge of the bed. Chase was all right. Tad. Adele. Her children were alive. But she felt as if one of her own children had just been ripped from her. "Ian?" she cried. "Not Ian Kendall?" When Seymour didn't answer, she said, "Poor Chase. We've got to go to her, Seymour."

"It's not like catching the subway, Nola." His hands ran frantically through his thick gray hair. "I can't get away. We have a deadline on a government contract."

She wanted to slap him. To throw the pillow at him. To disown him. "I hate your job," she said, her voice rising. "It's driven wedges between us before, but never like this. Chase needs us, Seymour Evans. Do you hear me?" She was screaming now. "For once in your life forget that job and think of your family."

"Honey, stop yelling. Think of the neighbors," he warned. "Your daughter is all right."

"Chase may have just had her heart torn out, Seymour. Doesn't that matter to you?"

His hand went unsteadily to the dresser top. "I'm so sorry, Nola, but there's no way to get in touch with Chase. We don't have the racing schedule. We don't know where she's staying. Cities. Villages. Who knows where?"

"The press room," she said, her voice quieting. "There has to be a central place for the journalists."

"I'll have my secretary check."

"No, Seymour. Just this once, do it yourself." She held out her arms. "Chase needs you. . . . I need you."

He came across the room, his hands like ice as he touched her. "I promise you, Nola, I'll turn Europe upside down to locate her." He would, she knew. She felt his tears against her cheek. "Do you think she really cared about him?" he asked.

"I think she loved him, Seymour."

It was time for Seymour to get ready for work, but he kept on holding her. "I'll make reservations for the first flight out to Paris. We will find our daughter, Nola, and comfort her." He smiled grimly. "Or there will be the devil to pay."

❀❀❀

On the island of Corfu, Vasille Golemis was overcome with grief. Unconfirmed media reports indicated that the American rider had died in a tragic accident on the mountainside. He knew better. He snapped off the radio. The villa sitting room never seemed darker, even with all the sunlight flooding through the windows. His legs buckled as he made his way around the room, forcing him to clutch the chairs until he reached his desk.

He lifted his face to his son's portrait. Alekos! The thick lips seemed pursed to speak, but Vasille clapped his ears, dreading his son's condemnation. For a moment he wished that the sea behind Alekos would wash the portrait away and take the reproving look in those dark eyes away forever. *Forever.* That's how long his son would be gone. That's how long Ian Kendall would be gone. He reached up and tried to yank the portrait from the wall.

"Don't, Vasille. It would not change things."

His wife's ponderous steps came up behind him. He turned to face her. She looked straight at him as she had always done.

"Molly and Marcella have gone, Vasille," she said.

"Because of me?"

"Molly is going home because her husband needs her."

"I need you, Olympia." He wanted her to smile, to hold him against that massive bosom of hers, to put her chin against his shoulder. She made no effort to come to him.

He had to make her understand. "You were here when I hired Salvador Contoni to stop Kendall from winning."

"And I told you it would dishonor your son's name."

"Olympia, I didn't hire Contoni to kill Ian Kendall."

When she answered, her voice was barely a whisper. "But you chose a man who thought nothing of killing."

"I was wrong." Her gaze never faltered. He weakened under it. Looking around, he said, "I wish Thymous were here."

"He is in France with Zoe."

"I know. They are there against my wishes."

"They wanted to stop Mr. Contoni from harming Alekos's friend . . . but obviously they were too late."

Vasille stared at his wife. "What have I done?" he asked her. "What have I done?"

"You have had your revenge. That should comfort you."

He palmed his hands to his cheeks, the tips of his mustache touching them. "Forgive me, Olymbia. Forgive me."

As she opened her mouth, her crooked front tooth caught at her lip. "You are asking the wrong person for forgiveness." She lifted the shawl from her shoulder and formed a crown around her head, highlighting her sad, empty eyes.

"Where are you going?" he asked.

"To church. To pray."

His legs went wobbly. "Take me with you, Olymbia."

She shrugged indifferently. "Why now, Vasille? You have not entered the church for years."

"Then surely it is time for me to go." His knuckles went white as he pressed his hands against the desk. "Please, Olymbia, take me with you. I cannot bear to be alone."

Now she allowed herself to look up at her son's portrait. Vasille saw her tears brim over and watched helplessly as she dabbed at them with the corner of her shawl. "He was so young," she said. "So alive—like Ian Kendall. But perhaps they are together now. That would be a blessing."

As she turned back to Vasille, the hard glint in her eyes softened. "Come, Vasille. Alekos would never want us to be at odds." She held out her hand, and he took three halting steps toward her to grasp her fingers.

🦉🦉🦉

In Isigny Monique Dupree and her father stared at the television as the unconfirmed media reports echoed through the farmhouse. They kept their eyes fastened on the screen as the scene was repeated over and over. The pileup. The injuries. And the helicopter lifting and carrying the young man's body with it. Her father's face was troubled, creased with wrinkles, suddenly old. He pointed to the screen. "There—there. Look, Monique."

She panicked. Had he seen Salvador among the fans? "Turn it off. Turn it off," she begged.

"That rider beside Kendall—who is he?"

She forced herself to look again. "They all look alike."

"His name, Monique. You have watched this race every day. What is that man's name—the one riding closest to Kendall?"

"Marcus Nash," she whispered. "He was a last-minute replacement on the British team."

"He caused that accident."

"Oh, *pere*," she cried. "I begged Sal not to get involved."

He gripped her arms. "Salvador Contoni? What do you mean?"

She shrank away from her father's grip, cold, numbing fear paralyzing her. Her father shook her, his lined face scornful, his voice harsh as he said, "Speak up. What about Contoni?"

"He—he was hired—hired to stop Kendall—any way he could."

"You knew this?" Her father's face turned purple with rage. "You knew and you didn't stop him?"

"How could I? He has been good to me—good to my sons."

"Oh, Monique, you are such a foolish woman. We thought you had learned your lessons with Harland Smith. But you grow more like him every day. . . . You won't change. You will never change. You are a disgrace to all of us, a failure to your sons."

As he reached for the phone, her fingernails dug into his wrist. "*Pere*, what are you doing?"

"I'm calling that American in Paris. What was his name? The American—the man I tried to frighten off the farm."

Her lip trembled. "Gregory. Drew Gregory."

"He may not be in Paris, Grandpa."

They whirled around. Anzel stood in the door, his boyish face taut, his body wispy-thin, his eyes staring coldly at them.

"Then who do I ask for, Anzel? Someone who can speak French. Someone who will listen to this poor peasant."

"Tell him, *Maman*," Anzel told her, his tone high-pitched. "If you and my friend Sal are in trouble, tell my *grandpere*."

Monique's gaze went back to her father. She was losing Anzel. Losing Salvador. "Mr. Carwell. Troy Carwell." Her father waited, his eyes demanding more. "He's the head of the American CIA in Paris. Their station-chief. The man over Mr. Gregory."

Strands of thin gray hair fell across her father's forehead as he dialed. He shoved blindly at them, his voice crackling as he said, "It is my duty to call. You won't, Monique, but Monsieur Carwell will want a full description of Salvador Contoni."

"Please, Father. Don't. I can't risk being involved. What if something happens to me? Please think of the boys."

He stared across the room and held out his hand to Anzel. "I am thinking of them, Monique."

"Salvador promised me not to come back here. Ever."

"But you will go to him. To Paris. Milan. Greece. Where will it be this time, Monique?"

"It does not matter, *grandpere*," Anzel said as he crossed the room. "Giles and I will be safe here with you."

🌀🌀🌀

In London Lennie Applegate stared in horror at the television screen as Ian Kendall careened wildly toward the stone wall. And then he was airborne, his body and bicycle soaring over the wall and spiraling down out of sight.

The riders kept coming. Three of them racing together. A pack of six behind them. The peloton in the distance. One by one they crashed, a massive pileup of young bodies and cycles. Fifteen at least. For a second even the commentator said nothing. Thousands of fans stood gawking, speechless. Lennie screamed, breaking the stillness of her quiet neighborhood. And then a second later, panic and bedlam erupted on that road in France. Lennie's eyes remained fixed on the television. Motorcycles and bicycles. Team cars and fans. Others were scaling the wall and disappearing out of sight as they scrambled down toward Kendall. The cameraman swung away from the wall and zoomed in on the twisted cycles and on the young faces contorted with pain.

Lennie clasped her mouth, shutting off the scream that tore at her throat. Only moments before the accident, she had seen her nephew pull up, pedaling furiously alongside of Kendall as they crested the steep mountain. She saw the astonishment on Kendall's face turn to shock as Marcus edged him toward the crowd. The cameras were on them as they took the descent at fifty miles an hour. A second later Kendall reached out to ward off Marcus's attack. Kendall's bike began to weave. Just before the impact, he made a dramatic effort to correct his wheel as he veered across the path of the oncoming peloton.

As Lennie's nephew descended the mountain, his wheel locked with the rider ahead of him. Marcus skidded out of control. She watched in alarm as he fell, his leg scraping across the surface of the road. As he crawled out from under his twisted bike and stood, the cameraman caught a close-up of the fury on Marcus's face. He adjusted his helmet, his mood as black as his hair. As he brushed the dust from his hands, she noticed the missing glove and cringed for the pain he must be feeling with gravel embedded in his palm. He exchanged cycles with one of the team mechanics and rode off as others lay bleeding. And then—as Lennie brushed the tears from her eyes—the camera switched from Marcus, swept once more over the pileup behind him, and panned down the mountain to the limp body of Ian Kendall.

Marcus. Why, Marcus? Is winning that important to you that you can ride away and not look back at Ian Kendall? She had been so proud to have her nephew riding on the Gainsborough team, and now the love she had felt for Marcus turned to loathing.

Lennie backed away from the television and called in sick for the third time in her embassy employment. She sounded sick. She felt sick. Nausea welled up from deep inside her. Her temples throbbed. The receptionist said, "But, Miss Applegate, I have you listed as coming in late after a medical appointment."

I changed my mind, Lennie thought, and for the third time in ten days, she said, "I am having trouble with my eye."

"You're alone. Do you want me to call the doctor for you?"

"No."

"Should I give Brianna Wilson a jingle?"

Brianna? No. "I am quite all right. I just need rest. I want to put a cold pack to my eye." *Don't you understand?* she wondered. *My eyelids are swollen from crying. There's been an accident—a horrible accident.*

"I worry about you, Miss Applegate. Ever since the other—"

Lennie still cringed over that humiliating exodus from Mr. Fairway's office strapped to a stretcher. The laser treatment at the hospital had stopped the hemorrhage, but she would have permanent cloudiness in that eye.

"Let me send someone to be with you."

Lennie dropped the receiver in place. As she hung up the phone, she glanced through the crack in the lace curtain and stared out the front window. Mr. Fairway already had a man on duty. The same man was there again this morning. Watching. Observing. Keeping her under surveillance. Should she burn the memo in her briefcase? No, it no longer mattered. Radburn had called her from France and asked her, no, demanded that she take one more memorandum—the one that would clear his name. Not hers.

She considered going out to the country to her parents' home, out where there was no television, but even there she would be followed. Behind her the radio and television blared out the news again, the commentator's grave voice saying, "The helicopter bearing the body of Ian Kendall—"

Dead! He's dead? Someday it would be her name on the lips of the journalists. But not yet. Right now it was Ian Kendall's moment to be remembered. She tried to remember him coming to the embassy to see Mr. Gregory, a handsome young man with sandy red hair. But she couldn't fill in Ian's features. It was as though they had been blotted out when his cycle crashed over the stone barrier in the Pyrenees Mountains.

Chapter 24

In Paris Miriam Gregory and Maggie Carwell spent the afternoon browsing in one of the elegant couture shops just off the Champs Elysees. Collette's Couture Shoppe was scented with Chanel No 5 and mirrored on three sides, giving the room depth. One corner was comfortably arranged with two blue velvet wing chairs, a bound volume of the latest fashions on the table between them.

The instant they walked through the door, the manager rushed up, hands outstretched. Within minutes she was showing them the fall evening dresses in baldacin and crepe de chine and the last of the summer sheaths in the brightest of colors. The racks bulged with the latest fashions, feminine and overpriced. Maggie insisted on trying on everything that caught her fancy. They giggled like schoolgirls, the saleslady standing patiently by, confident that Maggie would not go away empty-handed. Finally she made her selections.

As she waited for her parcel, Maggie tried on another dress and was examining herself in the mirror when the door was thrust open, jarring the usual lilting melody of the chimes. In the mirror they could see Troy Carwell striding briskly toward them.

"Maggie, put that dress back on the rack and go home."

"I have to change first, darling," she said lightly.

Troy did not smile but said sternly, "Change then—and go home and wait for me. I must talk to Miriam alone."

"Drew?" Miriam gasped. "Has something happened to Drew?"

As Maggie darted into the curtained dressing room, Troy

reached out and steadied Miriam. "We have to talk," he said, spiriting her out of the shop.

Outside, she saw the long gray embassy limousine waiting by the curb, a small flag fluttering from the chrome ornament. She stopped. "I won't go another step until you tell me. Is it Drew?"

His face was ashen. "Drew is all right. It's young Kendall. There's been an accident in the Pyrenees."

He propelled her toward the car. She moved, her legs numb as the embassy driver opened the door for her.

"To St. Mercy Hospital," Troy told the driver.

Not to the morgue. Then Ian was still alive. She dared to hope, to pray. She fell against the seat back, her eyes closed as though she could block out what was happening. Troy comforted her with his hand gently over hers. She opened her eyes again and fixed her gaze on the fine red hairs on his hand. "I'm ready," she said. "Tell me."

He squeezed her fingers. "The news media already announced the accident, but within an hour they will report a fatality from that tragedy in the mountains." His grip tightened. "Several were involved. Only Ian careened over the parapet."

"Was it bad?"

"They almost lost Ian twice en route to the hospital. Once there, we arranged for an immediate medi-evac on to Paris."

Her furtive glance went to the tinted bullet-proof window and then back to Troy. "You took a chance moving him," she said.

"The plane was fully equipped, trained staff on board. We feared a spinal injury or, worse, head trauma. We had to get Ian to a place where he'd get the best medical attention available."

She shuddered.

"We had to move him, Miriam. The news media reported that Ian's body was transferred to London."

"They think Ian is—dead?"

She fought her old revulsion of the CIA. The Agency was controlling a dying boy. She pulled her hand from Troy's and pressed her eyes to keep the tears from coming. "Is the news media in on your deception?"

"No. We just want the terrorists to think he's dead—"

His words sank in. "Then it wasn't an accident, Troy?"

"No. Ian's status is very guarded. His grandfather insisted that the family needs you. We had no choice but to involve you."

"And Ian's father and brother?"

"Aubrey and Grover are flying in early in the morning." He crossed his lanky legs, his cap-toed oxfords polished to a shine. "We are keeping the truth from them until they arrive."

"That is cruel, Troy. Aubrey is flying here expecting to take his son's body home? How could you be so cruel?" She glared at him. "What about Nedrick Russelmann? Is he with Uriah?"

"Uriah's stepgrandson? He won't leave Uriah's side."

"He may when Aubrey gets here," she cautioned. "Aubrey and Nedrick never got on well."

Troy reached up and spread strands of gray across his bald spot. Miriam felt overpowered by the scent of his cologne and knew that always in the future when she thought of this day and the tragedy on the mountain, she would remember the smell of Tiffany and hate it.

As the driver switched lanes, Troy said, "Kendall may not make it out of surgery." He touched her hand again. "We can only hope Ian lives long enough to reach the recovery room—long enough for his father to reach his bedside."

"Have you told Drew?"

"Not yet. We saw no need—"

"Of course not," she snapped. "Hold the truth from him, and he'll stay with the race and come up with answers for you."

Troy nodded, his face still ashen. "And now who is being cruel?" he asked. "Not knowing may keep your husband alive."

She quieted, forcing the words, "And the girl? Dear Chase. We have to send for her. She will want to be with Ian."

Troy patted her hand. "Please, Miriam, try to understand. We want Miss Evans to stay with the race. If we allowed her to come here and see Ian, the terrorists might get wind of it."

"What makes you think you can persuade her to stay with the race? Do you expect her to go on as though nothing happened?"

Carwell shifted uneasily. "There's no official engagement." He avoided Miriam's gaze. "And right now there's no reason for the terrorists to think that Kendall and Miss Evans were more than friends. I think she will help us."

He twisted his shoulder against the seat back and faced her.

"Drew and Chase saw the accident. Kendall was in the breakaway group, riding well, wearing his yellow jersey."

Bitter tears stung Miriam's eyes. She wondered if she would ever like the color yellow again. "They saw everything?"

"Yes. We're gathering information from film and video cameras. Photographers and fans began shooting the minute the crash occurred. We want to know who rode beside him."

She wanted to shake him. What did it matter where Ian rode or who rode beside him? "What good will all that do, Troy?"

"Faces in the crowd. We're looking for one face in particular—and anyone else that looks suspicious."

She pressed her fingers to her lips. She would not break down and cry, would not crumble in front of this man. Nor did she want her eyes to be red-rimmed when she faced Uriah.

Troy sounded more confident now. "Some terrorist group will probably take credit, but nothing yet. We do know one thing— they have an accomplice among the riders, someone Ian trusted. Possibly someone on his team."

He hesitated as though weighing his words again. "Ian took a poison pellet at close range. That's what made him lose control."

Troy took a lingering look out the tinted window as they sped through the snarled traffic, weighing his confidences again. "If Drew's theory is right, the terrorist who fired that pellet was in that group of fans. We hope the films will help us."

The driver took the exit off the motorway, barely slowing to the speed limit. The wheels squealed. He glanced at them through his rearview mirror, and then, with the car in control, he turned to the right. Three blocks later, they pulled up in front of a flagstone hospital on the edge of Paris.

"Miriam, if you make me a list, Maggie can pack a suitcase for you."

"I'm to stay here—at the hospital?"

"That's what Uriah wants—you here with the family." He smiled wanly. "Apparently you have always been close friends. And, Miriam, we've cordoned off an entire wing for Ian's safety."

He helped her from the car. With his hand to her elbow, they went staunchly up the steps and through the plate glass doors of St. Mercy's Hospital. A uniformed gendarme stood just inside the doors, an indiscernible smile on his lips as they passed him. *You know Troy,* she thought, and felt a measure of comfort that he would not be the only police officer on hand.

No one stopped them. No one questioned them as they walked through the lobby down the main corridor. One or two people nodded briskly at Troy. When they reached an elevator marked emergencies only, he stopped. "Ian won't be out of surgery for an hour or two, but Uriah is waiting in his room."

"Which room?"

He nodded to a nurse who had come up beside them. "She will take you up, Miriam. If you need me, let the gendarme on duty know. He will get in touch with his own commandant, Francois Pellier, or with me. I'll stay in touch with Drew. I promise."

"Will you tell him the truth?"

"As soon as I dare."

"Please, don't let anything happen to Drew or Chase."

She knew he could not promise safety for them any more than he had been able to provide safety for Ian. She ached for Chase. Chase's pain must be unbearable. Young love. First love. Miriam had guessed all along that Chase cared deeply about Ian. But no one should have to think that the man she loved was dead—not for a minute, not even for the CIA. Yet knowing her own fickle heart, Miriam knew that Chase would leave the Tour and fly to Ian's bedside—alerting the terrorist that he was alive. Right now Chase was in a key position to help Drew and to help Ian's team, but at what price?

She turned her anger on Troy. "If Ian doesn't make it, Troy Carwell, I will never forgive myself for not calling Chase."

"We will all bear your guilt," he said.

Seeing the pain in Troy's face, she sought safer ground. "What will you tell Maggie when I don't return to the house?"

"Absolutely nothing. She will have heard the news reports."

"Then she will clamor for details."

"Which I won't be able to give. She will sulk, but Maggie knows better than to question me." He sighed wearily. "We will take our meals at separate tables tonight—me in the dining room and Maggie in the kitchen with our house girl, Maggie chatting aimlessly about the latest fashions."

"And in the morning, will you be speaking again?" Miriam asked softly.

He smiled. "Our truce will come long before that. We need each other, and that will bring us together."

She watched him go, so striking in his familiar rich brown suit—a kind, practical man, not unmindful of the woman he loved. He did not look back. Miriam smiled faintly up at the nurse. "I'm ready," she said.

They stepped into the lift and pressed the button for the fourth floor. As the door opened, she saw Uriah Kendall and Nedrick standing behind him, both of them exhausted and uncertain. Uriah called out, "Oh, Miriam. Thank God you have come."

They ran to each other, arms outstretched, their tears unchecked.

۞۞۞

At the American embassy that night, Brad O'Malloy sat slouched in the chair across from Carwell's desk. He was wearing his tight stone-washed denims and threadbare gray sweater in spite of Carwell's rules that called for a strict dress code. It was after hours, the sun long set, and O'Malloy was more interested in going back to his apartment for a good night's sleep.

With his eyes at half-mast, he gambled on speaking first. "Have you notified Gregory that Kendall made it out of surgery?"

"He doesn't know Kendall is alive. Someone might risk another assassination attempt if he thought Ian had survived." Wearily he said, "We have to keep it under wraps."

"Carwell, Gregory saw the wound on Ian's neck. He's smart enough to know what happened. And if you don't—"

"Don't threaten me, O'Malloy."

"Just waving a caution flag. Miriam Gregory didn't sign a loyalty oath to this Agency. Her husband comes first."

Carwell eased back his shirt cuff and glanced at his Gucci watch. "One in the morning! It's too late to call him back. I'll call him later this morning."

"Before the riders leave the start-ramp? I think Mrs. Gregory will give you that long."

"Forget the Gregorys. My job is to interpret the message that Ian Kendall carried. We can't question Kendall yet—he's still unconscious, but as soon as we can—"

O'Malloy shook his head. "You don't trust the kid. I met him, Carwell. Kept his bike in shape. I was with him when he headed for the start-ramp, and I swear he wasn't carrying anything but his grandmother's Bible verse taped inside his helmet."

"Whether he's involved or not," Carwell said stubbornly, "as a result of that message, we know that Jiri Benak may be in the middle of the race somewhere. The terrorist threats are still coming. The latest promises to finish the job in Paris—here in the City of Lights before the riders cross the finish line."

"A threat like that in Paris—how can we stop him?"

"French Intelligence traced him to a Basque village. They arrested a friend of his named Ignasius. We'll get Benak."

"Before he gets to Paris? Poor Kendall. He never had a chance, did he?"

Carwell agreed. "But things are coming together, Brad. Langley is taking the threats seriously and working under the assumption that the man called Parkovitch will be in Paris. They aren't ruling out the possibility of an international crisis."

"So far the threats are being poorly executed."

"Or deliberately thwarted, O'Malloy. The red phone lines between Washington and Moscow have been hot for the last twelve hours. The president in Moscow is denying any knowledge of a plot to disrupt the race. The White House is pushing hard for answers."

"With any results?"

"Orders from the White House were to interrogate Kendall. We told them we can't interrogate a dead man."

"They think he's dead, too? They'll have your head, Troy."

"Langley is handling it. It still took three phone calls before Moscow acknowledged the existence of an Ivar Noukov. He's head of a Russian contingency in Bosnia—a recent replacement for a general killed in a traffic accident in Tusla."

"Another untimely accident? Do you plan to arrest him?"

"The Russian president will have something to say about that, if he's well enough. If necessary, Brad, we'll take old Ivar out with an accident of his own, but only as a last resort."

"And Parkovitch?" O'Malloy asked.

"Outright denials. Nothing more. So far Parkovitch is just a name, but our own agents are at work, trying to get a line on any of Noukov's old cronies. Or on why he was sent to Bosnia."

"Exiled there maybe. You don't have long to find answers, Carwell. If you want the best out of Gregory, tell him the truth."

"Aubrey and Grover Kendall are due at Charles de Gaulle in a few hours. Grover is booked on a flight to Bosnia four hours later."

"The grieving brother. And the wayward general. I have a feeling I'm flying to Bosnia. Right?"

"We booked you on the same plane with Kendall. First class, the seat right beside him."

"Do I shake his hand or ignore him?"

"You decide. Just keep your eye on him. And you'll contact two of our agents there. They'll put you in touch with Noukov."

"So my work is cut out for me? Guess I miss the end of the Tour de France. Shame. I was getting so I liked it. And getting really good at fixing the bikes while the riders were pedaling."

O'Malloy crossed his legs, and the worn sole of his walking shoe irritated Carwell. "Any report back on Nash's fingerprints?"

"A match." With an uncommon smirk, Troy added, "We'll send copies to Bosnia and The Hague but not until the race ends."

"So the Serbian war criminal rides all the way to Paris?"

"All the way."

"What about Gregory?" O'Malloy asked as he stood. "He needs to know about Nash and Ian Kendall."

Troy glanced at his watch again. "I can't wake the man up."

"Gregory won't be sleeping. Wait until later and you'll miss him. He'll be in some out-of-the-way cafe drowning himself in coffee. Ten cups and the sports page, and then he's approachable."

His flippant approach alienated Carwell. Carwell allowed silence to fill the room, and then veering his gaze away from O'Malloy, he patched through a call to Drew. Moments later, his words stormed across the wires. "I don't care what your hotel rules are. This is an emergency. Ring Mr. Gregory's room now."

Chapter 25

D rew lay on top of his bed fully dressed, wondering why he had been unable to reach Miriam. He wanted to pack it all in and go immediately to Paris to be with her. When the phone rang, he grabbed it before Vic awakened. "Drew speaking," he said.

"Carwell here. I have news for you."

Drew bolted to a sitting position. "Is it about Kendall? Have they done the autopsy?"

"That won't be necessary. Ian was shot with a poison pellet, but he's alive—at a private hospital with police protection."

"Alive?" Drew shouted. "But it's been broadcast all over the world that he's dead. His father is flying over to claim his body."

"We had no choice, Drew. The fewer who know the truth, the better. The threats are still coming in, more bizarre than ever."

Alive! Drew felt raw rage, rage that at this moment not even a prayer could mellow. "We've talked twice before, Carwell, and you've known this all along? Why have you kept us in the dark?"

Vic swung his lanky legs over the side of his bed, his eyes wide. Drew held up his hand to silence any questions.

"Drew, Ian is critical. At first we weren't certain he'd make it out of surgery. But that wife of yours is one terrific lady. Miriam is spending every minute with the Kendalls. She's like a rock."

"Then Chase and I are heading for Paris right now."

"No, Gregory, you can't tell Miss Evans. And you and Vic stay with the Gainsborough team. You're there to find a terrorist."

Carwell hesitated. "Washington and Langley are handling the

message that O'Malloy brought out. The search for Jiri Benak has intensified. We have no lead on Parkovitch, but Moscow has a General Noukov stationed in Bosnia."

"Is Nedrick Russelmann at the hospital with Uriah?"

"Uriah depends on that young man. He accepts Russelmann as flesh and blood, but we expect trouble when Aubrey and Grover get here."

"The old sibling rivalry," Drew said.

"Maybe that's why Grover has a reservation to take him right on out to Bosnia. He's traveling with some businessmen."

"Bosnia? Troy, can you keep him there for me? I want him to check on Lennie Applegate's family, especially her nephew."

"If you mean Marcus Nash, we've done that, and he's not Lennie's nephew. That's straight from Glenn Fairway in London. Seems Miss Applegate saw the accident on television and blamed it on her nephew. She says he ran Ian off the road. The sad thing is, he's not really her relative, but she doesn't know that yet."

"Then who's the man riding with the Gainsborough team?"

"A Serbian Intelligence officer wanted for war crimes. Lennie's real nephew was killed in the war. The town records were destroyed, but the men and boys in the village were killed execution style. Nash simply took over his identity."

"So I'm to keep my eye on Nash?"

"All the way to Paris. We want to know every move he makes. In the meantime, O'Malloy is on his way to Bosnia to get a line on General Noukov. He can check on what happened to Applegate's family for you."

"That means O'Malloy is sitting in your office right now. When does he leave?"

"On the same plane with Grover Kendall."

"Will Grover come out unscathed?" Drew asked.

"It depends on whether he's involved politically—"

The line in Paris went dead before Drew could slam the receiver in Carwell's ear.

"What was that all about?" Vic asked

"The biggest medical hoax I've ever been involved in. And Carwell, blast that man, has involved my wife in his deception."

"Miriam? Wow! So Kendall's really alive," Vic said.

"And we can't tell anyone, not even Chase. Carwell's orders.

And we're to stay on and ride to the finish line. But we're to make certain Chase stays with us so the terrorists don't get wind of Ian's condition. Everybody plays dead."

"Where are you going, Drew?"

"To see Chase."

"It's two in the morning."

"She'll be awake. She thinks the man she loves is dead. Not very conducive to counting sheep."

With a faint smile on her chubby face, Basil Millard's wife drew back the door and allowed Drew to enter. She nodded toward the bedroom across the hall. Chase was snapping her luggage shut; the rest of her clothes lay in neat piles on the bed. Basil Millard sat there straddling a straight-back chair, his arms braced on the chair back. Neither of them seemed aware of Drew leaning against the door frame.

"I wish I could say something to help you," Basil said. "My wife and I hate to see you go. We may never see you again."

"My reason for staying is gone."

Millard's face shadowed. "I called Franz in London. He already knew. Heard it on the BBC news."

"Is his lung infection better?" she asked.

"Yes. Said to tell you he was sorry—about the accident. He apologized for abandoning the race—said maybe if he had stayed with the team, that all of us together might have protected Ian."

"That's sweet." Her voice faded. "Franz is not responsible for what happened. None of you were. It was an accident."

Wrong, Drew thought.

Millard licked his upper lip, the tip of his tongue swiping across his thin blond mustache. Without his helmet and goggles, Millard's face looked rounded like his wife's. "The team may be pulling out of the race," he said quietly. "It doesn't seem right to go on without him."

"Oh, Basil, Ian wouldn't want you to do that." She toyed with a blouse, her face turned from him. "You knew Ian so well. Do you think he's with God? If—" Her voice faltered again, and Drew ached for her. "If I knew that for certain, maybe—"

"I'm not much on things like that," Basil admitted. "But I rather imagine if you want to ask God something, you can just talk to Him. Maybe my wife knows."

Chase began throwing her things into another suitcase.

"So you're really leaving?" Drew said from the doorway.

They turned, startled to see him.

"Oh, Drew. I told you I was going. Vic offered to drive me to Paris."

"I need him here. And I want your help, too, Chase. Ian would want you to stay. The race meant everything to him."

She tossed her head, her chestnut hair shimmering in the lamplight. "I thought *I* meant everything to him," she said softly.

"You do—you did." Drew crossed the room and lifted her chin, forcing her to look at him. "Ian would want you to see it through to the end—for him."

"Don't ask me to do that, Drew Gregory. I can't.... I won't. I'm going to Paris to find Mr. Kendall."

"Ian's grandfather? The Kendalls are private people. You know that, Chase."

She crumbled visibly. "All right then," she whispered. "I'll talk to your wife, Drew, before I fly on to London."

"Are you going on to New York after that?" he asked.

"I want to say good-bye to Beatrice Thorpe before I leave.... I should tell her what happened. . . . Drew, I suppose you're staying on? Everything for the race and Monsieur Chambord."

"The problems are still here, Chase. They didn't go away." He waited until she faced him again. "I've been on the line with Paris," he told her. "Talking to Carwell. They tried to bring Ian back on the flight in." It sounded so hopeless, but it was all he could offer. Part of the truth.

The floodgates opened again. A fresh flow of tears washed down that already puffy face. "During this whole race terrorists threatened Ian, and then a stupid accident—"

"It was no accident," he told her.

She collapsed on the edge of the bed, her back against the suitcase. "What do you mean, Drew?"

"Ian was injured before his cycle went out of control." He watched Basil from the corner of his eye and saw his scowl deepen. "He was injured with a pellet gun, Basil."

Drew didn't say a poison pellet. He spared them that, but he couldn't throw off the sight of that puncture wound in Ian's neck. "Ian was stunned before he went over that wall."

Millard's fingers dug into the chair back. "That's impossible, Gregory, at the speed we ride those bikes. People tried to stop the riders in the old days with nails and tacks when the Tour first started but not in our modern-day races. We don't try to put each other out of the competition."

"Someone did."

Drew glanced at Chase, not wanting to add to her pain. "Ian had a wound on his neck—" Drew hated the tremor in his own voice. He could not allow his personal involvement with Ian and his family to color the job that lay before him. "There was the wound," he repeated, "and a scrap of paper that tumbled from Ian's helmet during the accident."

"Another terrorist threat?" Millard asked.

"We think this message was given to Ian by mistake. I sent it to Paris with Brad O'Malloy."

"The Gainsborough mechanic? Don't tell me he's another intelligence officer." Millard knocked the chair over as he stood, and in his anger he left it toppled. "Ian carrying a code of some sort? I don't like what you're suggesting, Drew."

"And I didn't like Troy Carwell's report when I talked to him on the phone. Ian was definitely shot with a pellet gun. Metal fragments penetrated just beneath his skin."

"No," Basil cried. "That means ricin poison in his bloodstream. Then he was dead before he ever went over that cliff." He shook his head, his voice shaking with anger. "Isn't that how they took down a BBC broadcaster some years back?"

"The Bulgarian exile? Yes, the same scenario. But he was jabbed by a sharp point carried in the ferrule of an umbrella."

Millard's gaze turned cynical. "Drew, we just carry bottles of water on our bikes. There's no place to conceal a weapon. The pellet had to be fired by someone in the crowd."

Uneasiness crept over Drew. He had fixed his suspicions on Marcus Nash, convinced of the link between Lennie and her "nephew." Nash had ridden Ian's back wheel just before the crash. But the video films that Drew and Vic had played over and over pointed to another unwanted possibility. A pack of six men had been riding together, Ian's friend Orlando Gioceppi riding among them.

Now, facing Millard and that round cherub innocence and the guileless blue eyes, Drew's questions ran wild. Basil Millard had gone to the top of Mt. Ventoux with Ian—and Millard knew too much about poisoned pellets. Had the whole Gainsborough team conspired against Ian? Franz was the only member of the team who had dropped from the race, his body racked by a lung infection—yet abandoning sooner than they had expected. Had Franz disagreed with the plans to stop Ian?

Drew forced his attention back to Chase and Millard, but the doubts kept coming. Jiri Benak and Coach Skobla had known each other in Czechoslovakia. Were they in this together? Or was the accident only one step in a plot that went beyond the Tour to Moscow and to General Noukov and Parkovitch, whoever they were?

"Millard," he said, and his voice turned gruff and unkind, "do you know someone by the name of Parkovitch?"

"No."

"Or General Noukov?"

Millard's tone sharpened. "I don't know any generals. Is this some kind of joke, Gregory?"

"I don't think the note in Ian's helmet was intended as a joke. It named names. Suggested problems all the way to Paris."

All color drained from Chase's face. "Ian never had a chance. The terrorists won."

"No," Drew said. "The terrorists only win if we all quit the race."

Drew gathered Chase against his chest much as he would have done with Robyn if she had been there. He let Chase cry, wondering why he himself had not shed a tear. The stoic Drew Gregory holding his own, sloughing off emotion, being the invincible one.

"What do you want from us, Gregory?" Millard asked. "Alekos Golemis and now Ian—and still you want us to ride? Didn't you hear the news reports? The whole world believes it was a fatal accident. Accident, Gregory. How can you ask us to finish the race as though nothing happened?"

"Fold it in now, and we will never know the truth." He had to keep the team in the race. Carwell's orders. And by some miracle, he still had to convince Chase to unpack her suitcases and ride with the Tour to the finish line—all because something bigger was about to happen, quite possibly with a terrorist riding on the Gainsborough team.

Chase's convulsive sobs were quieting now. Still he held her as though he himself might find comfort in hugging Ian's girl. He took his handkerchief from his pocket and wiped the tears from her cheeks. "Blow," he said.

He almost smiled. She sounded like a baritone horn blown through dry lips.

"Chase, I know you want to leave. I understand. But we'd be in Paris in just a few days. By then the investigation will be over. Carwell will have answers for us."

"I can't—"

"Would you do it for me? Would you just trust me and stay?"

"Drew," Basil said, "I may have seen the man who gave that note to Ian—right after we signed in this morning."

Chase caught her breath. "Not Salatori?"

"No, it wasn't the journalist."

Benak then, Drew thought. "Fortyish. Medium build. Blond. Beige raincoat. Perhaps even smoking a cigar."

"Late thirties or forties, all right. But this man was not a particularly strong-looking man." He held up his hands. "I don't think Ian knew him. When they told us to line up, Ian tucked the note under his headgear."

"What happened to the man?"

"I don't know. I didn't pay that much attention. Orlando was there. He might remember more."

Basil's wife stood in the door now, their crying baby in her arms. In four long strides Millard was at her side, wrapping his arm around them. Above the top of his wife's head, he met Drew's gaze. "The man spoke in broken English—an accent of some sort. He warned Ian to be careful."

"Did Ian seem alarmed? Frightened?"

"Not afraid. Startled."

As Drew left the room, he said, "Chase, I'll try to reach Miriam tonight and let her know you're coming to Paris."

"Don't bother calling her, Drew. I changed my mind." She began emptying her suitcase. "Without Ian, it doesn't matter where I am. I'm going to stay and help you if I can. Ian would want me to do that."

Chapter 26

Bosnia. Two days later, Leopold Bolav tossed his khaki fatigues and his worn turtleneck sweater on the narrow unmade bed, stowed his gun beneath the pillow, and then dressed with great care. For the first time in months, he wore a white dress shirt and tie and the best of his serge suits, the only one salvaged from the war years. The shirt was frayed at the collar, one button missing, but tucked into his trousers, the missing button did not show. Four years ago, his wife would have used the shirt for a dust rag, but that was the distant past when she and his family and his job were his whole life.

He gave himself a final inspection in a cracked mirror and was startled at the emptiness in his eyes hooded by bushy gray brows and at the sulky protrusion of his thick lip. At forty-seven he had grown old. The war had done that. He could do nothing about the ravages of war any more than he could undo the killings that he had ordered. Now there was little he could do with his face or his bulbous nose, but he brushed his bowl-cut gray-blond hair to the left and slicked it down with water.

His Persian cat had taken possession of his sweater and lay curled in its armpit. He leaned down and scratched her neck, smiling as she purred back. "Your dish is empty," he said, apologizing for the watery milk that she had licked dry. It was time. Past time. He left the small quarters where he and General Noukov were housed and made his way to the town meeting.

Leopold entered the conference room, mingling among the foreigners and engineers and town officials who wanted only to forget the war and build their cities again. No one spoke of the Tour de France. No one seemed to care who raced or who won. Not one man in the room mentioned the rider who had died. Aimlessly Leopold picked up a coffee cup brimming with thick black coffee, the strong aroma filling his nostrils and scalding his throat. He clung to the cup for confidence, and when the others took their places at the table, he joined them.

The count would be accurate. He was there to replace another engineer, a man he had once worked with, a man too sick to make his appearance. Leopold had been part of conferences like this long years ago, sitting with a Muslim neighbor to his right and a Croatian across the table from him. Friends then. Drinking and smoking together and rolling out the blueprints for the 1984 Olympic Winter Games in Sarajevo. They had laughed back then, making jokes about the venues going up on the site of the assassination that had led to World War I. In those days of planning for the Winter Games, the turmoil and chaos was in Beirut—not Bosnia, Yuri Andropov was dead, and Professor Ivanski was unheard of in Russia.

And now they were here again, not to plan luge or bobsled runs or ski lifts, but to speak of foreign investments and foreign corporations controlling some of the rebuilding projects in his own country. He hated them, these strangers with names he didn't even know—unwilling to come four years ago to help stop the killings, but here now to grab at the opportunities to build up their own coffers. But no matter how clever or rich these men were, they could not erase the pockmarks and bullet holes in the conference table or plaster over the memory of the cracked walls, the broken windows, the shattered lives in their war-torn towns.

He folded his big hands on the tabletop to stop the tremor in his left hand and to help force the fury inside of him back down into the pit where it belonged. The town mayor was introducing the foreign guests now, the interpreters coming to the rescue of the Americans when language failed them. Pompous, well-dressed businessmen with their cuff links and silk ties. Portly gentlemen. Pleasant ones. And then his eyes settled on the American lawyer who had accompanied them, the name plucked from memory before the executive officer could say, "Grover Kendall."

"Sir," Kendall said, "it is good to see you again."

Their gaze locked. Kendall was well-groomed, smartly dressed. He wore no wedding band on his finger, just an expensive watch that he kept twisting. His voice was calm, unemotional as he asked, "Your daughter Ozella—how is she?"

As Leopold stared at the young man, memory tunneled back through the war years to five years ago when his daughter had come home with Grover Kendall. Kendall had traveled to Yugoslavia—it was still Yugoslavia then—and had left the country carrying propaganda pamphlets, not because he was political, but because he was smitten with Ozella.

She had been beautiful, convincing, bewitching. "Ozella." There he had said her name aloud. His only child. The room had gone silent as though everyone hung on Leopold's answer. He lifted his chin defiantly. "My daughter is dead," he said. "My whole family is dead."

The young man's expression crumbled. "I'm sorry. Truly sorry. I was hoping to find her on this trip."

And marry her? Leopold wondered. *Or did you plan to smuggle more political pamphlets out of the country?* He saw sympathy in the young man's eyes, as though he had stepped back in time and memory to that bursting joy of youth and first love.

Leopold looked away. *You know who I am,* he thought. *And it will not take you long to realize that I am the Leopold Bolav wanted on the war criminal list. Yet you will not interfere because of my dead daughter—and because you are here to help rebuild my country, to be part of a foreign takeover.*

When you discover where I live, will you knock on my door, or will you betray me? Or will you go back to The Hague and report where I am and who I am? Leopold was weary, too tired to think of fleeing. The seventeenth stage of the Tour de France had come and gone. That was the day when their plans should have come together— when Professor Ivanski was to have his imperial kingdom and the Serbs of Bosnia could go back to the battle line. But was that what he really wanted? Or was this—this chance to rebuild the cities of his country—what goaded him?

Three hours later the meeting ended, and Leopold rose stiffly from his chair. He braced his hands on the pocked surface of the table and risked a final glance at Grover Kendall, framed by the cracked walls of the room. Kendall avoided his gaze, but as

Leopold left the conference hall, he was certain that the footsteps behind him were youthful and determined. Yes, his daughter's first love was following him.

❧❧❧

Bordeaux. That same evening, Drew found Chase by the side of the road. She sat with her legs drawn to her chest, her face buried against bent knees, a solemn dejected silhouette in the moonlight. Shock was giving way to grief.

"Chase, it's Drew." He slipped up quietly and dropped down beside her. "You shouldn't be out here alone."

She lifted her face, the tears sparkling in the light of the moon. "Nothing happened these last two days of the race. And my hotel room is so crowded. . . . Everyone is so concerned about me. Drew, I can't stand all the questions and sympathy."

"You could have called me."

"At two in the morning?"

"It wouldn't matter. I keep late hours. Besides, I'm always grumpy in the morning. But honestly, Chase, you shouldn't be out here alone. It isn't safe."

"I speak French."

He laughed gently. "You're still in a foreign country." He handed her his handkerchief. "Can I help?"

"If you know how to scream," she said.

"I could give it a try. Are you just wanting the hills to echo back?"

"No, I've been screaming at God."

"Did He holler back?"

"He didn't say anything, Drew. My grandmother Callie was right—He doesn't even exist. In spite of what Ian used to say."

Drew's throat tightened. "What did Ian say?"

"He was quoting his grandmother, I think. He said, 'You can never be alone in the moonlight, not with God looking down on you.'"

"That's why you came out here?"

She opened her mouth to scream.

"Better not," he said. "You'll have the whole town awake. That's why I'm here. I heard that screeching noise—thought it was some wild animal."

Meekly she said, "Just me. Trying to get God's attention."

God had Drew's attention. The moon and stars lighting the vastness of the night, the whole universe cried out to Drew, convincing him once again that Someone had it all together. But how could he convince Chase? He said, "It was like this for me, too, Chase, when I settled things with God in the mountains of Sulzbach. 'Cept I didn't have a brilliant moon like that. But I had a canopy of clouds and the trunk of an evergreen to lean against." He chuckled lightly. "I would have fallen over without that tree for support. . . . I kept trying to swallow my heartbeat and make excuses."

"You were all alone?"

"Yes. I figured it didn't concern anyone else."

"Is that when Ian was in Sulzbach with you?"

"Yes. The day after his friend Alekos died."

"Were you angry at God?"

"Then? No. Just scared without Him. And my son-in-law was smart enough to give me space. In fact he gave me the whole mountain."

"Don't leave me, Drew. I'm scared. I didn't get to say all those things to Ian that I wanted to say. On the rest day when I met Zoe Golemis, she told Ian that he was always like a bird in flight, always wandering. Drew, I'm like that. My father says I'm always chasing the wind."

She held up her hands to the evening breeze. "Dad says I'm never earthbound. I was just beginning to think the wind was blowing with me—that I had found in Ian all I'd ever wanted."

Drew squeezed her hand, icy cold in his. It was the wrong moment to tell her that what she wanted was inner peace. "I think Ian knew that you cared about him," he said.

"But, Drew, he didn't know—Ian didn't know I loved him."

He watched her in the darkness. Saw her tears. Felt her pain. Gently, he asked, "You're sure you loved him? It's not what happened? You're not confusing grief for a friend with love?"

"I think I knew all along. He was different from all my other dates, even in the hills of Gascony. But it was just my pride. My degrees. My selfishness. My infatuation with Luke Breckenridge. I even wondered if Ian were good enough for me."

"He wondered the same."

"Did he tell you that, Drew?"

"A couple of times. I told him if it was meant to be—it would happen."

She rolled her hands over the path, clutching at a stone lying there. "So God didn't mean it to be?"

"I'm not wise in God's purposes, Chase."

She tossed the stone. They watched in silence as it disappeared over the cliff, soundlessly—as Ian had disappeared. "Do you think about where Ian is now?" she asked.

What could he say? He couldn't tell her that Ian was still in a coma, fighting for life. Alive, but barely. When she finally knew, she would hate Drew, hate the Agency, hate all of the lies and betrayal. This fragile moment with her—this moonlight night when she was sitting here doing some real heart-searching would come crashing down on her. Crashing down on him. It would be okay for her to hate him. But to hate God because they had all betrayed her! Drew could not tell her the truth, and Ian had no way of telling her. He was still in a deep sleep from which he might not wake up.

She turned her head to face him. "Well, Drew, do you know where Ian is? Can you promise me he's all right?"

"Chase, I try not to make promises that I can't keep. I don't always have answers—and even when I do, I can't always share them."

"Did Ian tell you about his dream?"

"His dream?"

"On the rest day—the day before—before the accident he told me that he kept dreaming about his grandmother. All in white. Waving to him. Beckoning Ian to come to her."

Drew blinked hard, shutting out the moonlight, trying desperately to escape the moment. What if Ian never awakened from his coma? What if they robbed Chase of the chance to go to his bedside while he was still alive? He agonized inside, shifting slightly.

"Drew, if I thought Ian were with Olivia, it might not hurt as much. Oh, Drew, if only I knew God existed."

"Try Him."

"How?" she whispered.

"No big deal," he said huskily. "That day on the mountain at

Sulzbach, I just told Him who I was—just in case He didn't know. And I told Him what I wanted. I figured God knew what a mess I had made out of my life without giving Him a rerun." He counted stars for a few seconds before saying, "Funny thing, I didn't think much about the blackness of my life—just the void and the emptiness."

As she leaned her head against his shoulder, he said, "I ended up thinking that God saw me for what I would be—could be—not for what I was. Chase, He's got the whole canvas of our life in full vivid color. That's the way He views us."

Another soft chuckle slipped past his lips. For a moment he wondered whether he had turned the confessional back to his own needs. "God saw me as worthwhile, Chase. Had to. He was dumping all of eternity into my lap."

"You don't sound much like a preacher, Drew."

"Deliver me. My son-in-law does a better job at that."

She pushed away and stared up at him in the darkness. "You really believe there's an eternity?"

"Positive." He reached over and cupped his hand over hers. "The way I have it figured out now is that God's Son sits on the right side of the Father kicking in a lot of prayers for us. I keep Him pretty busy."

"Do you think He is praying for me?" Chase asked, marveling.

"Yeah, you too. You can't go wrong on that. I'll leave you, Chase—I'll just go a shouting distance away. Your moonlight protector. But you're not alone. This is a private matter between you and God."

"But I'm mad at Him—if He does exist. Oh, Drew, He didn't have to take Ian."

Drew went cold inside. Truth mocked him. He couldn't tell her that Ian was still alive. Drew squeezed her hand. "Sometimes God asks us to trust Him with pretty big things. Not just our own lives—but with those we love as well."

He felt her shoulders convulse, heard the deep sob well up within her. He stood—tears in his own eyes—and smiled down at her. "You won't even have to scream—unless you're calling me."

Chapter 27

tage twenty: The day before Paris. A morning mist rose from the river, the city veiled by the sweeping ash-gray fog. Drew could have done with seeing the sun this morning. The coffee at the hostel had been bitter, and the pot was empty before he could pour his third cup. The fine drizzle and this thick haze added to his unrelenting headache. A dull pain pressed his temples, and spasms tugged at the back of his neck. He couldn't shake it—hadn't since the tragedy in the Pyrenees.

Two days had gone by without incident, but he didn't trust the terrorists. The morning after Ian's accident, the Gainsborough team had turned up at the start-ramp, seven somber faces showing the stress they were under. Millard had looked crestfallen, his jaw twitching nervously. Nash remained aloof, several feet from the others, a sneer catching the corners of his mouth.

Drew could still hear himself—not Jon Gainsborough or Coach Skobla—but Drew choking on his lie as he stood before the international press, saying, "The Gainsborough team has made the decision to finish the Tour in memory of their teammate."

Basil Millard rode off full throttle with a skill he'd never demonstrated before. Even today Basil was no longer riding support to Ian, but riding to win, doing better than Orlando Gioceppi. For twenty-four hours there had been no warnings, and now one had arrived along with the morning mist—the terrorist promising the riders a big surprise in the City of Lights.

"Call the race off, Chambord," Drew had urged.

With meticulous care, Chambord pocketed the message in his

blazer and walked off. In spite of his indifference and the inclement weather, stage twenty was going well. There had been no unexpected attacks. No daring breakaway by unknowns. No pileups along the ravine. No major injuries. The remaining 133 cyclists rode cautiously with the mist hanging low over them and the heady aroma of grapes surrounding them as they rode through wine country.

Drew was in the Fiat when Orlando Gioceppi pulled to the side of the road and waited for the team car to reach him.

"I can't go on," he said when they slowed and stopped.

"A flat?" Skobla called out impatiently.

"No. I'm quitting the race."

"You must not quit."

"I'm sorry, Coach. I'm sick."

Gioceppi looked more troubled than ill, his eyes dark and shadowed. When he caught Drew's eyes on him, his gaze veered ahead to the bike mounted on top Chambord's car; Ian's helmet was strapped to its handlebars and the number 19 boldly attached. The tendon in Orlando's neck throbbed as someone tore the placards from his shirt and bike. He turned back to the way they had come, cycling off and disappearing around the curve into the mist.

For a meeting with Jiri Benak? Drew wondered.

Drew had no one to follow him. He glanced at Raunsted. "Gioceppi is refusing the Broom Wagon. But I don't understand. Why would he abandon now? He could have made it."

Dr. Raunsted nodded. "Delayed depression or exhaustion. No other medical reason. Guess he just didn't want to go on."

For the next six hours Drew's thoughts centered in on the terrorists. He couldn't even recall who took the stage win. Drew did not like Salvador Contoni, but he could not in his wildest imagination continue to link him to the bombing of stage eleven or even to the accident in the Pyrenees. It was not like Contoni to work with a man like Jiri Benak. They worked best alone. Benak was greedy for power, a destructive madman. Contoni was more of a survivalist, bent on his own safety and the lure of the sea.

It was true that Contoni had worked for Monique Dupree's husband—had even sailed the yacht where arms deals had been negotiated—but Drew could not picture Contoni disrupting an international cycling event for mere pleasure. It was not Contoni's style. Yet where was the man? He had not returned to the press room since the bombing—had not even been seen since that horrible moment in Nordlune. It sounded crazy—even to Drew himself—but he saw some good in Contoni. He had come from good roots in Milan, and in his own gruff way he'd been kind to Monique Dupree's sons.

Even as Drew pondered over the threats against the Tour and over the possible surprise attack that awaited them in the City of Lights, Salvador Contoni and Yuri Ryskov were back in the car with the Amsterdam license plate belting down the motorway toward Paris.

For two days Sal had kept his ears tuned to the television, expecting to see his name blasted across the screen by the media. But neither Salvador Salatori or Salvador Contoni made the headlines. With the car serviced and his fears subsiding, he left the hotel in Bordeaux and struck out for Paris. Sal was surprised that the Russian had stayed with him; but he rather liked a man who could speak of nothing more than freedom.

Yuri had slept for the last 100 kilometers, his breathing as raspy as a sick man's. Now as Yuri rallied and shook sleep from his eyes, Sal took note of the car three lengths behind them. They were being followed. On impulse he took the cutoff toward Orly Airport. It was time to dump the Russian. Together, they would be taken. Alone, they each had a chance to escape.

Sal pulled into the terminal parking lot, pocketed the keys, and whipped out a flask of whiskey. He poured two small shots and handed one to Yuri. "To freedom, Yuri. Yours and mine."

Ryskov took it and swallowed. "To freedom. It appears that we have come to the end of our journey together." Wiping his lips, he asked, "Where will you go, Contoni?"

"A night in Paris and then to Italy." He capped the flask and put it back in the glove compartment. They walked inside the terminal and up the steps to the viewing balcony to watch the jets coming and going. The planes were specks in the sky on takeoff, a blur of unchecked speed as they landed.

"Can you find your own way from here, Yuri?"

Yuri nodded. "There is always a plane back to Moscow."

"Paris is fourteen kilometers south. Your call, Ryskov."

On the spur of the moment, Sal took out his father's business card and handed it to Ryskov. "This is an open invitation if you are ever in Italy. The Contoni Vineyards are just outside Milan . . . in case you don't go back to Moscow."

Sal saluted and disappeared toward the stairs.

ⓦⓦⓦ

Yuri crossed the wide corridor to the massive plate windows at the front of the building. Lifting his mini-binoculars, he watched Contoni move stealthily through the parking lot to the car with the Dutch license plate. No one followed him.

Yuri smiled. *Italy, Mr. Contoni? Or Amsterdam? Or do you have other plans?* Disappointment stole his smile. He would never see Contoni again, a man who had understood his cry for freedom.

He waited. Still the car did not move. Car trouble? No, Salvador was stepping from the vehicle and striding briskly back toward the terminal.

Maybe he is coming back for me, Yuri thought. *He will take me all the way to the Avenue Gabriel.*

"Ryskov," said a harsh voice in Russian.

The binoculars slipped from Yuri's hand and dangled from the strap around his neck. Guardedly, he turned to face a tall, wiry man in his thirties with a half-inch black beard. His almond eyes were cold. "Mr. Parkovitch is waiting in the car for you."

Yuri's death warrant. The crowd had thinned, his escape route already denied. "Why are you at the airport, Ryskov?"

"I am catching a flight to Moscow."

The man's smile turned cunning. "Is Professor Ivanski waiting for you on the other end? You know what happens to traitors in Moscow." He jerked his head toward the stairwell. "We must not keep Parkovitch waiting."

As Yuri looked around, the man said, "Let me warn you, I am armed with a silencer in place. Walk ahead of me."

Yuri's insides felt on fire as the whiskey burned his stomach. He was fourteen kilometers from Paris—fourteen kilometers from the American embassy. He broke into a run, crashing toward the stairs, the man's steps thundering behind him.

As Yuri slid down the railing toward the landing, Salvador looked up and grinned. "Something told me you needed my help."

Sal stepped aside as the Russian sprinted toward them, his gun aimed at Yuri. Sal was still grinning as he tripped the assailant. The man lost his balance and rolled down the cement steps, the back of his head cracking against the bottom.

Yuri tore his binocular strap free and twisted it in his hands. He reached out to wrap it around the man's neck. "No need for that," Contoni warned. "He is out cold. Bleeding. Go. Take a taxi. You will be in Paris before he wakes up."

Yuri glanced around the empty stairwell. They were still alone. "Parkovitch is waiting outside for me."

Sal kicked the inert body. "Parkovitch expects you to appear with this bodyguard." He touched his fingers to his brow in a salute. "To freedom, Yuri," he said, stepping over the man.

As he neared Paris, Salvador thought about Monique. Without her, life was meaningless. Without his freedom, she would never agree to move to Milan to live with him on his father's estate.

Since Kendall's accident, Salvador had grieved for the young man, grieved even more that Monique would blame him for it. But if Ryskov could be believed, there was more danger ahead, the risk of more deaths on the Champs Elysees. If Sal could send out a warning—if he could convince Monique that he had done so—it would awaken her sympathies and increase his chances with her.

He picked up the cellular phone. It was one of those European models that could cut across the boundary lines, giving him distant access. He toyed with an idea and counted the risks. With his decision clear, he asked the operator to help him. His French was weak. He risked Italian. *"Puo aiutarmi?"*

"You want my help?" the operator repeated. But silence followed except for her persistent, *"Bonjour. Bonjour."*

"Parla inglese?"

"*Oui*. Yes, I speak English."

He enunciated each word. "I must speak to Drew Gregory at the American embassy. This is an emergency. *Per favore*."

"Monsieur Greeg-or-i. American embassy."

"On Avenue Gabriel."

The phone line crackled and hissed. For a moment, Sal thought it had gone dead, and then a deep voice said, "Gregory is unavailable. This is Troy Carwell. How may I help you?"

Sal said, "I am Salvador Contoni. I want to barter for my freedom."

He relished the boldness of his own words. Carwell's silence slapped at him. He held on, putting his elbow to the horn and weaving through the traffic with one hand. Carwell would try to tap into the line and signal someone to start recording.

Go ahead, Sal thought. *It's a rented phone. Under an assumed name. It will take you precious time to trace the number to Amsterdam. But you don't know I'm in a private vehicle, thanks to the diamond cutter in Amsterdam.* "Carwell, I'm in a hurry."

"So am I," Carwell answered. "I'm a busy man."

"And a smart man. I have information on the Tour de France, on tomorrow's glory ride down the Champs Elysees."

He sensed the man bristling on the other end, but his voice remained calm. "I'm listening, Mr. Contoni."

As much as he hated Drew Gregory, if Gregory guaranteed Sal's freedom, there would be no doubting him. But could he trust Carwell? He had to risk it. "Signor Carwell, I have a reliable informant. I can give you names. The threats against the Tour are not over. One signal from the men in that crowd, and a coup in Moscow will go off as planned. Late, but it will take place."

Renewed interest filled Carwell's voice. He no longer acted as though he had a crackpot on the other end. "I'm listening."

"Don't trace this call," Sal warned. "You'll never find me."

Carwell chortled. "The traffic around you is heavy. But the names, Mr. Contoni. If lives are at risk, give me the names."

"You must remove my name from Interpol's wanted list!"

"I'll leave that up to Gregory."

"Good." He could trust Gregory. "The Russian's name is Boris Ivanski. He has a British contact here in Paris."

"So you are in Paris, Mr. Contoni."

He had blundered. He kept talking. "There's a Serbian point man. The two may connect tomorrow in Paris." Urgently, he filled in the details. What Carwell did with the information was up to the American embassy. "And you will want to contact the covering forces in Bosnia. Advice them to pick up General Ivar Noukov, the ranking Russian military officer in Bosnia."

Sal could hear sirens behind him. Two lanes over. A police vehicle riding the fast lane with its lights flashing.

"You see, Mr. Contoni, we have traced your call."

But the police car sped by him, racing toward Paris, looking undoubtedly for a rented vehicle. "No more tricks, Carwell," he cautioned. "Do you want my information or not?"

"Why should I believe you?" Carwell asked.

"You cannot risk doubting me. There's another Russian agent. Less than an hour ago we drank to freedom." Sal paused. "He sees the American embassy as his only hope for that freedom. If he shows up there—and I think that he might—he will confirm the names and places that I gave you."

He severed the connection and picked up speed. Had he won his right to freedom? His mouth was still dry as he began to whistle. He licked his lips, and the music improved, muffled a bit by the truck riding his bumper.

Sal had gone six kilometers when the phone rang. He smiled as he rolled down the car window, grabbed the phone, and dropped it on the pavement while it was still ringing. In his rearview mirror, he saw it smash on the motorway and disappear beneath a huge truck's grinding wheel.

"That's to my liberation from Interpol," he said aloud, and then he went on his way whistling, his tune quite merry.

⚗⚗⚗

Yuri was breathing rapidly when he tumbled into the back of the taxicab at the Orly Airport. "Paris," he told the driver. "The American embassy."

The Frenchman shrugged. "Avenue Gabriel is a one-way street. I will take you as close as I can," he offered.

Seven kilometers into Paris the driver announced, "We are being followed."

Yuri glanced back. Parkovitch was at the wheel, two car lengths behind them. Yuri turned his gaze back to the meter. Six kilometers away. Five. Three. One. They had reached the Champs Elysees. Yuri took a fistful of francs from his wallet and dropped them over the back of the seat beside the driver. The taxi wheels scraped the curb as the vehicle screeched to a stop.

"Go through the park. The embassy is on the other end."

The driver roared off before Yuri could slam the door.

Sweat formed on Yuri's upper lip. He took off. Glancing back, he saw Parkovitch pull to the curb. Step from the car. Run.

Yuri raced over the walkway that wound through the trees. He shoved past couples walking leisurely through the park. The gun! He must not be found with a weapon on him. He released it from his holster and tossed it. Parkovitch called out behind him, but he kept running toward the Avenue Gabriel, his long legs stretching double time toward freedom.

He reached the narrow one-way street and was midway across when he heard the gunfire erupt. It came from behind him like an explosion in his ears. His neck snapped. The back of his head throbbed. He felt the sudden dampness on his shirt.

He tried desperately to pick up speed, but his feet would not obey his commands. His arms and legs flailed in slow motion. They clawed at nothingness above the pavement, a pavement smeared with blood. The deafening roar of the traffic on the Place de la Concorde merged with his muffled cry for help. Yuri no longer heard Parkovitch behind him. He blinked at the blurred image of French guards rushing toward him with firearms cocked. Screaming, commanding him to stop. The French sounds thundered in Yuri's ears. High-pitched. Indistinguishable. Meaningless.

More gunfire split the air. More blood, his own blood splattered on the curb. He spun and stumbled toward the gendarmes as pain caught every nerve fiber along his spine. For a millisecond, the dullness of the embassy beyond the iron gate turned to the glowing white of the chapel on the Sulzbach mountain. Colonel Trotsky's mountain. As suddenly, it was the mute gray of a distant building again, an American flag flapping above it. Yuri fell forward, facedown, his fingers stretched toward the American embassy, freedom too far away for him to grasp.

🏺🏺🏺

Monique Dupree parked behind the honey-colored stone complex and walked around to the front entrance that overlooked the
River Seine. As she put her key in the brass lock, someone pulled
the door open. She stepped inside and looked up into Sal's troubled face. "I thought I would find you here," she said, smiling.

"Your father hung up on me when I telephoned."

"I know. That's why I came to Paris."

"Go away with me, Monique."

"Not without my boys—"

"We can take them with us. I will be good to them."

She went to him and allowed him to hold her, her thoughts on
the sea that would lure him away from her. As Sal held her, she
thought about Anzel refusing to go with her—of her father saying
that she would always make the wrong choices.

"I can't go, Sal," she whispered.

"Is that why you came here—to send me away? We can go to my
parents' home in the vineyards near Milan. We will be safe there,
Monique. My mama is fond of you; she would be fond of the boys."

Her palm covered the stubble of beard on his well-chiseled
chin. "We would be bad for each other," she said softly.

"I would be good to you, Monique. I love you."

He nuzzled the top of her head. She wanted to believe him—
wanted to run away with him. "You must go, Sal. My father will
guess that I came here. He will notify the Surete. He knows about
Ian Kendall—knows that you . . ."

He clasped her shoulders, his eyes piercing. "But I didn't hurt
Kendall."

"You killed him," she said quietly.

"No, no. Someone else did it."

"You were there in the crowd. I saw you on the television."

"Thousands of people lined the race. How could you see me?"

"I would know your face anywhere. I see it all the time. In my
dreams. When I'm alone or reading to Giles just before he falls
asleep. And I see your face when Anzel glares at me."

"So you cannot get me out of your blood. Go away with me."

"Sal, don't force me to choose between you and my sons."

"You know I have always loved you—even when your husband

Harland was alive." He pulled her against him, his muscles tens-
ing. Despair filled his voice. "And now you are a widow. But Anzel
has you, and I do not. Why must it be this way between us?"

"Go, please."

Slowly, he released her and stepped back, his eyes hardening.
Then he turned and snatched up his car keys.

"Drive carefully, Salvador."

"I am always careful."

"Where will you go? So many of the streets are already blocked
off for tomorrow's race."

"I will find a way out and drive straight through to Milan."

"But it's not your car."

"There's no time to think about that. My father will reimburse
the man in Amsterdam—"

"Take my car instead," she offered.

"And leave you stranded? No."

For a moment their eyes held. *Go,* she thought. *Before I change
my mind.*

The weather-lines around his mouth deepened, his gray eyes
wistful. "If you change your mind, Monique, I will be in Milan."

No, she thought. *The sea will lure you back.* She wanted to say, *I
tried to love you. I wanted to love you.* But the words did not, would
not come.

Without speaking again, he strode across the room, stepped
outside, and slammed the door behind him. She stood motionless, yearning to run after him. No man had ever excited her as
he had. Her knees buckled. She slid to the floor with tears running
down her cheeks. "Salvador. Salvador."

For an hour she sat collapsed on the floor, rocking back and
forth, her face puffy from the tear-wash. Salvador would stay a
few steps ahead of the law, but not forever. She would never
know when they found him, so he would always be alive to her.
She would think of him standing tall and handsome with droplets
from the Mediterranean Sea kissing his suntanned face, his skipper's cap pushed back revealing those marvelous cool gray eyes.
Just keep that memory of Sal in your heart, she told herself.
*Remember him at the helm of his ship, his wild and windblown spirit
free as he sails over the chicory waters.* She still tasted the sweetness

of his lips against hers. And yet he would never be hers. He would always belong to the sea.

Thirty more minutes ticked away. Still she sat hunched over the hardwood floor. As if awaking from a dream, she gradually became aware of her surroundings—her uncluttered apartment tastefully decorated with its seventeenth-century antiquity. She had chosen each piece of furniture with care and always with Harland's approval. Now it seemed so unimportant, so meaningless. Even the private garden off the bedroom that she had shared with her husband—that she had even dared share with Salvador—had filled with weeds and wilted flowers. All through her marriage to Harland, she had been at home working the soil, delighting in her garden. Now it was overgrown with thorns and deadwood like her life, a life cluttered with poor choices.

Outside, she heard the distant chimes of the cathedral, like a clarion call to her soul. She possessed everything, more houses and lands than she needed. But in the restless chamber of her heart, she possessed nothing. Her father—a poor peasant farmer at best—had refused the tainted wealth she offered him, choosing instead the simple honest way of life that she had known as a child. Back then, she had been barefoot and free, a rosary her only true possession. Then Harland walked into her life offering an eighteen-year-old the glitter of Paris.

Her parents had fought her leaving home. Even now they had everything Monique wanted—the old stone farmhouse where she had grown up, the land that they had plowed year after year. And they had what Monique wanted most—peace and the affection of her own sons. The pealing of bells in the cathedral tower stilled, but the ringing in Monique's ear persisted. She cupped her ears and tried to stop the noise before she realized that it was the telephone.

She crawled across the room on her numb legs and grabbed it. "Salvador?" she whispered.

"No, Monique. This is Thymous."

Thymous Golemis. She brushed her straggly hair back from her tear-stained face. "Thymous, where are you?"

"My sister Zoe and I are in Paris until after the race."

He doesn't know, she thought. *He doesn't know that Ian Kendall is dead.* "Thymous, Kendall isn't—"

"I know. I was there when it happened. And I cannot face my father unless I know the truth about Kendall's accident."

"He's dead, Thymous."

"Is he? I will know more after my appointment with the Surete this afternoon. I'm meeting with Officer Pellier."

"Will you tell him that your father hired Salvador?"

"If I have to. My sister and I promised our brother that we would be here for him." Thymous paused. "After Ian Kendall's accident—we felt compelled to stay on for Alekos and Ian both. Once they were good friends, you know."

Monique eased into a chair, her heart pounding unevenly. "Are you all right, Thymous?"

"I would be if I could see you."

"You wouldn't want to—not if you could see the way I look now." *Limp from crying. Puffy cheeks. Swollen eyelids. My skin blotched.* "Thymous, go back to Corfu with your sister. Be with your family. You need one another."

"I can't forget you, Monique. Come with me. I want you and your sons to visit the villa. I want my family to know you better."

They wouldn't like me. I've made such a mess of my life.

"Monique, come for a week or ten days or a month. My mother says it takes a month to dig deep roots. The rest would do you good. You can relax and sunbathe. I will take the boys swimming and boating and show them how we work the olive orchards."

"You don't even know my sons."

"I want to know them. I want to know everything about you, Monique."

"But your parents—"

"It would do them good to have children around." His voice wavered. "They need someone to help fill the void that Alekos left behind."

She felt his pain across the telephone connection and gave him a moment to recover.

"Monique," he said, his voice still unsteady, "you will bring gladness to my mother. She will take you to market on Saturdays and to church on Sundays. Father Papanikos considers her one of the faithful."

"And would your father welcome me? I don't think he liked me very much on my first visit."

"Give him time. . . . Will you come? Come for a month, Monique. Come forever."

"Thymous, would you still want me if you knew that Salvador Contoni was just here?"

It took him thirty seconds to answer. "I must confess—I was parked in a taxi across the street. I saw him leave, Monique."

"And you didn't try to stop him?"

"I am not Contoni's conscience. When I saw him, I thought there was no chance for me. I went back to my hotel." He managed a weak laugh. "It took me two hours to find the courage to call you. Will you have dinner with me tomorrow evening so we can talk about Corfu?"

"Not tomorrow. Paris will be teeming with people."

"The crowds will thin out by nine. The race will be over. We can have a late meal. Can you be ready by then?"

She twisted the phone cord. Her answer should be no, and yet, unlike Salvador, Thymous had made the right choices in life. The faithful son. Stalwart. Gentle. She couldn't make him any promises, but she wanted to know him better. She remembered her first impressions of him—a handsome Greek with black hair and sad, dark eyes that mirrored his own deep pain. She thought of the cleft in his chin, the strength in the unbroken lines in his face, the respect that he had for his family. She pictured Thymous doing what Harland had rarely done—carrying Giles on his broad shoulders or tossing a ball to Anzel.

"Are you certain you want all three of us to visit your villa? I must tell you—Anzel is a picky eater. Like I am."

"I will tell the cook."

"Giles is afraid of bugs."

"I will teach him not to be afraid."

"He's spoiled."

"So was Alekos, and we loved him."

"I'll ask them. The boys might come for a little while."

"Come for as long as you will stay. Forever, I hope."

I won't live with you, she thought. *I won't do anything else to embarrass my family. And once you know me, you won't want it to be forever.* "I can't make any more wrong choices," she said.

"My mother won't let you. What about dinner tomorrow?"

Monique closed her eyes and pictured Salvador—his white

skipper's cap pushed back, long strands of his sun-bleached hair blowing freely. *Dear Salvador—wild and free.*

"Monique," Thymous said anxiously, "are you still there?"

"Yes, Thymous. And dinner tomorrow sounds wonderful."

Chapter 28

Paris. Across town from the Arc de Triomphe, Jiri Benak continued his relentless drive through the streets of Paris in a stolen florist van filled with carnations, gladioli, baby's breath, and delphiniums. The gas tank moved toward empty. He must fill it again before he rode the Champs Elysees to deliver his floral tribute to the Tour de France.

Another man's white coveralls stretched tightly across his chest, and a cap emblazoned with "Pierre's Flowers" sat jauntily on his head. How eagerly the young florist had agreed to weave two massive floral wreaths together and wire them to their stands with special wire provided by Jiri. Jiri had helped him carry the flowers to the shiny blue van. As the man turned back, smiling, Jiri's gun smashed down on his skull. Quickly, he shoved the florist into the back of the van and took his check from the man's pocket. Then climbing into the truck, he attached a cone-shaped plastic bomb to each wreath, positioning a third one snugly behind the passenger's seat.

With the bombs in place, he drove through the inky blackness of night on toward the dusky gray that came just before dawn. Drawn at last to the quiet street that led to St. Mercy's Hospital, he slowed to a creeping crawl as he reached the somber facility. For a moment he considered dumping the florist off at the emergency room, but right now, it was too risky to enter St. Mercy's.

Racing the dawn, he drove on to an isolated spot a few blocks from the hospital and pulled to the side of the road. He circled round to the back of the van and opened the doors. There among the floral pieces lay the three cone-shaped cylinders filled with explosives. He checked the detonating caps at the end of each cartridge, saw the fine wires extending from them, and felt satisfied at how neatly he had made them part of the iron stands.

As he hauled the man's inert body from among the floral pieces, blood seeped from his head wound. Without remorse, Jiri dragged the florist to the cliff and lowered him over the hillside. He stood there, lighting a cigar and smiling as the man's body rolled down the slope and jammed against the rocks.

The pale pink rays of dawn broke at last, spreading across the horizon—the metal frame of the Eiffel Tower and the domes of Sacre-Coeur still darkened silhouettes. Now faint streamers of coral and melon jabbed the charcoal sky, piercing through the rippled clouds and turning to the glorious golden glow of day. Jiri's big day! He flicked his cigar down the hill toward the injured man, and at the same relaxed pace climbed into the van and drove away. He still had plenty of time to make his delivery.

Troy Carwell and Miriam Gregory rode the emergency elevator from the fourth floor down to the lobby of St. Mercy's. In spite of the dark circles beneath her vivid deep-set eyes, Miriam looked elegant. How she managed her stunning appearance he could not imagine. She had run on catnaps for the last three days. This was day four, and she was still going strong.

"Miriam, I never meant for you to get so exhausted," Troy said. "But Uriah says that Aubrey listens to you—that with you there, he's calmed down quite a bit since arriving in Paris."

She laughed. "Aubrey still wants to sue the U.S. government, the French president, and the directors of the Tour. He may have added others while I showered this morning."

"Will he follow through on his threats?"

"All Aubrey wants is for his son to get better. Besides, his wife won't let him sue anyone. Jill's very good for Aubrey."

Taking Miriam's hand was like gripping an icicle. Troy knew at that moment that much of her outer strength was a facade. She was nearing exhaustion. "Miriam," he said as they reached the lobby, "I can have Drew back here by six or seven this evening.

Just as soon as the race is over, Francois Pellier has promised to send Drew and Chase by police car. Sirens wailing."

"Does Chase know yet?"

"She will soon." He squeezed her icy fingers again. "There's a beauty salon down the block. Why don't you go have a manicure—or whatever you women do?"

"I can't leave Ian that long."

He grinned. "I think the nurses can handle it in your absence."

"So you want me away from the hospital?"

"Yes, for an hour or so."

She glanced at her nails. "All right."

"Good girl. By the time you get back, we'll have Ian moved down to the regular Intensive Care Unit."

"Moved? From the fourth floor?"

"We just—well, we thought it would be easier on Drew and Miss Evans to see him in a normal setting."

"Intensive Care is not a normal setting."

He shrugged, leaned down, and kissed her on the forehead. "Ian's nurses will transfer with him. Everything will be okay."

"Troy, are you expecting more trouble?"

He met her question honestly. "In the last memo from the terrorist—postmarked here in Paris—he promised us one final surprise in the City of Lights." Her grip on his wrist sent a chill down his spine. "Miriam, if anyone on staff leaked out information on Ian's hospitalization, the terrorist could find him. But if something happens, it will be on the fourth floor, not down in Intensive Care. Now go—and get beautiful for Drew."

She started toward the glass-plate entryway. He pulled her back. "We'll use the emergency exit. I have a police escort waiting there for you."

Outside the hospital, his attention was drawn to the unconscious patient being wheeled into the emergency room: skin colorless, scalp bloody, the code paddles balanced on the stretcher beside him. Troy glanced toward the policeman waiting for them. "An accident case?" he asked.

"Some vagrant. Found him dumped down a hillside nearby."

"Is he a candidate for intensive care?" Troy asked sharply.

"Where else? The man's fighting for his life."

Troy turned back to Miriam. "Sorry you had to hear that."

She sent him a trace of a smile. "After my last fours days here at St. Mercy's, nothing shocks me."

"Then I'll leave you in this officer's care. Any message for Drew? He's meeting me at the embassy in another thirty minutes."

"Oh, Troy, give him a big hug for me."

Carwell chuckled. "I won't go that far, but I'll tell him you sent your love."

ⓢⓢⓢ

In the heart of Paris the Champs Elysees was being cleared of all unofficial traffic. Steel barriers marked the dividing line between riders and fans. French flags and banners snapped above the Arc de Triomphe. A three-tiered platform stood to the left of the monument with an empty bandstand in close proximity. The twelve main arteries that fed into the Place Charles de Gaulle were secured with police cars. Robot bomb disposal units lay on either side of the Arc—one near the Avenue Kleber, the other looking like the British Marauder on the Avenue de Wagram. McDonald's restaurant was doing a booming business with the first of the half-million spectators already lined up on the tree-lined boulevard. A half-million people—and only a few aware that a contact between enemy agents was about to take place.

Francois Pellier's blue-uniformed gendarmes were ready and alert for whatever might happen—stoic young officers determined to keep the crowd back, to keep them safe. Motorcycle police roared up and down the avenue, clearing the remaining truculent drivers out of the area on threat of arrest. Pellier scowled as a florist vehicle drove up the Avenue Victor Hugo and parked near one of the bomb units. Armed police ran toward the driver as he stepped down. But he waved amiably as he opened the back of the van.

Pellier grabbed the walkie-talkie from his belt and flipped it on. "Get that truck out of here," he yelled.

"Looks clean," came the answer. "Proper I.D.—just a last-minute delivery. . . . Two floral wreaths ordered by the tour director the driver tells me. . . . Yes, Maurice Chambord."

"Then get them delivered and get that truck out of here."

Still he felt uneasy as two of the gendarmes helped lift the flowers from the truck. They balanced one of the wreaths between them and carried it to the Tomb of the Unknown Soldier sheltered beneath the Arc. The driver bore the second massive wreath in his own hands. At the Arc the driver paused, still pleasant as he thanked the officers. He knelt to adjust the wreath, but they waved him away. He hesitated, still touching the flowers, and then Pellier watched him whip off his cap, his hair snow-blond in the sun. For an instant, the man stood reverently before the eternal flame as the honor guard marched rigidly past him.

"Get him out of there," Pellier mumbled to himself.

The driver picked up the second wreath again and went alone to the platform and secured the flowers against the podium. The man's fingers moved deftly, Pellier noted. *Adjusting the arrangement perhaps,* he thought.

Within seconds the commandant paced in front of the podium, admiring the flowers, giving his orders, thumping the palm of his gloved hand with his walking stick. Now he noted with pleasure that the flowers were the brilliant colors of the French flag! Red carnations, white gladioli, and deep blue delphiniums! As he touched a carnation with his stick, the wires that held them gleamed. Uneasiness swept over him. Pellier wanted the race to be over with, not hours from ending. He just wanted to hear the national anthems of the winners—he didn't care who won—and be free to disperse the crowd. The terrorists had threatened a surprise for Paris, and no matter how he had protested, the race had not been canceled. His mustache twitched in agitation. He strode to the police van. "Where is Monsieur Gregory?" he demanded. "And where are the cyclists?"

"On the outskirts of Paris, sir. The man in the yellow jersey is leading a pack of 127 riders."

"Are they all right?"

"So far, sir. Just had a report that a train filled with Dutch passengers is racing them into Paris. Half of Holland should be here."

Pellier sighed. So in this first leg of their ceremonial ride into the city, the outcome was already decided; the Dutchman had held on to his overall points. The tense competition of the last three weeks had given way to celebration for at least 127 of them. They had made it all the way, and Pellier wanted nothing more than to have them beat the terrorists to the finish line. These riders were still his responsibility.

He groaned and paced again.

Five hours earlier and forty miles from Moscow, Professor Ivanski watched the television coverage in his library, his mind distracted by the silent phone and the haunting face of his wife staring down at him from the picture on the mantel. Dead, and yet her image pricked at his conscience, filling him with doubts, condemning his dream to take Russia back into imperialism. *You would have opposed me,* he thought. *You whom I loved and wanted to reign by my side. You would have disapproved.*

Outside a commotion shattered the quiet. He flicked the curtain back an inch and peered out. Unmarked vehicles roared across the lawn, stopping yards from the farmhouse. Men tumbled from the vehicles in riot gear. Behind them other *Militsia* stood guard—sharp-looking young men in their blue and gray uniforms.

Ivanski shouted for his housekeeper. She appeared at once, her dish-reddened hands fingering her apron pockets.

"What's going on?" he demanded.

Before she could answer, the police charged through the front entry. "You didn't lock the door," he shouted.

A smile twisted her lips. "General Noukov's orders."

You and General Noukov! He gave a defeated shudder, and then he closed the file of the Phoenix-40 and met the gaze of the man standing across the desk from him. He was dressed in a plain dark suit, his face ruthless, his eyes burning like dark coals.

"You will come with us," the man said.

To Moscow? Ivanski wondered. He had planned to drive to Moscow today—in triumph, not in custody. *Or to the notorious Lubyanka prison, the old KGB headquarters? No, the KGB was abolished by Yeltsin. To the Gulag then,* he thought bitterly, *to one of the labor camps in the wastelands of Siberia.* Weariness engulfed him as he rose from his leather chair. The room filled with men. His books were torn from the shelves, his desk drawers dumped upside down. He stared transfixed as his wife's picture swayed on the mantel, her shrewd eyes gazing down at him.

The police did not allow Ivanski the courtesy of reaching for his jacket or changing from his slippers into his shoes. A soldier in riot gear shoved Ivanski's face against the wall.

"What do you want? I am Boris Ivanski. I'm a national hero."

"You are under arrest," the man said as he shackled Ivanski's wrists and thrust him out of the farmhouse and down the steps to the waiting black car.

He had only seconds to glance back at his home. Another dozen young men crashed through the front door. He felt himself slammed against the backseat and trammeled inside the car. He watched in terror as the man in the black suit climbed in beside him. But he spoke out once more. "We must go back to the days of the czar, back to an Imperial Russia," he shouted.

The man flicked a shred of lint off his trousers and gave Ivanski an ingratiating smile. The car lurched forward. The professor closed his eyes. It was over. He had lost everything.

🪔🪔🪔

At the American embassy, Drew Gregory barged into Troy Carwell's office. "Troy, I'm pressed for time," he said. "I'm meeting Chase and Pellier within the hour. So tell me and tell me fast—Ian, how is he?"

Carwell's brows furrowed. "He's alive. Responsive off and on. Don't worry. Gendarmes are all over the hospital."

"And they're also in full force on the Champs Elysees?"

"They are. Bomb squads included with their canine units sniffing out every building on the boulevard, even McDonald's." He tried to coax a smile from Drew, saying, "The canine unit may have wiped out the hamburgers."

"Troy, the second this race is over, I'm going to tell Chase that Ian is alive, and she won't thank us for deceiving her."

"We'll give you a police escort to his bedside. Guaranteed. Now sit down, Gregory. We need to talk."

"I prefer standing."

"Just take a look at this." Troy handed Drew a police photograph. "This man died outside the embassy gates yesterday."

The grotesque features in the police photo were barely discernible. And yet something in the gray face stirred a memory in Drew. "Who was he?" Drew asked.

"Yuri Ryskov. The Russians haven't claimed him yet. But he was shot in the back with a Russian model 9mm. He carried little I.D.—just a postcard of Notre Dame in his pocket and some religious beads. Do Russian Orthodox have rosaries, Drew?"

"Don't ask me."

"He also had a detailed map of the Tour. The Alps marked off. Stage seventeen circled. And five stars on today's stage."

"More trouble?"

"That's how Pellier and I read it. The terrorist promised us a big surprise here in Paris. We also found a scratch pad with your name on it. Misspelled, but clearly your name, Gregory."

Drew stared at the picture again. "Why me?"

"Pellier thinks he was targeting you. I think the poor devil was just trying to defect. If he was, he wouldn't have enjoyed his freedom very long." He handed Drew the preliminary autopsy report. "Not much to go on. Male. Late thirties. Poor dental care. Gastric contents, half-digested breakfast—and carcinoma cells. He would have been dead within a year. He was a sick man."

"Ryskov. Yuri Ryskov. That name sticks in my craw." Drew frowned. "Sulzbach! That's it, Troy. He was part of the Russian team sent there to take Colonel Nicholas Trotsky back to Moscow."

"A friend of Colonel Trotsky?"

"Hardly friends. More like part of an assassin team. If he's one of the men from Sulzbach, he'd have reason to hate me. I know that someone in Ryskov's team murdered Alekos Golemis."

Troy whistled, startling Drew. Carwell was a stickler for good impressions. Whistling was out of character for him. "Ian Kendall's friend Alekos! Could that be our Russian connection?"

"You tell me. Ryskov could have taken Ian or me out without the elaborate plans to disrupt an international cycling race."

"At least we can breathe easier about Professor Ivanski. The Russians picked him up early this morning and took him to Moscow for questioning."

"Not to Siberia?"

"What they do with him is not our problem, Drew."

"Sweep it under Red Square, eh?"

"Whatever," Carwell said. "But they did confiscate Ivanski's records on the Phoenix-40. Dudley Perkins had a good man there, risking his life for good old England. Sacrificed it actually."

"I was foolish enough to think the Phoenix-40 died on the Sulzbach mountain." Drew looked down at the gray mask of death in the photo. "It ties in. This Ryskov was part of the Phoenix-40. One of the old hardliners. So he could have worked with Ivanski."

"The red lines in Washington and Moscow have been ringing off the hook. Chances are with Ivanski out of the running, we've stopped a major crisis." He jabbed his finger under his collar. "A toppled government would be too risky for America and the world."

"They're a formidable foe, Troy."

"Politically and militarily perhaps. They have a capable air force. But come in out of the Cold War, Drew. That's over. Forget the past. I was posted to Russia for a few years. They're a good people. They want peace and friendship, a chance at the good life. But a few men like Ivanski can ruin it for all of them."

"Apparently Ryskov feared another revolution." He glanced at his watch. "Sorry. Time to leave. I promised to meet Pellier."

"Before you go," Troy said, "if Parkovitch is here in Paris—if he exists—he won't know that Ivanski was arrested or that Ryskov is dead. But he may be waiting for someone else."

"That's why I still have my eye on our Serbian rider."

"Marcus Nash rides well," Troy reflected.

"Too well."

Troy walked Drew to the door. "We had a phone call from an old friend of yours. Salvador Contoni offered us some answers in exchange for his freedom—including Ivanski's name."

"He called the embassy?" Drew asked.

"Talked to him myself. Told him his freedom was up to you."

"I don't give freedom to any man."

"Is that a sermon coming? Or do I just accept that as your agreement to keep Contoni on Interpol's list."

"Both," Drew said.

✪✪✪

In Bosnia the Americans had been placed on tactical alert. Grover Kendall and a Humvee full of men in military fatigues pulled up in front of Leopold Bolav's small apartment. They clamored out of the jeep, but the apartment stood empty, Leopold and General Noukov both gone. Only a scrawny Persian cat hissed back at them as they broke down the door.

"All right, Kendall," the officer in charge snapped. "You said they would be here. So where are they?"

Grover stared back with sleepless eyes. His clothes looked rumpled after an all-night interrogation. "Mr. Bolav would never allow you to take him," Grover said.

"You warned him?"

"No, Lieutenant, I have no personal interest in Mr. Bolav."

They were back in the Humvee, the motor running. "Where to next?" the lieutenant asked as he pulled his lanky legs into the vehicle.

"There's an old war shelter on the edge of town. Bolav told me he'd go there if he had to and fight it out to the finish."

The lieutenant patted his rifle. "If that's what the man wants, we can accommodate him. It would save us the expense of another trial for a war criminal."

"Bolav lost everything. His daughter. His whole family."

"You can weep for him, Kendall. I won't." The lieutenant turned his attention to a radio communication with his headquarters and asked for backup. That accomplished, he turned and said, "Get out here and go back to your nice, fancy hotel room."

Kendall jumped down and faced the officer. "I thought when you asked me to help you, that you would just arrest him."

For a flash the lieutenant was sympathetic. "I know about Bolav's daughter, Kendall, and I'm sorry." He offered a casual salute. "We will do what it takes. If Bolav and General Noukov choose death over capture, we will battle it out with them."

Another civilian rode in the back of the Humvee in oversized fatigues and white running shoes, hardly military issue. "I'll get out here, too," he said, and with unexpected agility sprinted out of the backseat to stand beside Grover.

"Take care, O'Malloy," the lieutenant said.

"Was just going to tell you the same thing. It's a big one, Lieutenant. Just sorry we can't tell you any more."

"I just take orders, sir. Glad to be of help." He saluted again and with a nod to his driver sped off in the direction of the bombed-out shelter.

"Kendall," Brad O'Malloy said, "I know it's tough trying to separate the father of a friend from the man Leopold Bolav became. Don't blame yourself. War does strange things to men."

Grover brushed angrily at the wrinkles in his suit. "That's right, we can blame the war."

O'Malloy shrugged. "Are you staying on in Bosnia?"

"Our group heads back to the States tomorrow to write up our proposals and throw in our bids. After that we wait to see what happens. But first I'm flying into Paris to be with my family, if they'll still have me."

O'Malloy's brash grin was self-assured. "Funny thing, I'm heading back there myself. Catching a military flight out. Maybe I can get you on board. I'll call you, but pack up and be ready."

O'Malloy took off at a sprint, rounding the corner and disappearing from sight. Seconds later Grover heard the hum of another jeep and knew that someone had been waiting there for O'Malloy. He shoved his hands deep into his pockets and turned in the direction of the hotel. It wasn't fancy or first class, but it was all that was left for tourists in this war-torn city.

Grover walked block after block, down the empty streets, past the silent houses to the corner store where he had first met Ozella Bolav. He paused with a lump in his throat too big to swallow, and then he went on facing the future alone.

ⓢⓢⓢ

Paris at last. The 127 riders rode past the Eiffel Tower and through the streets of Paris, pedaling steadily. As they reached the Place de la Concorde, their competitive spirit emerged again. Sly glances passed between the riders. The eight laps on the Champs Elysees offered that final chance for individual glory. The Dutchman tightened his grip on the handlebars. Marcus Nash sprinted ahead, Basil Millard riding his wheel. Others took up the chase. It was time to steal a final victory before someone else sprinted across the finish line first. Time for Ian's teammates to race with everything in them.

Chapter 29

Drew edged Chase toward the podium where Parker, Chambord, and Pellier were standing. He nodded to the French commandant as they reached him. "Pellier," he said, "this is Chase Evans."

Pellier, an articulate man with a handlebar mustache, lifted Chase's hand to his lips. "We're ready, my dear," he said. "We're just waiting for Monsieur Gregory's signal."

Drew said, "Let the Serbian ride all the way to the finish line—just in case he contacts Parkovitch before the race ends."

"If such a man exists, Gregory," Parker said.

Drew kept his eyes on Pellier. "You'll take him—even if he's the man in the yellow jersey?"

"We will be discreet," the commandant said. He smiled kindly down at Chase. "I'm sorry about your young friend. He rode well."

Drew broke in. "Francois, why is that florist van parked by the bomb unit? I thought—"

Pellier's gaze swept over the crowd. He grabbed his walkie-talkie. "What is that truck doing there again?" he shouted. "Check it out. Bring in the canine units. Patrol the boulevard." He waved his arms. "Get rid of that truck. Where's the driver?"

"Gone, sir."

The first of the cyclists barreled down the Champs Elysees to the cheering of the thousands. Still distraught, Pellier said, "It looks like your Marcus Nash is riding well."

"That's our man," Drew told him.

Pellier scowled at Parker. "One of the Gainsborough team?"

Drew ignored Parker's fury as he replied, "Nash is Yugoslavian by birth. Serbian Intelligence by profession. I'm certain he's our man."

Radburn snapped back, "That's the first I heard of this."

On the second floor of a building not far from the McDonald's restaurant, Jiri Benak watched the riders pedaling over the hot pavement. He adjusted the field glasses strapped around his neck and glanced down for the third time at the attaché case braced between his feet. His beige raincoat lay neatly inside it with the Burmese walking stick folded in two and the firing mechanism and ricin pellets easily retrievable. He felt growing anger. Where were his Russian contacts—Ryskov and the elusive Parkovitch? Had they really betrayed him?

His resentment smoldered as he glanced toward the Arc and the podium where the floral wreaths stood. Gendarmes guarded the bottom of the steps, keeping the excited fans at bay. Standing room on the three-tiered platform was reserved for three young men, strangers to Jiri. Once the Tour winners stepped on the platform, their weight would activate the sensor timing device. Jiri imagined the band conductor lifting his baton and the triumphant notes of the Dutch national anthem filling the air. And then the blast. Death and chaos would follow. Within seconds the wreath beneath the Arc would blow, and fifteen minutes later the van would be sky high—Jiri's final tribute to the race, and his mocking message to the men who betrayed him. If the blast took their lives as well, all the better.

He must leave before the last rider crossed the finish line, five or ten minutes before the winners mounted the podium. Jiri needed that margin of safety, but he regretted that this final surprise would not have his trademark. A blast as destructive as this one should bear a man's signature.

The excitement of the half-million fans on the sidewalks below him peaked. Six laps to go. Marcus Nash was riding well. Jiri shoved the last bite of a McDonald's hamburger into his mouth and washed it down with the chocolate milk shake. He preferred a Czechoslovakian dish, a plate of *veprovy rizek* or even a bowl of *polevka* and a *salat*, but the American fast food, French version, had satisfied his gnawing hunger. He lifted his binoculars. The faces in the crowd sprang toward him, their features brought so closely into focus that he saw the mole on the fat man's cheek and the hair on the upper lip of the woman beside him. Out there in that crowd was the man called Parkovitch, the man who had guaranteed Jiri safe passage to Moscow.

🔱🔱🔱

"Drew," Chase said, "that's Orlando Gioceppi over there."

Orlando. Every nerve fiber in Drew's body tingled. Orlando Gioceppi, not Marcus Nash. "We were wrong then. It wasn't the man posing as Lennie's nephew. Chase, stay right here. I'll be back."

He pushed through the throng and made his way to Ian's teammate. "Orlando," Drew said.

Orlando spun around, surprise in his jet-black eyes. "What are you doing here, Gregory?"

"I was just about to ask you the same thing. When a rider abandons the race, he heads home. What brought you here?"

"I'm waiting for someone."

Drew felt sick. "Waiting to meet Parkovitch?"

"What? I don't know anyone named Parkovitch. Take off, Gregory. You'll ruin everything. You have to get out of here."

"It's over, Orlando."

"For Ian, yes. But Basil and I figured out what happened. We know who caused Ian's accident. We have an account to settle."

"You were riding well. Why did you abandon?"

He smiled ruefully. "I agreed to drop out and come here to keep my eye on Nash and any contacts he made. Basil's overall points were high enough to stay in the race and try for one of the first seven positions. It was the best we could do for Ian."

Orlando's gaze drifted back toward the boulevard. Marcus Nash and Orlando seemed to spot each other at the same time. Nash spun around on his bike, almost causing a pileup as he rode like a salmon going against the stream. Before Drew could stop him, Orlando hooked Nash's bike with the crook of his umbrella and sent the man sprawling. He was on Nash before he could crawl away, throttling him with his bare hands. "This is for Ian," he said, pounding Nash's face again.

Drew pulled them apart. "Let the gendarmes handle this."

As they waited for the police, Drew took the shredded glove from his pocket and thrust it in Nash's face. "I found this by Ian's body. It wasn't his."

Nash focused on the glove with total indifference.

"Do you recognize it, Marcus?" Drew asked. "Because I do. I saw the video films, and you were wearing this glove just before you sent Ian crashing over that cliff."

Two gendarmes stood politely, waiting for Drew's orders, as 126 riders took another lap up the Champs Elysees. Orlando wrenched Nash's arm behind his back. "Gregory asked you a question." He twisted again. "Answer him, Nash."

Nash winced in pain; sweat and blood coated his face. "I warned Ian off my bike. Otherwise, he would have taken us both over the cliff." He held up his free hand, the bruised fingers still swollen. "My glove was threadbare. Kendall ripped it from my hand just before he careened over the stone wall."

As they marched Nash back toward Pellier, the crowd made a path for them, their eyes curious. When they reached the others, Drew saw the cunning smile on Radburn Parker's face fade. At the sight of Marcus Nash, Parker shrank back.

Nash's fury erupted as he glared at Parker. "Parkovitch, you . . . you . . . This was all your doing, Parkovitch."

Nash! Parker! Drew had no doubt that the Serbian Roadrunner and the British Lily-trotter had just come face to face!

Five laps to go! Jiri Benák was certain that the Serbian rider strove for a stage win. Now on the fourth lap, he watched in horror as Marcus Nash turned in the opposite direction and rode against the traffic. Seconds later he was wrestled off his bike and dropped to the ground. Without Nash, Jiri would never identify Parkovitch. The McDonald's hamburger knotted in his stomach. Yes, that was Drew Gregory confronting Nash and Orlando Gioceppi securing Nash's hands behind him in a manacle grip.

Leave now while you have a chance, he told himself. *Take your margin of safety.* But he kept his binoculars on the scene below him and watched Gregory manhandle Nash toward the podium. *Lap three. Lap two.* Jiri kept his binoculars on Nash's face. And then a uniformed man with a whiskery ruffle on his upper lip stepped forward, smiling. Nash was obviously screaming out in protest, his fury directed at a big man in a tweed jacket. *Parkovitch! It could be no one else.* Jiri focused his binoculars on the square, self-assured face and watched the man's arrogance turn to fear. Parkovitch lifted his umbrella in self-defense. As the umbrella was snatched from his hands, he grabbed the young woman standing beside him. Chase Evans! Yes, that was Chase Evans, and Parkovitch had taken her as a human shield.

Jiri did not wait for them to be arrested, handcuffed, marched off to a police wagon—and he dared not wait for the winners to step up to the podium. He grabbed his attaché case and made his way back to the pavement below. The noisy crowd pressed against him as he worked his way along the storefronts, moving rapidly away from the Arc de Triomphe.

❂❂❂

"Let Chase go, Parker," Drew demanded.

As Parker locked Chase against him and dragged her backward toward the podium, he waved a gun in his free hand.

A Russian model, Drew thought as he inched toward them. *A double-action 9mm. Possibly a Makarov. The kind of gun that killed Yuri Ryskov.*

By the cheers erupting around them, Drew knew the race was over. Maurice Chambord strutted forward, his green blazer splitting at the seam. His mind was so occupied that he was unaware of the gun in Parker's hand. "Parker," he shouted, "stop fooling around. Let Miss Evans go. We must get on with the ceremony."

Chambord waved the three Tour winners toward the platform and nodded to the band conductor. The man lifted his baton.

Drew grabbed Chambord's arm as he reached the platform. "Parker is not fooling, Maurice," Drew cautioned.

Chambord's agitation turned to astonishment. "What—what's going on?"

From the corner of his eye, Drew looked at Basil Millard moving toward the steps. "Don't let those young men on the platform," he cried out.

Chambord gaped. "Why not, Gregory?"

"I don't know why. Just keep them off. Something isn't right." He nudged Pellier as he shot a glance toward the bomb unit. The unmanned florist van was still there. "These flowers—where did they come from?" he asked.

"Monsieur Chambord sent them," Pellier said.

"I never send flowers."

Drew winced at the fear in Chase's eyes. He peered down at the wreath. His mouth went dry as he spotted the fine wires extending up from a cone-shaped cartridge. "There may be a bomb in that wreath," he warned. "We've got to get the people away from the podium."

Pellier shouted more orders. "Bring in more dogs. Move the robots in. That blue van delivered two wreaths—"

The mass of people seemed mesmerized, unwilling to turn and run. They gawked in disbelief as the robot unit rolled in.

Parker swung Chase around. Her skirt brushed across the massive wreath. A sniffing canine rounded the steps, tugging at its leash. As the German shepherd neared the flowers, it sniffed and snarled and then began barking furiously, pawing the ground where Parker was standing.

Parker recoiled. "Get those dogs off of us."

The police officers braced to a standstill. The barking turned to a low growl. There was no color left in Chase's face. Her eyes were dark and hollow; emptiness and fear filled them. The old spunk had gone out of Chase. She no longer struggled. She had given up. As far as she knew, Ian was dead. In Bordeaux she had said she wanted to be with him. "Chase, don't you dare give up," Drew yelled. "Hang in there. Ian is alive. Ian is alive."

🌸🌸🌸

"Ian?" Chase's voice was barely a whisper. "Ian is alive?"

Across the barren space between them, their gaze held. "He's in the hospital," Drew said. "He needs you."

Her tears brimmed over.

Drew inched closer, infuriating Parker. "Let her go, Parker. Take me instead."

Parker's grip tightened around Chase, his fist catching her beneath the chin. She gasped for air. "Stay back," he warned. "All of you. I want transportation out of here, Gregory. Now."

"You won't get very far, Parkovitch."

"But Miss Evans goes with me." His viselike grip hardened.

"Don't believe Gregory," Parker whispered. "Kendall is dead."

No, Ian is alive! I feel it, but Drew lied to me. She hated him. She loved him. Some of the gendarmerie stood with guns drawn, powerless to help her. If they used their weapons, Drew was in the line of fire. Drew would die. She would die.

Oh, God, she cried inwardly. *Where are You? You were there on the hillside in Bordeaux. Where are You now?*

With each step Drew risked, Parker's rage mushroomed. He placed his cold revolver against her neck. "Tell them to clear a path for me, Miss Evans. Or you are dead."

She could not utter a word. She looked frantically at Drew. His gaze veered off, came back. He mouthed the words again, "Ian is alive. He needs you."

Ian is alive! Other voices assailed her. *Nola, dear, she is always chasing the wind.* Her father's disapproval. *I love you, Chase. I can't think about anything else.* Ian's voice close, tender as though he were there. *They tried to bring Ian back on the flight in.* That was Drew Gregory lying again.

Parker swung Chase around, trying to keep the dogs at bay. Her skirt snagged on a wire in the floral arrangement He yanked it free, and then his eyes fixed on the wreath.

"A bomb," he said. "It *is* a bomb!"

For an instant his grip loosened as someone in the mesmerized crowd took up the cry. "A bomb. The man has a bomb!"

The word echoed through the crowd. "A bomb! A bomb!"

"I want safe passage to the airport," Parkovitch called. "Or she is dead, Gregory. We're all dead. There's a plastic cylinder in that wreath. Jiri Benak's work. We'll all blow any minute."

"I know. I saw it." Drew glanced around at the people, thick as a stone fortress, unmovable. "Pellier, evacuate everyone," he urged.

Pellier shouted another order. The robot bomb units moved

forward, away from the Tomb of the Unknown Soldier, advancing steadily toward the people.

"A bomb!" someone shouted again.

Numbing fear swept over Chase. Her throat went dry. The robot unit moved toward them looking like a marauder in battleship gray, its iron jaws and hooklike tentacles extended. Chase watched its caterpillar tires make tracks across the lawn, coming in slow motion, coming relentlessly. Her tongue felt too thick and dry to wet her lips. For an instant she thought the iron claws were reaching down for her. But its X-ray eye was aimed at the floral wreath.

The voices assailed her again. *Chase can do anything she sets her mind to do.* Her father's voice coming out of the past. And over and over, Drew's words, *Ian is alive!*

She wanted to go to Ian. She felt the fire come back into her spirit. She dug her long, lanky legs into the ground, and then she kicked backwards wildly. She hit the podium first and then landed a good one on Parker's shin. He groaned. The dogs kept barking.

A bomb! The words rolled like a wave over the people. They tumbled over each other, a frenzied mob blindly rushing toward the Place de la Concorde. As Parker's hold tightened, Chase bit his wrist just above the Zodiac watch, and then she put her narrow heel into his shin again. She kicked him a third time and cried out hoarsely, "That one is for Lennie Applegate, Mr. Parker."

Sweat ran down Drew's face as the arm of the iron robot swept past Chase and scooped the floral wreath up into its jaws. Now the wreath was lowered gently into the metal container. Sand poured over the flowers. The massive lid lowered and clamped shut. The robot retreated. Slowly. Slowly backing away. Minutes passed. Eternity rushed past for Drew.

He nodded to the cyclist creeping up behind Parker. Millard took a flying leap onto Parker's back. The Makarov 9mm exploded as it went sailing through the air. Drew saw Chase stumble forward and fall facedown. One of the dogs stood guard over her, gently licking her outstretched hand. Drew was there now—without remembering the steps he had taken. "Are you shot?"

"I don't think so. Just scared."

He lifted her up and rocked her. "Chase," he said, "Ian is alive. He was injured severely, but he is alive."

As the gendarme restrained Parker, the robots disappeared behind the Arc de Triomphe, moving their cargo slowly away to a safe area. The commandant smiled. "Chambord, in another hour you can go on with your ceremony."

"But the crowd is gone."

"We'll put out word over the television. They'll come back." Pellier turned from Chambord and tapped Radburn Parker with his stick. "That was foolish, Comrade Parkovitch," he said, "frightening Miss Chase like that."

"The name is Parker," Radburn said stiffly.

"Very good, monsieur. Whatever. But first some questions for you about the Phoenix-40. And you two," he said to Drew and Chase pointing his stick, toward a waiting car, "be off."

As they raced to the waiting police car, Chase cried out, "I don't even know who won."

Drew grinned. "Basil Millard came in third. That's what matters. He did it for Ian."

Jiri Benak crossed over to the back streets and passed by the first three subway stations. But where was the blast? He had heard nothing. The fury of failure rose like bile in his mouth. He had failed, but he would survive. *Just keep going,* he told himself.

As he boarded the Metro, he felt less oppressed. The mission had failed, but for now, he must think only of escaping to the Normandy coast, to Dieppe or Calais. From there he would cross the Channel, riding the Stena Sealink Line or the Hoverspeed. Or perhaps he would catch the Eurostar through the tunnel to England and from there on to the Cotswolds. How he would live, he did not know, but for a while he would hire out like Ignasius as a sheepherder. And then? Well, time enough to think about that later as he sat by his cozy fireplace in the Cotswolds. As far as Jiri

Benak was concerned, he had all the time in the world to think about his future.

Chase sat in silence as the police car sped toward the hospital. Forty minutes later, she stood in the door of Intensive Care, afraid to go in. In the cubicle by the nurses' station, Ian lay on his back, his long arms limp against the spread, his face a chalky gray, those piercing blue eyes closed. There was no movement, no sound except the steady drumming of his heart monitor and the grind of a machine rotating his knee joint, forward, backward. She tried to see beyond the bottles and machines, tried to shut out the deafening beat of the monitor, to block out the erratic green and red lines on the wall screen above Ian's head.

She gasped as a couple peered around the cubicle curtain, two well-remembered faces. Nola Evans ran toward Chase, Seymour right behind her. Nola opened her arms wide, and Chase tumbled into them. Her father ruffled her hair and cried out gently, "Oh, baby, baby, are you all right? We wanted to come to you, but Mr. Carwell insisted that we wait here in Paris for you."

"I would have come days ago—" Chase took a deep breath and glared up at Drew. "How can I ever forgive you for not telling me that Ian was alive? I should have been here with him."

"No, dear, Mr. Gregory did what he thought was best. There's no time for regrets now," Nola said soothingly. "Ian needs you."

"But I'm afraid—afraid of all those machines."

"It's still Ian. Go on. Go to him." She hugged her daughter again. "We'll have lots of time to talk later."

Her father patted her rump, the way he had done when she was a child and he wanted her to brave the diving board or the ski run for the first time. "Do what your mother says. We'll be here waiting for you," he said, his voice still choked with emotion.

"No, we'll be waiting by that other bedside," Nola told him. "That patient has no one. They don't even know his name. And no one, not even a vagrant should suffer alone." Nola kissed Chase's forehead. "Go on, darling. Go to Ian. And remember, we love you."

Chase ran across the room. She took Ian's hand and tenderly

kissed those bruised, skinned knuckles. His face was swollen, a purplish bruise ran across his cheek; one arm was thickly bandaged. *But he's alive,* she kept thinking. *That's what matters.*

She leaned over the side rail. "Ian," she cried as she kissed the dry, white lips, "it's Chase. I'm here with you now."

A nurse stole into the cubicle on soft soles to check the IV pump that fed into Ian's upper chest. Chase bit her lip. She had to look into Ian's beautiful eyes, had to convince him that life was still worth living.

"He's been asleep like this most of the time, in and out of consciousness." The nurse's long, tapered fingers touched Ian's brow. "He's only said a few words since the accident. . . . Calls out for his grandmother every now and then."

A quiver shook Chase's body. The dream again. Ian's grandmother beckoning for him to come. "Lord," Chase cried, "don't take him from me, not when I've discovered how much he means to me."

"I should have been here with Ian," she told the nurse.

"He hasn't been alone. His family—your family—have been with him the whole time. They made a great fuss, especially his father. And all of them refusing to leave Ian by himself." Her eyes twinkled. "So the doctor wrote an order to cover them being here twenty-four hours a day. We just work around them."

"Did he ever ask for me?" Chase whispered.

Across Ian's hospital bed, their eyes met. "You must be Chase! He's asked for you more than anyone." She smiled across at Chase, a comforting human gesture, and then she was gone.

Alone, Chase brushed the locks of tousled hair from Ian's forehead and ran her fingers gently over the swollen face. She willed him to hear her. "Ian, it's Chase. I love you."

The seconds dragged by with unbearable stillness. And then painfully, with the muscles of his neck taut, Ian's face turned toward her. His eyes blinked open. His wandering gaze focused on her. He struggled to make sounds and then whispered hoarsely, "I thought . . . you . . . would never come."

Chapter 30

A ugust 1, London. The streets narrowed as Drew neared Lennie's address. When he turned onto Ivershire, the homes were crowded together, the shingles cracked and weather-beaten, the lawns nothing but tiny strips between the pavement and the five stone steps. Dowdy white curtains hung at the windows, blocking out the summer breeze. He checked the number in his address book. It was Lennie's place, but where was the garden she had bragged about? One chipped flower pot sat on the top step filled with pink begonias; a twisted vine of string beans dragged across the worm-gnawed tomato plant that grew against the railing.

He hesitated, not wanting to intrude on Lennie's private life. This modest dwelling—not her acts of betrayal—must have been the reason she refused his rides home even on cold winter evenings. He knocked. The door creaked open, and she stared out at him, a 9mm gun gripped in her hand.

"Oh, Mr. Gregory, it's you." She looked frazzled, her eyes darting, the gun still aimed at him. "I was afraid Radburn would come back now that the race is over."

"He won't be able to, Lennie."

She glanced beyond Drew, her eyes wary. "Where is he?"

"Lennie," he said quietly, "quit pointing that thing at me."

She looked down at her hand, surprise registering on her face. She lowered it. "Oh, I'm sorry, Mr. Gregory."

"Please, may I come in?" he asked.

She used the door for a shield as he stepped inside. "Did Mr. Fairway send you?"

"I volunteered to come." He took the gun without any resistance from her. *Another Russian 9mm Makarov,* he noted, *almost too big for her to handle.* She clasped her hands in front of her. Now she looked like the old Lennie in a straight skirt and old-fashioned blouse, her skin as white as flour.

"Mr. Fairway promised that I could talk with you first—to tell you about Parker," Drew said.

"Is he dead?" There was relief in her voice at the prospect.

"No, Lennie. The gendarmes arrested him in Paris at the close of the Tour de France."

"I didn't see that happen, and I was watching the television."

"The cameras were on the riders, Lennie."

"Yes, I suppose you're right." Her words sounded pinched, flat as she said, "The gendarmes, you say? Then they saved me the trouble. I would have shot him with his own gun if he had come back here. Radburn taught me to fire it."

Drew tried to picture this mousy woman at a firing range, missing the target. He followed her into her cracker-box sitting room—drab and colorless except for the potted plants in every corner. From the center of the room, he saw a tiny kitchen in one direction, Lennie's tidy bedroom in the other. The sitting room sofa was faded; a shattered picture frame lay on the worn rug beside it. Lennie's typing table had been drawn close to the desk, a half-filled sheet of paper fed into the typewriter. Several medicine bottles were lined up in a row on the top of the desk, a vase of dying red roses beside them. The Bible that Miriam had given her lay open on the desk. He emptied the chamber, pocketed the bullets, and placed the Makarov beside it.

"Parker should never have given this to you."

Glancing at it, she said, "I was terrified in the beginning, but I'm a good shot now, Mr. Gregory. Radburn always said if I had to, I'd know what to do with it."

He focused on the emptiness in her eyes as she said, "I wanted to go mountain climbing, too. I'll never get to do that now."

"I suppose not," he said. "But it isn't fun climbing alone."

"I have always done things alone—all my life." Before he could sympathize, she rubbed her forehead. "I'm sorry about your Mr. Kendall. I really wanted him to win the race."

He wanted to tell her that Kendall was still alive, but she might take refuge in that and hold back the information they needed. "You didn't ask why Parker was arrested."

A faint twist of her lips allowed that familiar prim and proper smile. "I already know. Did *you* have him arrested?"

"I was there."

"Did Radburn still have the Bosnian file?"

"Not on him." *No,* Drew thought, *we found that in the boot of his car along with the folder on Prague and copies of my own personal records of the Phoenix-40. And two one-way air fares from Paris to Moscow. Did Lennie plan to go all the way to Moscow with him? Or was Marcus Nash to be his traveling companion?*

"Lennie, were you planning on a plane trip?"

Her eyes widened. "Oh, no. I'm terrified of flying."

"That sounds like Miriam. My wife hates flying, too."

Lennie's cold finger touched the back of his hand. "Was my name in your Bosnian report?"

"It is now—a coded reference only. But all along we knew a British family was tied in with a Serbian war criminal."

"Family roots go deep, Mr. Gregory."

"I know, Lennie." It was impossible to hate her.

Miriam had said, "Pray with her. At least offer her hope."

The thought of praying for Lennie left him tongue-tied. He should confront her with a long account of what her deception had cost America. How many Russian agents and Bosnian *assets* would still die because of it? How much had they paid her for working for them? "Don't judge her," Miriam had warned. "If you must go see her, Drew, don't judge her."

He felt weak-kneed. What had he expected to accomplish by coming here? Assume her guilt? Hear her confession? "Lennie, did Porter Deven recruit you?"

"Radburn recruited me, Mr. Gregory." In the tiny kitchen the kettle kept whistling. "Would you like some tea, Mr. Gregory?"

"Only if you're having some."

She shuffled off to the kitchen like an old woman, her bedroom slippers flapping at her nude heels. It was the only time he had ever seen her in anything but dark lace-up shoes. He looked again. Were there blood stains on her slippers?

As she stood at the stove, he took three quick strides to the desk to check the labels on the medicine containers. *Enough sleeping pills for a permanent rest.* He dropped the bottles into his pocket beside the bullets, thinking, *Not this way, Lennie.*

When she came back into the room empty-handed, he led her to the sofa and urged her to sit down. As they sank onto the broken springs, she hunched over like a rag doll, her face as white as the curtains. She was thinner; he was certain of that. Eating poorly. Not sleeping. Already serving her life sentence.

"Lennie, I think you cut your heel."

"I did that yesterday when I stomped on Radburn's picture."

He could see the deep gash now, dried blood caked around it. "You may need stitches."

"Right. I will have it looked after later."

"Lennie, why didn't you tell me you needed money? I could have loaned you some."

The rag doll stiffened. "I never borrow money or take loans, Mr. Gregory. I would have no way to pay them back."

"But your family was ill."

"Just my mother. Radburn helped me find a less expensive nursing residence for my parents out in the country."

"Will they be all right?"

"Not when they find out what I've done."

She wrung her hands, her upper torso rocking back and forth. Drew half expected her to creak like the rocker in the corner.

She saw him eyeing it and said, "I promised Mums that I'd take that old chair to her. And now—"

"I'll make sure she gets it if you give me the address."

She pointed toward the desk—and seemed suddenly aware that something was missing. "My medicine," she cried out.

"I have the pills," Drew said. "It's not the answer."

She lifted her face. "Is that what you thought I would do?"

"I couldn't take a chance, Lennie."

"I never meant to steal the memorandums, Mr. Gregory."

He stared at the faded wallpaper again, dull against the bright gloxinia in the corner. "Lennie, why did you do it?"

"For my family," she said simply. "Mr. Fairway introduced me to Radburn. Radburn flattered me—took me to dinner, bought me flowers. And then he came to my apartment late one night and told me my nephew was on the war criminal list in Bosnia—that he'd be executed if they found him. Radburn guaranteed my nephew's safety if I copied the Bosnia file for him."

"And after that, it was one file or disk after the other?"

"Yes," she whispered. "You can't imagine how frightened I was at hearing all the rumors about the thefts at the embassy—you hear things like that in the powder room—and knowing that I was the one they were talking about."

Her face remained solemn. "He made me so many promises, Mr. Gregory. By then I was in too deep. He told me if I stopped bringing the files, he would break off seeing me and turn me over to Mr. Fairway." Her gaze strayed to the shattered picture of Radburn lying on the floor. "I loved him. When that no longer mattered, he threatened to hurt my parents or ruin your career. I couldn't let that happen. I had to find every file, every disk he wanted. . . . You always told me I could find anything. Better than Sherlock Holmes, you used to tell me."

"I did tell you that, didn't I, Lennie?"

The chalky face turned a cherry red. "I never thought you'd marry Miriam again. I always liked you, Mr. Gregory. I thought . . . when you sent me on that trip to Scotland, I half expected you to be there waiting for me."

Drew's stomach turned, and for a second he thought he might vomit right there on Lennie's threadbare rug. Had this poor woman been in love with him? What had he done to give the wrong impression? A couple of opera tickets. A holiday ticket to Scotland—a nice Christmas bonus. "Lennie, for me it was always Miriam," he said gently.

"I know. It's just—you were so kind to me. Such a gentleman." The cherry coloring touched her cheeks again. "That's why I turned to Radburn while you were on your honeymoon."

You were lonely and vulnerable, he thought miserably. *No wonder you fell for everything Parker said and did.* Drew took Lennie's icy hands in his; it seemed to be what Miriam would expect him to do. The heat from his own hands barely penetrated the chill. "Did he ask you to steal the memos?" he asked.

"Just to copy them." She pulled free, her hands dropping limply to her lap. "But we both had security clearance, so taking the folders from the embassy was my idea." She hesitated. "At least Radburn told me it was my idea. Sometimes with my awful headaches, I can't remember clearly."

"And after that?" he asked.

"I put the files back the next day. 'No harm done that way,' Radburn told me. And then he convinced me to just use the copier machine. It eliminated the risk of returning the files, but it seemed more like stealing—not just borrowing." She rubbed her fingers together. "You're ashamed of me, aren't you, Mr. Gregory?"

"Would it matter?" Drew asked.

"What you thought of me always mattered."

He was certain that she would tear the skin from her fingers if she rubbed them anymore. "I knew he was using me when he accused me of stealing useless reports. He boasted that the others were copying much more sensitive material for him."

Others? Was the whole embassy infiltrated with traitors? "Who are they, Lennie? Tell me. We must know."

"I never knew. Radburn wouldn't tell me."

"Why?" Drew asked wearily. "Why, Lennie? I trusted you."

"Radburn told me I owed him everything for bringing my nephew out of Bosnia alive. So many of my father's family had died during the war. But saving my nephew's life was one of the nicest things Radburn did for me."

One of Parker's charming tricks, like sending you flowers, Drew thought as he noticed the dying roses again. "Lennie, your nephew is dead. The rider on Jon Gainsborough's team was not the real Marcus Nash. He took your nephew's papers and I.D. when your nephew was killed during a Serbian attack on his village."

"That can't be. . . . It all started with my nephew. He was a nice young man. Dark and handsome. Frightening, but so polite."

And so deceptive, Drew thought.

"Marcus had all the right papers when Radburn brought him to the house. And pictures of my father's family."

"That nice young man was a Serbian Intelligence officer. He stole your nephew's identity in order to get out of Bosnia before the NATO forces moved in. Radburn helped him."

She collapsed against Drew, sobbing. Drew patted her shoulder and did what Miriam had told him to do. He prayed for mercy for both of them, prayed for peace.

Her muffled words cut off his prayer. "Don't. I'm not worth it. My father told me that we had to help Marcus. He was all we had left—what can I tell my father? He trusted that young man."

Drew wiped the tears from her cheeks. "Someday, Lennie, I'll get to Bosnia when things are more settled there. I'll find out what I can about your family. Maybe arrange for a proper burial."

"You would do that for me—after all I've done?"

"Everyone needs a friend." He stood. "If Miriam and I can help you in any way—"

"No, we'd better say good-bye here. I'm sorry, Mr. Gregory."

"I am, too, Lennie."

"Will they come for me soon?"

He reached out and helped her stand. "Soon. They can't risk waiting any longer. Parkovitch didn't work alone."

"Parkovitch? Who is Parkovitch?" she asked.

"That's what the Phoenix-40 called Radburn Parker in Moscow." He saw by her expression that she had not known the extent of Radburn's contacts—didn't know that he was a member of the Russian Phoenix-40. "Lennie, Parker had other agents here in London who will want to silence you."

"What will happen to me?" she cried.

"You will be arrested and tried for espionage—a bit tricky since you were selling U.S. secrets, but the British government will back us." His fears were as deep as her own. "I don't think it will be a long trial, Lennie. Parker will be interested in saving his own neck, and he has the money to back him—unless you are willing to testify against him."

"Oh, I couldn't do that, but if all this gets back to my parents, it will kill them."

It won't, he thought, *if I arrange to have them transferred to the isolation of the Eagle's Nest—to Margot Hampton's care.* "I'll see what I can do," he said.

"Mr. Gregory, would you thank your wife for the dinner invitation? She invited us for after the Tour. Tell her that Radburn and I won't be able to make it now." Her voice was empty, detached. "Tell her some other time."

He nodded. "She'll understand."

"It's the first time I was ever invited to a private home in Chelsea. I was so looking forward to it."

"So was Miriam," he said.

A police car cruised by as Drew went down the five stone steps. He glanced back and saw Lennie's curtain fall into place. *She knows,* he thought. *Knows that they are coming for her now.*

Five minutes later three cars pulled to a stop in front of him. Perkins and Fairway stepped from the first limousine. "Is she all right?" Fairway asked.

"She's frightened."

As Perkins nodded to the officers in the first car, police in plain clothes, Drew asked, "Dudley, could they let her walk out on her own, unassisted, unrestrained?"

"No handcuffs? Of course." Perkins turned and barked some instructions.

Drew watched the police climb the steps. As they reached the flower pot, they heard the gun go off, the first blast so violent that it blew out the window. As a second shot rang out, Drew and Fairway ran, Perkins puffing behind them. They found Lennie sitting at the desk, alone as she had always been, her fingers still locked around the Makarov. Her loose hair draped across the box of extra bullets. Drew had emptied the chamber, but Lennie had outwitted him.

She had known exactly what she was doing. One shot to the window to warn them to stay clear and a single shot to the temple leaving her colorless cheek streaked with blood. Lennie's distorted face lay against the shattered frame with Radburn Parker's picture in it. A letter was braced against her open Bible, Drew Gregory's name in bold print on the envelope.

He took out her unfinished letter—knowing that it would contain the highlights they had already shared—the pathetic confession of a lonely, misguided spy. He leaned over Lennie's lifeless body and read the eleven words that she had underlined in the Bible that Miriam had given her: "Have mercy upon me, O God . . . for I acknowledge my transgressions."

🕎🕎🕎

The next morning as Drew passed the checkpoint at the embassy, he saw Old Glory flying at half mast. He was still frowning as he reached his office. The room had been freshly painted, the carpet newly laid. Even the desk had been replaced, the deliberate water damage completely obliterated. Vic Wilson stood in front of Lennie's cubbyhole office, the room completely sealed off. "What's going on in there?" Drew asked.

"They're giving the room another once-over."

"Lennie didn't know how to plant bugs or any of the trick espionage techniques."

"No, but Parker was an expert at those things."

Drew glanced out the window, grateful that he could see through the tinted windows. "What's with the flag, Vic?"

"Glenn Fairway's idea. The ambassador agreed."

"A cover-up?"

"The good kind, Drew. We couldn't afford the scandal so soon after the Porter Deven betrayal, especially with your uncovering Deven and Lennie being—well, your secretary. Fairway concocted this forty-eight-hour salute to an employee who met her untimely death when her revolver discharged accidentally."

Drew whirled around. "That's a new definition for suicide, a new excuse for espionage, and a blatant misuse of the rules for flying the American flag."

Vic shrugged. "We're a crazy lot here at this embassy. But only a few of us knew that Lennie was under investigation."

"She was a British subject, Vic."

"But our employee."

The wind outside snapped at the flag. It fluttered and unfurled to its full colors, a touch of America on foreign soil. The brilliant red stripes were like scarlet ribbons hiding Lennie's betrayal. Perhaps it was the least he could do for failing her. "Tell Fairway thanks, will you, Vic?"

"I'll do that. Are you heading back to Paris again today?"

"Yes, Miriam's picking me up. I'm scheduled to meet with Carwell and French Intelligence for a full report. After that, Carwell told me to take ten days. Miriam and I will spend part of that time at the hospital visiting Ian."

"Fairway says there's talk of flying Ian back to Maryland for treatment. Does that mean a lifetime in a wheelchair?"

"No, you old fool," Drew said, giving a solid, playful punch to Vic's arm. "For rehabilitation. Another year or two, and there's going to be a Kendall back in the Tour de France."

"And Chase Evans?"

"I'd say she'll be in the crowd somewhere, cheering him on."

"And wearing a yellow jersey herself?"

"Yes, Vic, that sounds like her, doesn't it?"

Epilogue

Wednesday, August 6, Paris. Chase reached Ian's hospital room wearing a sleeveless powder blue sheath cinched at her narrow waist and a stylish floppy-brimmed hat that accented her dark velvet-lashed eyes.

"Ian, I'm here. Did you miss me?" She stopped in the doorway, surprised to see Miriam and Drew Gregory standing by Ian's bedside. "Miriam! Drew! I didn't know you were here."

"We're just leaving, aren't we, darling?"

Drew tilted his head and frowned. "Leaving? We just came."

Miriam tucked her arm in his. "And we're just leaving."

"Oh, yes. I see. Guess you kids want to be alone. Miriam and I did have some things to do—a late lunch with Ian's grandfather for one."

"Huh?" Ian peered around and winked at Chase. "Oh, yes, Uriah will like that. . . . Chase, come here."

"In a minute. Let me see the Gregorys off."

As Miriam pulled Drew toward the door, he grabbed an orange and peeled back the rind with his teeth. "Your folks brought the fruit basket, Chase," he said.

"I'm amazed that they're still here. Dad's never been away from the office that long before."

Miriam laughed. "Your mother threatened to leave him if they went home before Ian was really out of the woods."

"Drew, is everything ready?" Chase whispered.

"Your father and Aubrey Kendall have the phone line set up. Everything is ready to go."

"What do I do?"

"Push the speaker button. Ian won't have to hold the phone."

"That's good—because I'll be holding his hand. You're certain everything is set up."

"Positive."

"Trust Drew," Miriam said. "At least trust him this time."

Across the room, Ian was growing restless. He held out his bandaged hand toward Chase. "What's all the secrecy?"

Chase blew him a kiss. "Be right there." Still she stayed by the door, tears welling in her eyes as Miriam hugged her.

Miriam said, "Ian had a steady stream of visitors this morning. Even Jon Gainsborough and Maurice Chambord put in an appearance. And his team brought Ian the winner's silver bowl."

"But a Dutchman won. He's not on the Gainsborough team."

Miriam said gently, "The accident brought all of the riders together."

"And made them generous," Drew said. "A check for half the winnings came with the bowl for Ian's medical expenses."

"And Ian is so much better. You're good medicine for him."

Chase blushed. "His eyes are brighter now."

"And yours," Miriam said. They hugged again. "Will we see you before you leave for the States?"

"If you have some free time. I'm flying back to New York with my parents this weekend. On the Concorde." She glanced at Ian and tried to smile, but knew that it was little more than a tearful grimace. "I had no choice, Ian. Dad took his credit card back. And graduate school begins in ten days."

Ian's face looked white against the backdrop of hospital linens, strands of his unruly red hair falling against the pillow. "It's okay," he said flatly. "I understand."

"I don't," Drew grumbled, his voice low. "You can't walk out on Ian now. You're his major chance for a full recovery."

She whispered again, "I'm taking him with me. He just doesn't know it yet." She stood on tiptoe and kissed Drew before he could give her news away.

"You're serious? He won't be well enough to leave."

"And he won't get well here by himself. I'll explain later."

"Over dinner?" Drew insisted.

"All right. Over dinner. But I'm not leaving Ian until the hospital puts me out tonight."

"That's eight o'clock," Miriam said. "I fought the staff on that every night."

"Did you win?"

"Usually."

"Then we'll have dinner at nine." Drew checked his watch. "We'll wait for you in the hospital lobby, Chase. Nine sharp."

Chase watched them leave arm in arm. When they reached the end of the corridor, they turned and waved, Miriam's enormous dark eyes bright with laughter. Chase would miss them when she left Paris. She faced the closed door for a moment, and then with a warm smile walked across the room to Ian. "Do you think we will be as happy as the Gregorys twenty years from now?" she asked.

"What chance do we have?"

"None if you keep a gloomy look on your face."

"Where have you been for the last two days, Chase? I kept waiting for you to come."

She touched Bea's necklace at the hollow of her neck. "I flew to London and drove up to the Eagle's Nest. You told me to visit Beatrice Thorpe the first chance I had. Bea's worried about you, Ian. She said it wasn't like you not to come and see her."

"Poor Beatrice."

"She thought you were dead."

"So did half the world," he said.

"She saw the accident on the TV screen, so the staff snatched her television out of her room and wouldn't tell her what happened. After that, she refused to eat. She's very frail, Ian."

"She's very old. Ninety-five on the last count."

She squeezed his two unbandaged fingers. "Bea cried for five straight minutes when I told her you were alive—and how sick you had been." Chase leaned down and kissed him. "She sent her love. Now rest for a while, Ian. I'll be here."

She sat at his bedside, holding his hand as he dozed. Twenty minutes later when he opened his eyes, she said, "Are you finally awake, sleepyhead?"

"I was dreaming about the beautiful girl at my bedside."

She flushed with pleasure. "Ian, do you want to talk about the Tour yet?"

"How can I? I really wanted to win," he said.

"Do you know one of the Gainsborough riders came in third?"

"No one told me. Oh, not Marcus Nash?" he asked miserably.

"No, Basil Millard."

"That's impossible, Chase. He was here this morning. He never said a word. Basil never came in third in his life."

"He was never so inspired before. He did it for you. Besides, you told him he had never ridden to his full potential."

"He's a great guy."

"That's the way he feels about you. He couldn't even speak when we told him you were alive. Your teammates supported Basil—against Marcus Nash's better judgment—and then they gave it everything to try to win that race for you."

"But they couldn't beat out the favorites?"

"Not this year's winner. . . . But I don't want to talk about the team anymore, Ian. It's time to talk about us."

"Us? Is there anything left to say?"

"Everything!" She fluffed her hair and locked some strands behind her ear. Their eyes met and held. "Ian Kendall, will you marry me?"

He bit his lip, his face pensive, his blue eyes piercing. "Don't, Chase. You don't have to do that. I didn't keep my end of the bargain. I didn't win the race. I didn't even finish."

"There will be other races."

"For me? I might not walk normally again, let alone ride."

"Is that what your doctors said?"

"Not exactly, but I doubled over and fainted the first time they got me up."

"So you're quitting?"

"No, they tried again, and I screamed the whole five steps."

"Well, I'll be with you today, and we'll scream together."

He touched her, the gauze wrap on his hand rough against her cheek. "You can't gamble your life away on me. Not now."

"Four weeks ago you were willing to take a chance with me."

"Chase, four weeks ago I planned on winning a race for you. Look at me now, a physical wreck."

"I'm looking—you're still a handsome hunk to me. Ian, get used to it. I always make up my own mind. I want you in one piece, too. So we need a second medical opinion. That's why my dad flew in two orthopedic specialists from Columbia Presbyterian."

"Not those two doctors who woke me up this morning? One of them said he was a neurologist."

"Possibly. I get specialists like that mixed up."

"What good can they do?"

"Well, they won't pamper you. That's my job. They specialize in nerves and bones. My dad told them they'd better earn their money." She laughed as she ran her finger across his lip. "You may not like my dad, but you'll have to tolerate the doctors. One of them is a cycling enthusiast who lost money on you this time. He expects you to race again—so he can recoup his losses."

"That will never happen. I think I've lost twenty pounds."

"Then you'll have less weight to carry up the mountain." She tapped his IV monitor. "Just blame your weight on your transfusion diet."

"My legs still feel numb—useless when I try to stand up."

"Ian Kendall, your cycling hero Greg LeMond came back from a near-fatal hunting accident—he won the Tour after that, too."

"That was an incredible comeback."

"Yours will be, too." She kept Ian's hand against her cheek. "LeMond didn't ride a marathon a week later, you know. It was weeks before he could stay on a bike for twenty minutes a day."

"How would you know, Chase?"

"I called him from my hotel room." *At least I dialed his stateside number. Oh, dear Lord, forgive me. I'm already stretching the truth . . . and I've just been with Bea.*

"From here in Paris? LeMond took your call?" Ian asked.

She hesitated. "He's human, you know."

"Chase, I don't want to be a second-rate rider."

"LeMond didn't either. And he didn't succeed by frowning."

Ian's tired eyes smiled wanly. It seemed to take all his energy to work up a smile. Next month when he finally rode his first mile again, she would tell him the truth—the complete truth. Or by then—or even this afternoon—maybe she would find the courage to really dial Greg LeMond. Right now, Ian believed her. She saw hope spark in his eyes.

"My gut hurts, Chase, worse than the broken bones."

His spleen or his liver, the doctor had said; but in the joy of finding him still alive, she couldn't remember for certain. "Pretend like it's a stomach virus. Flu always goes away."

"These miracle doctors of yours—what did they say?"

"That any more surgery will have to be done in the States. They've studied your X-rays. They have big egos and reputations to live up to. They'll have you out of here by this weekend."

"Sounds like I've got a great team behind me."

"Well, there are a couple of feisty players. Your dad and mine are having a go at it. But it's only because they care."

"Tell your father that my dad can be a tiger."

"Your brother Grover calls them both bobcats. My dad has to help you. He says when he gives me away, the man I marry has to be standing at the church altar." Ian's eyes brightened; she took courage. "It was the wrong time to remind Dad that I plan to marry in mother's rose garden with you standing at the arbor."

"You're crazy. What about finishing your doctorate, Chase?"

"I'll work on that while you're in rehab. That's why I have to fly back to New York so soon—but you're going with us, Ian."

"Like this?"

"Well, I hope you don't wear that ugly hospital gown."

"I can't even take five steps on my own."

"You ever hear of stretchers? They'll carry you on board."

"Absolutely no stretcher—or I won't go."

"A wheelchair then—or they won't release you from here."

"What would I do in New York, Chase?"

"My dad wants you in the best rehab hospital in New York City—so I'd be home on weekends. Oh, Ian, New York will be in all of its autumn glory right after we arrive."

"So will Maryland," he said wistfully.

She felt his longing. "Then you're not going to New York?"

"I can't. Not if my dad wants me hospitalized near home."

"He does," she said. "Your dad and Uriah have been burning the wires to Maryland trying to find a better rehab center there. If you go there, I'd have to fly to Maryland each weekend."

"Can you get your father's credit card back?" he teased.

"He promised me one of my own."

"I love you, funny girl."

She choked up. "I thought you'd forgotten—"

"How could I? You are in my mind all the time. I thought about you when Marcus Nash rode against my cycle. That's when I realized I might not see you again. . . . I remember the stab in my neck—and then my bike started to weave, and after that—" He ran his bandaged hand through her hair, the gauze catching several strands. "After that I don't remember anything until I woke up in the hospital screaming with pain."

She forced tears away and said softly, "Oh, Ian, I should have been here with you."

"My grandfather was here . . . and my father. Yes, my dad! They just held me down until Miriam could run and get the nurse."

"And then the nurse came and gave you a shot?" Chase asked.

"One that put me back to sleep—but at least I could dream about you and forget that awful pain."

His bruised face broke into another smile. He reached up and pulled her to him. "I love you, funny girl," he said again.

As she rested against his shoulder, she heard the pulsating beat of his heart through the thin hospital gown. "Ian, I'm serious. Will you marry me?"

She felt his heartbeat race. Huskily, he said, "Let me think about it. Give me a second."

She pushed away, just far enough for their lips to be touching and whispered, "Well, what did you decide?"

He was so somber that she laid her head against his chest again, ready to tell him she understood, perhaps was even ready to let him go, if it came to that.

He blew on her ear. "Could you give me a year to be back on my feet—back on my cycle and racing again?"

Chase blinked back happy tears. "What about next July—after the Tour de France, darling?" she suggested.

"Sounds about right to me."

"That gives Mother time to get her rose garden ready for our wedding."

The phone rang. Chase pushed away from Ian and reached blindly behind her for the speaker button. "Hmm," she mumbled.

"Ian!" The crackling sound was not the phone line, but the wavering voice of Beatrice Thorpe.

"Beatrice," Chase cried. "Ian is right here."

Ian tried propping himself up on his elbow with Chase still leaning against him. "Bea," he said. "Bea."

"Oh, dear boy, are you all right?"

His bandaged arm tightened around Chase. "I'm fine, Bea. I'm going to be all right. And I've got good news."

"Tell me at once."

"It's about Chase and me."

"I guessed as much, you ninny."

Chase smothered a chuckle and brushed her cheek against his. The thumping of his heart pulsated as one with her own.

He smiled. "Bea, we're going to be married . . . next summer in New York."

"New York." Wistfulness filled Bea's quavering voice. "I've always wanted to see New York."

"Then come to our wedding," Ian urged. "We'll put you on the front pew as part of the family."

"I don't have a proper birth certificate. These folks at the Eagle's Nest don't seem to know where it is." Her sigh vibrated over the speaker. "And I certainly don't remember."

"We'll work it out," Ian promised, his gaze on Chase.

"Cherish each other," she said. "Keep on loving each other. And, Ian, dear boy—"

"Yes."

"Give Chase a great big tender kiss for me."

"I'll do that," he said.

And he did. Ian was still smiling, his lips parted, his azure eyes bright and lively. Chase slipped her arms around his neck as their lips met, the sweetness of that kiss fervent with the promise of years to come.